TRANSCENDING JERUSALEM

by

Peter Stockton

1

Published in 2008 by YouWriteOn.com

Copyright © Text Peter Stockton

First Edition

Published by YouWriteOn.com

This book is dedicated to my wife and children
Khawla, Aisha & Zainab

"Read! In the Name of your Lord Who has created (all that exists).
He has created man from a clot of blood.
Read! And your Lord is the Most Generous
Who has taught (writing) by the pen.
He has taught man that which he knew not.
Nay! Verily, man does transgress
Because he considers himself self-sufficient.
Surely unto your Lord is the Return."

(Qur'an 96:1-8)

"In the olden days there were men who saw the face of God."
"Why don't they any more?" The student asked.
The rabbi replied, "Because no-one can stoop so low."
A quote from Hyam Maccoby, in 'The Day God Laughed'

Contents

Prologue: Background to a dream   9

Introduction   12

1. Adam and Eve   20
2. Adam's Family - Cain and Abel   38
3. Noah   48
4. The Family of Abraham   60
5. Jacob   92
6. Joseph   106
7. Moses and Aaron   113
8. Job   148
9. Jonah   158
10. Joshua   163
11. David   173
12. Solomon   188
13. Elijah   205
14. Elisha   210
15. Isaiah   216
16. Jeremiah   232
17. Ezekiel   236
18. John the Baptist   241
19. Jesus   248
20. Muhammad   285

Conclusion   307

Prologue

Background to a dream

For everything there is a season,
and a time for every matter under heaven:
a time to be born, and a time to die;
a time to plant, and a time to pluck up what is planted;
a time to kill, and a time to heal;
a time to break down and a time to build up;
a time to weep, and a time to laugh;
a time to mourn, and a time to dance;
a time to cast away stones,
and a time to gather stones together;
a time to embrace, and a time to refrain from embracing;
a time to seek, and a time to lose;
a time to keep, and a time to cast away;
a time to rend, and a time to sew;
a time to keep silence, and a time to speak;
a time to love, and a time to hate;
a time for war, and a time for peace.
          (Ecclesiastes 3: 1-8)

I first went to Israel in 1981, on the way to India, intending to remain for a month. I stayed six. Hoping to find a cheap flight to my destination, I went down to Egypt but was robbed twice, and suddenly realised I had had enough and wanted to go home, via Israel. I raced from Cairo across the Sinai to Rafah and arrived at the Rafah/Gaza strip border on 5th June 1982. There I experienced what I grandly like to call my Road to Damascus conversion to an awareness of the Palestinian problem when I heard on the radio that Israel had just invaded Lebanon.

The next day I hitch-hiked, quite safely under the circumstances, through the Gaza Strip, wearing Doctor Martens and army trousers. Then I entered Israel, a very different Israel that was now at war. As I went further north, back to my old kibbutz, I got swept along by the curious sort of bonhomie that grips Israel-at-war, the lifts, the cake stalls at the side of the road: all of this was mine too.

I knew an officer in the UN, and he told me that Israelis were using phosphorus bombs up in Tyre and Sidon. At some point I knew I was going to have to come back and see the other side, the Palestinian, the Arab side.

At university I had felt very affected by the world, particularly the arms race and starvation. One evening, watching the Ethiopian famine unfold on TV, I cried in despair and prayed to God to make me an instrument of His Peace. Use me as Thou wilt, I prayed.

In 1985 I went to work as a teacher in Gaza and then the West Bank. Palestine for me was always a difficult place to be. I had always had a tendency towards psoriasis and after about seven months my face started to break out in angry red patches. People thought I had been burned. There in Jericho, at the world's lowest point, I felt like the world's psychic garbage sorter had just overloaded.

At some point in all this I started writing a book that aimed to resolve the whole Israel-Palestine, Jewish, Christian, Muslim, me thing once and for all. I called it 'Facing the Shadow' and ended the book with the Biblical quotation above and immediately heard it on TV. Despite such signs, that book, and the situation in the Middle East, did nothing to improve my life. When I went back to Palestine in 1988 I wrote in a poem:

Lying on hard, stone airport floors
But all is well –
There is a time 'twixt the time to reap and the time to sow
That is something that anyone with the slightest knowledge of the relevant Biblical passage
Should know

That monstrously elongated anticipation of 'the point of it all' in the penultimate line, that was my life that was. I was not ready to 'arrive'. I was trying to understand God from a position that was somewhere between Judaism, Christianity and Islam, while knowing that that was no solution, for either myself or the Middle East.

10

In 1993, I went back again to Gaza as a teacher. I also went down to Sinai for a week under the stars. In what felt like a replay of the border incident of '82, I hurried back across Sinai at the end of the holiday and arrived at Rafah too late to cross. I found a Palestinian on the Egyptian side who offered to look after me for the night, and we watched the news of the day: Arafat and Rabin were shaking hands on the White House lawn. I was beginning to think this was all my fault.

At some point after I had left, I had a dream. At the time, I was living in Stamford Hill, an Orthodox Jewish area of North London, and had recently seen the film *Schindler's List* when it came out in 1993, during a late show in a Hampstead cinema with a significantly Jewish audience. I found it shattering. I had the dream during Lent, as I was travelling through France, after I had seen the news of the Hebron massacre, where 29 Palestinian worshippers had been killed by Dr Baruch Goldstein in the city's central mosque. Staying in the mountains in southern France I felt hypersensitive to this three-sided monotheistic collision which I'd been following since I first came to Israel when I was 18; and I dreamed this dream. With hindsight it prefigured my own conversion to Islam and, in another way, it explains the big 'why' that, for me anyway, hangs over Israel and Palestine.

In the dream I was driving a horse and cart around Stamford Hill. The area had been made into a ghetto and I was transporting Jews around it. I then made a trip outside, with one Orthodox Jewish man sitting in the back of the cart. The streets outside were lined with people venting their rage against him. For me, this moment had a Jesus-on-the-road-to-trial quality. The people were screaming, 'World War III against the Jews!' I felt for him and stopped at a roadside stall to buy him, of all things, an iced bun, recalling my wartime cakes of '82. When I turned away to buy the cake the man was dressed entirely in black, jacket, trousers and fur hat. When I turned back to offer him the cake he had become an Arab, dressed in sparkling white *kaffiyeh* and *jalabiya*, headscarf and robe. The question did not immediately pose itself but did this transformation represent my destiny? That of the Jews? Both?

There was perhaps the question of who was going to go first. During the mid-'90s I met a Palestinian woman on one of my trips to Palestine, and liked her. In 1995, when I became a Muslim, we married. This book is, in a way, about the other possible interpretation of that dream.

INTRODUCTION

*We are regarded as a metaphor. Since we started as a nation we were a
big story, we are the Bible, and if you are already a story you are not
real. Israelis are addicted to this condition and it makes it difficult for
us to be normal, to adapt to the pettiness of routine.*
    (David Grossman[1])

*And do not dispute with the people of earlier Scriptures, but in a good
manner, except with those who do wrong.*
    (Qur'an 29:46)

It is a truism often repeated that Jerusalem is a Holy City for all three
faiths but, in looking at the stories of the Prophets associated with it, I
intend to look afresh at the significance of Jerusalem to Muslims. The
Qur'an says that Islam is the religion of all mankind, and it is my
contention that Jerusalem and the land around it is the key to
understanding why this statement is true.

On 28 September 2000, Ariel Sharon visited the *Haram Sharif* in
Jerusalem, accompanied by hundreds of soldiers. His message was that
the place would be eternally Jewish, and that the City would never
again be divided. The intrusion triggered the Al-Aqsa *Intifada*, by far
the bloodiest episode in the struggle between Israelis and Palestinians.
In February 2001, Sharon was elected Prime Minister. The man who
had been held significantly responsible for the massacre at Sabra and
Chatilla refugee camps in Lebanon in 1982 proceeded to crack down on
Palestinians in the West Bank and Gaza Strip. He received some
nervous censure from the international community for his policy of
political assassinations and disproportionate response. However, many
Israelis regarded him, in the midst of suicide bombing attacks, as being
not hard enough (though his policy of an eternally unified and Jewish
Jerusalem was one that was fine even with many quite left-wing, pro-
'land for peace' Israelis). And all this after peace had seemed so near.

There have been attempts since then to restart the peace process, but
each time it seems that hope is quickly destroyed by the violent acts of

---

[1] Grant (2004)

13

one side or the other. However, this book is not ultimately about such failures. I take no pleasure in the seeming pessimism of my politics, but this book presumes the nature of that 'hope' to be illusory, being based on a secular, non-religious approach to the whole profound matter of the Holy Land. From the secular point of view, all allegedly ultimate truth is relative, and 'deep causes' are numbers and names: 1982, or '67, '48 or even 1917; Begin, Ben Gurion, Balfour. Seeing a solution in the form of two states, and particularly a redivided Jerusalem and all that that means, is, on this logic, understandable and even imaginable. Yet it would depend on Jewish Israelis accepting the notion that they have something approaching equal rights with the Palestinians, and would require of Palestinians, particularly refugees, that they renounce hopes that have sustained them for over sixty years: hopes of a return to what once was, a return that, as it becomes more unlikely through human offices, assumes ever greater religious significance.

This pairing of improbabilities makes such a solution extremely unlikely. The majority of religious Jews believe that their Chosenness implies greater rights to the Land; and, while the majority of secular Jews may have discarded most of their religion, many have not discarded the idea of privileged ownership of the land that their religious co-religionists claim.[2] This provides, in a way, a fossilised part of their identity that is impervious to secular argument. History has also created a feeling of vulnerability where Israelis, and many Jews in general, see the world always acting against Israel. Arguments in defence of Israel are often based on security, and whether legitimate or exaggerated, they often carry the feeling that Israel has been singled out uniquely for persecution. Thus, counter-arguments, whether legitimate or exaggerated, are perceived as an insidious or overt form of anti-Semitism, which only serves to 'harden the fossil'.

A mixed secular and religious cast of mind operates for Palestinians too. Both the Al-Aqsa Mosque in Jerusalem and a *Hadith* of the Prophet Muhammad have conferred a special sense of importance on Palestinians and, as a result, the inspiration to struggle and sacrifice has often been religious, even though the *aspiration* has been national.

---

[2] As the old joke says: Israelis believe they have a right to the Land because God gave it to them, even though they do not believe in Him.

There has also been a similar sense of grievance that the world has ignored Palestinian demands for justice. All of this has created a similarly fossilised part of the Palestinian identity, particularly as it relates to how a solution is perceived.

The result of this is that there is a rigidity to both of these mindsets that finds great difficulty in seeing beyond the Israeli Jewish/ Palestinian Muslim paradigm. As this is something of a 'given', something that cannot simply be wished away or removed by external intervention, it seems that we are meant to go deeper and, if we wish to transcend the enormous problem that has grown within the Holy Land and especially around its symbol, the city of Jerusalem, we must dive really deep, and go way, way back, even to the extent of remembering God and accepting that this reality is His Will.

If we do this, whether we are Muslim, Christian or Jew, we will have to let something go. In the emblematic judgement of Solomon, which we will ponder in more detail later, the point, on one level, is that one cannot divide a child if it is to live, and that real love is expressed by the one who lets go of her claim so that the child can survive. Some commentators insist that one cannot apply this to the Holy Land – the Land will not die if there are two separate states. But this is justice on the purely human level. To explain Israel, to solve Israel (and I believe that Israel is a problem to be solved, and a soluble one at that) one must accept that God is One and that his truth is ultimately not relative but unitary, and that a deeper level of justice exists that is ultimately not contradictory, but transcendent, because so many people have suffered deeply, and they will not know peace if this is not true. The fact that Muslims and Jews (and, in a way, Christians) believe in One God should ease the task; but who is the mother of the baby, so to speak? What is the religious significance of Israel? And, simply put, who is right?

The answers are not immediately obvious, and it seems that even the question has been obscure until very recently. However, we need to believe that it is God's Will that Jews have been allowed to return to the land, at enormous sacrifice to themselves, and that they have the opportunity to do what their ancestors did not do, and to do what they were expelled for not doing in 70 CE and before in 586 BCE, which is to submit to God. For that, they would literally have to stop being 'Israel', because Israel was how Jacob was named when he 'struggled with God'. The difference between now and 70 CE, from a Muslim point of view, is that this time Jews (and all of us) have a uniquely clear and authentic message from an authentic messenger, these being respectively, the Qur'an and the Prophet Muhammad. The solution, as the graffiti indicates, is Islam, which means submission to God. There may be some tweaking needed to the image we project that might make this seem more attractive, but as a solution, this seems far more likely to succeed than any current peace process, not least because it seems to be not only what God says in the Qur'an, but what the Bible actually says too.

The Bible itself, upon which much of this book draws, is an extraordinary collection of material, from the sacred to the profane, at times sketchy, at times over-detailed, profound, contradictory, illuminating, perplexing, misleading. What it has, and probably what has kept it as the core book in Western culture, is a return, again and again, to the notion of One God, and to the idea that humanity is on a journey back to that One God. In older, and some might say simpler, times, the enormous mass of material that did not support this perceived straight and narrow path was perhaps considered in private with angst, but in public at least, it was attributed to God's unknowable side. Today we live among few sacred cows, and the faults of the Bible have become fair game. Consequently, former Biblical heroes are studied in microscopic detail, their moral failings psychologised and their stories dissected by grammarians, redaction critics or comparative ethnologists. Whether this is done in order to understand, or to dismiss, or to appreciate these people as fully rounded human beings, or because, in the light of post-modernism, it is simply interesting and amusing, the underlying assumption is that there is no alternative source of wisdom.

As Muslims, of course, we believe that there is. In their telling of the stories of these same figures, from Adam down the many generations, the Qur'an and *Hadith* offer a different primary source and a very different approach.[3] The 'voice' is another voice and, because Islam means submission, it is in the nature of the Islamic approach to our sacred texts that we accept what we read as the literal word of God in the case of the Qur'an, and the literal word of His last Prophet, in the case of the authentic *Hadith*. This literalistic understanding is something that very few Jews or Christians still share. Most see the Bible as having been written by many specifically human, non-prophetic hands, many years after the events described. In the case of the Gospels of Matthew, Mark, Luke and John, for example, the form of the story each tells reflects the political reality of the different contexts in which each telling was written. The same is true of the Hebrew Bible. By contrast, the parameters of biography in the Islamic sources are defined and, apart from some nuances in interpretation, are not really the subject of speculation and deconstruction.

Yet it is not true that there is no divergence within Islamic interpretation. For the purpose of our argument we can say that there are two schools, one that subscribes to the doctrine of prophetic infallibility and the other that acknowledges that the Prophets, all save the last,[4] committed some transgression, through which both they learnt and we can learn. It is, after all, through the weakest point in the earth's surface that the growing plant seeks the light.

It seems likely that the prophetic infallibility school has achieved an unspoken supremacy because of the nature of the Biblical text. If we look, as we will shortly, at what the Bible says about the lives of David and Solomon, we find scandal upon scandal. The prophecies of Isaiah and Ezekiel offer contradiction upon contradiction. The life of Jesus gives us more contradiction and, in the end, a deep uncertainty. What we are given is neither clear personal example nor message, nor a 'fully rounded human being' that we can relate to as a being like ourselves. It is as if the weakest points of the Prophets have allowed their stories to become choked with metaphorical weeds that leave the message or the *exempla*, not in light, but in deep, deep shadow.

---

[3] Also, though the Qur'an looks superficially similar to the Bible in its account of the creation of the universe, its account can be synthesised with scientific discoveries in a much easier way than the Bible can.

[4] Though even he was not very wise about date farming.

Much of this, I would say, reflects the very human nature of the Bible. The Bible doesn't simply tell us about the Prophets. Rather, it tells us about the nature and concerns of the Bible's authors and the times in which they wrote. At its worst this can lead to what seems like self-justification, complacency and special pleading on behalf of the Chosen People, as if the authors wanted, at the same time, to chide the people for their sins, convince them that their chosenness was an innate birthright and evoke the hallowed name of the forefathers to emphasise these points. This sets up a tension that is never really resolved in the Biblical texts.

In the Islamic sources this tension, at this level, does not exist. The moral limits are defined, and keeping to them is stressed as our responsibility, and the Prophets are examples. The same message can be found in the Bible, but heavy pruning is needed throughout. This leads us to the profoundest point of comparison between the Holy Books. Muslims see God as the One, the Eternal, and the purpose of life as being to praise and worship and please Him. It is a relationship that is expressed in the name Islam. The Prophets all came to teach this to people, or, rather, to bring them back to this Adamic relationship. The Qur'an and the *Hadith* are thus God-centred. It is this, perhaps more than anything else, that has been lost in the writing of the Bible by human hands. What we have in the text is a multiplicity of bad relationships with God, or perhaps just one long, bad one. The best that can be said for it is that it develops.

To paraphrase Tolstoy, there is one way of doing the right thing, but infinite ways of doing the wrong, and the Bible often seems like a history of doing the wrong thing. Why else would it be so long? (The Qur'an is much shorter, and compared to the history it sketches, it is slim indeed.) In its length and sometimes salacious detail, the Bible almost plays to the myth of individuality so dearly held in the West. This modern myth holds that intimate and carefully analysed details of deviation are more valuable, interesting and important, than the idea that there is a God, and that there is a way truly and joyfully to serve Him.

What the Bible reflects is precisely this lack of faithfulness, and its consequences, whether in the king or the people at large. As we shall see, it is a lack of faithfulness that is often described in terms of sexual infidelity or even prostitution. The Biblical relationship seems to be characterised by the archetype of Jacob's struggle with the angel, after which he was named *Isra'el*, 'he who struggles with God'. The Bible, therefore, seems very human-centred, or in the New Testament, Jesus-centred, but very seldom is it God-centred.

This goes back long before Jacob to the very beginning itself. For example, after Adam and Eve's eating of the forbidden fruit we immediately find the Creator of heaven and earth walking in the garden in the cool of day calling to them to find out where they are. Commentators, too, see God in terms of humans, rather than humans in terms of God. Of Abraham, Thomas Cahill says in 'The Gifts of the Jews'[5]: "Life was a wheel, and there was no escape. You were born fated. Nothing new was supposed to happen. But this one little desert tribe decided not to see life that way." In Islam such a conceptualisation would be unthinkable. It would be like saying that Muhammad had noticed that the Arabs needed a bit more attention in general, and a Prophet in particular, and so decided to do something about it.

This approach seems to have removed God, or Allah or El, from the centre of history; it is strangely symptomatic of the current secular global world-view that raises individuality above everything. Somehow, the solution to that problem is still to be sought in God, and for Westerners God is learnt about from the Bible. In the Bible there are Prophets, most of them are active around Israel/Palestine, and at least a few of them go to Jerusalem. For Muslims, Jews and Christians, this is why the Holy Land and Jerusalem are important. This is the place where the sacred and the profane meet. It is the great amphitheatre where the struggle is played out.

This study is concerned with all the Prophets who are either mentioned in the Bible and Qur'an, or have a connection to the Land, or both. I will discuss some of the differences between the Islamic and the Jewish or Christian understanding of their lives and teachings, and consider what wisdom can be drawn from them in terms of our natures, our shadow and our light, and the position we find ourselves in now.

---

[5] Cahill (1998)

Ultimately, my aim is to show how the message of all the Prophets points to the same straight path to God, to Allah.

In the end, this will lead us beyond Jerusalem and the Holy Land, to the point where Muhammad 'decided to do something about' the non-Jewish world not having a Prophet, or, as Muslims believe, to the point where God called upon a Prophet who would bring a message to all humanity, rather than merely to his own people. This happened in Mecca in Arabia, but the Prophet Muhammad's most sublime moment occurred on the Night Journey, as his journey to the holy city of Jerusalem and ascension to the heavens from there is known. Thus, I do not intend to leave Jerusalem and the Holy Land to the interpretations of the Jews and Christians. Rather, I intend to move beyond the dictum that Israel, Palestine, and within that, Jerusalem, Al-Quds, the Holy, is central to the three faiths, and see the place, not as the centre, but as the door to the faith, *bab al-din*.

Cahill, T. *The Gifts of the Jews - How a Tribe of Desert Nomads Changed the Way Everyone Thinks and Feels* (1998) Doubleday: New York
Grant, L. *In the Zone of the Living* (31 January 2004) Guardian: Manchester

1

ADAM and EVE

Adam and Eve were in the garden of Eden and one day Adam said, "Wow, Eve, here we are at one with nature and at one with God, we'll never age, we'll never die and all our dreams will come true the instant we have them", and Eve said, "Yeah, it's just not enough, is it?"
(Bill Hicks, American comedian)

What Bill Hicks said about Adam and Eve, Adam and Hawa in Islamic tradition, rings true, and is perhaps at the heart of things. As human beings, we are aware that we are creatures of appetite who are hard to satisfy, even though our better selves may tell us, even as we complain, that we have, "Enough already."

So, why are we like that? What drives human behaviour? What can we learn from these ancestors of ours? How is it that the children of these parents can include both oppressor and victim, sinner and saint, even within one body? Hitler and Hillel, Gandhi, Goethe and Genghis Khan, Martin Luther, Martin Luther King, King David and those who blew up the King David Hotel or a pizza parlour in Jerusalem.

In this chapter I intend to pause briefly on the nature of truth, and then to consider human nature as given to Adam and Eve, and to consider their stories as we find them in the Bible and Qur'an, with their differences and meanings. Then, once we've looked at the parents, we can see to at the children.

Adam and Eve spent generations as our unchallenged parents until the 19th Century, when scholars began to question the supposed literal truth of the Bible, and scientists, such as Charles Darwin, began to offer an alternative scientific and, apparently, more compelling explanation. Even today, in popular consciousness, a belief in Creationism is often regarded as eccentric.

However, this rejection has been criticised on at least two counts. The first is that it diminishes us and how we see our selves. For some, this

21

rejection has been considered partly responsible for atrocities committed by people whose philosophies are centred away from Biblical and Qur'anic ideas of relatedness and who hold closer to Darwinian ideas of inferior species. This has been true most particularly with the Nazis, but also with Stalin and Pol Pot's communists.

Secondly, it has been criticised, as science itself has advanced, for being wrong. In January 1988, Newsweek reported on a study of women from a wide ethnic range who had identical stretches of mitochondrial DNA, which is inherited only from the mother. The report also said: "Most evidence so far indicates that Eve... was more likely a dark-haired, black-skinned woman (who) lived in sub-Saharan Africa." A further study of the Y-chromosomes of a mixed-race group, established that all men have a common ancestor "of African origin" who lived less than 200, 000 years ago.[6] This opposes "the theory that mankind evolved in different regions of the Old World from an earlier ancestor, Homo Erectus (apes)."

This unity of origin corresponds with religious tradition in many cultures. In both the Qur'an and Bible, Adam is made of the earth and Eve from Adam. In Hebrew, Adam means both 'earth' and 'red', while in Arabic, Hawa (Eve) "signifies a brown colour, redness inclining to blackness or a colour intermixed with the blackish red dust like the rust of iron."[7] In 'Occidental Mythology', Joseph Campbell lists the many traditions, including Egyptian, Palestinian, Australian, Tahitian, Maori, Greek, Californian and Indian, where the first man is made of earth, and often red earth at that.

In both traditions, this earthen figure is given life by God breathing into it, at which point 'it' becomes 'he'. This pairing, of base material and pure spirit - the earth and the Divine breath - is what makes the human being unique. We are neither like the animals, creatures of instinct and appetite, nor the angels, pure beings of light, incapable of independent thought nor able to do anything that is not God's will, nor the *jinn*, creatures made of fire. This duality creates what Hassan Gai Eaton calls the "Human Paradox" in his book entitled, significantly in this context,

---

[6] The Times (23 November 1995)
[7] Lane (1993), p.661

'Islam and the Destiny of Man'. This is the paradox of our containing both light and shadow. However, what we find in the Biblical and Qur'anic stories, and the religious commentaries that have followed, is something of a time lapse between the manifesting, the unfolding, of this paradox. Although humanity is acknowledged to be a mixture of the earthly and the divine, light and shadow, within this time lapse, there is a period when Adam and Eve are purely glorious figures. It is their honeymoon period, and so ours.

In looking at the "truth" of this, and much of what follows, I am indebted to Gai Eaton for his retelling of the story, which I can do no better than paraphrase, perhaps adding some parallel thoughts. He discusses the Christian, Muslim and, implicitly, Jewish debate about whether Adam and Eve should be understood literally or metaphorically, with the telling rider, specifically aimed at Muslims, that we know, "if (we) are wise – that both points of view lie safely within the great circle of truth."

Muslims are less disturbed by this paradox than those of a Western mindset (perhaps I can extend this to a *religious* mindset). What he means by this, as he goes on to explain, is that Muslims believe the Qur'an to be infallibly true but also that we understand that God, Allah, communicates with us in the way we can best understand (as we shall see with the different manner in which the Prophets brought the same essential message). We believe that whatever we understand is only a small part of the truth, the reality, and whatever conceptualisation we may have, God's is always far greater. Hence, "Allah akbar!" which literally means that God is greater. I would add that this includes the way we see our faiths. Though as Muslims we believe that Islam is the final and only universal faith, we also need to be able to find the patience and humility to allow for the existence of faiths, in this particular case, Christianity and Judaism, which seem to contradict that. This, I believe, is more than simply toleration, which implies a grudging acceptance of wrong-headedness. Rather, it is a joyful acceptance of the paradox we find ourselves in, a paradox that is only resolved within God, in His infinite wisdom, and in the Destiny He has willed for us. That, God willing, is the spirit with which I hope to write and, with this in mind, the creation of Adam can be understood on a number of levels and from a number of viewpoints.

The making of Adam is described in the Qur'an and the Bible in a similar way. In the Bible we read:

"And the Lord God formed man of the dust of the ground and breathed into his nostrils the breath of life; and man became a living soul." (Genesis 2:7)

In the Qur'an, we find two tellings of this. In one, it says:

"Truly, I will create a man from clay. So when I have completed him, and breathed into him of My spirit, then fall down to prostrate to him. And the angels prostrated, one and all, save for Shaytan, who was too proud, and disbelieved. He said to him, 'O Satan, what prevented you from prostrating to what I have created with My two hands? Are you arrogant, or too exalted?' He said, 'I am better than he; you created me from fire and him from clay.'" (38:71-76)

In another, we find that the angels, by nature utterly obedient to God's will, question the wisdom of this:

"And when thy Lord said unto the angels: Lo! I am about to place a viceroy in the earth, they said: Wilt thou place therein one who will do harm therein and will shed blood, while we, we hymn Thy praise and sanctify Thee? He said: Surely I know that which ye know not." (2:30)

Then, before the command to prostrate, another important event is described, where the angels' limitations are shown to them, so that they subsequently bow down without demur:

"And He taught Adam all the names (of the creation and of His own names and attributes), then showed them to the angels, saying: Inform Me of the names of these, if ye are truthful. They said: Be glorified! We have no knowledge saving that which Thou hast taught us. Lo! Thou, only Thou, art the Knower, the Wise. He said: O Adam! Inform them of their names, and when he had informed them of their names, He said: Did I not tell you that I know the secret of the heavens and the earth? And I know that which ye disclose and which ye hide." (2:31-3)

24

Following this, the angels realise that some particular qualities are, as Yusuf Ali elaborates in his commentary on these verses, outside their natures, such as the abilities to love and plan, and also to conceal and suppress. Consequently:

"And when We said unto the angels: Prostrate yourselves before Adam, they fell prostrate, all save Iblis. He demurred through pride, and so became a disbeliever." (2:34).

Here we may notice the broad similarities and the subtle differences of the specific creation. In the Qur'an, the breathing of God's spirit is specified, rather than implied, and the "created with My two hands" is emphasised. This has been interpreted by Islamic scholars as a symbolic way of expressing God's special concern;[8] Adam was the only human to have been made this way.

This is one of the lines that has perhaps been imaginatively interpreted to give this special aura that Adam has within Islam and, for similar reasons, in Judaism. In Jewish tradition, Adam has, as Eliphas Levi describes him, "the most gigantic proportions. His forehead touches the sun's zenith, his right hand touches the east, his left, the west. When he lifts his foot to walk, the shadow of his heel causes an eclipse of the sun."[9]

In Islamic tradition there is a similar scale of majesty. When God tells the angels to bow down to Adam, the angels carry him on their shoulders "so that he towered above them." As he passes by, he greets them with, "Salaam aleikum", (Peace be upon you), and they reply, "Waleikum salaam wa rahmat Allah wa barakatu," (And upon you be peace and the mercy of God and His Blessings,) O Chosen of God, His preferred one, the masterpiece of His creation!" As we read this, we should somewhere in ourselves feel a stirring, a feeling of the majesty of humanity, for Adam is, in a sense, us.

---

[8] *Tafsir al-Fakhr al-Razi.* Reprint (32 vols. In 6), (Beirut: Dar al-Fikr) (1985) 26, 231-32
[9] Levi (1973) p.58

The "naming" is found in the Bible[10], where Adam gives names to all the animals, though a more profound significance could easily be inferred.[11] This part of the story highlights a profound connection between the human and animal members of the creation, through which we can understand that we somehow 'contain' this animal part, that it is not entirely 'other'. As humanity has lived in the presence of this 'other' and we have realised our dependence on it, we have perhaps also 'learnt' from it, or seen ourselves reflected in it: fierceness; loyalty; co-operation; even wisdom. Thus has been established an anthropomorphic tendency that could lead to deification, legendary status, fairy stories and, finally, a massive fortune for Walt Disney. However, the Biblical and Qur'anic stories humbly suggest the one who was, so to speak, top dog:

"All the inhabitants of heaven were summoned, rank upon rank, before him and ... he was endowed with a voice which reached them all. That day he was clothed in a garment of brocade light as air, with two jewel-encrusted girdles anointed with musk and ambergris. On his head was a golden crown which had four corner-points, each set with a great pearl so luminous – or so transparent to the divine radiance – that its brightness would have put out the light of the sun and the moon. Around his waist, encircling his very being, was the belt of God's 'Good Pleasure' (ridwan), and the light which came from it penetrated into every one of the chambers of Paradise. Adam stood upright before the celestial assembly and greeted them. Then God said: 'O Adam! For this [saying] did I create thee, and this saying shall be your greeting and that of your descendants until the end of time.'"[12]

Eaton continues, describing how Adam's radiance is even increased as he comes down from the pulpit and that here he is given grapes to eat, his first heavenly food. After eating, he says "Al-Hamdulillah!" (Praise be to God), to which God responds: "O Adam! For this [saying] did I create thee, and it shall be customary for thee and thy descendants until the end of time."

---

[10] Genesis 2:19-20

[11] The naming also recalls the singing into existence of the creation by man, as believed by native Australians. The following of the Songlines is like a ritual re-enactment of this belief.

[12] Eaton (1986) p.196-197

26

This is perhaps his first sensory experience and when Iblis, Shaytan, hears of this, he says: "Now I shall be able to seduce him!" This he does, through the forbidden fruit, and thereafter, through the sensory appetite.[13] The relationship between humanity and Satan is the second part of the human creation story quoted above. It does not exist in the Bible but in Islam it is central to our understanding of the capacity of human beings for sin and evil.

In the film 'The Usual Suspects', the character played by Kevin Spacey says, "The greatest trick that Satan ever played was to convince people that he didn't exist." It is a line that gives the film an aura that keeps you going, through the times when you feel that you are watching a film that tries to be a bit too clever for its own good. Think about it and read it again.[14] The Devil, or Satan, Shaytan, is a figure that has generally passed out of serious consideration, even in religious circles. He is more the stuff of horror films and is seen as a way in which folks-of-old would conceptualise or explain bad things happening.

In Islamic understanding, though, he is seen as very real, and his refusing to bow down to Adam is an event of cosmic significance. Firstly, he has the effrontery to disobey a direct command from God, based on his egotistical calculation that fire is a superior substance to earth, making himself the embodiment of arrogance. Secondly, and more importantly, he takes this on as his role. He says:

"Grant me, My Lord, a reprieve until the day man is raised again. Since you have thrown me out, I shall now waylay man on the straight path you have laid and make him commit sin, from the right hand to the left, from before him and behind him; you will not find in Adam and in most of his progeny, gratitude for your bounties." (7:13-17)

---

[13] In some narrations of the story, it is the eating of wheat that leads to the loss of primeval purity. This seems to be in line with the use of the narrations to advance the cause of the pastoralists at the expense of the sedentary farmers, as in the case of Cain and Abel. It seems, though, that the wheat/pastoralist telling and interpretation diverts attention away from a more fundamental story about the nature of human beings.

[14] A similar idea, though more rudely expressed, is found in Auden's poem 'Song for the Devil.'.

In other words, Satan offers to prove that man is not worthy of being bowed down to, and God accepts. There is also a *Hadith* of the Prophet Muhammad, which says that all human beings have their hearts touched at birth by Satan, and therefore have a tendency towards weakness, all except Jesus and his mother Mary.

We might legitimately ask here: Why? Why did God agree? Why did He effectively permit the existence of evil, when, being All-Knowing, He would know that even His beloved Adam would soon fall from grace? To answer this, we must consider how the fall from grace occurred.

Before this, however, we also need to consider the creation of Adam's mate, who will have an important role in what comes next. Like Adam, Eve is given a position in the telling of her story that is both elevated and humbling; the Qur'an says that she has a "like nature" (4:1). She was made, after all, of the same material.

Both the Bible and the *Hadith* literature say that Eve was formed from one of Adam's ribs. Abu Hurairah relates that the Prophet Muhammad said:

"Treat women kindly. Woman has been created from a rib and the most crooked part of the rib is the uppermost. If you try to straighten it you will break it and if you leave it alone, it will remain crooked."[15]

Thus, like her husband she is also of a miraculous creation and, as Mekaeel Maknoon says, has "much the ability as he to acquire knowledge, reason, articulate and exercise free will to discriminate morally." As Gai Eaton says, the chroniclers also depict her in a glorious light, with auburn tresses that were so long you could hear them rustling and thighs that were so plump that they "chafed when she walked."

"This is my handmaiden, and thou art my servant, O Adam! Nothing is dearer to me than ye twain, so long as ye obey Me."

---

[15] Bukhari and Muslim

God loved them so much that He Himself performed the marriage ceremony, witnessed by the angels. Marriage, we read in the *Hadith* literature, is half of our religion – and fear of God, *taqwa*, the other half – and the nobility of this ceremony reminds us that, as Eaton puts it, though we are created in pairs, "that duality as such is divisive and that two must be one in their act of union or a dynamic unity constantly renewed." Jewish tradition is very similar here, with Rabbi Hiyya Ben Gamda[16] saying: "A man who has no wife is not a complete human being, as it is written, '...and [God] blessed them, and called their name Adam.'"[17]

After this, God tells Adam and Eve that they can stay in the garden of paradise and eat fruits of any tree, except one. "There is one to which you shall not go nor shall you eat its fruits. For indeed, it will be a transgression." (2:35) They are also warned that they must be aware of the dangers of Shaytan.

For a time, they live in a state of satisfaction, but that genetic refrain "it's just not enough, is it" manifests at some time, caused or exploited by Satan. As we will recall, it is the eating of celestial grapes, the sensuality of that act, that had given him hope of misleading Adam in the first place So now he tells them that they should enjoy their nakedness together and that the tree has been prohibited because God does not want them to become immortal: "O Adam, shall I lead you to the tree of Eternity and to a kingdom that never decays." (20:120)

Satan is often called 'the Liar' and it could be that this was his biggest lie, the lie that this was not the fruit of eternity (which it seemed Adam

---

[16] Genesis Rabba, section 17, part 1

[17] Mordechai Ettinger and Joseph Nathanson bring together ideas concerning our unity and diversity as a reflection of God in a commentary. It has some shared ideas with Islamic notions on the same, though part of it sounds essentially Kabbalistic: "The word *Elohim* (God) is in plural form... Nonetheless, it refers quintessentially to a single being that that is not plural in nature by any means. Although several influential forces branch out from God, only one, unique God exists. When God created a human being, He created a male and a female, who, as it were, were in God's image: Although Adam also contains a plurality – male and female – and branches out into different individuals, all these individuals must regard themselves as a single being. There should be love and fraternity between them, as if they were a single human being, composed of several organs. This is a higher principle than '...but thou shalt love thy neighbour as thyself.'" (From *'Tziyyon Yerushaliyim'*)

and Eve had already) but that the forbidden fruit was the opposite: nothing more, but nothing less, than earthly fruit. Eating it, which they do, begins the whole process of digestion and excretion and hunger. The human body would now know the physiological truth of the digestive cycle, the internal separation of the pure from the impure, and it would now know appetite. The kingdom they would fall to, unlike their heavenly one, is precisely one that *would* contain the decay of all things.

This is like a physical symbol of what happens when, as the Bible says, they now "knew good and evil." Both the Qur'an and the Bible state that their first action is to cover themselves. This has been interpreted as the birth of consciousness and the awareness of that paradox of the self, the self that knows and feels the presence within the self of the divine attributes, but also knows and feels the, literal here, pull towards things earthly. God, in His wisdom, had made it so. It was in their nature to be tempted and to fall. It was their, and our, destiny.

In a way, the Bible stops there. Adam and Eve are not so much expelled from their paradise on earth, which is where it is located in the Bible, as ordered to live in the same place but in its new, cursed form, a place of thorns, thistles and weeds, painful birth and painful toil.

"The Lord sent him forth from the garden of Eden, to till the ground from whence he was taken." (Genesis 3:23)

For Jews, explicitly in Kabbalistic Judaism, the Jewish people were created to mend what is regarded as this "disunity in the godhead," a disunity that was vanquished momentarily at Mount Sinai through Moses but then increased by the worship of the Golden Calf. For Christians, it is believed that it is only the blood of Jesus that washes away this primordial sin.

For Muslims, though, this is, apart from anything else, theologically unnecessary. In the Qur'an, Adam and Hawa are also expelled, but they repent of their sins, and God is Merciful:

"Our Lord, we have wronged ourselves, and if you do not forgive us and have mercy on us, we will surely be lost." (7:23)

30

They are told the following, and thus begins humanity's journey back to the final destination, our final destiny:

"If, as it is sure, there comes to you guidance from Me, whoever follows My guidance will not lose his way, nor fall into despair. But whoever turns away from My message, certainly he will have a life narrowed down and We will raise him up blind on the Day of Judgement." (20:123-124)

This gives the essential aim of humanity from this time onwards, and the challenge that we faced and face. We are beings endowed in small measure with the attributes of God and the nobility of Adam and Eve. We are essentially good, but, and it's a big but, we are made of earthly material, and this is our weakness. Through the very substance that Satan despised, he can tempt us. We are also called *'insan* in Arabic, a word which has its root in the verb 'to forget'. These are givens from our inception, but we are assured that we will not be alone in our path through this life, this history. Prophets will be sent who will bring messages that will remind us of where the straight path lies. It will be the same message, submit your selves to God, the literal meaning of the word Islam, though its form may vary, as will the personalities of the Prophets who bring those messages. This is the Islamic understanding.

In Judaism and Christianity something similar happens, with guidance coming from the Prophets. In Judaism, the greatest of these is Moses, and, in Christianity, Jesus. Though these are both venerated in Islam, and the Qur'an has much to say about them both and others, as we will see, the unfolding of the story suggests, at least from an Islamic perspective, that the final revelation only comes with the Prophet Muhammad (peace be upon them all), and the Qur'an.

For Muslims, the differences that exist between the beliefs of the three faiths we are considering here are often considered to be caused by the mistakes, inaccuracies or possibly self-motivated intentions of those who have recorded the *Tawrah* and the *Injeel*, as the Torah and New Testament are called in the Qur'an. We have already seen how some small variations occur in the telling of the story of Adam and I have implied - I would because I'm a Muslim - that they are 'better' in the Islamic version. It is important to understand here that, though the Qur'anic message came after the others, it is not seen as having been taken nor adapted from the Christian and Jewish versions, as is sometimes assumed or believed by non-Muslim scholars. Rather, it is seen as a corrective version, directly revealed to the Prophet Muhammad by God, and thus, by definition, faultless.

One example, relevant to the essence of human nature, the nature of angels, the nature of sin, and also its cause, may illustrate this.

Salaam aleikum and *Shalom alekem* are the formal forms of greeting in Arabic and Hebrew respectively. What is interesting about them is that they are grammatically plural in form but are used whether you are greeting one or greeting thousands. The reason for this is that when you greet someone in this way you are not addressing only them personally but also the angels that sit at their right and left shoulder. This is relevant here because the stories of Adam in both the Bible and the Qur'an tell us much about the nature of humans and angels.

Muslims believe that the two angels are responsible for transcribing all our deeds. The angel on the right shoulder records our good deeds, while the angel on the left shoulder records our bad ones. Jewish belief is similar, but there is a subtle difference that becomes clear in this story:

"Come, come, my beloved, let us go to meet the bride, to meet the Sabbath Queen and to welcome the Sabbath. Two angels accompany the Jew on Friday evening from the synagogue to his home - a good angel and a wicked angel. When he comes to the house and finds a candle burning and the table set, the good angel says: 'May it be also the coming Sabbath' and the wicked angel responds: 'Amen' (so may be His will) against his wish. And if he does not find in the house a candle burning and a table set, the wicked angel says: 'May it be also the coming Shabbat' and the good angel responds against his will 'Amen'. In his home the Jew welcomes the angels and blesses them in this way: 'Peace be upon you, may your coming be in peace, angels of

G-d, the angels of the Shabbat who come to me as the messengers of the king of Kings, blessed be He."[18]

The New Testament, for its part, describes each person as having a protective angel (Matt. 18.10; Acts 12:15) and these are shown as having the freedom to make moral choices - they require judicial supervision (1 Cor. 6:3: Jude 6). In the Jewish Bible, Isaiah says, "How art thou fallen from heaven, O Lucifer, son of the morning!" (Isaiah 14:12), the first reference to Lucifer, the Devil or Satan, as a fallen angel.

In Islam, angels are totally obedient to God and have no will of their own. Shaytan, also known as Iblis, is a *jinn* whose arrogance prevents him from bowing down to God's creation, Adam, an order that the angels questioned, but followed. He is cast down from paradise for this and is given permission by God to prove his point - that human beings are not worth being bowed down to. Thus, sin in humans is not seen as innate. We are not fundamentally flawed, though we have weaknesses, and we are subject to temptation, of appetite or ego. This weakness to temptation is the weak point through which Shaytan tries to draw us away from God. To say that this is just a fairy story that has no validity in modern life could be seen as just the sort of thing that Shaytan would want us to believe, as Kevin Spacey says.

In the Biblical story, the Fall is seen as fundamental in explaining the existence of evil but the moral universe of the story is also confused. For example, God seems naïve: He walks around the garden unaware of what Adam and Eve are doing until He finds out what has happened. He then explodes, and here the punishment is unmitigated. The means of the Fall is the serpent, the symbol of wisdom, which does not have any connection with the devil until much later. However, the fault is attributed to Adam, who then blames Eve. Thus, the impulse to sin is seen as internal, though also transferrable. Though the good and wicked angel image is never fully developed as a philosophy, we can see human beings as being as inclined towards good just as much as towards evil, with the two angels seeming like projections of an internal state. When we study the stories of the Children of Adam in the Bible, whether the immediate children, Cain and Abel, or the Prophetic

---

[18] Rosen (1973)

successors, we find again and again that the best of men are also the worst of men.

This is certainly not the case in the Qur'an. Just as Adam succumbed to temptation, most if not all of the Prophets are tested. Essentially, however, they are exemplary beings whose aim is to praise God and to call their people to do the same. The angel at their left shoulder did not have much writing to do.

If we believe that we Muslims have the more authentic message, we should nonetheless recognise our potential weakness in living with it. Even our understanding of our message is limited by our limited ability to understand. However, the ability to reason is one of the gifts granted to Adam, and we can use it to reflect back on our own beliefs and our understanding of them. If we do this with open minds and open hearts, we can appreciate that much of the wisdom of the world can be contained within the parameters of Islam. We should also be prepared to have those parameters stretched.

When I first began to try and write about the religions and the Holy Land, I was interested in, and influenced by, the little that I knew of both psychology, particularly Jungian, and Taoism (I was an acupuncturist at the time). The essence of the latter particularly struck me:

"Tao begets One; one begets two; two begets three; three begets all things. All things are backed by the Shade (*yin*) and faced by the Light (*yang*), and harmonised by the material breath (*ch'i*)."[19]

It is very similar to the essence of the Biblical and Qur'anic stories, and strongly reminiscent of the Qur'anic verse:

"And of everything, created We pairs: that you may reflect." (51:49)

What this philosophy has explicitly is the idea of the harmony of light and shade, from which Jung, among others, developed the psychological notion of the shadow as a way of understanding and

---

[19] *Tao Te Ching,* Chapter 42

integrating the darker side of human nature. This idea throws light on the Judeo-Christian understanding of humanity which is, at best, a balance of light and dark, while the balance within Islamic understanding is more towards the light. What this has meant is that while Islamic thinking has been accepting of human nature as it is, non-Islamic thinking has either had to accept a faulted paradigm within the religious framework, or dig deeper into and around it in order to reclaim the treasures that somehow it is felt have been lost. Thus, an important psychological mechanism has been the shadow, the hidden part of the self, the unconscious, and the dangers of not integrating it have been a feature of our story.

If we see the Genesis story in terms of a defining myth, we can see that the self, as represented by Adam, has been given an inadequate outlet for dealing with feelings of sin and guilt in the form of the Other. In Genesis, the blame for the expulsion from Eden is passed on. God asks Adam if he has eaten the fruit of the Tree of Knowledge. Adam replies that the woman gave him the fruit and he ate. When Eve is asked, she says that the snake beguiled her and she ate. In both cases, the blame for sin in the world is "someone else's fault." Part of the rest of this story will be concerned with looking at how this pattern has been repeated again and again through history, where the stronger party disowns what is effectively part of its self. If we did all come from one person, this is what is happening when we use or abuse any one of a different gender, race or religion.

The hatred of women because of Eve is a phenomenon much written about by feminists, and the antagonism between faiths is one that will be a recurring theme of this book. One example of racism that is pertinent is the already mentioned possible origin of humanity in Africa. We can read something into how people of the past have tried to come to terms with this mythical story, where myth may be a conglomeration of various stories that carry the essence of truth. In this way, the Garden of Eden can be interpreted symbolically as part of the process of humanity's out-of-Africa migration, a migration that was at once geographical, psychological and spiritual. Simon Magus, a Gnostic writer, interpreted Eden in such a way:

"Grant paradise to be the womb; for scripture teaches us that this is a true assumption when it says, 'I am he who formed thee in thy mother's womb' (Isaiah 44:2).... Moses...using allegory had declared Paradise to be the womb and Eden the placenta." More recently, in comparing the stages of growing maturity in human life with the stages of growth in the Jewish people, Rabbi Daniel Smith said that a baby is "a sort of slave in Egypt, a slave to his desires and totally ruled by his instincts."[20]

In this interpretation, Africa can be seen as the womb, and Eden, whether in the Sinai or somewhere in the Middle East, as the place through which the "child" had to pass into the world. The dominant feature of Africa in mythology is that it was a paradise. The findings of natural historians, who say that it was once far greener than it is now, gives historical credence to this. Africans themselves have generally been seen by Europeans, in a way that has worked against them, as primal, unredeemable, in the Western sense, savages - something between animals and children. However, as the original parents they were closer to the source, where it was experienced on a more unconscious level, without the dubious benefits of monotheistic, dualistic "enlightenment." This enlightenment manifested literally as light skin, an enlightened vision of the transcendent unity, of God, and a lighter, less reverent feeling for the earth. As Alice Walker puts it:

"Guess what.... Folks in Africa where Nettie and the children is believe white people is black people's children.... They say the white missionaries before Nettie and them come tell them all about Adam from the white folks' point of view and what the white folks know. But they know who Adam is from they own point of view. And for a whole lot longer... the first man that was white. Not the first man."[21]

As mirror image, ethnic shadow, Africans were the budding monotheists' original Other, "beast" of our "humanity", which is how Alice Walker interprets that archetypal buck passing:

"From what Nettie say, them Africans is a mess. And you know what the bible say, the fruit don't fall too far from the tree. And something else, I say. Guess who the snake is?

---

[20] Smith, *Religious Life and Personal Growth* in Cooper (1988)
[21] Walker (1982)

"Us, no doubt, say Mr.-.

"Right. I say. Whitefolks sign for their parents. They was so mad to git throwed out and told they was naked they made up they minds to crush us wherever they find us, same as they would a snake."[22]

Adam and Eve's responses to being questioned about the eating of the fruit are true as far as they go, but they stress someone else's responsibility and avoid accepting that a choice was made. It is like a child admitting to having done something, but saying that they did it because someone, usually of superior status, told them to do it, as if because of this they had no choice. There is a choice, however: Adam and Eve could have lived, it might be supposed, in a state of unconsciousness in Paradise, symbolised by their uncoveredness, but the snake promised that if they ate, they would not die, as they had been told, but their eyes would be opened and they would be like God, "knowing good and evil" (Genesis 3:5). Adam and Eve had free will, and they chose this course, to grow, to develop. They chose consciousness, enlightenment, and the polarity of experience that that brought. In doing so they began history as we know it. Consciousness, and the sense of personal responsibility that goes with it, flickers like a candle flame through this whole story. When the strain of that burden has become too much, which it often has, "snakes" have been found

The Islamic version lacks this complexity, but it is hard to look at the Bioblical version as a Muslim and discard it as something without any truth or merit. In His wisdom, God, Allah, has willed all this so, and it is to us to try and perhaps integrate it into ourselves and make our peace with it by reconciling our selves with our Others, and in doing so, realise that we are all one, as indeed is God. That will be the subject and aim of the rest of this work, insha'Allah.

Cooper, H. (ed.) *Soul Searching - Studies in Judaism and psychotherapy (*1988) SCM Press Ltd: London
Eaton, H.G. *Islam and the Destiny of Man* (1985) Islamic Texts Society: Cambridge

---

[22] *Ibid.*

Jeffery, A. (ed.) Al-Kisa'i, *Qisas al-Anbiya*, in *A Reader on Islam* (1962) Mouton & Co.: The Hague

Keller, Nuh Ha Mim, *Evolution Theory and Islam* (1999) Muslim Academic Trust: Cambridge

Lane, E.W. *Arabic-English Lexicon, Book 1, Part 2* (1993) Kazi Publications: Chicago

Lao Tsu, *Tao Te Ching*

Lau, B. *Interpersonal Relationships are Holy* (27 April 2007) Tel Aviv: Haaretz

Levi, E. *The Book of Splendours.* (1973) Red Wheel/Weiser: Newberryport

Maknoon, M. *The Universal Significance of Adam (A.S.)* (May 1998) Qalam

Rosen, A. *Thousand Hebrew Words* (1973) Achiasaf Publishing House: Tel Aviv

Walker A. *The Colour Purple (*1982) Women's Press: London

2

ADAM'S FAMILY - CAIN and ABEL

The Lord was our shepherd. We did not want. He fed us in green and fat pastures, gave us to drink from deep waters, made us to lie in a good fold. That which was lost, He sought, that which was broken, He bound up, that which was driven away, He brought again into the flock. Excellent, excellent, had we been sheep.
        (Howard Jacobson)[23]

... which they were not. Very soon after the birth of humankind, the angels' concerns for potential blood spilling and Shaytan's low opinion of humanity's self-control seemed to be confirmed. The event was the death of Abel (Habeel in Islamic tradition) at the hands of Cain, (Qabeel in Arabic tradition). A bad start. The fruit, it seemed, had not fallen far from the tree.

Children often reflect their parents' characters, and the original parents, Adam and Eve, who encompassed the whole range of human characteristics, had children who reflected both the extremes of human nature and, in fact, contemporary employment opportunities, though with differences between Qur'an and Bible.

The Biblical Adam and Eve produced two sons who were active and passive, older and younger, farmer and shepherd, Cain and Abel respectively. However, they were "Fallen" parents and their children reflected this. Though Cain is the obvious villain, Abel is not portrayed as a viable alternative. Though "righteous Abel" (Matthew 23:35) was a title later attributed in the New Testament to the younger brother by Jesus (the Church fathers saw him as a forerunner of Jesus), Abel in Hebrew means 'breath', 'transient' or 'nothing,' and nothing is precisely what he says while alive. His blood crying out from the ground means he is only heard after his death. The "he himself" in "And Abel also brought, he himself" (Genesis 4:4) hints that the offering he brought for God was more personal, but that is all we learn of him. The spectrum of human possibilities is, in fact, rather negative

---

[23] Jacobson (1982) from the chapter *'Cain Remembers a Birthday'*

and runs from violence through to weakness. Eliphas Levi, in a Kabbalistic interpretation of the Bible, says that neither was just enough to remain alive before God. With irony he bemoans the fate of their ancestors:

"Happy are the souls who descend in a great line from the great Adam! For the children of the useless Abel and those of the criminal Cain are no better one than the other: they are the unjust, the sinners. True justice unites goodness and strength, it is neither violent nor weak."[24]

The Qur'anic parents, slightly different in the balance of light and dark within, also produce differing sons, one of whom we can characterise as good, while the other, despite committing murder, responds differently afterwards to his parallel character in the Bible.

Versions of the story in both the Qur'an and the Bible are quite short and similar in outline, though they differ in details. If we compare the narratives, we find that the Bible is more detailed about the identity of the two. Cain is the older and "a worker of the ground", Abel, a shepherd. The Qur'an refers to them simply as the "sons of Adam", the naming being part of tradition. In both versions, an offering is made, as befitting the occupation of each son in the Bible, but without specification in the Qur'an, (the word *qurban* could imply either an animal sacrifice or a crop offering). In both, only the offering of Abel is accepted by God.

Cain is then very angry, and here a major difference arises. In the Qur'an, Cain/Qabeel speaks with his brother, while in the Bible, God speaks to Cain. In both cases, Cain is given warning but takes his anger to a logical conclusion by murdering his brother. In the Bible after the murder, Cain disowns the crime, saying: "Am I my brother's keeper?" In the Qur'an, Cain is full of remorse at the killing and further humbled by a raven showing him how to bury the body. The echoes of shame in the Bible are external when God says: "The voice of your brother's blood cries out to me from the ground."

---

[24] Levi (1973)

40

The crucial points of these narratives are the moments before the crime – when Cain and Qabeel are offered a moment's reflection before they introduce murder into the world. In the Bible, God says:

"Why are you angry? And why has your face fallen? If you do well, will you not be lifted up? But if you do not do well, sin is crouching at the door: its desire is for you, but you can master it." (Genesis 4:6-7)

Understandably, much is made of this line, and, according to psychotherapist and rabbi, Howard Cooper, it is one of five sentences in the Bible that is impossible to unravel. Yet what it seems to say is that if you do the right thing, in this case to patiently accept the infallible Judgement of God and to learn from it as a test, you will be uplifted, or rewarded. If, however, you do not, you will open yourself to temptation. Crouching at the door of your heart is none other than Satan, to use the Islamic and later Judeo-Christian understanding. However, if we allow that the Biblical text was human and written, at least partly, to serve its own position (certainly a more controversial approach for Jews, particularly Orthodox, than for Muslims), this is not an obvious response. What may be happening is an unconscious attempt by the writer to bring back the story to its authentic form – the form it has in the Qur'an, where Abel spells out what is implied in the Bible. In the Qur'an, Abel says:

"God accepteth only those who are pious. Even if thou stretch out thy hand to kill me, I will not stretch out my hand against thee to kill thee for I fear God, the Lord of the Worlds. I would rather thou shouldst bear the punishment of the sin against me and thine own sin and become an inhabitant of the fire. That is the reward for those who do evil." (5:27-29)

In some way, he restates the lesson of his parents - that we are sometimes tempted, and that we have the responsibility to do the right thing, to "ward off (the) evil" crouching at the door. In the light of his words, we can see what happens to Cain/Qabeel as a test - after the forbidden fruit, this is humanity's second one - and he fails. It is stressed that it is preferable to do right because the sinner will be rewarded with the fire. The moral universe that was created with the parents is thus seen in operation with the children. They can choose righteousness, or they can choose sin.

Again we find that the Qur'anic message is simpler, a reason why the text is so short and the commentaries far fewer than on the Biblical text. Though the latter is only slightly different in essence, it has required much more debate and soul-searching.

A number of interpretations of Cain and Abel's (and God's) motivations have been made. Admiel Kosman, writing in the Israeli newspaper *Haaretz*, says that Philo of Alexandria points out that a sacrifice should be of the finest quality.[25] The Biblical text specifies that Abel brought "the first born of his flock and their best parts" and also that "he himself" brought them, while Cain merely "brought of the fruit of the ground." For this reason, God preferred Abel's gift. A similar story from early Islamic scholar, Ibn Kathir, goes further, stating that bad feeling began with rivalry over an intended spouse (there obviously were not many possibilities) and that Cain offered some of the worst produce he had grown. The marital rivalry also occurs in Jewish tradition with Rabbi Ivo interpreting the word "field" as being a reference to woman. (The same meaning is also found in the Qur'an).

To decode the end of the story, particularly the part where "Cain said to Abel his brother... and it came to pass that when they were in the field..." (Genesis 4:8), other Rabbis have speculated about what, if it was not about marriage, Cain said in the field. A *Midrash* of the Rabbis of Aggadah says that "the field" meant they were discussing a division of the world, where one takes the land, the source of crops, while the other takes the moveable property, such as the sheep. At this, Cain then tells Abel to strip, and is told to get lost. He then attacks Abel.[26] Bruce Chatwin quotes a *Midrash* that says that the same division led to Abel accusing Cain of trespass.[27] Quoting the Aggadah *Midrash*, and reminding us of Bill Hicks - It's just not enough, is it? - Kosman says:

---

[25] Kosman (2000)
[26] *Parashat Raba 22:8*
[27] Chatwin (1987) p.214

"How much bitter truth is contained in this description of two brothers, given the whole world as a gift, who cannot divide it up without fighting."

Some have seen the story as part of the historical tension between pastoralists and agriculturalists. Joseph Campbell calls the murder a duplication of the Fall motif, where the murder stops the ground's strength coming to Cain,[28] and is thus the opposite of other ritual murders in agricultural myths, that led to increased fertility.

It is also opposite in where the preference goes. He quotes an old Sumerian cuneiform text that reads:

Shepherd:
The farmer more than I, the farmer more than I,
The farmer, what has he.... more than I?
If he pours me his first date-wine
I pour him my yellow milk...
If he gives me his good bread,
I give him my honey-cheese...
More than I, the farmer, what has he.... more than I?

Goddess:
the much-possessing shepherd I shall not marry
I, the maid, the farmer I shall marry:
The farmer, who makes plants grow abundantly,
The farmer, who makes the grain grow abundantly...[29]

Inveterate nomad that he was, this idea appeals to Chatwin, whose 'Songlines' is a meditation on the roots of his own rootlessness, and whether nomadism is not the authentic state. He mentions the roots of the names Cain and Abel, which come from, respectively, the verb *kanah*, which means to acquire, get, own property, and so, to rule or subjugate, and *hebel*, which means breath or vapour, and hence, as Howard Cooper says, transient or nothing. (Abel, we recall, did not

---

[28] Campbell (1964) p.105
[29] Kramer (1944) p.102

43

speak). Chatwin also says that 'Cain' means 'metal-smith', and that the words for violence and subjugation in many languages (he mentions Chinese) are linked to the discovery of metal.

The Biblical version can thus also be seen as an attempt by a nomadic group, the Hebrews, to legitimise their ascendancy over a sedentary group, in this case, interestingly in terms of the name, the inhabitants of Canaan. Related to this is that other theme of Genesis, the preference of the younger brother over the older, as in Isaac and Jacob. There is also in Genesis, the parting of the ways between the two groups when Lot, given first choice, chooses the more fertile land of the Promised Land, leaving Abraham with the rougher land of the hills, land that is only suitable for pasture.

However, most geographically specific of all the Jewish interpretations is the view of Rabbi Joshua of Sikhnin who, following his teacher, Rabbi Levy, said:

"Both of them possessed land and moveable property. So what was the dispute about? This one said: 'The Temple will be built on my land.' Where is the allusion in the Bible? In the verse 'and when they were in the field...' The 'field' is the Holy Temple. As it is written: 'Zion shall be plowed as a field.' (Micha 3:12)"

Kosman explains that Rabbi Levy before had felt that it was illogical that two brothers with the whole world at their disposal would fight over the division of land. He thus explains it as a religious dispute, and ironically comments that the idea of spilling blood over land in order to be "nearer to that which is spiritual" is not unknown in our day.

Perhaps it is the incompleteness of all these interpretations within the rabbinic interpretations that have led to the later development of what Kosman calls "mirror image" stories. He quotes one from Israel Costa's *Mikve Israel*[30] that is well-known, appearing also in a poem by Christian writer Kenneth E. Bailey.[31]

---

[30] Costa (1851) section 59
[31] Chapman (1983) p.220

44

In this *aggadah*, God chooses the site of the Temple after an incident that took place between two brothers who were farmers. One was rich and had a wife and children, while the other was poor and single. At harvest time the brothers worked together and divided the crops between their two granaries, but that night, neither brother could sleep. The poorer brother thought that his brother's need was greater, because of his family, and the richer brother thought his brother's need was greater, because of his poverty. Both crept out in the darkness to take some of their own sheaves to their brother's granary. In the darkness, as Kosman relates, their paths cross and, "realising the goodness and purity of their sibling's intentions", the brothers fell into each other's arms and cried tears of love. The *aggadah* concludes: "God desired this place, where two brothers thought fine thoughts and performed good deeds. Thus it has been blessed by the people of the world and chosen by the Children of Israel to be the home of God." [32]The home of God in this context is, of course, the Temple Mount, Al-Aqsa, and by extension, Jerusalem.

Commenting on the most important difference between this story and the Biblical, Kosman says that whereas in the Biblical narrative the brothers fight for their right to control the religious site, in the "mirror story" they are more concerned about their sibling's welfare than their own, "which is precisely what turns this godforsaken and insignificant mountain into the dwelling place of God." He concludes with this:

"What God is asking (when he asks Cain, Where is Abel your brother?) is how sacred labels have become attached to inanimate objects, empty of significance, and how, in consequence, man's heart has been drained of that which is genuinely sacred."

In Jewish interest in this passage, we may suppose there is a certain amount of identification with Abel. He is apparently the favoured of God but this has tragic consequences, just as Jews would feel was so as a consequence of their chosenness. Howard Cooper broaches the subject of whether Abel actually attracts the persecution by bringing the best offering and this raises the question of the shadow as a means to

---

[32] Costa, ibid, 30b

understand both the dynamics of human behaviour and the archetypes that operate within cultures.

It is here that Biblical Abel's silence is particularly interesting. As we observed in the story of Adam and Eve, in the Bible, evil, and blame, lie elsewhere. Either they are externalised (Adam blames Eve blames the serpent) or they are suppressed into the unconscious mind. In the Islamic version, Adam and Hawa own responsibility for their actions and ask for repentance. In the Cain and Abel story, there are similar patterns. The Biblical Cain is spoken to by God and ignores, or, if like commentators since, does not understand the warning. The Qur'anic Cain is spoken to by Abel, and has the consequences of his impending action spelled out.

As we have said before, these two sons are from one; they are microcosms of the endlessly multiplying essence of Adam. They are two halves that make a whole. Among many complementary pairings, they are victim and oppressor, but the difference is that the victim-self in the Qur'anic story tells the oppressor-self what he is doing, while in the Biblical story, the victim-self says nothing. So necessary is the desire to speak that the New Testament will have Jesus say, when he is oppressed, "Forgive them Lord, for they know not what they do."

Here, with the response to this first crime, two patterns of thinking are set. One is incredibly complex, it is fascinating, and it is not only to be found among Jews and Christians, though it finds its fruition philosophically in Judeo-Christian thought. I would even go so far as to say it is why this half of the philosophical tree that has produced the novelists and playwrights, and it is why I was so struck by the words spoken to playwright David Hare by an Israeli actress who became religious:

"All theatre is wrong. All fiction is wrong. God makes the stories. What right have we to invent new ones? Why rival God? Why fabulate?"[33]

---

[33] Hare (1997)

One writer of fiction, Herman Hesse, had a main character of his novel *Demian* say of the "Mark of Cain":

"Rather there was some hardly perceptible mark, a little more intelligence in the eyes than people were accustomed to. This man had power and they all went in awe of him... Men of courage and character always seem sinister to the rest. I consider Cain to be a fine fellow..."

Colin Wilson, commenting on this passage in *The Outsider* much later, also says: "Perhaps Cain was not simply an evil man who killed his brother out of envy; perhaps there was something about him."

I'm not going to say *all* fiction is wrong, but, sorry, this is the sort of stuff they said about Hitler.

This mode of thinking is essentially dualistic, and half of it, at least, is like the part of the iceberg under the water, invisible and unknowable (and much bigger). It is only understandable by God, who spoke to Cain.

For Muslims, it is simpler, though there are fewer novels. God, Allah, is One, His creation is one. We are reminded over and over that this is so, and taught that this is precisely what all the Prophets came to tell us.

There is, though, clearly a danger that we could get over-triumphalist about this, that our egos might be puffed up, which is exactly when we are most vulnerable to the whispers of Shaytan. We should remember the last part of the story of the two sons of Adam. As Muslims we often quote this, as proof of our belief in the Unity of Creation and humanity:

"If anyone killed a person not in retaliation of murder, or to spread mischief in the land – it would be as if he killed all mankind, and if anyone saved a life, it would be as if he saved a life." (5:32)

What we often forget, or find inconvenient, are the first few words of the same verse:

"Because of that (the murder of Adam's son) We ordained for the Children of Israel..."

In the *Mishnah*,[34] we find:

"That is why God created one man, Adam, rather than creating the whole race together. It was to show that if anyone causes a single soul to perish, it is as though he causes a whole world to perish; and if anyone saves alive a single soul, it is as if he had saved alive the whole world."

It was also the inscription on the ring given to Oscar Schindler's by the Jews he had saved.

Campbell, J. *The Masks of God - Occidental Mythology* (1964) Viking: New York
Chapman, C. *Whose Land is Palestine?* (1983) Lion Books: Oxford
Chatwin, B. *Songlines* (1987) Picador: London
Hare, D. *Via Dolorosa* (1997) Faber: London
Hesse, H. *Demian* (1965) Harper & Row: New York
Ibn Kathir, I. *Stories of the Prophets* (2003) Darrusalam: Riyadh
Jacobson, H. *The Very Model of a Man* (1992) Penguin: London
Kosman, A. *Even then, it was all about the Temple Mount*, Haaretz: Tel Aviv (2000)
Kramer, S.N. *Sumerian Mythology* (1944) The American Philosophical Society: Philadelphia:
Levi, E. *The Book of Splendours* (1973) Red Wheel/Weiser: Newburyport
Mishnah Sanhedrin, 4:5
Wilson, C. *The Outsider* (1956) Gollancz: London

---

[34] Sanhedrin, 4:5

3

NOAH

God gave Noah the rainbow sign,
No more flood
The fire next time.
      (African American hymn)

One version of the first time went something like this:

"The world bellowed like a bull" and the gods were so sickened by this behaviour that they decided to exterminate the world. Only one of them felt sympathy for the humans and he decided to warn one of them. Build a boat, he said. "Let her beam equal her length, let her deck be roofed like the vault that covers the abyss. Build seven decks." There was feasting and self-anointing on the boat as the storm broke, with wind blowing from the south and water coming from above and below. The storm raged for six days and six nights until all mankind was turned to clay, but then the gods were shocked and repented. On the seventh day, the boat came to rest on a mountain and a dove was released. It returned. Then a swallow was let out. It returned. Then a raven was released which ate, flew around, cawed and did not return. A sacrifice was made and "when the gods smelled the sweet savour, they gathered like flies over the sacrifice and vowed to remember." The goddess of the heart rebuked Enlil, the god of wells and canals.

There is flood evidence from 2900 BCE in southern Iraq at the site of Ur, the Biblical home of Abraham, and flood stories in many traditions, from the Babylonian 'Epic of Gilgamesh' told above and from non-Semitic Sumeria. There are also similar stories from India and further afield, from East Asia, Cochin, China, the Pacific and America. This fact, and the sometimes striking similarities among them, has been used to suggest all these, Bible and Qur'an stories and all, are folk tales that, over the years, have picked up bits of truth here and lots of storytellers' licence there.

As Muslims, we cannot do this. We can allow for a little of Gai Eaton's allegorical truth at a stretch, but we are fundamentalists by definition –

we believe that the Qur'an is the literal word of God as revealed to the Prophet Muhammad. If it says it in the Qur'an, it *is* necessarily so. If it seems a little difficult at times, that is a problem of our limited perception rather than any shortcoming of the author.

This means that with, say, the Gilgamesh story, we would notice the salient similarities with the Qur'anic story of Noah, or Nuh, and even allow their existence to be a cause of affirmation in our own book, but where they contradict our version, we infer the Babylonian storyteller working his or her art, or assume some chain of narration that is not sound, and that has served the purposes of storyteller and audience over the years. The story often tells us more about the storyteller than it does about the subject of the story. More, but not everything. Some of it could even be true.

So in the Bible we read that when the number of descendants from Adam and Eve became very large, God began to repent that He had made humankind whose "every inclination of the thoughts of their hearts was only evil continually." (Genesis 6:5)

Because of this, God decided that He would "blot out" all living things on the earth except for the family of Noah, a man who "found favour in the sight of the Lord." Noah was a *tsaddik*, "a righteous man, blameless in his generation" (Genesis 6:8-9) and God promised to establish His covenant with him and his family. (Genesis 6:18)

God instructed him and his sons Shem, Ham and Japheth, to make a huge Ark so that they and their families would survive the coming deluge. They were to bring seven of every clean animal into the Ark and two of every other, along with all types of foods so that they would have supplies for the Ark, and food to begin again when the flood had finished.

The rains fell for forty days and the springs overflowed and covered the mountains. The flood continued for a hundred and fifty days after which time God made the waters abate, leaving the Ark on Mount Ararat. Noah sent out a dove that returned, first with nothing, but then, on a second journey, with an olive branch, so Noah knew that the waters had subsided. He waited a little longer before leaving the Ark.

When he did, he built an altar and sacrificed one of each of the clean animals that he had taken on board. When God smelt the pleasing odour, He blessed them with the sign of the rainbow and said to Himself:

"I will never again curse the ground because of humankind, for the inclination of the human heart is evil from youth; nor will I ever destroy every living creature as I have done. As long as the earth endures, seedtime and harvest, cold and heat, summer and winter, day and night shall not cease." (Genesis 6:21-22)

This was to be a new start for humankind and God established His covenant with Noah, Japheth, Shem and Ham, the youngest and the father of Canaan. The people of the earth are all descended from the three sons but the three were soon to have their standing in this world stratified. Once he was back on dry land, Noah planted a vineyard and got drunk on the harvest and lay naked in his tent. Ham discovered him and told his brothers who covered their father without seeing his nakedness. When Noah woke and realised what had happened he said:

"Cursed be Canaan; a servant of servants shall he be unto his brethren. And... blessed be the Lord God of Shem; and Canaan shall be his servant. God shall enlarge Japheth, and he shall dwell in the tents of Shem; and Canaan shall be his servant." (Genesis 9:25-27)

Thus, the sons of Shem would be the owners of the land, with the sons of Japheth merely having dwelling rights, though their forefathers' action had been the same. For his role, the discovery of his father drunk and uncovered, the generations that followed Ham would be "servants of servants."

In the Qur'an, we read that over the years after the death of Adam, humankind began to forget their first duty, to worship God, and they began to worship idols to other gods such as, according to Islamic tradition, Wadd, Suwa', Yaghuth, Ya'uq and Nasr. These are explained in a *Hadith* as being statues of five well-known men who had lived at different times and had had different qualities. After their deaths there had been legends and then the statues, built to honour and inspire. However, Shaytan had prompted the following generations to worship them and before long they were seen as being responsible for rain and crops, which led to rituals and prayers, until eventually God was almost forgotten. He was angry at this ingratitude and sent a messenger to them to counsel them: "Warn your people before a painful punishment comes to them." (71:1) He also spoke words of encouragement "in public and secretly", saying "ask forgiveness from Your Lord, for He is forgiving. He will send rain to you in abundance; give you increase in wealth and sons; and bestow on you gardens and rivers." (71:11-12)

Well, they got the rain in the end, but before then, the leaders of the people ignored him, saying:

"This man is only a man like you, who wants to put himself over you; and if God wanted, He could have sent down angels. We have not heard anything like this in the case of our forefathers. He must only be a man possessed by *jinn*, so just watch out for him for a while." (23:23-25)

Noah knew that such a warning had to come from a man, and not from an angel, so that people could relate to him as one of themselves and see him as an example:

"Are you surprised that a reminder from your Lord should come to you through a man from among you, so that He can warn you, and so that you can have *taqwa* (fear of God) and perhaps find mercy?" (7:63)

When people do not want to hear something they invent any number of excuses for not hearing it. "They push their fingers in their ears and wrap themselves in their garments and persist." (71:5) In this way, the leaders of the people focused on what they imagined were Noah's political ambitions, as well as his lowly birth.

"We do not see any one following you except the lowest of us, unthinkingly, and we do not consider you to be any better than us. Indeed, we think you are a liar."(11:26)

Noah responded that he sought no reward and that if he was making up stories then he would pay for his actions, but the people did not listen.

The Qur'an has many, many retellings of this persistent warning in different parts of the text and it is a suggestion that Noah delivered the same message again and again, persistently and patiently, until finally the people said:

"'Oh Noah, you have argued with us and argued with us again, so bring what you have threatened us with if you are telling the truth.' He said: 'God will bring it to you if He wills, and you will not be able to frustrate it.'" (11:32)

We can infer that it was still not immediately, because Noah lived for nine hundred and fifty years before the flood. Finally, though, even he had had enough and it was revealed to him that none further would believe who did not believe already so he should not address God on their behalf any more. God also said:

"Build the ship under Our eyes and Our inspiration; and then when Our command comes and water comes gushing out from the ground, then put a pair of every kind in it, and your family – except the one of them against whom the Word has already been passed – and do not plead with Me with those who do wrong, for they will be drowned." (23:27-30)

The people continued to laugh at Noah while he built his ship of planks and palm fibre. Even when the rains came and "the fountains of the earth gushed forth" (11:40) they still did not believe that Noah was telling the truth, including some members of Noah's family. One of his sons, while "waves like mountains" were crashing around him, ignored his father's pleas to leave the disbelievers, saying that he would go up a mountain which would save him from the water. (So there is differentiation between the sons, but by God, rather than Nuh.) When he saw this, Noah *did* plead with God to forgive and save his son. God replied:

"O Noah, he is not one of your household for surely his action is not righteous – so do not question Me about what you have no knowledge of. I am protecting you so that you do not become one of the ignorant." (11:46)

Noah's wife also rejected him and drowned, learning like the others that "there was no-one to help them save God." (71:25) and becoming a warning to those who rejected signs and warnings. Noah prayed that God "leave not even one of the disbelievers on the earth. For if you leave them, they will lead astray Your slaves and will not beget any but wicked, ungrateful ones." (71:26-7)

After many days, God commanded that the rains cease and the earth swallow up its waters. The boat came to rest on Mount Al-Judi, and God said:

"Now you are far away from the people who did wrong." (11:44)

Though Noah thus saved the good portion of the people from his area, his story was to be a sign "for all the worlds" (29:15). He was blessed, as were his descendants: "And We rescued him and his family from the grievous distress; and made only his progeny to endure (on the earth). And We left this blessing for him among the generations to come. Peace be upon Noah among the nations." (37:76-81)
However, there was a warning in the blessing too:

"O Noah, go down in peace from Us and blessings will come from those who are with you – and there will be other nations to whom We will give pleasure for a long while, and then a painful punishment from Us will overtake them." (11:48)

	Gilgamesh	Bible	Qur'an
Location	Euphrates area implied	The world	The land of Nuh's people
Reason for flood	"The world bellowed like a bull" – bad human behaviour implied	Inclination of people's hearts to evil	People worshipping other gods
Ark builder	Shurrupak - no special characteristics or warning role	Noah - a *tsaddik* - a righteous man, warning implied	Nuh - a Prophet, warned the people for a long time (see

	mentioned	below)	
Ark	Dimensions specified	Dimensions specified	Dimensions implied?
Storm	Water from above and below for seven days	Water from above and below - 40 days rain, 150 days flood	Water from above and below for "many days"
Resting point	Mount Nisir	Mount Ararat	Mount Al-Judi
Birds	Swallow–returned Dove–returned Raven–didn't return	Dove–returned Dove–returned with olive branch	None mentioned
God's promise for the future & Blessings	Sacrifice-pleasant smell->gods vowed remember	Sacrifice-pleasant smell->God vowed never to do it again Noah blesses two sons and curses a third	No sacrifice mentioned God promises blessings on descendants but a painful punishment for some

Table 1: Table showing key similarities and differences between three Ark stories

If a Jewish, Christian and Muslim child were to summarise the story as it is taught to them at school, they may tell something very similar, and would recognise the Babylonian child's version, too. As can be seen above, there are some major similarities – a man is told by a god to build a boat to save himself and a few others from the flood that will soon come. The flood comes from above and below, from rain and overflowing ground sources, and when it ends, the boat has come to rest on a mountain. The survivors are then promised a better future.

People who have wished to dismiss all religion, at least as being from God, have said that this simply suggests that these are myths that have mutated through time and cultures. From an Islamic point of view, this has validity inasmuch as the Qur'anic story is the original one, one that is then revealed long after the others as a corrective for those others.

Such a claim has attracted a number of criticisms and hence controversy, because there are not many positions that exist between believing that the Prophet Muhammad received direct revelations from God which have been exactly recorded in the Qur'an (the Muslim position) and calling him a liar, which is what claims that the Prophet Muhammad recycled Bible stories he had heard to suit his purposes are often seen.

The 'Prophet Muhammad as author' claim is refuted by Muslims for a number of reasons which include: the Qur'an says the "Revelation (is) from the Lord of the Worlds" (5:77 among others); he had lived forty years showing no sign of poetic flair and was, in fact, illiterate; he had no material motive – he died with very little; and, if power and glory had been his motivation, he could have accepted a deal from the Quraysh that offered him everything (except recognition as a Prophet). To a Muslim, and God willing to non-Muslims too, the evidence of his character and circumstance, points to his genuineness.

Christians and Jews might equally take such an exclusivist position, but in terms of the religious content of the message, at least one aim of this book is to show that the message of the Prophet Muhammad, the Qur'an and the *Hadith*, can comfortably contain much of the essence and beauty and narrative of Judaism and Christianity in a way that Judaism and Christianity cannot contain that of their 'Others'. As we have seen in the stories of Adam and Eve, and Cain and Abel, one way that Islam can contain other faiths, particularly when dealing with the same narrative, is that in terms of the purity of the story, the Qur'an is often quite specific, whereas in terms of the fleshed-out, "roundedly human" details of the characters, it is the Bible that is often shockingly detailed. Not much airtime is given to Noah's drunken nakedness at many Saturday nor Sunday schools, for example.

In the Biblical story of Noah, we find a central character who, we are told, is an upright man but who shows himself to be seriously flawed (as his forefather Biblical Adam was) at the end, and at the end, we find the similar sort of psychological opt-out that we have seen before. As a response to the shameful state Ham finds him in, Noah curses his son. Ham thus becomes the bearer of the shame of Noah's deed and is cast into a shadow role, ethnic as well as psychological, because the Hamitic line is traditionally seen as being African. The significance of this will become manifest later. Even the treatment of the brothers Shem and Japheth is differentiated, though their actions are the same. This might be expected to have the effect of creating an unsatisfactory alliance between the two that is based on their both benefiting from the servitude of Ham and both being "white", but also characterised by a sense of injustice between the two, not least because it is "family." (This pattern of resentment and oppression can be seen amongst the "sons of Shem" today - European Jewish Israelis, non-European Jewish Israelis and Palestinians – though you will not necessarily find agreement that Arabs are Semitic). If the theological role of the Flood was to cleanse the earth of corruption, the Biblical story immediately re-establishes it, by having the main protagonist, Noah, literally corrupting himself with alcohol, then repeating the blaming of another and finally failing to integrate both sides of himself, which, in religious terms, is done by begging God for forgiveness. Instead he re-establishes a pattern of blessed and cursed that is based on rather arbitrary moral considerations.

It is details like these that make the Bible seem such a humanly constructed text, and allow the Qur'an to be seen as what it claims itself to be, what God, Allah, claims it to be, namely, His Word. The Bible, nonetheless, is based on truth (one of the articles of faith of a Muslim is belief in *Tawrah* and *Injeel*, the Torah and New Testament respectively, though in their original form), and purity and holiness are certainly found there, but not always so clearly.

In the case of the Noah story, we can see that the Bible says: "Noah was a righteous man (*ish tsaddik*): he was blameless in his generation..." (Genesis 6:9) Interpretations of this have varied from Rabbi Yehuda saying that Noah was merely righteous compared to those around him, whereas Rabbi Nehemiah says that if he was that righteous then, he would have been so much more righteous had he lived later. Moshe Kohn, who quoted the above two opinions, also says that the use of the construction *ish+man/person* means that he also tried "to teach and warn the people of his time to become righteous people too."[35]

---

[35] Kohn (1999)

He also lays great stress on the word used for lawlessness in this time being *hamas*. Though not spelling out the obvious current political resonance for most Israelis, he explains that the word means to unlawfully take less than a penny's worth, while robbery means to take more than a penny's worth. As this was not punishable under the law, the Flood was God's response to this deviousness, a "sentence without trial", as he quotes Rabbi Levi saying.

A concern with words and their purity is a feature of both Kohn and Rabbi Shlomo Riskin's understanding of the Noah story. Both mention the instruction by God to bring some animals in pairs and some with seven males matched with seven females,[36] the distinction being between the seven pairs of animals that are pure and the pairs being "...of every animal that is not pure." Kohn mentions that many Rabbis have understood that God modified words in order to avoid saying impure words, and thus said *einena tehora* (not pure) rather than *tamei* (impure). Kohn draws from this that people should keep their language clean, while Riskin says that people should do this because "elegant words lead to elegant deeds," just as bad language had led to the violent behaviour of Noah's day.

Riskin then engages in what might be called an esoteric interpretation of the text. Firstly, he points out that the word used in Hebrew for the Ark is *teva*, although the usual word for ship would be *onia* or *sfina*, and then uses a form of numerology discovered by Baal Shem Tov, the founder of Hassidism, in which each Hebrew letter has a numerical value that depends on its position in the alphabet.[37] The measurements of the Ark given in the Bible are 300 cubits by length, 50 by breadth and 30 by height and by taking the letter equivalent of each of these values, 300 (*shin*), 50 (*nun*) and 300 (*lamed*), a word, *lashon*, can be made. *Lashon* means language, so, as Riskin says, "the Hebrew *teva* means 'word' and its measurements embrace us with 'language'." It is language, he continues, that separates us from animals.

On the subject of the boat's specifications, one of the curious details of the Gilgamesh text is the survival of some fairly specific building

---

[36] Riskin (1999)

[37] A similar system exists in Arabic – see Jarrar, B. *Irhassat*, (2000) Noon Books: Ramallah.

58

instructions. Although the Qur'an has nothing specific by way of measurements, "Build the ship under Our eyes and Our inspiration" (23:27) could be taken as being specific enough to infer that particular measurements were important, at least then.

If the Jewish analysis so far has been quite positive, this is not always the case. Riskin closes with a criticism that has been made against Noah by some commentators, that Noah's *teva* saved only his family and that, according to the literal text, Noah did not protest, (nor warn the people to change either). It was to Moses that a wider mission would come.

Thus, at the end of the Noah story, from a Muslim point of view, we are obliged to confirm that, similarities notwithstanding, the Noah of the Bible seems to serve the writer's purpose most obviously, which is ultimately to advance a particular ethnic position. Divine truth may be accidental or incidental, and Divine purpose in all this is perhaps not yet entirely clear. The only story that presents a man who is worthy of admiration, who is worthy of being called a Prophet, who brought a message from God, is the Noah of the Qur'an.

Frazer, J.G. *Folklore in the Old Testament* (2003) Kessinger Publishing: Whitefish MT
Ibn Kathir, I. *Stories of the Prophets* (2003) Darrusalam: Riyadh
Jarrar, B. *Irhassat* (2000) Noon Books: Ramallah
Kohn, M. *Keep Your Language Clean* (15 October 1999) Jerusalem Post
Riskin, Rabbi S. *Man and Beast* (15 October 1999) Jerusalem Post
Roberts, M. *The Ancient World* (1979) Nelson: Oxford

4

The FAMILY of ABRAHAM

God said to Abraham, 'Give me a son'
Abe said, 'Man, you must be puttin' me on.'
God said, 'No!'
Abe said, 'What?'
God said, 'Do what you wanna do but
Next time you see me comin' you better run.'
Abe said, 'Where do you want this killing done?'
God said, ...
(Bob Dylan – 'Highway 61 Revisited')

Bob Dylan had it as being Highway 61. Look at an Israeli map and you'd have to drop that to Highway 60, in Jerusalem or, if you are a Samaritan, on Mount Gerizim, overlooking Nablus. A Muslim would head Deep South to Arabia and Mecca. Bad enough already, never mind which son. Was it Isaac or Ishmael, Is'haq or Isma'il? Is it necessary to have a certain opinion on this in order to *get* Abraham, Ibrahim?

Most would say yes, because, as all traditions agree, Abraham is of profound significance to Jews and Muslims, Christians and Samaritans, because of his life and as the father of the faithful through his sons. In both Biblical and Qur'anic sources, as well as from elsewhere in the traditions, there are many stages in the story of Abraham that superficially have striking similarities. However, on closer analysis, there often, though not always, appear to be big differences, so there is much to be gained in comparison.

Origins
According to Islamic tradition, Abraham was born in the city of Ur on the banks of the Euphrates. Unlike all of the people around him, including his father, he was a *hanif*, which means that he recognised the true nature of existence and worshipped God only. At some point in his life, we assume before the confrontations he had with his people, he went through a process of questioning the nature of his Lord, in which he first considered his Lord to be a star, but the star set; then the moon,

60

but it set too; then the sun, but that also set. This confirmed for him that God was above and beyond the things that the people around him associated with Him, and that He "encompasses everything in His knowledge." (6:80)

The Qur'anic Abraham tried to persuade his father Azar and those around him not to worship "what does not listen and does not see and does not benefit you at all" (19:41) but his father threatened to stone him if he did not leave him "for a long while." Abraham withdrew, promising to pray for his father, but when it became clear that his father was "an enemy of God" (9:114) he disassociated from him completely.

When he asked his father and his people why they worshipped these objects that they themselves had made, they said that it was because they had found their fathers doing the same. Then, when the people were away out of town at a religious gathering, Abraham, who had excused himself from going through feigned illness, smashed all of the idols, except the largest. When the people asked who had destroyed their gods, Abraham said, "This, their chief, hath done it. So question them, if they can speak."(21:63) Obviously, he knew that they could not, and that the people knew that too. In their anger, they cried out to burn Abraham to avenge their gods. "Build a pyre for him and throw him into the burning fire."(37:97)

This was the final moment between Abraham and his people and he called out: "Lo, you have chosen idols instead of God. The love between you is only in the life of this world. On the Day of Resurrection, you will reject each other and curse each other, and your abode will be the Fire and you will have no one to help you." (29:25) Then, Abraham and Lut (Lot) were saved from the fire of this world by the order of God, and the flames of the fire were "coolness and peace" for them.

It was on this day that one Muslim commentator, Suddi', said Abraham had the argument that is mentioned in the Qur'an. Nimrud, who believed himself to be all-powerful because he had power of life or death over his people, was the ruler of the place where Abraham was punished. Abraham told him that it was God who gave life or death and that it was as natural that it were so as the rising of the sun. "Can you make it (the sun) rise in the west?" (2:258) he asked the puzzled king, to show him how powerless the king really was, and how limited his idea of all-powerful was. The king, though, like many others, was destined to remain in ignorance and was unable to let go of his own arrogance. After this, Abraham and Lot escaped to "the land, which We have blessed for (all) peoples." (21:71) Here there is a divergence of views as to whether this was the land of Palestine or Arabia, not the only multi-faith ambiguity in the Qur'an, as we shall see.

In the Bible, Abraham was born in Ur on the Lower Euphrates but left his birthplace along with his father Terah and nephew Lot. They travelled northeast, settling in Haran, an area near the border of Syria and Turkey. Terah died here, whereupon God told Abraham to resume his travels to an unnamed destination to "make you a great nation" (Genesis 12:1-3). One of the biggest differences between the two tellings of the story will be the recurring specific geographical promise of the Bible, and it is to this place that the Bible takes the Patriarch, his wife and his nephew Lot.

Unusually, the Qur'an has more detail up to this point. However, there is at least one story in the Jewish tradition that fills in some of the gaps in the tale between Ur and Canaan. As told by Moshe Kohn,[38] Abraham's father was actually a maker of idols (Joshua 24:2) and one day when Abraham was in charge of his father's business, he smashed all of the idols except the largest and, when asked to explain, he said they fought over a bowl of cereal that a woman had brought. His father retorted that idols could not do such a thing and Abraham said: "Do your ears hear what your mouth is saying?"

As a result of this, his father gave his son to the King, Nimrod, so that he could be dealt with as a heretic. Nimrod decided to burn him to death but first offered that if Abraham would worship the fire then he would be saved. Abraham said: "I will worship the water that extinguishes the fire."

Nimrod made the same offer with water, and Abraham replied in the same way, saying that he would worship the clouds that bring the water. So it went on, through clouds, and winds that disperse the

---

[38] Kohn (1999)

clouds; and wind, and man who endures the wind. In the end Nimrod became angry and said that as *he* worshipped fire, he would throw Abraham in the fire and let God rescue him, which He did.

Here, then, we have different stories that are found in the Qur'an, the smashing of the idols and its punishment, the argument with a tyrant and the chain of association in defining the creator, coming together as two parts of the same story in Jewish tradition. The latter part is quite different in context, an internal debate of genuine speculation in the Qur'an and a public call-and-response to make a point in the Jewish tradition. None, though, seem much out of character - the disputations all have the same mocking tone that Abraham/Ibrahim uses when asked about the fate of the idols.

In that story, there is exactly the same context but there are some subtle differences in its unfolding. In the Jewish story, Abraham is actually working for his father, and then carries out the smashing at least in front of the woman who brought the cereal. In the Qur'an, the act is done when the people are away, though the culprit is obvious because Abraham has already made serious attempts to put his father on the right path, to the point where it is impossible to imagine him helping his father in the idol-making business. This, in fact, is probably the most significant difference between these two particular stories and the Biblical and the Qur'anic Abraham in general. As we found with Noah, the significance of the Qur'anic Prophets is that they do actually warn. The Biblical Prophets and Patriarchs, and this became an issue with Noah's cursing, are often primarily, or even only, associated with connecting the Land and the People.

What we have in this Jewish story is the echo of the Islamic stories within the Jewish tradition. In this case, the story may have gone from Qur'anic story to folk tale, though its standing is not mentioned in the article in question. This would depend on when the story appeared in Jewish tradition. Something similar in reverse happened in Islam in the early years when a small number (the number 39 is the most specific I've seen in an Islamic knowledge card game) of Arabian Jews converted to Islam and they brought with them their own knowledge of the Bible. The body of literature within Islam that grew up around the Biblical traditions is known as the *Isra'iliyyat*, and in some instances it complements and amplifies what exists in the often-briefer stories of the Qur'an and *Hadith*. However, there are occasions, as we will see, where the *Isra'iliyyat* versions stand in contradiction to, or at least in tension with, the Qur'anic story. This is particularly the case with the stories of Abraham.

More helpful than the "who copied whom" argument is to see the stories as being different versions of the same event. As a Muslim, it is quite possible to believe that the Qur'anic version is true, the Jewish version contains elements of truth, and that common elements were not copied, but are simply surviving parts of the original story.

Canaan and Egypt

According to the Bible, after leaving Haran, Abraham next went south through Shechem (now Nablus) to Hebron and thence to the Negev. He and Lot were quite wealthy but as their wealth was dependent on the size of their flocks, they were also dependent on the fall of rain to sustain them. When famine befell the area, Abraham went south to Egypt where he stayed for some time.

It is here that we find another significant parallel story. In the Bible, while in Egypt, Abraham feared that the Pharaoh would covet his beautiful wife and kill him to get her, so he asked her:

"Say, I pray thee, thou art my sister: that it may be well with me for thy sake: and my soul shall live because of thee." (Genesis 12:13)

As Abraham feared, the Pharaoh was taken with Sara and took her into his household and gave many good things to Abraham. However, God inflicted many diseases on the Pharaoh so when he discovered Abraham's trick he returned Sara and ordered them both to leave.

By way of contrast, there is a sound *Hadith* that records that the Prophet Muhammad said:

"Abraham did not lie except three times: (the first being his excusing himself through illness as we have heard and the second being his claim that the big idol had destroyed the others)... and one regarding Sara. He came to a land of a tyrant, along with Sara, and she was the most beautiful of people. He said to her: 'If this tyrant knows that you are my wife, he will defeat me and take you away from me. If he asks you (about the relationship between us), tell him that you are my sister, for you are my sister in Islam, for I know no Muslims in the land except you and I.' When they entered his (the tyrant's) territory, a member of the tyrant's family saw her. He went to him and said: 'A woman has come to your land, and she should be for none other than you.' He sent for her, and she was brought to him. Abraham resorted to prayer…"

Dr Mustafa Abu Sway points out that the concerns of the Biblical Abraham are rather selfish and material, while those of the Qur'anic Abraham are for his wife and that his response, prayer, is spiritual. Also, the lie is simply a play on words. Details as small and apparently insignificant as the reporter to the tyrant/Pharaoh are very similar – "princes" in the Bible and a family member in the *Hadith*, yet there is this huge difference in the moral content of the characters in the tales and this seems to affect the outcome. In the Islamic story, Abraham's prayers are answered – the tyrant has a fit each time he approaches Sara, declares her to be possessed and gives her Hagar (a *Hadith* transmitted by Abu Hurairah). In the Bible, Sara is "taken into the Pharaoh's house" (Genesis 12:15) and, given that Abraham is showered with all manner of gifts, we are not supposed to imagine this was for a cup of tea; Robin Lane Fox presumes she commits "rampant adultery,"[39] which is quite shocking to read but the only conclusion that can be drawn before plague strikes the unsuspecting Pharaoh. (The Dead Sea Scrolls, however, say that though she was with Pharaoh, he "knew her not" – a detail which could be seen to highlight the moral failing of the Biblical story).

This similarity in insignificant detail and difference in moral content is a significant and recurring pattern and it does beg the question, Why?

The very fact of Abraham's going down to Egypt is actually enormously vexing for Jewish commentators, though not for this reason. Rather, it is for the manner of Abraham's going there in the first place, and the debate does not show the Biblical Abraham in a very good light. One point of controversy is another repeated story, though

---

[39] Lane Fox (1991) p.408

this one occurs twice in the Bible. In Genesis 12:10, the Bible says that there was a famine in the land and Abraham went down to Egypt. This is placed alongside 26:1-2 where Isaac, Abraham's son, is faced with a similar famine and is told: "Do not go down to Egypt, stay in the land which I point out to you." In the Bible, the similarity of expression is so great that strong criticism of Abraham is implied. Nachmanides (Ramban), the Jewish commentator who lived in Spain in the 13th Century, after criticising Abraham for the "sister" story, took this further and said:

"You should know, that our father Abraham sinned a great sin, although by error, when he brought his pious wife into danger, because of the fear that he feared for his life, since he had to turn to God Who can help and save. Leaving the country because of the famine was also a sin, since God can save us from death by hunger. And because of this it was decreed upon his children to be in exile in Egypt in the hands of Pharaoh."

Elsewhere, it is the whole Egyptian thing that troubles. In the Babylonian Talmud of the 3rd to 5th Centuries, one rabbi sees the time in slavery in Egypt as punishment for Abraham detaching students from their learning to fight (based on Genesis 14:14) while the other, who he is disputing with, sees it as being caused, an echo of Dr Abu Sway's criticism here, by Abraham's not "bringing people under the wings of God" when he had the opportunity to – he agreed to the King of Sodom asking: "Give me the persons and take the possessions." (Genesis 14:14)[40]

One final explanation for the going into slavery that Jewish scholars have inferred is that Abraham lost faith in God, even if only briefly. When told in Genesis 15:1-7 that he will inherit the land of Canaan, Abraham demands that God give him a sign or a proof that God intends to fulfil His promise. A *Midrash* from the 8th Century picks out the repetition of the word *Eda'* in 15:8 ("Whereby shall I *know* that I will inherit it?") and the related words *Yado'a teda'* in 15:13 ("*Know* for certain that thy seed shall be a stranger in a land that is not theirs...") to

---

[40] Babylonian Talmud Nedarim (Vows) p.32a

make a direct connection between loss of faith and slavery in Egypt.[41] The *Yalkut Shimoni*, an *aggadic* collection of commentaries on the Old Testament, [42]also says on this passage:

"One must always be careful about one's words and actions, lest the slightest slip lead to sin. For because of Abraham's scepticism – 'How will I know…?' – his descendants went into exile in Egypt."

Furthermore, an Aramaic translation of the Bible mentioned by Professor Avigdor Shinan shows us that this particular criticism was not restricted to the learned but was taught to the public as well.

Thus, the 'Why?' Professor Avigdor Shinan, the Jewish writer who has highlighted most of the 'Egypt' criticisms above, makes the distinction between a perfect person, who is a model for adoration, and "a great person with small defects, deficiencies and disadvantages, side by side with advantages, merits and virtues", who is a model for imitation. He places Abraham in the latter category and notes his obedience, hospitality, pursuit of peace, prayers for others, his resistance to temptation and his willing acceptance of pain, as being highly worthy characteristics for *all* to follow. The flaws, he says, make him human and therefore imitable

The Islamic argument on the flawlessness or otherwise of the Prophets is very different. There are some who believe that the Prophets were flawless, while others believe that they (some or all) were tested at some weaker point, Adam being an obvious example. However, the flaws the Bible mentions in Abraham, among others, are simply too great, to the point where they almost seem to cancel out the merits and virtues, leaving simply the blood line and the land promise. As Muslims, we believe that the merits and virtues were there, untarnished, in the Bible originally, but that the Bible was changed, as the Qur'an itself says (2:59).

The reason it was changed, as we have mentioned, is at least partly because it was written at a particular time to standardise a non-canonical body of stories in a way that would serve a national purpose,

---

[41] Pirke de Rabbi Eliezer 48
[42] *Lekh-Lekha, 77; Mo'ed Kattan 25b*

that being to strengthen the claims of the Children of Israel to the Holy Land. In doing this, the new writers would have had a different set of priorities than were operative in what Muslims understand as being the original *Tawrah* (*Torah*). National struggles need to have their followers strengthened by their canons, so to speak, and this can lead to the nations' own myths or heroes being built up at the expense of their rivals. Certainly the Bible is at pains to create a duality out of every story – Cain/Abel, Shem/Ham - in a way that reflects the Jewish position at the time of writing. The self, usually represented by the Prophet, may not be so pure, but is better than the Other, having God on its side.

In order for the writers to accomplish this, it was necessary for them to gloss over or ignore the morally troubling questions that Chosenness brings. The reason for that, as we have seen with the Adam story, looks like a misreading, wilful or otherwise, of human nature and humanity's role, a role that in the Jewish reading became increasingly particularist, with one people being right, having "God on our side" to quote Dylan again, and the Other, carrying the literal and metaphorical rubbish (and hewing wood and bearing water as well). The key message of the human creation stories, though, is that our task is to unify that which has been split into pairs, whether this be as man and woman, or to integrate both sides of our nature, the conscious self and unconscious, and to learn from those who are different from us. What the message most profoundly is not, is that we should see humanity as either good or evil, nor to accept that evil as part of our nature. Sin is there to tempt us, but it does not define us.

Not acknowledging this at source effectively sets the reader of the Bible, whether Jewish or Christian, off on a journey with a faulty map. The traveller is left to try to explain why "bad things happen to good people" - themselves. The only explanation is to find someone else to blame, which is what the Biblical characters do - someone we are allowed to think of as being evil because it has always been easier to choose to remain unconscious of the faults of the Self and to blame the Other. This Other then becomes the repository of all the disliked personal qualities of the Self. This is a failure to accept both the responsibility and mystery of the destiny of humanity. Because we are all from One in the first place, that Other you are looking at is you, that is. He, or she, is a mirror.

However, by stressing the unimpeachable chosen nature of one people in the Bible at the expense of another, *and* portraying that same people and their Prophets as flawed, the writers of the Bible have created a kind of schizophrenic superiority/inferiority complex for its subject people to cope with. The warts 'n' all portraits of the Prophets are, in a way, worthy works of honesty, an acknowledgement of human frailty. However, given what the story says is at stake – the taking of an inhabited land and through it the blessing of humanity – it is as if the weight is too much for ordinary folk to carry. The Bible's writers are thus left with the problem of how to shift the load.

In the Bible, it is the motif of Egypt that represents this unintegrated unconscious aspect of the persona, this shadow that has been with the Biblical Prophets since Adam. We have already mentioned the connection of Egypt and punishment and we can note that in Kabbalistic Judaism, in the Zohar, going down to Egypt is seen as Abraham descending into the place where he "resisted being seduced by the demonic essences, and when he had proved himself, he returned to his abode."[43] It is no accident that Egyptians are the dark-skinned descendants of the cursed Ham; nor even that perhaps Adam was African; nor that wishing to go back to Egypt while in the Sinai was like the longing we have for going back to the innocence and lack of responsibility of childhood. It is for all these reasons that Egypt represents the People of Israel's ethnic and psychological shadow.

"You can master it", Cain was told of this psychological weight, with God's help. However, if you forget God, or lose faith, or become egotistical, putting your faith in material things, (textually implied of Abraham in the Bible), it will master you. From after Joseph until Moses it did, and the Children of Israel were literally slaves to Egypt. By telling the family history in the way they have, the writers of the Bible have thus condemned coming generations to the need for years of analysis. Freud would eventually even conclude that Moses himself was Egyptian.

---

[43] Levi (1973) p.45

That might make for an "interesting" journey, but "interesting times" is a Chinese curse, and seeking understanding of that journey is not necessarily all that it is cracked up to be either. As Werner Erhardt, of the *est* seminar training workshops, put it: "Understanding is the booby prize!" It's the sort of pithy one-liner that has stayed with me since I did one of those two weekenders when I was in Israel in 1982 and it has a validity. The fate of the world, as Jung put it, may hang by a single thread and that is the unconscious, but God help us if we all have to understand it for the planet to survive. We cannot all do therapy, nor *est* weekends, nor go to Egypt. It is to meet this need, to live and deal with the unintegrated part of ourselves, that seems to be a main part of religion's God-given function. God, Allah, effectively promises that, as it is put in *Pesikta Rabbati*, return as far as you can, and He will come the rest of the way. Human efforts that over-complicate, like the Bible, are more likely to be serving the purposes of the writers even if they are, by definition, God's Will, and in the case of the Bible, partly authentic. However, they are not, experience suggests, likely to work.

The Muslim belief is that Islam is *the* way to do this, to live with things we do not know or fully understand. Allah Akbar! God is greater than anything we can conceive. It seems, though, that as Muslims we need to better accept both the ways in which we fall short of perfection, without losing the sense of our blessed nature as human beings, and to recognise the way of all human beings in falling short of the practice of their religions, without losing a reverence for the God-given nature of those religions. All contradictions are resolved within God and all conflict is resolvable through patience.

Nonetheless, the profound similarities between the Biblical narrative and the Qur'anic do invite us to understand, or try. My guess is that, everything being the product of God's will, the Qur'an represents something like a strict, almost simplistic guide to life, while the Bible chronicles a life off that path in all its depth of feeling and wrong-headedness. For all that, it still contains the same call, Submit, and the paradox is that there is depth in apparent simplicity, and vice versa. There is much we can learn from the Bible, though not always in the way the writers intended. As the Qur'an says, speaking of the Jews:

"And they planned and God planned and God is the best of planners."
(3:54)

Hajar and Isma'il

If material wealth is seen to imply spiritual success, Chapter 13 of
Genesis begins well, with Abraham and Lot rich in cattle, gold and
silver. However, back near Bethel, Abraham and Lot decide to part
before they begin fighting. Lot chooses to settle in Sodom, wherein his
famous encounter with the city's inhabitants occurs, while Abraham
goes to live in Hebron, having been told by God that he and his
descendants will be given all the lands that he can see. Clearly, though,
there is a price to pay, and it is after this that Abraham has this doubt,
the one also mentioned above.

In a vision one night, God summons Abraham out of his tent and tells
him "I am thy shield and thy exceeding great reward." (Genesis 15:1)
He tells Abraham to look to the heavens and count the stars. "So shall
thy seed be." To seal the covenant, Abraham is commanded to take a
heifer, a she-goat and a ram, all three-years old, a turtledove and a
young pigeon, and to divide all except the birds in two and place each
piece against the other.

That night "a great darkness" falls on Abraham as he is told what will
happen to his descendants. They will be strangers in a land that is not
theirs for four hundred years and serve the rulers of that land. The
rulers of that nation will be judged and Abraham's descendants will
"come out with great substance." Abraham will live to a good age and
"go to thy fathers in peace," and "Unto thy seed have I given this land,
from the river of Egypt unto the great river, the river Euphrates."

One of the effects of the continuous repetition of the Promise by God to
the Biblical Abraham is to lessen the sense in which we feel Abraham
is tested. In the Qur'an, by contrast, guidance comes more as an
ongoing phenomenon, so we do feel that Abraham is confronted with
tests as his spiritual journey unfolds. This is certainly true in the way
that the Hagar and Ishmael stories are communicated.

In the Bible, as well as the cattle, silver and gold, Abraham and Sara
also come out of Egypt with a maidservant, Hagar. Given the role of

71

Egypt as the Other in defining Jewish identity, this is significant because the "Other" will, through Hagar, now become an inseparable part of the Self. As they still have no children, Sara gives Hagar, who is her servant, to Abraham "to be his wife" (Genesis 16:3) and Hagar duly conceives. Because of this, Sara begins to feel despised and she tells Abraham. Abraham tells Sara to do as she wishes so she "dealt hardly" with Hagar, resulting in the latter fleeing. An angel tells her to return, promising, "I will multiply thy seed exceedingly" (Genesis 16:10). Hagar returns but after the birth of Isaac it is the sons' rivalry - Ishmael mocks Isaac – that is the problem and Sara asks Abraham to send mother and son away. This time, God tells Abraham "hearken unto (Sara's) voice" (Genesis 21:12) and do as she wishes, even though he is unhappy about it. God here promises to "make a nation" of Ishmael because "he is thy seed." (Genesis 21:13). Abraham gives them bread and water and sends them to Bir Sheva where, the water having run out, Hagar sits a way off from Ishmael because she does not want to see him die. God hears her crying and commands her to "lift up the lad... for I will make him a great nation", whereupon "God opened her eyes" and she sees a well and they drink. After this "God was with the lad" (Genesis 21:18-21) and he grows up in the wilderness of Paran, where he becomes an archer and is given an Egyptian wife by his mother.

In the Qur'an, much of this is similar, though not all. We are told that Abraham is unable to have children by his wife Sara so he marries his slave girl, Hajar,[44] who bears him a son, Isma'il. In the Islamic tradition there is no rivalry mentioned, though Ibn Kathir tells the Biblical story to suggest possible filling for the spaces the terse Qur'anic and *Hadith* tellings leave. In these, simply, when Isma'il is a few months old, God commands Abraham to take Hajar and Isma'il to a desert valley called Bakka, in central Arabia. He does as he is commanded. When he comes to leave them, he will not answer Hajar's question as to why he is doing this until finally she asks him if it is God Who has commanded him, to which he replies affirmatively, an answer that Hajar accepts, saying: "Surely God will not abandon us." As Abraham leaves, he prays: "Our Lord, I have settled some of my offspring in a valley without any cultivation, by your sacred house, so they may establish regular

---

[44] The name in Hebrew and Egyptian Arabic is Hagar, while in Arabic elsewhere (mostly) it is Ha*j*ar, a feature of the languages in general in their pronunciation of the *g* and *j*.

prayers. So make the hearts of people yearn towards them, and provide them with sustenance that they may be grateful." (14:37)

Not long after he leaves, they run out of food and water. Looking for help, Hajar puts Isma'il down and runs off to the top of a nearby hill. Seeing nothing she runs to the top of another, then back to the first. In her distress she runs between the two hilltops seven times until she finally returns to Isma'il and prays to God. When she looks down she sees water welling up where Isma'il has kicked it. She quickly makes a wall of mud around it to stop the water flowing away and then they drink. Shaikh Sharawi explains that in doing this, God has shown that Hajar's faith does not prevent her from acting to help herself and her child, even though it has no effect on the outcome. The miraculous appearance of water then preserves in our minds God as the Ultimate Cause of all result in the universe, even though it is a young baby who "causes" the water to flow by striking the ground. In other words, though it is the foot of Isma'il that causes the water to flow, on the deepest level, it is the Hand of God.

The water attracts the attention of some birds that fly around the spot. These in turn are spotted by a passing caravan, which then finds Hajar and Isma'il. The water is so good that some of the travellers decide to settle there, after agreeing that the water belongs to Hajar and Isma'il. Thus, Mecca is founded, the town that will now be home to Isma'il and Hajar. The hills will become known as Safa and Marwa and the well as Zamzam.

In the two stories, the superficial similarities are again striking, particularly the mother separating herself from the child before the miraculous appearance of the water. The biggest difference, though, is that the Biblical story is driven by the presence of the Other, and has to take place after the birth of both sons for this reason. This means that the "lad" Ishmael is at least thirteen, according to the ages and events (such as Isaac's weaning) given in the Bible, and therefore, it is a little bit hard to see him as being in as vulnerable a position as is needed – at fifteen or so he might be as strong as his mother. In the Qur'an, the fact that the child is breast-feeding means that Isaac has not been born. The story simply seems to stand as the origin within the divine plan of the divergent lines within the house of Abraham. Within this context,

Hajar is assured that the leaving *is* God's will, while the Hagar of the Bible appears simply as a victim, or cause, of the jealousy of her mistress.

This has provided another troubling area for Jewish scholars. One, Rabbi Shlomo Riskin, sees the later intended sacrifice of the son as being punishment for Abraham, "measure for measure", so that he knows what it feels like to suffer for your child. He points to textual similarities (again we see the importance of the words) in the Hagar story and the sacrifice story – the rising early; putting food/wood on the back of Hagar/the son; then an angel rescuing.

All this comes after the earlier abuses within the relationship. Riskin mentions a Rabbi[45] writing that Sara's behaviour was "neither ethical nor pious" and that Abraham did not try to prevent wrongdoing. The Ramban said that the Ishmaelites in the future would want their measure for measure: "Our matriarch transgressed by dealing harshly, and Abraham also transgressed by allowing her to do so. And so, God heard her (Hagar's) affliction and gave her a son who would be 'a wild ass of a man' (16:12) to afflict the seed of Abraham and Sara."

The Qur'an stresses of the Prophets that God makes no distinction between any of them. In the Bible, this almost reaches the point where Isaac and Ishmael in the Bible are, as Riskin puts it, "mirror-images": they are both named by God and blessed and, while Isaac begets the fathers of twelve tribes, Ishmael begets twelve princes. He also points out that the place where Ishmael is saved is named Be'er-lahai-roi (Genesis 24:62) and it is here that Rebekah first sees Isaac, the man who will be her husband, and that he lives there. Rashi (Rabbi Shlomo Yitzhaki) writes that Isaac goes there to bring Hagar back to be with Abraham after Sarah dies, and that the woman named as Abraham's third wife in the Bible, Keturah, is actually Hagar.

The stories, though, serve different functions. While the Qur'an constantly asserts the unity of the Prophets in their message, the Bible constantly creates separation in its telling of the story of the Children of Israel. Yet it can only be said that it agonises over this separation even

---

[45] In the Radak of R. David Kimhi 1160-1235

while it is unable to let it go. When Abraham dies, the two brothers meet to bury him. This agonising is true of much of the Jewish discourse since. Shlomo Riskin was a rabbi on the West Bank settlement of Ariel when he wrote:

"Isaac begets Jacob/Israel, father of the covenanted nation but God will continue to hear the pain of the descendants of Ishmael (which means literally 'God will hear') if they are not treated properly by the descendants of Yisrael. Our ultimate redemption can only take place when the two sons of Abraham come together in peace."

Abraham and Isma'il

Once Ishmael and Hagar have left for the wilderness, they effectively fall outside the scope of the Bible. In the Qur'an, though, what happens next is central to why the mantle of Prophethood passes to the Ishmaelite line with the calling of the Prophet Muhammad, after the last of the Prophets from the line of Isaac has come.

After leaving Hajar and Isma'il, Abraham returns to the Holy Land, but he returns later and, with his son's help, builds a sanctuary at the place that God shows him near the well of Zamzam. It is named the *Ka'bah*, cube, because of its shape and it contains a celestial stone, which it is said was brought to Abraham by an angel from a nearby hill. "It descended from paradise whiter than milk, but the sins of the sons of Adam made it black," as Martin Lings puts it. Afterwards, Abraham prays there and God says, "Lo, I have made you an imam, a leader, for mankind," (2:124) thus confirming Abraham's universal role. Abraham then asks whether the same is true for his offspring, to which God replies, "My promise does not include wrong doers." As his offspring will include both Isma'il and Is'haq (Isaac), we can see that God clearly states that spiritual leadership is dependent on moral character and behaviour rather than the specific lineage of either of the sons.

While they are raising the foundations of the *Ka'bah*, Abraham prays:

"Our Lord! Accept from us (this duty). Lo! Only Thou art the Hearer and the Knower.

75

Speaking of his offspring, only Isma'il at this point, though God knew otherwise (as now do we), he continues: "Our Lord! Make us submissive unto Thee, and make of our seed a nation submissive unto Thee, and show us our ways of worship, and relent towards us. Lo! Thou, only Thou, art the Relenting and the Merciful."

Finally he prays for the coming of a Prophet to the Isma'ilite line: "Our Lord! Raise up in their midst a messenger from among them who shall recite unto them Thy revelations, and shall instruct them in the Scripture and in wisdom and shall make them grow. Lo! Thou, only Thou, art the Mighty and Wise.

"And who forsaketh the religion of Abraham except him who fooleth himself? Verily We chose him in the world, and Lo! In the Hereafter he is among the righteous.

"When His Lord said unto him: Submit! He said: I have submitted to the Lord of the Worlds." (2:127-131)

When Abraham finishes building the *Ka'bah,* God tells him to institute the rite of pilgrimage: "Purify My House for those who go the rounds of it and who stand beside it and bow and make prostration. And proclaim unto men the pilgrimage, that they may come unto thee on foot and on every lean camel out of every deep ravine." (12:26-27) Part of the rite of pilgrimage will be to re-enact parts of the story that connects Abraham and Isma'il to that place, including the passing between the two hills of Safa and Marwa and the stoning of Shaytan who tempted Abraham before the would-be sacrifice of his son.

Sacrifice
Some time around this point a narrative comparison of the Abraham stories becomes difficult, because the defining moment of Abraham's life – the sacrifice of his son - makes sense in the Islamic tradition probably only if that son is Isma'il (and we'll return to the "probably" later), and in the Biblical apparently only if that son is Isaac (and ditto with "apparently"). For now, if we look at the chronology of the stories we can see that the stories do make most sense if Isma'il and Isaac are the respective Qur'anic and Biblical sacrifices. Isma'il is central to the

idea that the Arabs have a special role as "children of a sacrifice", just as Isaac is central to the idea that the Jews have a similar special role: Isaac is specifically named in the Bible, and Isma'il is strongly implied in verses 37:99-113 where the news of the birth of Isaac comes *after* the mention of the sacrifice.

Qur'an (logical chronology)	Bible (literal chronology)
Abraham moves to Haran – tries to bring message	Abraham moves to Haran
Argument with father – idols - fire	(Smashes idols – argues with Nimrod – fire)
Goes to Arabia or Palestine then Egypt	Goes to Palestine then Egypt
Tyrant king and "sister"	Pharaoh and "sister"
Returns to Canaan (separates from Lut)	Returns to Canaan and separates from Lot under duress
	Hagar conceives, flees and returns
Abraham takes Hajar and Isma'il to Mecca	Abraham sends Hagar and Ishmael to Bakka
Abraham rebuilds *Ka'bah* with Isma'il	
Abraham told to sacrifice son	
3 angels come to tell of Is'haq and…	3 angels come to tell of Isaac and…
…imminent destruction of Lut's city	…imminent destruction of Lot's city
Abraham asks for mercy	Abraham argues for mercy
Is'haq born	Isaac born
	Abraham told to sacrifice son

Within the Qur'an there is an interesting, again almost complementary, differentiation between the characters of the two brothers that Ahmed Deedat points out, after quoting the two relevant *ayat* of the Qur'an when their respective births are announced. Of Isma'il the Qur'an says: "So We gave him (Abraham) the good news of a son ready to suffer and forbear" (37:101) while Is'haq is proclaimed: "Fear not! We give thee tidings of a son endowed with wisdom." (15:53)

Deedat elaborates: "The eldest son Isma'il, his character, characteristics and idiosyncrasies of his progeny, the Arabs, are being prophesised in the Word of God, the Holy Qur'an, as *Halim*, meaning humble, submissive, ready to forebear in the Way of God. And Is'haq the progenitor of the Jewish race, as a person endowed with wisdom, knowledge and intelligence with its accompanying responsibility."[46] It is a differentiation that echoes the respective meanings of the text, where Qur'an means to read, and Torah to teach. This suggests we should not rush to proclaim theological absolutes based on the story.

There is an interesting ambiguity in both texts, too, that discourages hasty judgement. In the Bible, the expression "thine only son" is used three times, when Isaac was never Abraham's only son. The only way to explain that is to cast Ishmael as some kind of illegitimate son, adding a (further) slur to the characters of both father and son. In the Qur'an, Isma'il is not mentioned by name and, in fact, many Islamic scholars believe the sacrifice was Is'haq. This is not simply because of *Isra'iliyyat* influence, because one of the scholars was Ali, the Prophet Muhammad's cousin, hence Shia Muslims believe it was Isaac. On the day I converted to Islam, the one resistant thought I had was that the sacrifice was Isaac. Though I now incline towards thinking of it as being Isma'il, I would concur with Sheikh Hamza Yusuf who says that it should not be an issue. The issue, he says, is the submission of Abraham and his son – the identity of whom is "not substantial to the story."

Perhaps the ambiguity is not a weakness, or an uncertainty, but part of the mystery at the centre of the faiths of the Peoples of the Books – Jews, Christians and Muslims – for to be able to say categorically that it is one might tend to question *any* validity within the other traditions. Rather, the ambiguity allows us to approach each other in humility. That, perhaps, is the greatest lesson of the sacrifice. As Abdul Hakim Murad says of sacrifice in its broadest and in this, its most specific, meaning:

"As well as their practical function in God's design for our world, they (animals) symbolise something. That something is the *nafs*, the ego, the lower impulse within each and every one of us which draws us, as though by a powerful magnet, towards immediate and selfish pleasure... The *nafs* is Shaytan's ambassador to the soul. As a *Hadith* puts it: 'Your greatest enemy is the *nafs* which lies between your flanks.'"[47]

---

[46] Deedat (1989)
[47] Murad (1999)

In quoting the Qur'anic *aya* - "He who purifies his *nafs* has triumphed." (91:9) - he approaches the defining act of sacrifice:

"This choice which Prophet Abraham faced on that arid mountain near Mecca seemed to be unbearable. On the one hand, he could honour and obey his God, who had stood beside him in every hardship, and had made him His Prophet and Friend. On the other hand, he loved nothing more than his teenage son. Despite the harsh choice, however, Abraham did not hesitate... Submission to God's will, which is the very meaning of Islam, is thus summed up in Abraham's momentous decision."

As often, it is generally easier, and more often accurate, to talk of 'the Islamic position', and no more so than in this case, which is such a defining moment. It would be an over-simplification to call this '*the* Jewish position' on Abraham, because there are several, though we do find the same idea in a Jewish text, Norman Cohen's *Voices From Genesis: Guiding Us Through Life*, in which he says:

"The sacrifice God wanted on that mountain that day was not Isaac. What Abraham had to sacrifice was his ego, the I, so that he could hear God's true call. Like other young people, Abraham had to transcend himself and move beyond his own ego needs to become the person he could truly be..."

Other arguments have been made, however, by Jewish writers as well as Christian (such as Soren Kirkegaard) that express anger at Abraham for his submission, when at other times he had no reservations about arguing with God. This has been a particularly poignant argument since the Shoah, when God appeared to demand the multiple sacrifice of 'Isaac', and did not intervene.

If, however, after all of this, it is the act of sacrifice itself that is "substantial" rather than the identity of the sacrifice, it is *this* that seems to be the ultimate sacrifice of the ego that is being asked of members of the faiths: the allowance of the possibility that the one whom Abraham

---

was ready to sacrifice was not exactly of our respective faith line, and that *that* submission is more important than our tribal allegiance.

If the object of the sacrifice is "not substantial", of more significance is the manner of the sacrifice itself. In both versions of the story, God says to Abraham, Give me a son, Abraham agrees and at the moment of sacrifice is given a ram to sacrifice instead. However, most striking is the difference in attitude of the sons themselves.

In the Qur'an when "his son was old enough to walk with him", Abraham dreamt that he was commanded to sacrifice him so he asked his son for his opinion:

"O my father" the son said, "Do what you have been commanded to do. Insha'Allah you will find me one of the steadfast." (37:102)

When it came to the moment of sacrifice, God called out: "O Abraham, you have indeed fulfilled the vision" (37:104-5) and sent a large ram to be sacrificed instead. Abraham had confirmed the essence of the dream in his, and his son's, willingness to submit to the will of God.

In the Biblical telling of the story, "God did tempt Abraham" (Genesis 22:1) by telling him to take his "only son Isaac" to the land of Moriah and offer him there as a "burnt offering." Abraham accepted what he had to do but persuaded his son to come with him through evasiveness and, at best, economy with the truth. After three days journeying they came to the mountain and Abraham and Isaac went ahead of the rest of the party. As they walked, Isaac asked his father where the lamb for a burnt offering was, to which Abraham replied: "My son, God will provide himself a lamb." (Genesis 22:8)

When they arrived at the place Abraham built an altar, laid the wood on it, bound up Isaac and then laid him on the wood. He was just about to slay his son when the angel of the Lord called out to him from heaven: "Lay not thine hand upon the lad, neither do thou any thing to him: for now I know that thou fearest God, seeing thou hast not withheld thy son, thine only son, from me." (Genesis 22:12)

Instead there was a ram caught in a thicket, which Abraham sacrificed. Then the voice from heaven called out again: "By myself have I sworn... for because thou hast done this thing, and because thou hast not withheld thy son, thine only son: That in blessing I will bless thee, and by multiplying I will multiply thy seed as the stars of heaven, and as the sand which is on the sea shore; and thy seed shall possess the gate of his enemies; And in thy seed shall all the nations of the earth be blessed; because thou hast obeyed my voice." (Genesis 22:16-18)

Here we note again the national significance that is attached to the act and its apparently greater importance than the moral point of submission. It is as if the author of this passage believes the blessing of this defining moment of submission is granted hereon as a genetic birthright, notwithstanding any contrary behaviour. Similarly, a Jewish legend quoted by Reuven Firestone states that Isaac's near-sacrifice attributes "the power of atonement for the entire Jewish people".[48] Abu Hurayra, quoted in Ibn Kathir, gives Is'haq's alleged post-sacrifice prayer as being: "O God, whoever dies and does not associate any partner with You, forgive him and bring him into Paradise." However, it is not a position he is in sympathy with, believing that the Isaac tradition was "taken into Islam uncontested and without proof" (the *Isra'iliyyat* position mentioned above) particularly by Ka'b al-Ahbar, a Jewish convert to Islam, in the time of Umar.

The idea of the benefits of a willingness to sacrifice being handed on as a birthright finds expression again in the Christian belief concerning Jesus dying for mankind's sins, and corresponds with the Adamic model of inherited guilt. As both of these sacrifices are believed, by Jews and Christians, to have taken place in Jerusalem (though the Samaritans believe Abraham took Isaac to Mount Gerizim near Nablus), I believe there is great significance in the Islamic model being more to do with personal responsibility for transgression, personal repentance, and Divine forgiveness. The aim of this work is ultimately to expand the horizon of readers beyond the Holy Land to include a different geographical centre and hence different understanding. A different location can be seen to represent the different nature of Abraham's sacrifice.

---

[48] Firestone (1952) p.133

We have, though, to suspend judgement on this for the moment, in the light of the ambiguity of the intended victim and accept that there may be a Divine purpose in this ambiguity. (There is a similar ambiguity, significantly, around the Crucifixion, as we shall see later). What the sacrifice really highlights is that Abraham, through his two sons, Ishmael and Isaac, is the point at which a division occurs. The line that comes from Isaac, the "Jewish" line, is characterised by an association with one place through one people and, as a whole, it is characterised by disobedience to God. This is a characteristic that, according to the Bible, both people and Prophets such as Aaron, David, and Solomon share. The significant characteristic of the Children of Israel from this point until the second expulsion of the Jews from the Holy Land in 70 CE is a stiff-necked refusal to submit to God, to trust in God and to worship only God. Prophets were sent, certainly, but only to correct this tendency.

On the other hand, the line that descends from Ishmael is, literally, the Muslim one, the submissive one. Through the seed of the first-born, this line submitted to its fate of, apparently, being displaced from the centre of things, from the Holy Land. (We shall see when we consider the Islamic significance of Ishmael what destiny the desert of Bakka actually held for Hagar and her son). The Qur'anic version of the sacrifice is thus far closer in spirit to a relationship to God that is based on total obedience and to the example of the last Prophet, in all that we know of him. While the Jewish Biblical tradition seems at once to venerate and ignore the message of the sacrifice, the very meaning of Islam is summed up in Abraham and Ishmael's acceptance of God's command. Having waited scores of years – he was 100 – to be granted a son, Abraham accepted the command from a far greater power to do something that went against everything he had felt and thought and believed within the limits of his own self. It is as if he recognised the essential insignificance of his own ego, his own *nafs*, as did his son. In a sense, the rest of the story could be summed up at this point thus: The Children of Israel were continually given guidance and continually refused it, so finally the guidance was offered to another, related, people, the Children of Ishmael. Of course, this is a little simplistic.

The announcement of Isaac's birth

What, then, is the function of Isaac, of Is'haq, and the significance of the announcement of his birth?

In the Bible, when Abraham was ninety-nine, "the Lord appeared to Abraham, and said unto him, I am the Almighty God; walk before me, and be thou perfect." (Genesis 17:1) Abraham fell on his face as God again told him his seed would be multiplied; that he would be the father of many nations and accordingly his name would now be Abraham, which means father of a multitude; that He would establish an "everlasting covenant" with the descendants as their God: that the land of Canaan "wherein thou art a stranger" would be an everlasting possession; and that "a token" of the covenant was that every male child be circumcised at eight days of age. Sarai was to change her name to Sara and Abraham was told that she would bear a son and be "a mother of nations." At thirteen, this is just at the point where Ishmael was moving from childhood to manhood. Some bar mitzvah present!

Abraham laughed at the thought of this and said "O that Ishmael might live before thee!" to which God replied that Sara's son would be called Isaac, which means laughter, and that the covenant would be established with him. God added that He had heard Abraham, and that Ishmael had been blessed and would be fruitful, begetting twelve princes and making a great nation. On that same day, after "God went up from Abraham", Abraham had Ishmael, himself and all the male members of his household circumcised.

Some time later the Lord and two men appeared to Abraham at midday as he was sitting in front of his tent. Abraham ordered a calf, bread, butter and milk (non-kosher then) for them and as they ate they told him that Sara herself would bear a son (news that he had already received in the previous chapter, Genesis 17:16). Sara heard this and laughed, for she was also old. When the Lord asked why she had laughed, she was afraid and denied it, to which the Lord said "Is anything too hard for the Lord?" (Genesis 18:14)

In the Qur'an, there is a similar narrative. Abraham returned to the Holy Land where he received some good news. He was by now a hundred years old and he and Sara had thought as long ago as Abraham's marriage to Hajar that Sara would never have children. One day though, Abraham received what appeared to be a group of young men. He greeted them and ordered a fatted calf to be roasted for them. When they did not eat he became suspicious but then they revealed that they were angels who had been sent to announce the birth of a knowledgeable son to him and Sara, and of a grandson Jacob after. When Sara heard the first of the news she laughed because she could not believe that it was true and Abraham himself had trouble believing it. The angels told them not to be surprised at the power of God, nor to disbelieve.

When Abraham asked what their business was now, they told him they were going to destroy the people of Lot's community, "to rain down stones of clay on them." (51:36) Abraham pleaded with them to spare the people there, to which they said:

"O Abraham! Forsake this! Lo! Thy Lord's commandment hath gone forth, and Lo! There cometh unto them a punishment that cannot be avoided." (11:76)

When Abraham said that Lot was there, they told him: "We know very well who is there – we are going to save him and his household, all save his wife, who is one of those who will stay behind." (29:32)

In the Bible, soon after the visit, Sara conceived. "The Lord visited Sara as he had said, and the Lord did unto Sara as he had spoken." (Genesis 21:1) At the "set time" she gave birth to Isaac and after eight days Abraham circumcised him. On the day that Isaac was weaned, Abraham made a great feast and Sara saw Ishmael mocking Isaac. Sara told Abraham to cast out the bondwoman and her son "for the son of this bondwoman shall not be heir with my son, even with Isaac." (Genesis 21:10) Abraham was upset but the Lord told him: "Let it not be grievous in thy sight because of the lad, and because of thy bondwoman; in all that Sara hath said unto thee, hearken unto her voice; for in Isaac thy seed shall be called. And also of the son of the bondwoman will I make a nation, because he is thy seed." (Genesis

21:12-13) This antagonism would lead to Hagar's final departure, as discussed above.

Thus, apart from the outcome of the birth, the differences seem slight: God is with two angels in the Bible while there are simply three angels in the Qur'an; none of the guests eat in the Qur'an, though they do in the Bible; and in the Bible there is a sustained argument between Abraham and God about the fate of Lot's city, Sodom, while in the Qur'an, Abraham's objection is briefly answered, rather than developed into almost a battle of wills.

It is in a short event like this, though, that we can see great differences in essence between the two narratives. Essentially, there is an underestimation of God in the Biblical story. He is visible, He eats, He is on His way to Sodom, as the Bible says... "Because the cry of Sodom and Gomorrah is great, and because their sin is very grievous; I will go down now, and see whether they have done altogether according to the cry of it, which is come unto me; and if not, I will know" (Genesis 18:20-1), so He is neither all-seeing nor all-knowing. Then, His justice is negotiable; Abraham haggles with Him over how many righteous people within the city would save the city, starting at fifty and coming down to ten. Given the theme of the Bible – the wayward People of Israel being constantly exhorted to submission to God by a succession of righteous Prophets – we might wonder that the writer of this Biblical passage had more than a historical interest in speculating whether the virtues of the few could compensate for the sins of the many. If that is so, then the Qur'an stands here, as in many other places, as a corrected and corrective version. The truth, it says, is much, much simpler.

The truth, then, of the Qur'anic Is'haq's purpose is simply that, as the Qur'an says, he would establish the practice of the faith among his descendants. Both he and Ya'qub (Jacob) would be born in Abraham's lifetime, and they were made righteous imams who did good deeds, gave alms and established worship, worshipping only God (21:72-73). The Prophethood and the Book were established among all their descendants (29:27) except the last, Muhammad, who was descended from Isma'il. This means that there was a large amount of prophetic activity at this time, with Abraham, Ishmael, Isaac and Jacob all alive at the same time, as well as the one other Prophet we have just mentioned, Lot.

Lot

Not since Nebuchadnezzar's hanging gardens went to pot,
Not since that village near Gomorrah got too hot for Lot,
No, not since Nineveh.
(From the musical 'Kismet')

As commented on earlier, the way in which the Biblical writers seem to cope with the moral failings of the main characters of the story is to have a subsidiary character, usually a relative, to be a kind of shadow bearer. They either carry the worst of the guilt of the moral failing of the "good" character which is the case so far with Eve, Cain and Ham, or they make the main character's failings look relatively small when compared to their own. Lot in the Abraham story is an example of this, and we will see this pattern recur later.

Lot was Abraham's nephew and they travelled together during Abraham's childless years, building up their flocks as they did. According to the Bible, however, the point was reached when they had to part before they started fighting each other. At this point, Abraham offered Lot the choice of the well-watered plain of Jordan or the harsher land of Canaan to the west. Lot chose the former and went to live in Sodom, which was a city of wicked sinners. During one of the many local wars he was captured, being released by an expedition led by Abraham. The grateful king of Sodom offered to reward him but Abraham turned him down, saying: "I will not take anything that is thine, lest thou should say that I (the king of Sodom) have made Abraham rich." (Genesis 14:23) Despite his hostility to Sodom, Abraham later bargained with God to save the city, with God finally agreeing that if ten good men could be found there he would not destroy it. Thus Sodom survived for some time longer.

Some time after Lot's return to Sodom, two angels disguised as men came to visit him. While there, all the male Sodomites surrounded Lot's house and demanded to "know" the guests. Lot offered his two virgin daughters instead, "to do ye unto them as is good in your eyes" (Genesis 19:8) but the offer was refused. Eventually the angels blinded the Sodomites and told Lot to leave Sodom and not to look back, as God was about to destroy it with fire and brimstone. He was told to flee to the mountains but Lot showed little faith or obedience and was extremely reluctant to go, saying, "I cannot escape to the mountain, lest some evil overtake me and I die." (Genesis 19:19) Lot warned his sons in law but they mocked him, so Lot escaped with only his wife and two daughters, considerably fewer than ten good souls, and this seems to be the only action he actually initiates. "And it came to pass, when God destroyed the cities of the plain, that God remembered Abraham, and sent Lot out of the midst of the overthrow." (Genesis 19: 29) While they were fleeing, Lot's wife looked back, as Lot had warned her not to, and she was changed into a pillar of salt.

Lot preferred a city that was both near and small and was permitted to go there so he left on the road to Zoar. In the end, though, he was too afraid even to live there, so he fled to a cave in the mountain with his daughters. There they feared that they would never have a man so they seduced their father by getting him drunk. They each bore a son, Moab and Ben-Ammi, who fathered the Moabites and the Ammonites, later enemies of the People of Israel, the sum total of his legacy.[49]

In the Qur'an, after King Nimrod had tried to kill Lot and his uncle, Abraham, Lot declared, "Lo, I am a fugitive to my Lord; and Lo, He is the Mighty and the Wise," (29:26) and travelled together with him from Babylon to the Holy Land. When they reached their destination, Lot was sent as a Prophet to the people of Sodom and Gomorrah to forbid them from the practice of sexual deviancy. The men there were the first people to have sex with men and they did not thank Lot for forbidding them. They dared him to bring down God's punishment on them and threatened to throw him out of their midst for being so pure.

When the people had been warned and had rejected the warning, angels came to visit Lot to warn him of the town's coming destruction.

---

[49] The cave was nonetheless made into a monastery.

However, the people of the town heard that Lot had guests and came to him, angry that he had received guests though forbidden from doing so, and desirous of having their ways with these newcomers. Lot did not know what to do, and said: "O my people! Here are my daughters; they are purer for you (if you marry them). So fear God and do not disgrace me with regards to my guests! Is there not among you a single right-minded man?" (11:77). It was an offer that the townspeople rejected scathingly and he wished that he had some power to use against them.

It was then that the angels revealed that they were from God and that the people would not be able to get near him. The townspeople were blinded and the angels told Lot:

"So travel with your household in the last part of the night, and follow on behind them, and do not let any of you look back – except your wife, for surely what happens to them will also happen to her too. Lo, their appointed time (for destruction) is for the morning, and is not the morning nigh?" (11:81)

As promised, at dawn the skies rained down stones of burning clay and the people died as they "wandered blindly in their drunkenness." (15:71) Lot and the rest of his family, except his wife, were brought into the mercy of God.

So, similar again, except that Lot was a warner, sent by God to mend the ways of the people of his city – he was a Prophet, not simply the relative of one, as he appears in the Bible. Also, come the destruction, he is told that his wife will perish. Just as with Noah's lost son there is a strong reminder here that simple family or blood relationship is no protection against God's punishment. In the Bible, this part of the story has the feel of the sort of temptation anyone might feel when told, Do not look (Genesis 19:26). Lot's wife appears to be unlucky, and the fact that God saves anyone is simply because He "remembered Abraham" (19:29). In being given instructions of how and when to escape, Lot in the Qur'an follows divine guidance, while the Biblical Lot whinges. Needless to say, at the end, the Qur'anic Lot does not drunkenly sleep with his daughters on consecutive nights.

It is perhaps these daughters who do provide an insight into the minds of these Biblical writers. If we take the Qur'anic story as authentic, we can grant that, when Lot says to the men of Sodom "Here are my daughters; they are purer for you (if you marry them)." (11:77) and "These are my daughters (to marry lawfully) if you must act so" (15:71), he is still trying to encourage a permitted expression of sexuality in a general way, though without the parentheses added by translators, these words still look a little stark.

The Biblical story, on the other hand, is not only shocking but fraught with contradictions. Lot offers his daughters "which have not known man; let me, I pray you, bring them out unto you, and do ye unto them as is good in your eyes" (Genesis 19:8), which is a far more explicit invitation. We then discover that the daughters are married because the sons-in-law refuse to heed Lot's advice to leave (19:14), meaning that either there is a direct contradiction, or Lot tries to save his sons-in-law even though they are so far off the path that they have not even consummated their relationships with their wives. This interpretation is perhaps borne out by the words of the daughter who suggests sleeping with their old father because, as the New English Bible puts it: "There is not a man in the country to come to us in the usual way" (19:31) However the contradiction resolves itself, it is hard to avoid the internal voice that keeps reminding the reader, this is supposed to be a moral, religious text.

Other
The other main differences between the two stories in the Bible and Qur'an are extra details found in the Bible. On one occasion, Abraham and Sara went to the south country (near Bir Sheva). Again Abraham pretended that Sara was his sister, so the king, Abimelech took her as a wife. However, before he had slept with her he had a dream that warned him she was a man's wife, so he pleaded with God: "Wilt thou slay also a righteous nation?" (Genesis 20:4) God accepted Abimelech's plea of integrity of heart and after Abimelech had given Abraham sheep, oxen, servants and a thousand pieces of silver Abraham prayed to God to heal the king's wife and maidservants of the closing up of their wombs that had happened as a result of Abimelech taking Sara as a wife. (A similar story *with the same king* later happens with Abraham's son, Isaac in Genesis 26:1-11)

Another story has geographical implications that are felt strongly to this day. When Abraham was one hundred and twenty seven, Sara died. Abraham mourned and wept, but, as a nomad, a "sojourner", he had no place to bury her so he offered to buy the cave of Machpelah from Ephron, son of Zohar, a Hittite who lived in the area of Hebron. Ephron offered the field for nothing but Abraham insisted on paying, the sum of four hundred silver shekels being agreed on in the end. On the basis of this, Hebron today remains, after Jerusalem, the most bitterly contested of religious sites.

Before he died, Abraham arranged marriage for his son Isaac to Rebecca and also married again, a woman named Keturah[50] who bore him six sons. When he died at the age of one hundred and seventy five years, he gave only gifts to these sons. Everything else, "all that he had" (Genesis 25:5), he gave to Isaac who, together with Ishmael, buried him in the cave of Machpelah with his wife.

Conclusion

Some Jews see human beings descending in quality after Adam, with Abraham the only one to raise himself above the normal level (Moshe Chayim Luzatto, *The Way of God*). Others talk of God moving progressively further away from mankind for seven generations after Adam, and then moving nearer to mankind for seven generations, culminating in Moses, the turning point being Abraham. Many rabbis identify Abraham as the original archpriest, who initiated many Jewish practices.[51] A modern Israeli play, *Va Yomer, Va Yelech* (*He spoke, He Walked*), although in many ways profoundly ill at ease with the Jews' relationship with God, ends with God's promise to Abraham. It is, as many Israelis often say, their "unarguable" title deed for the Land of Israel. Their point is that both despite and because of all this, the Land is theirs. "I will bless them that bless thee, and curse him that curseth thee: and in thee shall all families of the earth be blessed." And: "Unto thy seed shall I give this land."

---

[50] See p. 70
[51] Kuschel, (1995), p.54

This is obviously interesting from a Muslim point of view, because Muslims do bless Abraham at least five times a day in prayer, at the closing of each prayer cycle:

"God send blessings on the Prophet Muhammad and the family of the Prophet Muhammad as you send blessings on Abraham and the family of Abraham."

Also, as the children of Ishmael, Muslims are of the seed of Abraham too.

Burton, Capt. Sir R.F. *Pilgrimage to Al-Medina and Mecca*, vol. ii (1855) Penguin: London

Cahill, T. *The Gifts of the Jews - How a Tribe of Desert Nomads Changed the Way Everyone Thinks and Feels* (1998) Doubleday: New York

Cohen, N.J. *Voices From Genesis: Guiding Us Through Life* (1999) Jewish Lights: Woodstock

Deedat, A. *Arabs and Israel – Conflict or conciliation?* (1989) IPCI: Durban

Firestone, R. *Journeys in Holy Lands – The evolution of the Abraham-Ishmael Legends in Islamic Exegesis* (1952) State of New York University Press: New York

Frazer, J.G. *Folklore in the Old Testament* (2003) Kessinger Publishing: Whitefish MT

Hiro, D. *Sharing the Promised Land - The Tale of Israelis and Palestinians* (1999) Olive Branch Press: New York

Kessler, E. Bound *by the Bible - Jews, Christians and the Sacrifice of Isaac* (2004) Cambridge University Press: London.

Kirkegaard, S. *Fear and Trembling* (2005) Penguin: London

Kohn, M. *The Man on the Other Side* (22 October 1999) Jerusalem Post

Kohn, M. *The Crown of Age* (5 November 1999) Jerusalem Post

Kuschel, K-J. (Tr. John Bowden.) *Abraham – a symbol of hope for Jews, Christians and Muslims* (1995) Continuum: New York

Murad, A.H. *The Secret of Sacrifice* (April 1999) Meeting Point – the Newsletter of the New Muslims' Project: Leicester

Riskin, Rabbi S. *Measure for Measure* (29 October 1999) Jerusalem Post

Riskin, Rabbi S. *Man and Beast* (15 October 1999) Jerusalem Post

Scholem, G.S. *Zohar - The Book of Splendour: Basic Readings from the Kabbalah* (1971) Schocken Books: New York

Shinan, Prof. A. Lahham, Fr. M. & Abu Sway, Dr. M. *Abraham in the Three Monotheistic Faiths* (1999) Passia: Jerusalem

5

JACOB

A Little over Jordan,
As Genesis records,
An Angel and a Wrestler
Did wrestle long and hard.

Till, morning touching mountain,
And Jacob waxing strong,
The Angel begged permission
To breakfast and return.

"Not so," quoth wily Jacob,
And girt his loins anew
"Until thou bless me, stranger!"
The which acceded to:

Light swung the silver fleeces
Peniel hills among,
And the astonished Wrestler
Found he had worsted God!
          (Emily Dickinson)

The light tone of the poem belies the fact that it describes one of the two defining events, along with Abraham's sacrifice, of the whole Jewish Bible. One describes an act of submission to God; the other, an act of struggle with God. If the point of the Abraham story, and the whole of his story if we accept the Qur'anic narrative, is to show how we should relate to God, the point of Jacob's story, of which the wrestling is symbolic, can be seen to show what happens if we do not, particularly if we focus on the Biblical text.

At this point, it could seem that we are facing the apparently simple duality of struggle with, or submission to, God, which translates, literally, a little too neatly as Israel *versus* Islam. However, as with Abraham's story, there is an ambiguity of sorts that ought to prevent complacency. In Hebrew, the name, Israel, which Jacob is given while struggling with the mysterious man/angel at the stream of Jabbock, means "he who struggles with God", though Howard Cooper points out that Israel also means "he who struggles *for* God." Meanwhile, in Arabic, Ya'qub means "he who travels in the way of God", though, as the Prophet Muhammad said in a *Hadith*, travel is torture. So which is true? In a profound sense, they both, or all, are, for who is to say that in not submitting, the Children of Israel were not following God's plan, God's will. There was always the choice, but the Jews were Chosen, not in spite of, but because of being "stiff-necked", unless we wish that the All-seeing, All-knowing God had not realised that when he Chose them. Paradoxically, they fulfilled both struggle and submission. Struggle was a fulfilment of their own will in their own terms, and God's in terms of His. After all, it says of the Children of Israel in the Qur'an that they planned but God is the best of planners. Or as the Yiddish proverb puts it, "Man proposes, God disposes." These, as we will see, are the themes that are played out in the tellings of the story of Jacob.

The Biblical Jacob
Although Ibn Kathir tells a fairly full story of Jacob's early life, it is not attributed to any chain of *Hadith* narration and is certainly not from the Qur'an. Rather, it corresponds exactly to the Jacob story of the Bible and it seems that that is where it has come from, for it contains a number of Biblical features – flawed patriarch, promise of the land and, as we have seen before, the creation of an Other in the form of an enemy. This latter is where it, and the Biblical story, begins.

While the relationship between Ishmael and Isaac has traditionally been taken to represent the relationship between Muslims and Jews, the relationship between Isaac's sons, Esau and Jacob, is often seen as representing the relationship between Jew and Gentile, the *Goyim*, who are literally 'the nations', but are usually seen to be Christians or the Romans.[52] Esau also had a geographical connection with Edom, the area to the south of Judea, which was a kingdom the Children of Israel had a complicated relationship with, being one of the areas of the twelve tribes but also being an adversary in war. It was also where the Herodian dynasty originated, so there were resonances aplenty. The

---

[52] Interestingly, some Zionists tried to identify the new Israelis with the agricultural and not over-intellectual Esau. Poet Haim Gouri wrote of him as "Not too smart and not too holy... but, when you are needed and called upon to appear, you are suddenly there."

text implies that God wished it so; Isaac had prayed for children from Rebekah, his wife, who had been barren for twenty years of marriage and God had spoken to her, saying:

"Two nations are in your womb, and two peoples, born of you, shall be divided; the one shall be stronger than the other, the elder shall serve the younger" (Genesis 25:23)

Thus, right from the start there is a conflict of the sort that is not present in the Qur'an. As we have seen before, this could be explained by the fact that this story was written down at a time when the distinction between Jew and non-Jew in the Holy Land was highly charged – there being invasions and conflicts between the Children of Israel and those around them. It may therefore have been permissible (the writers felt), all being fair in love and war, for Jacob, whose name in Hebrew means 'trickster', to be treacherous in his youth. (The Prophet Muhammad himself described war as being, in some part, deception.)

This, however, reflects an ongoing debate within the Bible as to how the nation of Israel or Judah should survive. Isaiah, as we shall see, was not the only one who counselled faith, and Jacob, as we have mentioned above, is in many ways lack of faith personified. Thus, he tricks his brother out of his inheritance for a bowl of lentil soup, and tricks his blind father into blessing him instead of Esau, his favourite, by serving his father's favourite food, having disguised himself as Esau using animal skins.

In these events there is great play on the value attached to the surface of things and the major events that take place on the basis of them. Thus, Esau is so "living for the moment" that he gives up his birthright for a soup he only identifies as red, while his father Isaac redirects the whole course of human history simply because he cannot distinguish between the skin of an animal and the skin of his son. In the second event, Jacob is almost painted as a Cain-wise-after-the-event where this time he finds favour by getting there first with the offering of meat, having previously co-opted the agricultural symbolism with the lentil soup. However, it is neither an honest nor a personal offering. Nonetheless, Jacob receives his blind father's blessing:

96

"May God give you of the dew of heaven,
and of the fatness of the earth,
and plenty of grain and wine.
Let peoples serve you,
and nations bow down to you.
Be lord over your brothers,
and may your mother's sons bow down to you.
Cursed be every one who curses you,
and blessed be every one who blesses you!"
(Genesis 27:28-9)

Yet when his father discovers what has happened, he does not revoke his blessing on Jacob, but rather adds insult to Esau's injury. In a way whose shock recalls Noah's similar curse to his son Ham, Isaac curses his minutes-before beloved son with this, though it is also a warning to Jacob:

"Behold, away from the fatness of the earth shall your dwelling be, and away from the dew of heaven on high. By your sword you shall live, and you shall serve your brother; but when you break loose you shall break his yoke from your neck." (Genesis 27:39-40)

Because of this, Esau vows vengeance and when Rebekah hears this she tells Isaac that she does not want Jacob to marry one of the local Hittite women. To enforce this, she sends Jacob to live with his uncle and to marry there. The blessing Isaac gives includes the explicit prayer that Jacob will be fruitful and possess the land.[53]

On the journey Jacob receives further geographical encouragement when he rests the night with his head on a stone (now the British coronation stone) and in a dream sees a ladder that reaches from heaven to earth with angels climbing up and down it. In the dream, God tells him:

"I am the Lord God of Abraham thy father, and the God of Isaac, and the land whereon thou liest, to thee will I give it, and to thy seed. And thy seed shall be as the dust of the earth and thou shalt spread abroad to

---

[53] (28:3-4)

97

the west, and to the east, and to the north, and to the south: and in thee and in thy seed shall all of the families of the earth be blessed. And behold, I am with thee, and will keep thee in all places whither thou goest, and will bring thee again into this land; for I will not leave thee until I have done that which I have spoken to thee of." (Genesis 28:13-15)

When Jacob woke he made the stone into a pillar, anointed it with oil and named the place Bethel, which means the House of the Lord. Here he vowed:

"If God will be with me, and will keep me in this way that I go, and will give me bread to eat, and raiment to put on, so that I come again to my father's house in peace, then shall the Lord be my God. And this stone, which I have set for a pillar, shall be God's house, and of all that thou shalt give me I will surely give a tenth unto thee." (Genesis 28:20-22)

However, it is an incident which is not interpreted entirely positively. Despite his illustrious father and grandfather, Jacob still makes his acknowledgement or belief in God conditional. He has something in common with Abraham, though; according to Moshe Kohn, the rabbis have read a similar lack of faith into this dream as they did when Abraham fled to Egypt.[54] According to Rabbi Berechiah, God asked Jacob why he did not go up and Jacob replied that he was afraid that he would fall, to which God replied:

"If you go up, you will not fall down." But Jacob lacked faith and did not go up. [55]

Though there does not seem to be any Biblical basis for this extrapolation, it does suggest a mind - a confluence of reader, writer and protagonist - that is heavily influenced by feelings of guilt and unworthiness, that haunting melody that runs through much of the Bible.

---

[54] Kohn (19 November 1999)
[55] *Midrash Tanhuma: Vayetzeh 2*

This persists through the rest of the story. Though his mother had said that she would send a message to Jacob when Esau had safely forgotten what his brother had done, the events that take place when he arrives at his uncle's land seem to be written with the thought that what goes around, comes around and they guarantee that it is Jacob who has trouble forgetting, rather than his brother. In this place, his grandfather Abraham's original home, and really for the rest of his life, Jacob suffers. He has to wait many years in exile before he is able to return home. He is unable to immediately marry Rachel, Laban's younger daughter, the woman he loves; her father says he must wait seven years. Then, when the seven years are up, Laban swaps the daughters over without Jacob knowing and the marriage is consummated with Leah, the elder sister. Thus, Jacob has done to him almost exactly what he did to his brother. As if the transgressive nature of his own actions had not been highlighted enough by this, Laban explains he did this because "it must not be so done in our country to give the youngest before the firstborn," (Genesis 30:26), a sharp reminder that there are rights to the firstborn, and a contrast to many of the Biblical stories where the blessing, one way or another, goes to the younger.

Jacob then has to work another seven years and when he finally marries Rachel, she remains barren while Leah, "when the Lord saw that (she) was hated", produces six sons and a daughter. In the end, Laban tricks Jacob into staying and working unpaid for twenty years, so Jacob, to build his own wealth, has to trick Laban into parting with some livestock. In terms of children, finally, after arguing with Jacob, Rachel bears a son, Joseph, but then after they have fled, again through more trickery, she dies in childbirth at Bethlehem, giving birth to Benjamin. Jacob's favourite son, Joseph, is later dumped into a well by his elder brothers and taken to Egypt and for years Jacob thinks he is dead. He loses Benjamin for a time as a result, before finally the family is reconciled.

The intention of the writers in this therefore seems to be to show the people's eponymous patriarch as dishonest by necessity, divinely affirmed, both going into and returning from exile, driven by a will that is not his own and assured of an uncomfortable journey. It is the event on his return, where his name is changed from a personal one to the one that his people would carry, that makes this story so symbolic for all of the Children of Israel, and it is this we shall now consider.

Jacob becomes Israel

When Jacob neared his brother's land in the Edomite country, Esau heard of his brother's return and came to meet him with a large retinue. Hearing of this Jacob divided his party and sent ahead valuable presents, himself staying behind most of his party and hoping that Esau would be appeased by the gifts before he came upon his brother.

We are probably supposed to imagine here that Jacob was full of dread at the prospect of this. As he was always the less physical of the two twins, he had lived in constant fear that Esau's physicality would be turned upon him at some unspecified time in the future when Esau had the chance, as Isaac had foretold. Esau had effectively become Jacob's shadow, whether or not he knew or felt it. The victimiser, as Jacob was, is usually less conscious of their offence than the victimised because they stand to lose the power they had gained in the offence if they face it. (The fear that modern Israel suffers is a partial, though pertinent, current example of this). Yet the fear of the victim's anger, particularly if the victimiser becomes vulnerable, is always present on an unconscious level and it may struggle to show itself, appearing in fearful half-thoughts, dreams or external events. Thus, Jacob may have suspected that his parting of the ways with Laban, his former host, was his destiny, and that God had willed this return to meet the imagined murderous fury of his brother. We suspect that, sooner or later, we will face a comeuppance. As the sun's position changes in the heavens, at the end of the day, even if we stand still, we know we will have to face our shadow.

Thus, when messengers tell Jacob that Esau is come to meet him with four hundred men, Jacob is afraid, though there is an ambiguity (again) because 'meet' in Hebrew, means both to meet as friends and to meet in battle. Jacob's fear clearly makes him expect the latter so he prays to God for deliverance, and arranges the gifts to appease Esau. Finally, though, he is alone and the supernatural event occurs, as suggested by the Biblical language:

"And Jacob was left alone; and a man wrestled with him until the breaking of the day." (Genesis 32:24)

It is Jacob's dark night of the soul, a struggle that can be meaningfully interpreted on a psychological level as Jacob's reawakening consciousness, as well as on a theological level. Jacob refuses to give up the struggle even when asked and seems to ask for the meaning to his suffering, to the wound he receives from this man, this angel, this personification of his twin, this shadow. At the same time he owns his own tricksterhood when he is asked his name ('name' in Hebrew also means 'essence'). At that moment, according to the Bible, the man/angel says: "Your name shall no longer be Jacob, but Israel because you strove with (struggled, though also translated as 'had power with') God and with men, and prevailed." (Genesis 32:28)

Jacob understands this event as meaning he has seen God "face to face" and survived. (32:30)

This blessing is the moment of transformation, both nationally and personally. Howard Cooper, quoting Jung, explains the psychological significance of the struggle:

"Through that long night of struggle with the mysterious force carried in and by the unnamed man, Jacob gains for himself a blessing, thereby integrating that dark force of potential destruction into a life-giving, life-enhancing energy. Jacob's 'shadow contains valuable, vital forces' which need 'to be assimilated into actual experience and not repressed' - or projected."[56]

What the writers seem to have done through this event is to attempt a resolution, or a new configuration, of the conflict which they had set up from the first, between the Self and the Other. The previous patterns had included murder (Cain and Abel), subservience (Shem and Ham)

---

[56] Cooper (1995)

and banishment (Isaac and Ishmael). There is a recognition in the Jacob story that the Other is a part of the self, God-given and, like God, unknowable. The reconciliation with Esau even suggests that a resolution is possible, as hinted at earlier by the meeting of Isaac and Ishmael to bury their father Abraham.

Peace, though, if that is what the promise is, is not immediate. Importantly, this inner transformation does not lead to confidence externally. Jacob has won his inner battle but still fears Esau and his four hundred men who appear the moment that the struggle with God finishes. It is never said exactly when Esau reconciled himself with his brother, whether it was long before the messengers warned Jacob of his coming with the four hundred, or whether it was only when Esau saw his brother's countenance. We are left wondering if he too experienced a transformation during the night, a tiny shift in his heart from rejection to recognition, for this is what happens, and the two twins are reconciled. When they meet, Esau greets him warmly and refuses his gifts.

The story is ambiguous and paradoxical, some of which is lost in translation into English. Even in the reconciliation when Esau "fell on his (Jacob's) neck and kissed him", this could be translated as "bit him." In the context it is unlikely, but there is a shadow of doubt here that may be reflecting Jacob's internal state ("Am I really off the hook?"), and one which is actually far closer to the actuality of relations between Jew and Gentile.

Howard Cooper elaborates on the meaning of the passage in the context of Christian-Jewish relations by pointing out that Israel means both 'one who struggles with God' and 'one who struggles for God':

"In this sense we are all Israel. Once the Jew can recognise the shadow there can be some development, but there is no release from the struggle, the tension: it is just lived at a different level. And somehow, as the text enigmatically illustrates, all this has to take place internally (alone) and yet, paradoxically, in the presence of the other, the Christian."[57]

---

[57] *Ibid.*

Jacob's later years – the loss of Joseph

According to the Bible, on his return, Jacob settled first at Shechem and then Bethel and had one more son, Benjamin, by Rachel, who died giving birth to him at Bethlehem. Because he was Rachel's son he was much loved by Jacob, though Jacob loved Joseph, Rachel's first son, even more. It was this relationship that would dominate the closing years of Jacob's life.

The story will be told more fully in the following chapter but where it concerns Ya'qub's, or Jacob's, words and actions we can learn more about him, particularly through comparison, as the story is also told in the Qur'an. In the Bible, it is Jacob's unconcealed preference for Joseph - he gives him a many-coloured coat for example - that makes his brothers hate Joseph so much. Some rabbis have interpreted the preference as the reason why the Children of Israel were again punished through Egypt. As Moshe Kohn writes: "Rava bar Mehassia said in Rabba Hamma bar Guria's and Rav's names: 'One should never play favourites among one's children. For we see that because of the few hundred grams of superior wool that Jacob gave Joseph more than he gave his other sons, they burned with jealousy of him. One thing led to another and our forefathers went down to Egypt eventually to undergo the trials they underwent there.'"[58]

In the Qur'an, there is also a clear preference, which is also the cause of the suffering that Jacob suffers later. To offset this, we can see that Jacob explicitly recognises it as God's will and trusts in what is happening. Also, the preference could be understood as Jacob's recognition of his son's Prophethood, which is a possibility suggested by the father's advice to the son. When Joseph tells him of his dream, Jacob advises him not to tell his brothers but to keep patience. "Thus Thy Lord will choose you and teach you the interpretation of dreams and perfect His blessing on you and the family of Jacob, just as he perfected it on your forefathers, Abraham and Isaac." (12:6)

In contrast, in the Bible no such wisdom is dispensed and Joseph tells the brothers about his dreams in which his brothers' wheat sheaves bow

---

[58] Genesis Rabba 84:8; Shabbat 10b, quoted in Kohn (3 Dec 1999)

down to his, and where the sun, moon and eleven stars bow down to him. Jacob rebukes Joseph with what seems like disbelief and, although he observes the brothers' envy, he nonetheless sends Joseph to Shechem to see how his brothers are doing with the flocks. When he calls him to go, Joseph even uses the words, "Here am I," as used by Abraham and Isaac before the latter's would-be sacrifice (22:1; 22:7). When they bring back Joseph's bloodied coat Jacob believes that his son is indeed dead, saying: "It is my son's coat. An evil beast hath devoured him. Joseph is without doubt rent in pieces." (Genesis 37:33) Unless he was familiar with Jungian psychological symbolism, the "rent in pieces" suggests that Jacob really believed that the "evil beast" was literal, though the writers would seem to want the reader to make that psychological connection.

In the Qur'an, we can see aspects of Jacob's wisdom in the same situation. When his sons come to tell him the false story that a wolf has eaten Joseph, Jacob knows that they are lying but shows the same patience and faith that he himself counselled his son. As a Prophet, we can understand that he would recognise from the dream (knowing that dreams are a means by which God communicates with His Prophets) that Joseph, in fact, had a greater destiny than himself, for the sun and moon (Joseph's mother and father) bow down to their son.

In fact, he had anticipated the evil beast, saying, when the brothers *asked* to take Joseph (another key difference): "It grieves me that you should take him away with you, and I fear that the wolf may eat him while you are heedless of him." In the light of what happens and how they explain it, their response of: "If the wolf were to eat him while we were a group, then surely we are useless people," becomes effectively an admission of guilt. When they do give this excuse afterwards, they even say: "But you will never believe us even when we speak the truth." (12:17) There is actually something almost touching about this, that they had always simply wanted some recognition from their father. That they are not too bad is suggested by their later leaving one other brother in Egypt and their final forgiveness. And it is not simply blood that saves them; we have seen in the stories of both Lot and Noah that family ties are not in themselves enough to guarantee salvation.

The famine that is the key to Joseph's rise to power in Egypt is also the key to bringing him together with his father again, eventually. In the Bible, hearing that there is wheat there, Jacob sends his sons down to Egypt, though he keeps Benjamin to prevent mischief befalling him. The brothers are arrested by Joseph as spies and only released when they leave Simeon as a hostage while they return to Canaan to bring Benjamin to verify their story. When they show their father the wheat that they did not have to pay for, and tell him what Joseph had said, he forbids them from returning: "My son shall not go down with you, for his brother is dead, and he is left alone." (Genesis 42:38)

However, the famine continues and he is forced to relent, though not before he has told them off for handling the situation badly before, particularly their folly in saying there was another brother. He tells them to take the money that Joseph returned before in case it was an oversight and, as they leave, he prays for mercy:

"And God Almighty give you mercy before the man, that he may send away your other brother, and Benjamin. If I be bereaved of my children, I am bereaved." (Genesis 43:14)

In the Qur'an, when Joseph as the ruler of Egypt, tells his brothers to bring Benjamin to see him, Jacob is unhappy about sending his other favoured son after what had happened to Joseph before. When it is then discovered that the money the sons had paid for the wheat has been returned to them secretly (an act that would suggest to the Prophet that a benign hand was at work here), he trusts in God and allows his son to go, but asks the same faith of them. Firstly, asking more by way of surety from them than before, he makes the brothers swear before God that they will bring Binyamin back unless some calamity befall them - "unless you yourselves are surrounded (by enemies)." He also has them swear to "enter not all by one gate: Enter ye by different gates" (12:67) because eleven similarly dressed foreigners would attract unwelcome attention in such a time of famine. He, significantly, though, recognises that such advice is worthless if it runs against the will of God. This is perhaps another example of Jacob recognising that the Will of God that is being played out here is beyond his scope; if they follow his commandment and still get into trouble, as is the case (12:68), this will indeed seem to be proof that this is so.

105

Even when Binyamin is arrested for apparently stealing a cup, Jacob shows trust in God, even though the further loss makes his eyes go "white with the sorrow he was suppressing." (12:84) We can see that the Jacob of the Qur'an also suffers and is tested, despite his great wisdom and faith: "Go and search for Joseph and Binyamin. God's spirit is protecting them."

In the Bible, when the truth is finally known and Joseph asks for his father to come down to Egypt, Jacob first does not believe it. When he has decided to go he receives a blessing from God: "Fear not to go down into Egypt, for I will there make of thee a great nation. I will go down with thee into Egypt and I will also surely bring thee up again, and Joseph shall put his hands on thy eyes." (Genesis 46:3-4)

In the Qur'an, when the brothers return from Joseph and Binyamin with the request that he join them all in Egypt, although he is blind, Jacob's other senses have become more acute. He senses their coming soon after their caravan leaves Egypt, and when Joseph's shirt is placed on his face, his sense of smell confirms the trust he had felt, and his sight returns. At this he declares to his sons: "Said I not unto you that I know from God that which ye know not?"(12:96)

He then prays to God to forgive them. Jacob then goes down to Egypt and, after the reconciliation, spends the rest of his life there.

In the Bible, Jacob lives a further seventeen years with Joseph. Before he dies he calls Joseph to him and asks him to bury him alongside his forefathers. He also blesses Joseph's sons Ephraim and Manasseh, and includes them in his inheritance:

"God, before whom my fathers Abraham and Isaac did walk, the God which fed me all my life long unto this day, and the Angel which redeemed me from all evil, bless the lads, and let my name be named on them, and the name of my fathers Abraham and Isaac, and let them grow into a multitude in the midst of the earth." (Genesis 48:15-16)

It is an act that again establishes the predominance of the younger.

In the ceremony of blessing, Joseph leads the eldest, Manasseh, to receive the primary blessing but Jacob deliberately gives it to the younger, Ephraim, a fact that displeases Joseph, but Jacob says: "I know it, my son, I know it. He shall become a people, and he also shall be great, but truly his younger brother shall be greater than he, and his seed shall become a multitude of nations." (Genesis 48:17)

Finally, before he dies he gathers his sons to him and tells them their destinies. Reuben "shall not excel"; Simeon and Levi are cursed for their anger and told "I will… scatter them in Israel." To Judah he says: "The Sceptre shall not pass from Judah, and the Lawgiver from between his feet, until Shiloh come and to him belongeth the obedience of peoples." This is a blessing we shall have cause to look at later. Zebulun "shall be for an haven of ships"; Issachar "became a servant unto tribute"; Dan "shall be a serpent by the way"; Gad, "a troop shall overcome him, but he shall overcome at the last"; Asher would produce good bread and "he shall yield royal dainties"; Napthali "giveth goodly words"; the blessings of Jacob "shall be on the head of Joseph"; and Benjamin "shall ravin as a wolf – in the morning he shall devour the prey, and at night he shall divide the spoil." (Genesis 49:15-16)

After his death his body is embalmed and brought back with great ceremony to Hebron where it is buried alongside Leah, who was not his preferred wife but was the wife through whose son Judah the tribe of Israel would survive.

In the Qur'an, Jacob is often mentioned as sharing the same characteristics of spiritual power and insight as his father, as well as remembrance of the Abode, righteousness and truthfulness, and, like Is'haq, the Prophethood is confirmed through him and his descendants. This is shown at his death when he asks his sons: "What will you worship after me?" They reply, "We will worship your God, the God of your forefathers, Abraham and Isma'il and Is'haq: the One God. To Him we will surrender ourselves." (2:133) Unlike in the Bible, the parting words are simple confirmation that the message has been understood and will be passed on, the message's simplicity being highlighted in comparison with the complex motivations at work in the Bible. From the pedigree of the four patriarchs as they are described in the Qur'an, the ones who ultimately establish the "Jewish" line in Egypt, for that is where they end up, we can see that the messenger is not to blame for any error. Rather, it is the people who were at fault, the people to whom the message is brought, the descendants of this holy family in Egypt. They will face a fall from grace, from voluntary submission to enforced slavery, a process that will begin after the death of Joseph.

Cooper, H. *Dealing With Conflict: Jew and Christian* (1985)
Kohn, M. *Corrupt Public Servants* (3 Dec 1999) Jerusalem Post
Kohn, M. *Jacob Afraid* (19 November 1999) Jerusalem Post
Lau, B. *Living only for today* (24 November 2006) Tel Aviv: Haaretz

6

JOSEPH

After thirteen years of romantic mystery, the brethren who had wronged Joseph, came, strangers in a strange land, to buy 'a little food'; and being summoned to a palace, charged with crime, beheld in its owner their wronged brother; they were trembling beggars – he, the lord of a mighty empire! What Joseph that ever lived would have thrown away such a chance to 'show off'?
      (Mark Twain – 'The Innocent Abroad')

Yet in both the Qur'an and the Bible Joseph, Yusuf, does not do this. He does not show off.

A Roman woman demanded of Rabbi Yosse: "It isn't possible that a hot-blooded 17-year old boy like Joseph withstood that woman's beguilements! Surely the Torah is covering up for him." In response, the rabbi read her two passages where two of Joseph's brothers *had not* controlled themselves (Reuben and Judah, 35:22 and 38:12-30) and said: "If the Torah doesn't cover up for two full-grown men living with their father, why should you imagine that it is covering up for Joseph, a mere boy far from home?" (*Parashat Raba 87.6*)

Joseph was not simply a "hot-blooded 17-year old boy" - a *Hadith* says of him that "he was given half of the beauty (of Adam)."

God introduces it as one of "the most beautiful stories" at the beginning of Surat Yusuf, and it is the only story in the Qur'an that is told in one continuous recitation, rather than coming in different places in different chapters.[59]

---

[59] However, 14th Century Islamic commentator Ibn Taimiyya, well-known for his literal interpretation of the Qur'an, says that it is no more than the best in its class. Though Yusuf suffered, he was not persecuted for calling on people to worship one God; he merely responded well to things he had no choice about. He also believes that Yusuf's patience during imprisonment was more praiseworthy than his patience with his brothers. (*Jawab ahl al-iman fi tafadul ay al-Qur'an, pp. 11-13*)

In the Bible, Joseph is one of the few, perhaps the only, character who comes out of the telling of their story well. ('Well' being the operative word).

And he is the only Prophet to have had a successful musical written about him that people still might go to (*Jesus Christ Superstar* now being rather dated).

The evidence suggests that Joseph, Yusuf, was *really* special and that perhaps there is a special meaning in his story. In comparing the Qur'anic and Biblical stories, we will discuss, as well as the significant differences and similarities, how and why this might be so.

One of the most striking things about the two stories is, on first reading, how similar they are. The outline of that story is one that begins with Joseph's dream of the stars, the sun and moon bowing down to him, the son, making a convenient wordplay for English readers. After this, the brothers' jealousy moves them to the point where they decide to get rid of their brother. They dump him in a well and take his shirt (or coat), smeared with the blood of a goat, to their father.

Joseph is found in the well by some merchants who take him to Egypt where he is bought by a high ranking official who recognises the boy's worth. Significantly in both traditions, explicitly in the Bible and implicitly in the Islamic exegesis, the man is either a eunuch or impotent. This, it is implied, leads to his wife trying to seduce Joseph, and Joseph, with God's help, resisting. Shirts again play an important role in the story (not for the last time either) and as a result of the episode, Joseph is put in prison.

In prison, Joseph meets two of Pharaoh's servants – the wine bearer and the baker, who both have dreams that he interprets, though not before he has mentioned God in some way. The wine bearer, whose dream Joseph correctly interprets positively, forgets to tell Pharaoh about Joseph for a long time, despite being asked by his former cell-mate, until the Pharaoh himself has a dream about seven fat then lean cattle, and seven green then dry ears of wheat. Joseph is then called for, though in the Qur'an not before the minister's wife has cleared Joseph of any sin. On the basis of his interpretation of the dreams, Joseph is made the most powerful man in Egypt after the Pharaoh, and is given particular responsibility for setting aside some of the surplus from the years of plenty.

When the famine comes, its widespread nature brings Joseph's brothers down to Egypt for food for their people. Joseph tells them to return for more but to bring Benjamin the following time. The father, Jacob, is at first unwilling but finally agrees, as we have seen in the previous chapter. Joseph has Benjamin kept behind through the planting of the royal cup and a brother also offers to stay, Judah in the Bible and the eldest in the Qur'an.

At this point, Joseph reveals his identity and Jacob is invited down to Egypt where they live out their lives and establish the Children of Israel in that land.

So far so similar. On a closer reading, however, we find significant differences, where we learn as much about the author as we do about the story. Given that the author of at least one of these is regarded as being divine, we can say the God is indeed in the details. Between the Bible and the Qur'an (and I will use the names Joseph and Yusuf respectively to distinguish which is being referred to), there are different details and emphases. In the Bible, the favouritism of Jacob for Joseph is not portrayed as a sin in itself but as something that merely is the case. It is the giving of the 'coat of many colours' (or 'the coat with long sleeves' in some translations) that is the breaking point for the brothers. In other words, whereas the feeling is acceptable, basing actions on that feeling is not. When the brothers do get rid of Joseph, it is the eldest son, Reuben, who does not want them to actually kill him, so they put him into a dry well without food or water. This is the same brother who is mentioned above in the rabbi's defence, so perhaps this is intended to show him in a better light.

Also, unlike in the Qur'an, they actually sell him when a band of merchants appear, Judah (also mentioned above by the rabbi) suggesting the sale. In view of the central line of this thesis, it should be noted that the merchants were Ishmaelite, precisely the sort of detail that is never mentioned in the Qur'an unless there is a particular purpose. Here we can imagine that it has some significance for the writers of the Bible because, once again, it reconnects the destiny of the Children of Isma'il and the Children of Isaac, or Israel, as we can now call them, because if the merchants were Ishmaelites, they were close family, relatives of Joseph's grandfather's brother, Ishmael. This means that it was Islam's forebears who were unwitting agents of God's Will in placing the Children of Israel in Egypt, which was also the home, of course, of Joseph's great grandfather Abraham's second wife, Hajar.

There are further resonances when Joseph is sold, on Judah's recommendation, for twenty pieces of silver, ten fewer than the amount that Jesus is betrayed for by Judas in the New Testament, making some very obvious parallels in name, theme and even value (if we allow for inflation). If the twenty pieces of silver might have a forward resonance to the Jesus story, the blood of the kid (another oddly English pun in the story) has both a backward reference to the Abraham story where, in the place of a beloved son, an animal is killed at a defining moment, and forward to the story of Jesus, who is also called the Lamb of God, "who taketh away the sins of the world." Here the blood of the kid takes away the sin of the brothers.

The Qur'anic story, by contrast, is told in a less complicated way because there is no internal need within the story or its teller to do this, either to correct or excuse. There is, though, the return to Egypt, in physical chains. The subtext of the story from a Muslim point of view, is how both Joseph *and* Yusuf submit, literally, to their servitude and imprisonment and in doing so become free, and how this exactly parallels their internal submission to the will of God, and how this plays such a pivotal role both in their elevation as Prophets and in the destiny of their people. The place that Thomas Mann calls "the nether world, to which the pit had been the entrance" is the place where Joseph, Yusuf, eventually becomes "established in the land." The "nether world" can mean many things here, but in the Bible it is represented by a number of "Others": other people, other places, other religions. The deepest meaning of "the nether world", though, is that part of our selves that we are not usually conscious of, what has been referred to earlier as the "shadow." Joseph, Yusuf, will face all of these in his time in Egypt, and it is in this place that he first has a direct sense that there is a greater hand guiding him when he is told: "You will tell them about this deed of theirs when they do not recognise you." (12:15)

112

In Egypt, the Bible makes it clear that Potiphar, the rich captain in Pharaoh's guard who buys Joseph, is a eunuch, though we are left to imagine the effect of this on his young wife. Potiphar "saw that the Lord was with him and that the Lord made all that he did to prosper in his hand" (Genesis 39:3) and so was pleased with him and promoted him, though his trust was not great enough to survive his wife's false accusation of attempted seduction. He had said: "How then can I do this great wickedness and sin against God?" (Genesis 39:9) Joseph is imprisoned, incriminated by his shirt that is left in the wife's hands, but he is thus removed from temptation in prison.

Here again, though, he pleased those around him and he was put in command of the other prisoners. Two of the prisoners, Pharaoh's butler and baker, told Joseph of dreams they had had where the one was serving the Pharaoh wine, while the other was carrying bread in baskets on his head that was being eaten by birds. Joseph told them "Do not interpretations belong to God?" (Genesis 40:8) and interpreted them, saying that the butler would be restored to his post in three days, while the baker would be hanged from a tree and be food for birds.

The predictions came true and the butler promised to tell Pharaoh about Joseph. However, it took two years for the Pharaoh himself to have strange dreams before the butler remembered. He told the Pharaoh what had happened in prison and Pharaoh called Joseph to him. Joseph shaved and changed his clothes before hearing that in the dreams seven lean "kine" (cattle) devoured seven fat cattle, and seven dry ears devoured seven good ears of corn. After telling the Pharaoh that the answer was from God, Joseph explained that years of plenty would be followed by seven years of famine and that food from the good years should be stored in preparation for the coming bad years. Pharaoh was so impressed with Joseph's wisdom that he was made chief minister, was put in charge of the storage programme and was given Asenath, the daughter of an Egyptian priest, as his wife.

The famine affected the whole region, including the land of Canaan, and Egypt's reserves of corn were well known, so Jacob sent the brothers, except Benjamin, down to buy corn. In the Bible they travel through the desert by donkey (42:26), which is an inappropriate mode of desert travel though common to pastoralists, while in the Qur'an, they travel by camel (12:65, 70, 72, 82). Joseph recognised them and when they bowed down to him he remembered his dreams, but he did not tell them who he was. Instead he accused them of being spies and demanded that the other brother, Benjamin, be brought as proof of the truth of their words. The brothers saw this as retribution for what they had done to Joseph, unwittingly, speaking words that Joseph could understand. Simeon was left as a hostage and the brothers returned, though not before Joseph filled their bags with corn and secretly returned their money.

When he was told of Joseph's conditions, Jacob refused to let Benjamin go at first but the famine persisted and in the end, after Judah had guaranteed Benjamin's safety, he was left with no choice but to assent. Joseph was deeply moved to see his younger brother again but still did not tell the brothers who he was. Instead he concealed a silver cup in Benjamin's bag and had the brothers followed. When they were challenged, the brothers said they would kill the thief and become Joseph's servants if anything was found. Thus they all returned to Joseph, who said that he would not keep them as servants except for Benjamin. Honouring his promise to his father, Judah pleaded to be allowed to take Benjamin's place and therefore spare their father's grief. At this point Joseph sent all his servants out and finally revealed his identity saying: "Now therefore be not grieved, nor angry with yourselves that ye sold me hither, for God did send me before you to preserve life." (Genesis 45:5) It was not them who had sent him to Egypt, but God.

In the Qur'an, before the brothers return to tell Jacob, Joseph gives them his shirt to take, and the father smells this even before they are back. When he puts it over his eyes, his sight – lost through grief - is restored.

Pharaoh then invites Jacob and all his people to come down to Egypt where Jacob lives until his death seventeen years later. Meanwhile, Joseph increases Pharaoh's power by trading corn for the cattle and land of the people of Canaan and Egypt, and establishes a gift of the fifth of the produce of all lands, except those of the priests, that is to be paid to the Pharaoh from that time on. The Hebrew community in

Egypt will grow and prosper by the time Joseph dies in Egypt at the age of a hundred and ten. Before he dies, Joseph takes an oath of the people saying: "God will surely visit you and ye shall carry up my bones from hence." (Genesis 50:25) His embalmed remains are kept there until the Exodus, when Moses carries them with him through the Sinai.

At the end of the story, we can wonder at its significance. Is it the most personal of the stories that are common to the Christian, Jewish and Muslim traditions? Perhaps, with its themes of youthful "over-reach", rejection, temptation, loneliness and triumph in the face of adversity, grace under pressure, it is. If so, perhaps the significance of the story is that it gives us a post-Adamic fall model of how to be in the world. In falling low and submitting, we will be raised high.

Abu Salem, I. Milgrom, J. Neuhaus, D. *Joseph in the three Monotheistic Faiths* (2002) Passia: Jerusalem
Parashat Raba 87.6
Saheeh Muslim: Hadith
Ibn Kathir, I. *Stories of the Prophets* (2003) Darrusalam: Riyadh
Twain, M. *The Innocents Abroad* (2003) Penguin: London
Westermann, C. *Joseph – Studies of the Joseph Stories in Genesis* (1996) T&T Clark: Edinburgh

7

MOSES and AARON

As the song goes: What miracles you can achieve, if you believe. Or, as they say in Hollywood, It just shows what you can do if you have the staff.

(Jonathan Romney on 'The Prince of Egypt', 18 December 1998, Guardian)

Though Moses' story comes chronologically after those of Abraham, Isaac, Jacob and Joseph, one striking feature of his story is that the figure of Moses has far greater supernatural powers (including the staff) than the Patriarchs from the time Joseph Campbell calls "the Legendary Cycle". Another difference is that the Moses story sees the Children of Israel entering history as a people, in a way that is not the case with Joseph. During the Moses story, one Pharaoh dies, and a nation is, eventually, born.

This is reflected in both Bible and Qur'an, and the outlines and importance of the Moses story are similar in both books. In the Qur'an, Moses, Musa in Arabic, is mentioned 196 times, compared with 96 for Abraham and 27 for Jesus, and in both, Moses is unique (except for the Prophet Muhammad) in that God speaks to him directly. In the Bible[60] we read: "There has never yet arisen in Israel a prophet like Moses, whom the Lord knew face to face," while the Qur'an says: "God spake unto Moses, discoursing with him." (4:164). In this chapter, we shall consider the extent to which the Biblical and Qur'anic tellings of the story differ and concur with each other and with history, and also consider how far these can be reconciled with some of the psycho-mythical observations made of the Biblical story by Joseph Campbell and Sigmund Freud. We shall do this in the usual way of accepting that the Qur'anic story is correct, but also consider it from the other perspectives. Like the wandering in the Sinai it may be an interesting journey, but it will not take quite as long, insha'Allah.

Moses' Upbringing

---

[60] Deuteronomy 34:19

The stories of Moses in the Bible and Musa in the Qur'an are essentially similar. As we have seen, this is often the case. However, there are some, sometimes telling, details that are different, and plenty more detail generally in the Bible.

A difference from early in the telling of the story concerns the concealing and the finding of the baby Moses. In the Qur'an, Moses' mother is directed as to when she should put the babe in the river and is consoled after he is found (28:8), while in the Bible, Moses' mother simply does the concealment in an "ark of bulrushes and daubed it with slime and with pitch" (Exo 2:3). Her emotions concerning this are not mentioned. In the Bible, Pharaoh's daughter finds the child and knows it is a child of the Hebrews, while in the Qur'an, it is the Pharaoh's wife[61] who finds Moses. It is not specified whether the child's ethnicity is known, but she calls him "a comfort for the eye for me and for you (Pharaoh)" and says: "Kill him not, perhaps he may be of benefit to us, or we may adopt him as a son." (28:9). In itself the identity of the finder seems a minor detail but it prepares us for the important position held by the Pharaoh's wife in the Qur'anic story, where she comes to be seen as the embodiment of goodness in her new-found faith (she becomes a believer), while in the Bible she is not mentioned. The effect of this is to remind us that Moses' message in the Qur'an is as a warning and a call to all to worship one God and that the Children of Israel are no more nor less than the vehicle of the destiny of this message, rather than simply its sole recipients in a sea of evil and unshakeable polytheism.

In both tellings, Moses is raised in Pharaoh's household. In the Qur'an we are told what the outcome of this will be: "Then the household of Firaoun picked him up, that he might become for them an enemy and a (cause of grief)." (28:8) In both, through the artfulness of his sister he is breast-fed by his own mother, a convenient wet-nurse who is "found" to calm the distressed child, and in both books, the period of privilege ends with the killing of an Egyptian.

The flight to Midian
One day he entered the city where his people lived. Though he was a prince outwardly, Moses was inwardly still one of his people and his

---

[61] A detail picked up by the DreamWorks cartoon 'Prince of Egypt'

Israelite blood must have boiled when he saw two men fighting, one of his own, and one of the Egyptians. In the Qur'an, the former appealed to him for help and Moses instinctively leapt to his aid, striking the other man with his fist and killing him. He immediately realised that he had been misled by Shaytan and repented, begging forgiveness of God and said: "My Lord, I have wronged myself so forgive me." God forgave him, and Moses promised: "My Lord, as You have blessed me, I will never be a help to the guilty again." (28:16-17) In the Bible, the killing appears premeditated because, before he attacks the Egyptian, Moses "looked this way and that way and when he saw no man, he slew the Egyptian and buried him in the sand." (Exo 2:12)

The situation is repeated the following day, with the difference that in the Qur'an the same Hebrew is fighting another Egyptian, while in the Bible, another two Hebrews are fighting each other. Moses says that the man is surely a troublemaker but still goes to help his fellow Israelite, at least to seize the man who was "enemy to them both." The Egyptian, though it is textually possible that it is the Hebrew, taunts him for what happened the day before, even echoing Moses' vow never to help those who sin: "O Moses, are you going to kill me just as you killed a man yesterday? Do you want to be nothing but a tyrant in this land and not one of those who sets things right?" (28:19) In the Bible, Moses asks the wicked one why he is hitting his fellow, who says: "Who made thee a prince and a judge over us? Intendest thou to kill me, as thou killedst the Egyptian?" (Exo 2:14)

Both scenarios raise issues of justice and the responsibility of leadership, but in the Qur'an the questions are raised by an individual whose character is not very trustworthy, somehow raising Moses' moral stature. In the Bible, the Hebrews collectively are shown in a poor light. The unintentional irony of the wicked man who asks "Who made thee a prince and judge over us?" would not be lost on the audience, who would know that more of such insolence was coming, even when the answer to this matter is known. We could imagine Moses' thinking something like, Is this the thanks I get (and will get), for literally covering up for you people? As well, though, there is the truth of the question - You deliberately killed a man yesterday, and yet today you lecture us on the misuse of violence.

In the Bible, something of this collective disquiet has been perceived by scholars. Exodus 2:14 concludes with Moses thinking: "Surely the matter (the killing of the day before) is known." Quoting *Shmot Rabba 1:30*, Moshe Kohn writes: "Rabbi Yehuda son of Rabbi Shalom said in the name of the elder Hanina and the Sages in Rabbi Aleksandri's name: Moses thought: What sin did Israel commit that, of all the nations, it was confined to serfdom? Aha – 'the matter is known' – they were enslaved because gossip and informing is rife among them, making them unworthy of redemption."[62]

This is but one example of the sort of insolent rage that Freud believed suggested that Moses was actually killed by his own people. In the Bible, Moses flees in fear. In the Qur'an, it is a better-intentioned man of the Hebrews who warns Moses that "the matter is known" at the highest level, and that plans are afoot to kill him. As he flees, he prays to be saved from "these evildoers." (28:21)

In the Qur'an we have learnt previously that Moses has had bestowed on him *Hukm* (Prophethood and right judgement) and religious knowledge (28:14), but it is clear that these have not manifested fully in Moses' consciousness because, as he flees in fear towards Midian in the Sinai, he says: "Perhaps my Lord will lead me along the right way." (28:22)

In both the Bible and Qur'an, when he reaches Midian in the desert, tired, thirsty and anxious, he comes to a place where he helps two women (seven in the Bible) in watering their flocks, because shepherds are already watering their own there. He is introduced to the father and is soon married to one of the women – fearful flight becoming loving refuge. What is interesting is that the Qur'an, often terse in its storytelling, contains far more details of the encounter. After helping the women, Moses returns to the shade and, perhaps in hunger for both food and affection, prays: "O my lord! Truly am I in need of any good that Thou dost send me!" (28:24)

His prayer is immediately answered when one of the maidens returns, "walking shyly" (28:25), and tells Moses that her father wishes to invite

---

[62] Kohn (1999)

him in order to reward him for having watered their flocks. Obviously expectations on both sides are high and are not disappointed. Moses immediately trusts the father enough to tell him his whole story, at the end of which the father congratulates him on his escape and promises him hospitality and safety: "Fear thou not: (well) hast thou escaped from unjust people." (28:25) One of the daughters asks her father to employ Moses for wages and the father agrees to do so and to give Moses one of his daughters if Moses works for him for eight or ten years if he chooses. (The scholarly consensus is that it was the longer).

The Voice in the Burning Bush

This is the background to Moses' major confrontation with his destiny in the Voice of the Burning Bush. In the Bible it takes place after God has heard the anguished voices of the Hebrews following the death of the Pharaoh but while Moses is still tending his father-in-law's flocks. In the Qur'an it takes place after Moses' agreed time of working has finished. He and his family are passing Mount Tur in the Sinai when Moses sees a fire. He tells them to wait while he goes to get some information or, as he puts it, with unintentional irony, "some guidance" (20:10), or a burning brand to make a fire of their own. When he reaches the bush, he is told:

"O Moses! Verily I am thy Lord! Therefore put off thy shoes. Thou art in the sacred valley Tuwa."

He is then told in his first Divine revelation that there is but one God, and this God is speaking to him, and that regular prayer should be established for His remembrance. Moses is warned of the Judgement to come and warned of those who believe not and who "follow their own lusts" (20:16), an obvious reference to Firaoun, but also a warning that will be true of his own people.

The Biblical account is very similar in outline, though with some important differences. Firstly, there is something to do with turning aside, a detail that is mentioned twice in Exodus 3:3 and 3:4 that recalls that in the Qur'an we read: "When he saw the fire, he was called from the right side of the valley from a tree in the blessed ground" (28:30) From this, some Muslim exegetes have deduced that he was facing the Qibla in Mecca. As in the Qur'an, Moses is told to remove his shoes, being on holy ground. It is here that the identity of the owner of the voice and the reason for the call provide the biggest difference between the two stories. The voice of God in the Bible says, not I am the Lord of the Worlds, but "I am the God of thy father, the God of Abraham, the God of Isaac, and the God of Jacob." The primary message is to proclaim the deliverance of the people from the suffering in Egypt and the promise to bring them to a "good land...flowing with milk and honey." (Exo 3:8)

In both the Bible and Qur'an, Moses is uncertain about this responsibility, and in both stories, he is shown two signs that are to be shown to the Pharaoh. Firstly, God commands Moses to throw down his staff, whence it becomes a live snake, causing Moses to run away. In the Qur'an, Moses, conscious of his transgression many years before perhaps, is brought back by words that see what is in his heart: "O Moses, do not be afraid. Verily messengers are not afraid in my presence, except whoever has done wrong and then turned to good after evil. Verily I am Forgiving and Compassionate." (27:10-11).

The snake returns immediately to its former condition when Moses seizes it. He is then told to put his hand to his chest, near to his heart. When he draws it out it has become white. In the Qur'an it is shining with divine light, while in the Bible it is white because of leprosy.

Though continuing to follow the same outline, the Bible now tells a sort of shadow version of the Qur'anic story. In the Bible, in Exodus 4:8 and 9, God introduces provisos – "if they will not believe..." - while Moses seems to become increasingly reluctant. In the Qur'an, God tells Moses to "Go to pharaoh... and speak to him mildly, perhaps he may accept admonition or fear (of God)." (20:43-4)

"I am slow of speech, and of a slow tongue" seems to compare with a similar admission by Moses in the Qur'an that his brother Haroun (Aaron) is more eloquent and has a better voice; even Firaoun will later mock Moses for his speech (43:52). However, the difference is that in the Bible Moses is asking for someone else to be the messenger, while in the Qur'an, Moses is asking for someone else to help him. Thus, in the Bible, God angrily says that Aaron will be the speaker, while in the

Qur'an, God simply agrees to Moses' request to strengthen him through his brother.

Another difference is that in the Qur'an, Moses' response is immediately to pray for a bigger heart, the place where the emotions and the intellect meet to produce wisdom and compassion. He prays for this difficult task to be eased for him. He prays that the knot from his tongue be loosened, that his speech impediment be removed. And he prays that all this be done so that they can "celebrate Thy praise without stint, and remember Thee without stint" (20:33-34). And God grants Moses his prayer, telling him how He has already been active in Moses' fate in reuniting him with his mother and protecting him with love, with sparing him from affliction after the death of the Egyptian, and with testing him in Midian. And despite Moses' fear, God promises that he and his brother will be protected. With these outer transformations reflecting the transformation within him, Moses is now ready to go and confront Firaoun, who has "indeed transgressed all bounds" (20:24), and to free his own people.

Facing Pharaoh

The outline of the encounter with Pharaoh is again similar in both Bible and Qur'an: Moses delivers his message and plea to leave; there is a "magic battle" which the Pharaoh's magicians lose; the plea is still rejected; there are plagues; Moses is still rejected; the Hebrews flee; they are followed; they escape through water; Pharaoh follows and is drowned, boo hoo. The differences are subtle and follow the same pattern as before and, if we are so disposed, we can see a consistent ethnic position in the Bible and a corrective universalist vision in the Qur'an.

Though the cry "Let my people go!" has rung through history as a Biblically-inspired clarion call for freedom, Moses' first plea in the Bible is actually for Pharaoh to Let My People Go and hold a feast in the desert for three days. In the Qur'an, Moses requests that Pharaoh just let them go. While the Biblical Moses does this in the name of the God of the Hebrews, the Moses of the Qur'an does this in the name of the Lord of the Worlds. Pharaoh is moved by neither, though the Qur'an states: "They denied them (the signs) ...out of pride, though their souls acknowledged them." (27:14)

122

In an article entitled 'Facing Pharaoh',[63] Rabbi Arthur Waskow, says: "Moses and Aaron might have stayed focused on that universal name (YHWH), but they added an explanation of it as 'YHWH, the God of the Hebrews'." He then asks: "Why, precisely when they are trying to get an Egyptian king to pay heed, did they entangle an ethnic claim with a universalist assertion?"

He answers this by dwelling on the meaning of the word Hebrews (*Ivrim*), which means "those who cross over", and by saying that this was a God of those who cannot be pinned down, but in the end he does not really satisfactorily answer his own question. The reason seems to be that the Bible actually writes the God of Moses as an ethnic god, even if His name does transcend language and therefore ownership.

We can understand this as being a typical feature of the Bible, where the writers of the Biblical stories write what advances their own purposes, if we remember that all of this was written down many hundreds of years later. However, they do leave something of the universal story, some of which is reflected in the story and something of which is reflected in the Hebrew. Waskow gives an example of this, beginning his article by saying that, in Hebrew, God does not say "Go to Pharaoh", as the translations usually read, but *"Bo el Pharaoh"*, which means "*Come* to Pharaoh", meaning that God is already "within the Egyptian potentate." He elaborates on this by considering the phrase "... I have hardened his (Pharaoh's) heart" (Exo 10:27 & elsewhere) by looking at the root meaning of the word *kvd* which means to be hard or heavy, but also glorious or radiant. Thus, he says that this phrase can be as easily read as:

"'I, God, have put My radiance in his, Pharaoh's heart.' In other words: Come to Me – the Me who lives hidden inside Pharaoh. Do not be afraid. What looks like *his* radiance, *his* glory, is really *My* radiance, *My* glory."

In isolation, this could be argued, but in the context of the Biblical telling of the story, Pharaoh and his people are unrelentingly portrayed

---

[63] Waskow (2000)

as bad, as witnessed by the utterance about the hardening of the heart every time Pharaoh seems to be on the point of relenting. The implication is that God actually makes Pharaoh do something that he was not inclined to do. If we compare this with the Qur'an, we find Firaoun referred to as "an insolent tyrant" who should be spoken to "gently" in consecutive verses (20:43-44) in case "he accept admonition or fear of God." As Ibn Kathir says, though God knew what Firaoun would do, He nonetheless sent His best Prophets of that time and told them to speak with kindness. This is not untypical; elsewhere, the Qur'an says: "Invite all to the way of your Lord with wisdom and beautiful preaching, and reason with them in ways that are best and most gracious." (16:25)

An example of this is, when the brothers go to Pharaoh and ask him to let their people go, Pharaoh asks Moses about his past, about how he had been brought up by the Egyptian royal family, and had repaid this by killing an Egyptian. Moses says: "I did that then when I was one of those who are astray, so I fled from you because I was afraid of you, and then My Lord granted me wisdom and made me one of the Messengers - and that favour with which you reproach me now was only as a result of you having enslaved the Tribe of Israel." (26:18-22) Had he not been speaking mildly he might have mentioned the massacre of the sons of Israel that the Pharaoh had ordered that led to the original adoption.

Here, Firaoun's referring to the past creates a point that both Maurice Bucaille and Ibn Kathir mention in trying to date the story of Moses. Firaoun says: "Did we not bring you up among us as a child?" (26:18) Both writers take this to mean him personally, thus contradicting the Biblical version, which explicitly states that one Pharaoh dies while Moses is in Midian and a worse one takes his place. This may be the case because "we" could be a royal "we" that refers to the family as a whole, though Moses uses both the plural 'you' form in 26:21, and the plural in 26:22, which suggests otherwise.

One interesting similarity between the two stories is that in both Bible and Qur'an, it is not in the first meeting that the signs of God are put to the test. In other ways, though, they differ. In the Bible, Moses' request leads Pharaoh to increase the work and sufferings of the Children of

Israel, leading them to blame him and Moses in turn to blame God (Exo 6:21-23) In the Qur'an, Moses shows Firaoun the signs and Firaoun responds by saying he will bring his own magicians from all over the land, Moses appointing the time as being the day of the Festival of Adornment at midday, a day that everyone could attend, at a time when no half light could be used for trickery. (20:59)

When the day comes, Firaoun's magicians ask Moses who should throw first and Moses tells them to. However, when the magicians' staffs and ropes appear to move, Moses feels afraid that he cannot match this. On God's command, though, Moses throws down his staff, which swallows those of the other magicians. They immediately declare their belief in the Lord of Moses and Haroun, remaining strong in their faith even when the Pharaoh threatens to have their hands and feet cut off and to have them crucified for plotting this humiliation with Moses and Haroun. Even then, Firaoun will not believe that he is wrong.

In contrast, in the Bible it is Aaron who is commanded to cast the staff and then the Pharaoh's magicians cast theirs, which become serpents, rather than appear to become. (At no time is the white, leprous hand shown.) Aaron afflicting and the magicians trying to match his actions is a pattern that is repeated throughout all the plagues until finally they admit to Pharaoh: "This is the finger of God." (Exo 9:19) Moses' role is to entreat to God after each of the plagues that they be removed in return for him and his people being released. Pharaoh breaks his promise each time. In the Bible, much more time is spent discussing the Ten Plagues (blood; frogs; lice; flies; cattle plague; boils; hail; locusts; darkness; and the slaying of the first-born)

In the Qur'an following the display of the staff, Firaoun's chiefs advise him to kill Moses, though he also receives other advice from a relative, a believer in Moses' message, who says: "If he is a liar, on him will be the lie, and if he is truthful, there will befall you some of what he threatens you with" (40:28) He also reminds them that they believed in Joseph until he died, when they had said: "No Messenger will God send after him." (40:34) When Moses brings further signs, "years of scarcity, and diminution of fruits" (7:130), rather than make people more "mindful", it encourages them to think "This is our due" during the good times and to blame Moses in the bad. The *aya* continues:

"So We sent on them the flood and the locusts, the lice and the frogs, and the blood, self-explained signs, but they were arrogant and a sinful people." (7:133)

Only at this point did the people of Egypt say: "O Moses! Invoke your Lord for us because of His Promise to you. If you remove the punishment from us, we indeed shall believe in you, and we shall let the Children of Israel go with you." The punishment is removed but the promise is broken and, as the Qur'an says: "We took retribution on them and they were drowned in the sea." Perhaps a clue as to the identity of the Pharaoh is the following *aya*, which says: "And We destroyed completely all the great works and buildings which Firaoun had erected." (7:137) One Pharaoh who had his "great works" notably destroyed was Akhenaten, often known as 'the Heretic Pharaoh', because he believed there was only one god, though this god was the sun.[64]

Pharaoh's demise
In his book, *A History of the Jews*, Paul Johnson says:[65] "Something happened, at the frontiers of Egypt, that persuaded the eye-witnesses that God had intervened directly and decisively in their fate. The way it was related and set down convinced subsequent generations that this unique demonstration of god's mightiness on their behalf was the most remarkable event in the history of nations."

In the Bible, God finally tells Moses that he will send one more plague (the tenth) after which Pharaoh will beg him to leave. This is the slaughter of the firstborn where at midnight on the fourteenth night of the month the firstborn child in every family is taken by the plague, this being the basis of the Jewish feast of Passover. All houses except those of the Israelites, who have marked the doors of their houses with the blood of a lamb, lose their eldest, and as this includes Pharaoh, he finally orders Moses and his people to leave. They flee but, in a change

---

[64] Freud actually believed that Moses was an Egyptian survivor of the anti-Akhenaten backlash who wanted to take his own version of monotheism to a place of safety.
[65] Johnson (1997) p.26

of mind or a desire for revenge, Pharaoh follows them. They are guided by a cloud by day and a pillar of fire by night until they reach the Red Sea. Here the people again show lack of faith, complaining: "Is this not the word that we did tell thee in Egypt, saying, Let us alone, that we may serve the Egyptians? For it had been better that we serve the Egyptians, than that we die in the wilderness." (Exo 14:12) Moses then parts the waters using his staff and the Children of Israel cross. Pharaoh's army follows them but before they reach the other side, the waters roll back in, drowning them all.

In the Qur'an, God tells Moses to give the order for the Tribe of Israel to leave under cover of the night. They flee, but are followed by Firaoun's army, who catch up with them at sunrise. When the Tribe of Israel sees this huge Egyptian force on one side and the sea on the other, they believe they are about to die, but Moses is told to strike the sea with his staff, whereupon the seas part so that "each part stood like a huge mountain." (26:63) He and his followers cross but when Firaoun and the Egyptian army follow, the waves crash back in on them, drowning them all.

Thus far, the Biblical and Qur'anic accounts of the end of Pharaoh are very similar but the Qur'an has two additions concerning the death of Pharaoh. Firstly, as he dies, Firaoun cries out, at last: "I believe that there is surely no god except the one that the Tribe of Israel believe in. I am one of those who submit (to God)." (10:91) A "deathbed" conversion such as this is without value (as stated in 4:18) and elsewhere it says that Firaoun will go ahead of his people on the Day of Standing and actually lead them down into the fire (11:98). In this life certainly, it made no difference either. All that would remain of Firaoun would be his story and his body, which was embalmed, the other non-Biblical detail. "This day shall We save thee in thy body, that thou mayest be a sign to those who come after thee!" (10:92) In fact, the body of the Pharaoh most believe to be Moses' persecutor, Merneptah, the son of Rameses II who brought up Moses, was discovered in Thebes in the Valley of the Kings in 1896. Maurice Bucaille described it as having "multiple lesions of the bones with broad lacunae, some of which may have been mortal... he most probably died either from drowning... or from very violent shocks preceding the moment when he was drowned - or both at once." He observes that the body does not show much sign of deterioration from being in the water for too long.

Towards Mount Sinai

In the Qur'an, it says at three points following the crossing of the sea that the Children of Israel inherited the wealth of the Egyptians. The most explicit is: "And We gave the inheritance to those who had been abased, the eastern and the western parts of that land that had been blessed and perfectly was fulfilled that most fair word of your Lord upon the Children of Israel because of their patient endurance." (7:137) Elsewhere it says that "We bequeathed them (the treasures of the Egyptians) upon the Children of Israel" (26:59) and "We want to bestow upon those who have been oppressed, and to make them leaders, and to make them inheritors." (28:5) The initial picture of the flight is thus positive.

According to Medieval Islamic commentator Averoes (Ibn Rushd), it is Moses' receiving of the law on Sinai that makes him a Prophet, rather than the miracles that came before. It is also the beginning of his most serious problems. In the Bible, trouble begins straight away as the people head through the Sinai for the Promised Land. They complain to Moses frequently, firstly about food. God brings them water and food, in the form of quails and manna, but they still bemoan the loss of the fish, cucumbers, melons, onions, leeks and garlic (Numbers 11:5). After leading them against the Amalekites, Moses establishes judges to deal with disputes among the people, this at the suggestion of his father-in-law, to reduce the strain of leadership on him that these complaints cause.

In the Qur'an, there is a similar lack of faith described. Despite the blessings mentioned above, after crossing the sea, the Bani Israel come across people worshipping idols and ask: "O Moses! Make for us a god like the god they have." He responds: "Surely you are a most ignorant people. Surely that which they are engaged in shall be shattered, and false is what they have been doing." (7:138-9) The people also complain about food, asking Moses to pray for them "to produce that which the earth grows – its pulses, cucumbers, garlic, lentils and onions" (2:60). The Qur'anic text interestingly highlights the contrast

128

here between the foods of the earth and the foods of the skies, "the manna from heaven." There is a reminder in this of how Adam and Eve were tempted through their appetites, and how Shaytan was pleased to discover that their earthy, earthly natures could be touched by what they ate. Moses rebukes them, saying: "Will you exchange the better for the worse?" (2:61) and refuses to follow their wishes. In the end, they eat the food of heaven for the next forty years, with ultimately disappointing results.

This incipient rebelliousness of the people comes to a head when they all are at the Mount of Sinai. The story is similar in both versions. In the Bible, Moses withdraws for forty days to receive the commandments from God. When he returns with the tablets, he discovers that in the time he has been away Aaron has overseen the making of a golden calf that the people are worshipping. This is a massive transgression, "a disgraceful episode" which Jewish sages compare "to a bride who is unfaithful on her wedding night" as Benjamin Lau writes in a commentary on the Portion of the Week in the Israeli newspaper *Haaretz*.[66] Due to Moses' intervention, God does not destroy the people and Moses returns to the mountain for another forty days. He receives a second set of commandments (a different, stricter one according to the Essene Gospel of Moses), again written by him or God, (both are mentioned), and on his return he has the tabernacle built, he receives further instructions and laws, and he makes priests of Aaron and his sons. As Lau says, what is needed for "a nation of slaves that have been sentenced to liberty" is a set of very strict guidelines for living and worshipping, to facilitate the move from total, enforced submission to total, voluntary submission. Ironically almost, it is during the time that Moses is away receiving the new rules that the Children of Israel show how much they need them.

In the Qur'an, Moses is summoned to the mountain of the Lord for forty nights (thirty plus another ten) to receive the Book. While he is gone the people make a calf from their golden ornaments "of a saffron hue...which gave a lowing sound" (7:148) and which they pray to. They do this contrary to the warning of Aaron, or Haroun, (20:90) and at the proposal of a magician, As-Samiri. Though Ibn Kathir calls him

---

[66] Lau (9 March 2007)

Aaron Samiri, thus linking him to Aaron, others have said that As-Samiri is a title of a man rather than a name and that it may signify that he was a member of the people who were later to be called the Samaritans, the descendants of the tribe that would be called Israel. He tells them the calf is their god and even the god of Moses, which he has "forgotten." (20:88)

When Moses comes down, he calls their action evil and says: "Would you hasten the justice of Your Lord?" thus implying a prohibition on such actions that intend, or have the effect of, bringing the Day of Judgement nearer.[67] Moses then throws down the tablets he is carrying - they do not shatter in the Qur'an because he later picks them up – and he furiously asks Haroun what had prevented him from stopping the people. Haroun replies that the people had nearly killed him (7:150) and that he was frightened that Moses would say that he had sown discord among the people.

When Moses asks As-Samiri for his side of the story, the latter says that, perceiving something that the people could not see, he had taken some dust from "the messenger's trail" (usually understood to be Jibreel's) and thrown it in with the molten gold as his soul had told him to (20:96). This sounds like Shaytanic temptation, and Moses condemns him to be something like an untouchable from thereon, and he says they will burn the calf and throw it into the sea. For those who repent and believe in the One God, Allah, there is forgiveness. When his anger subsides, he takes up the tablets again and tells the people of the guidance he has received.

The most interesting difference here is the difference in the roles played by Aaron/Haroun. Muslim circles do debate how guilty Haroun was; when Haroun says: "Clutch not my beard nor my head!" (20:94), some see that Moses has not necessarily done this yet, or that he is only holding lightly. However: "He cast down the tablets, and he seized his brother by the head, dragging him towards him" (7:150) sounds less nuanced. In the end, though, the worst that can be said is that Haroun

---

[67] In another verse of the Qur'an, Allah says: "Man was created with a hasty nature. I shall show him My Signs, but do not hasten (them)." (21:37) The final injunction "ask me not to hasten" implies that God is talking about the fearful signs here, such as the Day of Judgement.

130

fails to stop them. The responsibility lies elsewhere, with the Samiri, who we will return to.

In the Bible, on the other hand, Aaron actively leads the people in their idolatry. Though a Midrash says that his actions were an attempt to divert the people that went wrong (which begs the question, Divert from what? What could have been worse?), the abiding impression is that Aaron is a kind of shadow prophet, (as was Lot to Abraham); one who advances the action in a negative way.[68] As Aaron has been given the staff to carry out some of the key actions in the story, he is actually essential. Significantly, his name in Hebrew means messenger or bringer of light, and, as we have seen, he was gifted with clear and beautiful speech. This made him a better mouthpiece for the word of God than his coarse-spoken brother. Yet somehow this bringer of light, this High Priest, agrees to make a golden calf, thereby sanctioning an idolatrous act that deprives the people of a law that speaks to and for the heart, if the Essene version is correct. It seems that the writers of this story were trying to resolve something inherent in the way they had told the story and the language they wrote in.

Some light is thrown on this by the thoughts of Jung, who experienced a dream in which he was carrying a flickering candle through a dark, windy night, aware that he was being followed. Suddenly he realised that what was following him was his shadow, and that its size was directly proportional to the light shed by the light he carried.

Jung used this to understand our relationship to God. Without us there would be only light, only God, but in carrying that light we become the instruments of the unfolding of God's will, and we can only understand ourselves, and hence God, by looking to our shadows. In Hebrew, the word *tsel* is the root of the words for both 'man' and 'shadow'. Particularly in the Biblical narrative, and in the minds of its writers – consciously or otherwise - we are the shadows that God's light casts.

Jung wrote elsewhere that the religious task facing Jews, Christians and Muslims, is to restore the fallen angel, Lucifer, to heaven. This in

---

[68] In 2003, David Grossman compared Shimon Peres to Moses and called Benjamin Nethanyahu "a descendant of Aaron" when he defeated him. They were polar opposites politically.

essence means that we must bring together the two sides of our natures, restore our shadows to ourselves, embrace fully our consciousness, for Lucifer, in Latin, also means the bringer or bearer of light.

In name, in essence, Lucifer, Satan and Aaron, are thus one and the same. The Star of David represents, in some traditions, the meeting of earth and fire, and the people of Israel have lived this duality, as a proud, unbending people, bringers of light (*nur legoyim*), chastised in the Holy Books for carrying out the sacred task of bringing the world to consciousness and restoring Satan to heaven, restoring our shadow to ourselves. Thus, in this primal meeting of the Jews with their destiny, the Jews, the People of Israel, embrace struggling for God, a task personified in Moses, and embrace struggling with God, in following Satan's temptation, as personified in Aaron.

Though it is hard to consider fully from an Islamic point of view, Freud's theory of the "twin nature" of the Prophet Moses/Aaron opens up an interesting line of thought. He believed that there were two Moses: one who was a non-Hebrew worshipper of the one god Aten, the sun god, who, as exiled governor of a border kingdom, led its inhabitants (the Hebrews) to a land where they could worship freely; and the other, a Midianite priest of the volcano god Jahve. He believed that the former Moses was killed by the Children of Israel and that the religion they followed after resembled that of the volcano priest. However, over time, the god they worshipped became more like the god of the original Moses. Retrospectively, the people began to revere the original Moses and this, Freud believed, was the source of the Jewish guilt complex.

What this highlights is that there were something like two religious models imposed on the Moses story, and this *is* consistent with the Islamic point of view. One of the most striking features of the Biblical story of Moses is how much of it – much of the Books of Leviticus and Numbers – consists of the laws of sacrifice and temple practice. Given the history of the books - they were "found" or written by temple priests around 623 BCE, the year of the first Passover - it seems possible to suggest that this priestly tradition was added much later to a known story and is effectively false. This appears to be made plausible by the fact that it is precisely this temple worship that is railed against by later Prophets, as we shall see. As Freud puts it in 'Moses and Monotheism':

"The priests, in their rewriting of the Biblical text as we have it, ascribe much too much to Moses. Institutions as well as ritualistic rules undoubtedly belonging to later times are declared to be Mosaic laws, with the clear intent of enhancing their authority." [69]

He also perceives a deeper motive as being to "establish a continuity between their own times and the Mosaic period" in order to fill the gap between the two. He goes on to explain the gap in psychological terms, comparing the initial resistance and later sudden acceptance of the monotheistic idea to a similar pattern that greeted Darwin's theories; there is an incubation period, or period of latency, before the initially difficult idea is suddenly accepted. [70]

It is significant, and perhaps *this* is the manifestation of the guilt, that it is Aaron who is named as the high priest in the Bible, and that he even loses two of his sons, who burnt incense in a way that was not prescribed (Leviticus 10). He is thus another "shadow prophet" who the Bible says initiates evil, explicitly, as we have seen with the case of the Golden Calf, and implicitly with the false introduction of the temple cult. Some Jewish commentators have argued that God commanded the Jews to offer sacrifices because, as Miron Izakson puts it, "they were incapable of serving him (*sic*) in any other fashion." [71] However, this seems to be rather a provisional relationship between God and His Chosen People. It is also one that will only be operable when the Temple is established, a long time hence. In this light, the whole edifice of Temple cultism starts to look like retrospective defeatism.

The Qur'an does not see the Prophets or their messages in anything like this way. Its view of the Prophets is that they, at best, all bring the same message and are all perfect, and at worst, that they bring the same message adapted slightly to the time and people they bring it to, and that are all tested at some point of weakness. Thus, the Qur'an does not distribute the responsibility in the same way as the Bible. Instead it

---

[69] Freud (1939) p.81

[70] He calls this 'Post accident stress guilt neurosis.' p 84

[71] Izakson (2006)

says, highlighting the key issues: "And We verily gave Moses and Aaron the Criterion (of right and wrong) and a light and a reminder for those who keep from evil."(21:48) In the Qur'an, it is either the Children of Israel as a whole, or the character of someone referred to as As-Samiri, who carry that weight.

Some Christian and Jewish writers have had a problem with this figure. One writer objects that a Samaritan is an anachronism at this time, and that features of the story are fabulistic. There is such a tendency with some writers to regard so any part of the story that is different from the Biblical version (conversely to my approach here). However, the writer does offer us one possibility to vindicate the Muslim position, which I am inclined to view with sympathy:

"There is a downside to this otherwise formidable objection: there are no manuscripts of Pirke de Rabbi Eliezer (the source from which the writer claimed the Prophet Muhammad took the story) which pre-date the career of the Prophet Muhammad. So a Muslim could propose that someone who knew the Qur'an's description of As-Samiri mischievously inserted the statement about Sammael[72] into the text of Pirke de Rabbi Eliezer. (For a discussion of Pirke de Rabbi Eliezer, see the essay by Dr. Lewis Barth at www.usc.edu/dept/huc-la/p...endas.html) I think it's exponentially more likely that the saying that Sammael causing the golden calf to moo was disseminated in Arabia long before the text of Pirke de Rabbi Eliezer was finalized, but that is of course difficult to prove. So although the ring of truth reverberates in the theory that the Qur'an's As-Samiri character is the result of a misunderstanding of a rabbinical saying about the archdemon Sammael, it is not empirically demonstrable."[73]

In the Bible, Moses tries to take the burden of the responsibility when God demands the total annihilation of the people, even though God promises to spare him and make him the father of a (different) great nation: "And now, if you will not forgive their sin, blot me out, I pray you, from the book that you have written." (Exo 32:32) Rabbi Shmuley Boteach ("America's most famous Rabbi") calls this offer a new kind

---

[72] An evil angel in Jewish tradition
[73]Waterrock
http://p099.ezboard.com/fsabdiscussionboardfrm19.showMessage?topicID=177.topic

of heroism and, recalling the slaughter of Abraham's *nafs*, he quotes the ancient Rabbis: "Who is a hero? It is he who conquers his own selfish inclination."[74]

However, the burden of the action ultimately falls on the people. In the Qur'an, even before Moses returns, they realise that they have done something terrible that will require divine forgiveness. When Moses does return he tells them: "O my people, surely you have wronged yourselves by your turning to the calf, so turn in repentance to your Creator and *faaqataloo nafsakum*." (2:54) This literally means "kill yourselves" and could thus by extension mean: "Slay the wrongdoers among yourselves", which would be consistent with the Biblical punishment where Moses tells those who take his side, the Levites: "These are the words of the Lord the God of Israel: 'Arm yourselves, each of you, with his sword. Go through the camp from gate to gate and back again. Each of you kill his brother, his friend, his neighbour,'" resulting in three thousand deaths. (Exo 32: 26-8) However, *faaqataloo nafsakum* could also mean something like "overcome yourselves" or "slay your egos," in the sense that we have seen with Abraham. This could be seen as the more likely, because the Qur'anic verse continues: "This will be better for you with Your Creator and He will relent towards you." (2:54) (Similarly, in the Bible, God says: "A day will come when I shall punish them for their sin," implying that the punishment would be later. The commentary adds: "And the Lord smote the people for worshipping the bull calf that Aaron had made," implying that it was not the Levites. (Exo 32:34-5)) Another telling of the scene in the Qur'an gives further strength to the idea that no major punishment was inflicted at that time, but that a severe punishment was threatened on a group of seventy:

"Lo! Those who chose the calf (for worship), terror from their Lord and humiliation will come upon them in the life of the world. Thus do We requite those who invent a lie. But those who do ill deeds and afterward repent and believe - lo! for them, afterward, God is Forgiving, Merciful. Then, when the anger of Moses abated, he took up the tablets, and in their inscription there was guidance and mercy for all those who fear their Lord. And Moses chose of his people seventy men for Our

---

[74] I read an article by him in 1997 *The Hero's inside you.* He later published *The Private Adam: Becoming a Hero in a Selfish Age* in 2003.

appointed time and place of meeting and, when the trembling came on them, he said: My Lord! If Thou hadst willed Thou hadst destroyed them long before, and me with them. Wilt thou destroy us for that which the ignorant among us did? It is but Thy trial (of us). Thou sendest whom Thou wilt astray and guidest whom Thou wilt: Thou art our Protecting Friend, therefore forgive us and have mercy on us, Thou, the Best of all who show forgiveness. And ordain for us in this world that which is good, and in the Hereafter (that which is good), Lo! We have turned unto Thee." (7:152-156)

God says that He has the power to both punish and forgive: "My punishment I afflict on whom I will and My Mercy embraces all things." As Moses says in 2:54, God accepted their repentance, implying that His Mercy is stronger.[75]

As to the fate of the Golden Calf, in both Bible and Qur'an, it is ground down. However, in the former, the resulting powder is to be drunk, while in the latter it is to be thrown into the sea. This corresponds to the two methods of portraying and dealing with wrong that we come across in Bible and Qur'an – respectively "owning" it and disassociating utterly from it.

Reaching the Promised Land
In both the Bible and the Qur'an this repentance was neither permanent nor wholesale, and its second great manifestation occurs when the people reach the Promised Land. After a year in the Sinai, the nadir is reached when Caleb and Joshua, who had entered the Promised Land, warn that the people there are very powerful. In the Bible, Moses and Aaron fall on their faces before the congregation and Caleb and Joshua both counsel:

"If the Lord delight in us, then he will bring us into this land, and give it us; a land which floweth with milk and honey. Only rebel not ye against the Lord, neither fear ye the people of the land; for they are

---

[75] In 7:157 this forgiveness is connected to believing in "the unlettered Prophet." Ibn Kathir mentions several *Hadeeth* where the Prophet Muhammad talks of the best Ummah (religious community) who will be the last of people but the first to enter Paradise. p. 400

bread for us: their defence is departed from them, and the Lord is with us: fear them not." (Numbers 14:8 -9)

However, the people want to stone these two and head back to Egypt.

Because of this lack of faith the Bible says that the Children of Israel will spend a further thirty-nine years in the wilderness and are told that they will never see the Land, except Caleb and Joshua. The people still complain, about food and water, and Aaron and Miriam complain about Zipporah, Moses' wife. There is even a rebellion[76] against Moses, led by a man called Korah and the Levite priests (that unresolved guilt again on behalf of the writers), and an unsuccessful invasion of the Promised Land from the south carried out without Moses' approval.

In the Qur'an, when they reach the borders of the Promised Land, Moses says:

"O my people, remember God's blessing upon you when He appointed Prophets from among you, and made you kings, and gave you what He had not given to anyone else in all the worlds. O my people, go into the Holy Land which God has written for you, and do not turn back on your heels – for then you would return as losers." (5:20)

However, the people fear the powerful inhabitants of the land, and prefer to wait until either they have left, or, preferably, Moses and his Lord have driven them out. They say that they will wait where they are in the meantime. Even with the counsel of two God-fearing men of their number (these are named as Yashu and Kalab - Joshua and Caleb - in the Islamic tradition), who say they will be successful if they enter trusting in God, the majority are still unconvinced, despite all that has happened before. Because of this God says: "For this it shall remain closed to them for forty years, while they wander aimlessly in the land." (5:26)

---

[76] The Oxford Companion to the Bible suggests that there were two rebellions, one religious and one secular, that the writers have made into one story that contains "awkward transitions".

To this point the two accounts are remarkably similar, and what follows bears comparison. In the Qur'an, Moses pleads with God to distinguish between the good and the bad but God tells him not to be saddened by the people who are disobedient because the punishment is theirs alone, even if the crime is extremely serious. The point is made by refering to the story of Kabil and Habil (Cain and Abel): "We decreed for the Children of Israel that whosoever killeth a human being for other than manslaughter or corruption in the earth, it shall be as if he had killed all mankind, and whoso saveth the life of one, it shall be as if he had saved the life of all mankind." (5:32) The offence was huge and had been committed as one so the people would all share the same destiny. The forty years in the wilderness would thence bind the people together as one.

In the Bible, the holistic nature of Moses' words is expressed differently:

"Behold, I set before you this day a blessing and a curse: the blessing, if you obey the commandments of the Lord your God, which I command you this day, and the curse, if you do not obey the commandments of the Lord your God, but turn aside from the way which I command you this day, to go after other gods which you have not known." (Deuteronomy 11:26-28)

Paradoxically, the power and the glory would be theirs if they submitted themselves voluntarily, a typically Islamic call, in fact. Despite the hardships and the miracles that Moses had led the people of Israel through, they were not yet ready to embrace this fully as a way of life, a full living of the laws of God. The light, the consciousness of self and of God, is a blessing, but it cuts both ways.

The Wilderness Years
The years in the wilderness that followed, however, are not a time of repentance, but a time of further complaint and disobedience, examples of which are found in both Bible and Qur'an.

In the Qur'an, when the people are told that they can enter the town and eat their fill providing they prostrate and say "Repentance" as they enter the gate, some of the people still say something else and are punished. On another occasion they are told to keep the Sabbath, and fish miraculously come to them when they do, and do not when they do not, enabling them to eat, yet still they lack faith.

On another occasion, when they are commanded by God through Moses to sacrifice a cow in order to establish the guilt of a murderer, they enter a long, mocking negotiation through Moses as to what sort of cow this sacrifice should be. (2:70-3) Islamic commentators Ibn Abbas, Mujahid and Suddi, among others, have said that God would have accepted the sacrifice of any cow had they sacrificed it immediately, but as they argue, He makes it harder for them. In fact, even when they receive an accurate description – a cow of middle years, yellow, not broken-in as a working animal, and flawless – they nearly do not sacrifice it.

The talk of calf sacrifice then leads into a comment on the nature of these people. The result of this episode is to harden the hearts of the people so that they became harder than stones – "As stones or even worse in hardness." (2:74) The verse continues, saying that stones at least sometimes produce water when struck. An example of this found elsewhere is when Moses strikes a stone and produces twelve streams of water, one for each tribe, an incident found both in the Qur'an (7:160) and the Bible. The implication of this is clearly that the Children of Israel still have a lot to learn, not least about their own opinion of themselves.

This need for learning is expressed in the Qur'an through the meeting of Moses with someone called Al-Khidr. According to a *Hadith* transmitted by Ibn Abbas and collected by Bukhari, the Prophet Muhammad said that one of his people once asked Moses if he knew anyone who knew more than him. Moses said that he did not, but God informed him that there was such a man, called Al-Khidr, the Green Prophet. To find him, Moses was told to take a fish with him, and that wherever he lost that fish, which would be at the point where two seas meet, there he would find Al-Khidr.

Moses and his servant accordingly met the man at the predicted place and Moses asked if he could follow him so that he could learn his righteousness. Al-Khidr said that he would need patience when

139

confronted with things he did not understand and told him: "If you are going to follow me, then do not ask me about anything until I tell you about it." (18:70) Moses, though, thrice could not contain himself when Al-Khidr first made a hole in a boat, then killed a boy and then repaired a wall that was about to fall down in a town where the people had refused to feed them. At that point Al-Khidr explained that the boat belonged to poor people and was about to be seized by a king. The boy was destined to oppress his believing parents and it was wished to exchange him for someone pure and less likely to be oppressive. The wall concealed treasure that belonged to two orphans of a righteous man who would have been denied their inheritance, had the wall fallen and exposed the hidden treasure. He concluded: "And I did not have it of my own accord – that is the meaning of what you could not be patient with." (18:82)

The people of the tribe of Israel also had to make a leap in their development. In Egypt they had been a distinct, enslaved group, but they had not yet become Jews, or even monotheists, before they left Egypt. According to the Bible, they carried God's promise of the land of Canaan, but they were separated from being able to fulfil that promise by more than the geographical distance between Africa and Eurasia. The Sinai desert that lay between the two lands was also like a psychological space, a state of transition, between the one-time "Paradise" (where there were still melons and cucumbers) where the polytheistic Hebrews had lived, but in which they did not belong, and the world, outside the womb of Africa. Joseph Campbell places the story within a mythical tradition, pointing out that the Children of Israel entered Egypt, in the form of Joseph, through water (a well), and exited through water (the parted sea). This could be seen to belittle and relativise the story to one of many variations. However, its status in both Bible and Qur'an, and its effect on history, could argue that God had "written" this story precisely so that it would be played out in a way that replicated powerful archetypal devices. Not least of these is the powerful geographical position. In their crossing of the Sinai, the Hebrews re-enacted the mythical migration that had been performed by our ancestors who had left thousands of years before. On a more conscious level than then, though still symbolically, they discovered who they were, on behalf of all those who lived, and would live, outside Africa, and how they should relate to God. In a sense, they were a transitional people.

In mythological terms a journey into wilderness stands as a passage to a place where the ego is stripped away from the traveller who is left to face their soul unprotected by the worldly concerns by which we generally define ourselves. (No melons, no cucumbers). In psychological terms wilderness represents a place where our repressed unconscious selves have no choice but to become conscious. In religious terms, it is in the wilderness that we meet God.

This usually occurs on an individual level but in the Moses story, it happens on a community level. It was Moses' destiny to lead his people through this process of becoming, and to give guidance through which a new identity could be maintained once the period of transition was over for the generations that migrated with him. As Joseph Campbell says:

"The individual has no relation to God save by way of this community, or consensus. God – the only God there is – is apart, and the body of His Chosen People is the one holy thing on earth. The individual apart from that is null."[77]

This transition was the transition from enforced submission in Egypt to conscious, voluntary submission in Canaan, as demanded by the covenant between God and Abraham. Writing in *Haaretz'* 'Portion of the Week', Miron Izakson delineates "three complex stages, each augmenting the previous one" of this wilderness transition. The Children of Israel move from a "vast and desolate... barrier... full of threats and perils" through a place where "spiritual and physical order can be created even in the largest of wildernesses." This is a place where: "The soul examines itself relentlessly, without the danger that outside influences might cause it to forget its spiritual qualities." The Bible mentions 42 places. There were 14 before the entering of the spies and 8 in the last year which means that there were 22 places in the intervening 38 years, time to establish some sort of community at each stopping place and ultimately not too taxing. Rabbi Shlomo

---

[77] Campbell (1964) p.139

Yitzhaki (1040-1105), better known as Rashi, the pre-eminent commentator on Jewish texts, commented on this: "God was merciful with the people even as He was punishing them."

In the process of the transition, the message that is transmitted is that the people can only survive with God's help. Only God's plagues had convinced the Pharaoh that the people must be allowed to go, and it is only through God that the people are fed and watered in the desert. However, the apparently inexplicable Biblical fact is that these people, whose line grew from the rather late-in-the-day arrival of Isaac and the tricksterhood of Jacob, the people who God chose to love above all others, very rarely bowed their "stiff necks" in submission. In both the Qur'an and Bible, it is Moses (with Aaron in the Qur'an) who embodies virtue, fear of God, faith and obedience, and the people who embody the opposite. On five occasions in the Bible Moses calls them "stiff-necked" and on one occasion says: "Circumcise therefore the foreskin of your heart, and be no more stiffnecked." (Deuteronomy 10:16) Clearly, mere physical circumcision as a sign of the Covenant, as established by Abraham, is not enough. Although they are finally granted the Promised Land, though without Moses, the People of Israel do not change, for all their years in the wilderness before and the chastisements they would receive within the Land in the years to come, as we shall see. This realisation is the third stage. Miron Izakson says: "Despite the consolidation of law and order, the more rebellious aspect of the wilderness remains. It is much easier to take the Jews out of the wilderness than to take the wilderness out of the Jews."[78]

However, it is not that the Children of Israel have acquired traits of the wilderness in the wilderness, but that the submission required in the wilderness has not removed the rebellious traits that were there in the first place.

Each miracle is a vivid reminder of how omnipotent God is and how relatively unimportant and insignificant the human ego is, yet the overriding impression of the time spent in the Sinai is that, despite this, the people keep lapsing into old ways and forgetting God. Almost the moment basic survival is assured by the manna from heaven, the people bemoan the loss of the foods they ate in Egypt. When Moses ascends

---

[78] Izakson (26 May 2006)

the mountain to receive God's commandments, the people ask his brother Aaron to make a golden calf to worship. The people seem to wish to literally remain in Africa, like a metaphor for remaining unconscious, and thus to avoid the responsibility their destiny has for them. Yet the message God imparts through Moses is that their destiny is elsewhere, beyond that, and that whether they like it or not is of little importance. They are required to become, which they do, in part, although there is always a resistance.

As we have mentioned, when it seems that, despite these unchanging stiff necks, the time has come to enter the Promised Land, it is as if some collective sense of unreadiness manifests. The men who go to spy out the land return warning that the people of the land appear far too strong for the people of Israel to defeat. For this lack of faith the people are told that for every day that the men were spying out Canaan they will have to spend a further year in the wilderness, for God is no longer among them. They are thus condemned to a further forty years in the wilderness, and that all those who had shown lack of faith in God's power to achieve great things through them would not live to see the land.

God not being among the people can be seen in two ways at this point. God can be seen to have actively withdrawn here because no faith is being shown. However, if God's power is understood in terms of presence, *minyan,* rather than action, responsibility for the withdrawal can be seen to rest with the people. Because they did not, or would not, acknowledge God's presence, because they could not consciously acknowledge God's power, God could not act through them. It was not that God refused to help them, but that God would only help them if they helped themselves, which they would have to do by submitting to God's will.

Ultimately, even Moses lets slip his perfection as an instrument of God. After the people are turned away from the land they run out of water and God commands Moses to tell the rock before him to bring forth water. Instead Moses questions whether it will happen, replicating his people's lack of faith. Though he strikes the rock with his rod and it does bring forth water, for this lack of faith he is told that he will not enter the Promised Land either.

Each of the Prophets, the greatest - Moses, Jesus and Muhammad - and the lesser, is a perfect instrument for the unfolding of the divine plan, but they are perfect in the sense of being complete, rather than perfect in the sense of being flawless. For something to be complete within itself is paradoxical. The paradox can be reconciled in the understanding that that self is a dynamic thing, a question in the process of answering itself, rather than a frozen moment of flawlessness. It contains within itself the flaw, or incompleteness, that keeps it growing towards its end, its death, when it is finally released from its mortal limitations. The Prophets seem, in the way they live their lives, to have an awareness that this is so, and it is this sense of a message that is to be completed by those who follow them that is the profoundest meaning of their lives.

Ibn Arabi, a Muslim who lived in Spain in the 12th Century, had a vision of the oneness of the Prophets and their teachings. He said:

"The son is the mystery of his father."

This can be interpreted in a quite literal way, that we as children live out the unlived lives of our parents. Paradoxically our parents, unconsciously, want us to live their unlived lives while at the same time they consciously wish us to affirm the lives they lead by living as they do, or at least as they say. Implicitly, we will make the same demands on our own children.

It can also be interpreted more symbolically. The idea, of constantly growing, moving towards completion, is there in the lives of the Prophets. Moses, stern, but disallowed from entering Canaan because of his doubt and anger when faced by the rock, was also prohibited because he had killed an Egyptian while he was in slavery. Yet according to the Bible, Joshua, who succeeded him, was required to kill thousands. Each was, in the Prophetic sense, perfect, but they were not the same, and there was essentially no way that Moses could have led the people as Joshua did. Somehow, the unfolding required that Moses doubt God, even if for a moment, and that, ironically, he be barred from leading an army that would kill thousands because he had killed one.

144

There is this same deeper unfolding when Moses ascends Sinai to receive the commandments. While Moses is receiving the Ten Commandments the people ask Aaron to make a golden calf to worship. According to the Essene Gospel of Moses it is because of this that the original commandments were destroyed and a sterner version given.

"It shall be a stern law, yea, it shall bind them for they know not yet the Kingdom of Light."

The pattern here is consistent with the pattern of the dynamic interplay of the two sides of our natures. With Moses gone, the people lapse back into unconsciousness. Their spiritual selves, rather than seeking meaning in their God, seek external and sexual satisfaction. The two are often paired in the Bible, for sex, with its implicitly creative energy, is the most "religious" act we can commit with another person, is essentially spiritually abusive when committed without love, and is less spiritual than our relationship with God. The people are punished by receiving different commandments, commandments that are more like strict rules, deemed to be the only form they could understand. It is implied that, had they been able to use their spiritual impulses consciously, they would have been ready to enter the Kingdom of Light. But they were not, at least not yet. They were only ready for laws that could be understood rationally, with the mind, not with the heart. With time, implicitly, following those laws would teach a submission that would engender love.

The sense is that it had to be so. They, and by implication, we, are not ready. Had the people waited patiently for the perfect commandments, the implication is that they would have been ready for them. It would have been as if human consciousness had come full circle. The land of milk and honey would be synonymous with a return to paradise externally and internally, rather than an inner aspiration of a flickering consciousness that was not reflected in the world outside. It would somehow have been too easy an ending to a story that did not really seem like it was about to end.

Arrival

In the last phase of his life, Moses led the people into what is now Jordan, fighting and defeating the people there and dividing the territory between the tribes of Reuben, Gad and half of Manasseh. Before he died, Moses gave a farewell address to his people, commissioned Joshua as his successor, ascended the Mount of Nebo to view Canaan and died at the age of 120 years. That he did not enter the Land is attributed in the Bible to both his responsibility (to convince the people) and the people's responsibility (to be convinced of Moses about God and thence to stop sinning).

When we consider Moses, we can see that he is clearly a great man, and Prophet, and leader, despite or because of the nature of his people. He was a statesman, lawgiver, and a creator of a people from a group of slaves. Moreover, they were a people who developed some sense of God and their own Chosenness in His eyes under Moses' guidance, though they were prone to lapse from it. In many ways he is like the Prophet Muhammad, and Muslims see this similarity stated in the Bible in a passage in which Moses tells the people what the Lord had told him:

"I will raise them up a Prophet from among their brethren, like unto thee (Moses), and will put My words in his mouth; and he shall speak unto them all that I shall command him." (Deuteronomy 18:18)

This Prophet, who Christians sometimes see as Jesus (Acts 3:21-22 says that this prophecy will come true when Jesus comes again), in fact, sounds more like the Prophet Muhammad. In many ways – in the nature of their births; their marital status; their political power; their direct message from God; the new laws they established; their acceptance by their people; their natural deaths - Moses was most unlike Jesus and much more like the Prophet Muhammad. As we will see in the words of Isaiah (29:12) while the Prophet Muhammad and Moses had words put in their mouths by God, Jesus spoke much more independently - the Word was in his heart. Further, "brethren" suggests something more distant than the use of the words "family" or "from amongst you" would, and this would imply the children of Ishmael rather than the children of Isaac. It was told of Ishmael that "he shall dwell in the presence of all his brethren" (Genesis 16:12) and "die in the presence of all his brethren" (Genesis 25:18), giving the exact sense of this phrase.

Before his death Moses gives this blessing to the Children of Israel: "The Lord came from Sinai, and rose up from Seir unto them; he shined forth from mount Par'an, and he came with ten thousands of saints; from his right hand went a fiery law for them." (Deuteronomy 33:2) Before he comes to blessing the individual tribes of Israel he says that, though God "came from" Sinai, his full glory would be from mount Par'an, a place whose only reference in the Bible is as the place where Ishmael and Hagar lived after being sent away by Abraham, Ishmael of whom the Prophet Muhammad and the Arabs were descended. When the Prophet Muhammad entered Mecca in victory he did so with "ten thousands of saints", and with him he brought the "fiery law" of the Qur'an. There has been no other such law since Moses.

The gentile, non-Israel, import of this message is emphasised by the words that follow: "Yea, he loved the people; all his saints are in thy hand: and they sat down at thy feet; *every one* shall receive of thy words. Moses commanded of us a law, *even* the inheritance of the congregation of Jacob." (Deuteronomy 33:4-5) In other words, while the words of Moses were solely for the "congregation of Jacob", the Children of Israel, the words of the other will be a universal message for everyone, a message to "every one", "to all mankind" (34:28).

There is, though, one significant difference between the Prophets Moses and Muhammad, peace be upon them. Moses died at the age of 120 *before* the arrival within the Promised Land, although he is described as being at the height of his powers. This can only be seen as profoundly significant in the message it conveys – the deepest meaning of the story of the Children of Israel is to be found in the journey. The essence of their Chosenness is to be found in the Wilderness. Arrival would still impose requirements of submission to God, as we shall see in the following chapters, but Moses actually founds the community while it is on the move. It would be more accurate to say that he tried to found the community, because the message that the Bible conveys is that even after the forty years, the Children of Israel were none too submissive.

In contrast, though the era of the Prophet Muhammad actually begins in flight from Mecca to Medina, the significance of Islam is that it is a universal religion that was founded in an established, urban community in Medina under the leadership of the Prophet Muhammad. The importance of migration is preserved in the ritual requirement of pilgrimage, Hajj is the fifth pillar of Islam, but the other four pillars, particularly prayer and fasting in Ramadan, actually require stability to be performed fully - when travelling, prayers can be shortened and fasting postponed.

In short, while Judaism is the model for life's journey and struggle, Islam, at its heart, is the model for submission, arrival and peace. We can take this on a personal level or on the level of the history of humanity. Though Jews may be like everyone else only more so, as the Qur'an says, we were all Muslims initially and we are all supposed to be so again ultimately, insha'Allah.

There is hope for all, and this includes the Children of Israel, stiff-necked or no. As the Qur'an says: "We gave Moses the Book , and We gave guidance to the Children of Israel." (17:2)

Ghazali, in his 'Renewal of Muslims I', gives an example of this. Moses is in the desert with the people, he says, and there is no rain so they pray but no rain comes. Moses prays to God to find out why and God says: "There is one among you who is sinning. While he is among you there will be no rain." Moses tells the people and asks the man to leave. No one moves. They pray again and this time it rains. Moses asks God why and God says that it is because the man has repented. Moses asks who it is and God says:

"If I wasn't going to tell you who it was while he was doing a wrong thing, I'm certainly not going to tell you after he has done such a good one."

Boteach, Rabbi S. *The Private Adam: Becoming a Hero in a Selfish Age (2003)* Harper Collins: New York
Bucaille, M. *The Bible, the Qur'an & Science* (1981) Seghers: Paris

Campbell, J. *The Masks of God - Occidental Mythology* (1964) Viking: New York

Cooper, H. (ed.) *Soul Searching - Studies in Judaism and psychotherapy* (1988) SCM Press Ltd: London

Deedat, A. *What the Bible says about the Prophet Muhammad (Peace be upon him)* (1995) IPCI: Durban:

Freud, S. *Moses and Monotheism* (1939) Vintage: New York

Garstang, J. & Garstang, J.B.E. *The Story of Jericho* (1940) Marshall, Morgan & Scott: London

Ibn Kathir, I. *Stories of the Prophets* (2003) Darrusalam: Riyadh

Izakson, M. *The two faces of Wilderness* (26 May 2006) Haaretz: Tel Aviv

Izakson, M. *A mighty voice, a tiny letter* (31 May 2006) Haaretz: Tel Aviv

Jones, J. *Portrait of the Week: Michelangelo's Moses (1513-16)* (8 Jun 2002) Guardian: London

Kohn, M. *Gossip enslaves* (1999) Jerusalem Post: Jerusalem

Lau, B. *A Nation of Slaves Sentenced to Liberty* (9 March 2007) Haaretz: Tel Aviv

Reed, C. *DreamWorks puts new spin on Moses Tale* (18 Dec 1998) Guardian: London

Seale, M.S. *Qur'an and Bible* (1978) Croon Helm: London

Waskow, A. *Facing Pharaoh* (17 Jan 2000) Jerusalem Report: Jerusalem

Dating Moses[79]

Reign	Key events	Date
2nd Intermediate Period		
Hyskos Period	Joseph	1650-1580 1600 (Rohl)
Dynasty XVIII:		**1570-1345**
Ahmoses I		1570-1545
Amenhotep I		1545-1524
Thutmoses I & II		1524-c.1502
Queen Hatshepsut	Pharaoh's daughter who saved Moses?	1501-1480
Thutmoses III	Contesting reign of Queen H. Exodus? (J.W. Jack's thesis)	1502-1448 1250 (Rohl)
Amenhotep II	Joshua enters Canaan (J.W. Jack's thesis)	1448-1422
Thutmoses IV		1422-1413
Amenhotep III	Aten heresy begins	1413-1377
Amenhotep IV (Akhenaten)	Amarna period: Habiru incursions Joseph enters Egypt? (Thomas Mann thesis)	1377-1358
Tutankhamun	Exodus? (Freud's thesis) Amun cult restoration	1358-1349
Ay	Harenhab the virtual ruler	1349-1345
Dynasty XIX		**1345-1200**
Haremhab		1345-1318
Ramses I		1318-1317
Seti I		1317-1301
Ramses II	Building projects: Pithom, Raamses; Exodus? (Bucaille & Albright's thesis) c.1280	1301-1234 1250 (Rohl)
Mereptah	Israelite Stele mentioning suppression of an "Israelite" revolt in Palestine – first appearance of term "Israelite" Exodus? Scharff's thesis c. 1240-1230	1234-1220 1200 (Rohl)

---

[79] The table is adapted from: Campbell (1964) pp. 136-7

Seti II	Exodus? Meek's thesis c. 1240-1230	1220-1200 (1214-1194 – Meek's dating)

David Rohl's 'A Test of Time' (1995) radically redates the timescale of the Pharaohs and corresponding Biblical events, including Moses, but also David and Solomon

8

JOB

I have no doubt
You realise by now the part you played
To stultify the Deuteronomist
And change the tenor of religious thought.
     (God to Job in Robert Frost's 'Masque to Reason')

Both Jewish and Islamic sources and traditions place Job, or Ayyub, before Moses in terms of chronology, but the former places him after in his position in the Bible as one of the 'Wisdom' books, because, as Frost implies above, the Bible until that point had missed something, something personal rather than national. Some go further, as does Gunnar Kopperud in the novel 'A Time of Light':

"The Book of Job can be read as a criticism of God, a criticism of a god who had become too abstract and who sent a son in order to become more concrete."

It was possibly written in the 4th Century BC, though Robin Lane Fox sets the parameters as being between 6th and 2nd Centuries BCE and says that the problem of evil, its primary theme, was not entirely new, having been explored both in other Near Eastern literature and in the Psalms, immediately after Job in the Bible, though probably written before.

Some Jewish traditions place Job just prior to Moses' time. For example, according to Rabbi Hiyya bar Abba, who said it in Rabbi Sima'i's name, three men were present when Pharaoh gave the order to slaughter all of the Hebrew boys. Balaam advised the Pharaoh to annihilate the Jews; Jethro, Moses' father in law, fled; Job said nothing. According to this line of thinking, what we read of his suffering in the story of Job is, by implication, punishment for this silence.

It is an interesting idea but seems to contradict any other commentary made on the story of Job. As Robert Frost puts it in the opening quotation, the story of Job changed "the tenor of religious thought"

152

because it endeavoured to answer the question that had not been answered in the Bible up to that point: If God is good, why do the righteous suffer and the wicked prosper? If Job had been guilty, even of a sin of omission, the question would lose much of its force. Noted Jewish exegete Saadya Gaon (882-942) considered it so important that he called his commentary on the Book of Job, written in Arabic, *Kitabu-l-ta'dil*, the Book of Justification (of God). The Book of Job does try to answer the question, and is thus widely quoted, as well as for being frequently beautiful and moving. However, for all that, many say that it falls short of its aim.

Central to the attempt to answer is Job himself. Once there was a man, we read, "perfect and upright" (Job 1:1), who was both God-fearing and prosperous, in fact "the greatest of all men of the east" (Job 1:3) As J. Bowker describes him, "Job is defined, artificially and completely" as innocent and also very, very good.[80]

One day Satan, as part of a group of "the sons of God," comes before God, who points to Job as a man unique in his righteousness and fear of God. Satan responds that it is only because of his wealth that Job is so good. "Touch all that he hath and he will curse thee to thy face," he says. (Job 1:11) Accordingly, God gives Satan power to inflict hardships on Job, Satan agreeing not to touch Job himself.

Satan begins with the taking of Job's livestock but progresses rapidly to add the loss of his children in a storm. Job's response is to fall to the ground and worship, saying: "Naked came I out of my mother's womb, and naked shall I return thither. The Lord gave, and the Lord hath taken away. Blessed be the name of the Lord." (Job 1:21) Such language and poetry the book has bequeathed us is perhaps one of the reasons it has such a place in the consciousness of the Judeo-Christian world. Also much quoted as a sympathetic portrayal of the human condition, from the darker, later part of the book, is: "Man that is born of a woman is of few days, and full of trouble. He cometh forth like a flower, and is cut down: he fleeth also as a shadow, and continueth not." (Job 14:1-3) Louis de Bernieres also cites two complementary proverbs: "The price of wisdom is above rubies", and "The fear of the Lord, that is wisdom."

---

[80] Bowker (1970)

Aminadav Dykman sees this "literary miracle" as being the result of a "linguistic alchemy" involving many words that do not appear elsewhere in the Bible. It is an alchemy that takes place in the crucible of a particularly refined soul.

However, after Job's angry rebuking of his wife for saying: "Are ye still unshaken in your integrity? Curse God and die," (Job 2:9) and the saying: "Throughout all this, Job did not utter one sinful word." (2:10), Job utters several.

The change comes after a second discussion between God and Satan, which sees Satan given power to inflict further misfortune on Job personally. This time Job is afflicted with boils and pains so great that three friends coming to him do not recognise him. They sit with him in silence for seven days until Job gives expression to all the anger and pain he feels. De Bernieres deems the term "the patience of Job" utterly inappropriate from this point because for all but the two preceding chapters of the Book, the discourse is more marked by the defiance of Job, his preferred title. In cursing the day he was born he effectively gives Satan victory in the latter's argument with God but the suffering does not end there. When Job finishes, the three friends, often called Job's comforters, but described as "possibly the most irritating characters in all of literature" by de Bernieres, advise him in different ways on how to ease his troubles.

The first, Eliphaz, says that God sends trials to those who deserve it: "Happy is the man whom God correcteth. Therefore despise not the chastening of the Almighty, for he maketh sore, and bindeth up. He woundeth, and his hands make whole." (Job 5:17-18) Job would receive six troubles, including famine, war, "the scourge of the tongue" (Job 5:21) and destruction, but the seventh would not harm him, he says. "At destruction and famine thou shalt laugh. Neither shall thou be afraid of the beasts of the earth. For thou shalt be in league with the stones of the field: and the beasts of the field shall be at peace with thee. And thou shalt know that thy tabernacle (covenant) shall be in peace; and thou shalt visit thy habitation, and shalt not sin." (Job 5:22-23) He even tells Job that he will have many descendants, despite the earlier loss of his children, and is thus almost prophetic in anticipating what will happen. However, he really misses the point and Job is not comforted by him because his comfort is dependent on Job accepting that his own iniquity has caused this, which it has not, either in terms of what is true (Job is innocent) or in what we know (that the punishment is the result of a wager). Job says: "My righteousness is in it (in question). Do I ever give voice to injustice?" (Job 6:29-30) and assures Eliphaz that his tongue can tell the difference between truth and lies.

Taking an initially similar line, Bildad says that Job and his children must have done something to deserve this: "Doth God pervert judgement? Or doth the Almighty pervert justice?" (Job 8:3) Job acknowledges God's perfection and accepts that he himself is not perfect but, that being so, God seems to destroy "the perfect and the wicked" (Job 9:22) with equal pleasure. Like Eliphaz, Bildad misses the fact of Job's blamelessness and thus adds insult to injury, leading Job in response to enquire of God whether this is "good unto thee that thou shouldst oppress." (Job 10:3) Again he asserts his righteousness and hence his confusion.

The third, Zophar, says that God knows much more than we do and that Job is actually being punished *less* than he deserves. Perhaps he even hints that Job's declarations are a sign of some vanity. (In fact, they do seem to be a little, because an assumption of one's own faultlessness does sound rather jarring.) Regarding the evil who seem to prosper, their happiness is brief, he says, and God brings them to justice in the end. Again, a perhaps understandable assumption that Job is not faultless means that he also misses the point. Job's anger is presumably fuelled by the fact that an all-knowing God would know that he, Job, is faultless. And maybe this is the problem, that the story cannot work as a source of instruction because it is trying to work out a philosophical point based on the hypothetical existence of a perfect human being when no such being can exist except, arguably (and only in Islam), among the Prophets.

Consequently, Job dismisses this, and the others, (and he later calls them all liars), with the words: "But I have understanding as well as you. I am not inferior to you." (Job 12:3) He then goes on to say that in fact thieves do prosper while the righteous suffer and that princes, kings and counsellors are all misled by God: "They grope in the dark without light and he maketh them to stagger like a drunken man." (Job 12:25)

155

Following this, Eliphaz, Bildad and Zophar on one side, and Job on the other, reprove each other for speaking so much, to which, by the end of a further twenty two chapters, one can only utter a heartfelt "Amen." Instead, "these three men ceased to answer Job, because he was righteous in his own eyes." (Job 32:1) At this point, another, Elihu, who had kept quiet because of the greater age of the others, reproved them all. People see his role in different ways: Robin Lane Fox attributes his argument to a later author "who found the original text too oblique"; Saadya Gaon regards him as having "reason and just argument," while, according to de Bernieres, he is "the most annoying of them all." He is angry with Job because he "justified himself rather than God" (Job 32:2) and angry with the friends for condemning Job without answering Job's argument. He concludes his (also very long) argument by saying that God is unknowable: "Touching the Almighty, we cannot find him out" (Job 38:23) and in doing so could be guilty of his own criticism of the others.

Saadya Gaon, however, defends him. He wrote at a time when Judaism was under attack from within from the literalist and heretical Jewish Karaite sect, and also needed to defend itself from the external arguments of Muslims. He was much concerned with mounting an orthodox defence and in instilling good behaviour in his congregation. In his response to the Book of Job he numbers three reasons why God allows suffering in general: moral and intellectual instruction, like a father to a son (ta'dib watafhim); punishment ('uquba) or purification (tamhid), to turn the sinner away from the sin; and as a test and examination (balwa wa mihna). For him, Job's suffering is of the latter sort. God means well by Job because: he allows him to achieve repentance after sin (tawba) – he does not specify, but this could be when Job is required to pray for his comforters; he is given a means of gaining reward (hasanat); and he is tested and given the chance to "pass."

Significantly, Saadya argues that Elihu hints/says that justice is done in the hereafter. It is hard to find where but Elihu comes closest to this in Chapter 36 when he says: "God repudiates the high and mighty and does not let the wicked prosper, but allows the just claims of the poor and the suffering" (36:5-6) but this stops short of mentioning the

156

afterlife. In his translation of the Book of Job into Arabic, Saadya was inclined to change words to suit his purpose. In 16:4 he adds a word that means *true* when Job talks about how he would speak if he were in the shoes of the comforters and that Job would nod his head *in sadness* rather than in disapproval when he uttered these words (of truth). His translation makes Job less selfrighteous in 22:18 and in the lines following the first quotation above, where Saadya has: "But if they do not hear (obey), they will be passed over at the resurrection and they will die without knowledge thereof", the modern English translation has: "But if they do not listen, they die, their lesson unlearnt, and cross the river of death." (36:12)

This seems to be where the reference to the afterlife comes from and it seems that Saadya projected his own thoughts onto the story because "the high and mighty" clearly do often prosper in this life, and concepts of reward, which are closely related to those of examination, only ultimately make sense if the concept of a Final Judgement is allowed for. The lesson or knowledge, referred to in the English text, is clearly about this life, while with Saadya's rearrangement, it seems to refer to the resurrection. Saadya is not entirely convincing in the end and, as he says, even Elihu ultimately cannot answer Job's question, so God intervenes.

Saadya praises the structure of the book highly – the dilemma; the refutation of three solutions; Elihu's speech; Divine explanation and restoration, and says it is designed to advance the position that the key reason for the suffering is as a test. However, given the answer that God gives at the end, it could be argued that Saadya's answer is less influenced by the text than the Islamic understanding of the people he lived among, which he had absorbed unconsciously into his own thinking. The structure is persuasive, but is grievously faulted by the content, in which Job is neither "everyman" nor patient.

He is, in fact, furious with God. "They are tricked that trusted" and "God thinks nothing amiss" if the wicked prosper, he says. The Book of Job as it is seems to raise more questions about God than it answers. As Carl Gustav Jung says: "The ambivalent God-image plays a crucial part in the Book of Job. Job expects that God will, in a sense, stand by him against God."[81] In fact He does, "admitting somewhat disarmingly to all of Job's indictments" according to de Bernieres and "comes out of this story as the most morally tarnished."

Finally, God speaks out of the whirlwind, asking rhetorical questions that emphasise the gulf that exists between man and God through 129 verses, though without answering Job's question. At the end of this, Job acknowledges God's omnipotence, repents in dust and ashes and is rewarded with the restoration of twice what he had lost, though this is an "almost accidental explanation", as Bowker puts it, in the Biblical text that is dependent on Job praying for the forgiveness of the three comforters. It almost seems as if Job, having failed to find answers within himself, the four friends' arguments and even in God, submits, though without much conviction. De Bernieres is ultimately not moved by the Biblical restoration and sees Job as "a classic existentialist hero." For him, a God who "absentmindedly does not restore to life the servants or the children killed off in chapter 1" is "a frivolous trickster... who even botches up the reparations when he decides to make them."

With the story not measuring up on a text level, some have tried to go deeper. Jung endeavoured to answer the question originally posed:

"Jung's answer places evil, finally, in God directly. God's nature is complex and bears its own shadow. It needs human beings, with their focused body-based consciousness, to incarnate these opposites in divine life and thus help in their transformation. In considering the Book of Job, Jung surmises that Yahweh suffers from unconsciousness, himself forgetting to consult his own divine omniscience. Job's protests against his unmerited suffering make Yahweh aware of his own shadow dealings with Satan and finally he can answer Job with the figure of Christ, who takes the suffering of human beings into his own life and pays for them himself."[82]

In his book 'An Answer to Job', Jung places Job on a continuum between Adam and Jesus. Answering the question as to why God

---

[81] Jung (1963) *p.242*
[82] Ulanov (1997)

should believe what Satan says about Job when He is supposed to be all knowing, Jung can only conclude, as others have done before and since, that God is somehow lacking. For Jung, this is decisively shown when Job's pleas for mercy are answered merely by God declaring His omnipotence. The implication is that this is as far as God can go without changing. The effect of all this on the image of a wise and powerful God, which the Bible at least purports to show, is bad enough, but the next is even more surprising.

Drawing on his understanding of mythical archetypes, Jung explains that this transformation is carried out through the agency of Sophia, a feminine figure who represents Wisdom, a theme of the end of the Book of Job (which as mentioned above is one of the 'Wisdom' books of the Bible). Jung sees Sophia as the prototype of Mary through whom, in Christian belief, God comes to understand human suffering by being born. He comes to understand that things have come to this pass because of the influence of Satan on Adam and Eve, and as Satan is associated with sex, God would have to be born of a virgin.

Though more or less intellectually consistent within itself we seem to be faced with the familiar Biblical interpretation of God being less wise than both those around him, and most particularly, less wise than human beings in general since then. Again it may be interesting or illuminating, but if illumination is achieved at the price of belittling God this much then the source of illumination needs to be questioned and a different perspective considered, such as the Islamic one.

According to Islamic tradition, Ayyub, as Job is known in Arabic, is descended from Is'haq, but not through Jacob so he is not a member of the tribe of Israel, thus putting him in the same pre-Mosaic timeframe as the Biblical Job. The essence of the story in the Islamic version is the same as in the Bible in that for the first part of Ayyub's life he is healthy, wealthy and pious. As a test from God, all this is taken away from him. He loses his family, his money and his health, his body becoming covered with sores. At first he is patient, accepting that everything is from God, although at some point his wife is not and criticises him for the persistence of his faith so in anger he vows to beat her. It is a vow he immediately regrets having uttered but he is sent a divine instruction: "Take some grass in your hand and beat with that so that you do not break your vow." (38:44) A tradition says that he had vowed to beat her a hundred times, so is told to take a hundred pieces of grass and beat her once.

Eventually, though, he can take no more and so prays to God for help: "Shaytan has indeed afflicted me with suffering and torment." (38:41) In response, he is told to strike the ground with his foot. The spring that appears there will bring him coolness and refreshment. The ordeal ends with the words:

"So We answered his prayer, and We removed what was afflicting him, and We gave him back his family, and with them the equivalent of them, as a mercy from Us and a reminder for those who worship (Us)." (21:84)

The Islamic version is much shorter, I would contend because it did not need to "change the tenor of religious thought," and is not so much a version as an apparent corrective or highlighter to a story that, as some Orientalists such as Montgomery Watt have suggested, was quite well known through the telling of the Biblical tale. Leaving aside two name-only mentions, Job's story is effectively dealt with in six verses in the Qur'an. Assuming the basics from a common tradition, the highlightings or corrections seem to be three. Firstly, Ayyub's anger is recognised, understood and forgiven, through God allowing him to carry out a binding vow in a harmless way. In the Bible, Job's wife tells him to curse God and die, to which he replies: "Thou speakest as one of the foolish women speaketh," though he is soon doing both. In the Qur'an, though it is not stated why he is angry with his wife, we could infer that it is for a similar reason to the Biblical telling of the story. His vow to beat his wife, showing that he does feel some anger and impatience, is seen compassionately by God so he is allowed to beat her with a piece of straw, thus obeying the letter of the vow. This incident aside, he is patient throughout.

Secondly, he says that Shaytan has afflicted him, though this does not contradict the idea that all is from God. Finally, "We gave him back his family, and with them the equivalent of them," means he received twice what he had at the start, as in the Bible, but that this includes what he

160

had at the start, rather than it all being replacements. De Bernieres should be pleased to find that God does not "botch" it up in this version.

However, he may be less happy about the conclusion, which is that the arguments given by the comforters seem to have it about right: God is just; He tests and heals; He knows far more than we can about all things; we should not be angry at the chastisement we receive, and, if Elihu does in fact say it, all is resolved in the hereafter. All this is consistent with the Islamic position; it says in the Qur'an that no one is tested beyond what they can bear. Thus, it seems that the fault is not in the comforters, nor even in Job, but in the writers who inferred the possibility of faultlessness within human beings by placing this characteristic within him, alongside a complete lack of humility, surely a fault in itself. Given that the story was written at a time when the Children of Israel were facing trials of their own, the motivation might be an unconscious attempt to avoid taking responsibility for themselves and their position.

Bowker, J. *The Problems of Suffering in Religions of the World* (1970) Cambridge University Press: London
De Bernieres, L. *The Impatience Of Job* (19 Sep 1998) Guardian
Dykman, A. *The Wondrous Sublimity Of Grief* (25 Feb 2000) Haaretz: Tel Aviv
Jung, C.G. *Answer to Job* in Joseph Campbell (ed.) *The Portable Jung*, (1971) Penguin: London
Jung, C.G. *Memories, Dreams, Reflections* (1963) Random House: London
Rosenthal, E.I. *Saadya's Exegesis of the Book of Job*, in *Studia Semetica I Jewish Themes* (1971) Cambridge University Press: London
Ulanov, A. *Jung and Religion: The Opposing Self* in Young-Eisendrath, P. & Dawson, T. *The Cambridge Companion to Jung* (1997) Cambridge University Press: London

9

<u>JONAH</u>

*The historical Jonah, if he can be so called, was glad enough to escape
but in imagination, in day-dream, countless people have envied him. It
is, of course, quite obvious why. The whale's belly is simply a womb big
enough for an adult. There you are, in the dark, cushioned space that
exactly fits you, with yards of blubber between yourself and reality,
able to keep up an attitude of the completest indifference, no matter
what happens... Short of being dead, it is the final, unsurpassable stage
of irresponsibility.*
    (George Orwell – 'Inside the Whale')

The story of Jonah, or Yunus in the Qur'an, is very much about the
responsibilities of Prophethood. In the Bible, Jonah is told by the Lord
to go to Nineveh to preach against the wickedness of the people there.
Instead, he takes a ship from Joppa (Jaffa)[83] that is going to Tarshish
(Tarsus) so that he can escape his calling or, as the Bible says, "the
presence of the Lord." (Jonah 1:3) Obviously there is no escape and the
Lord sends a storm that threatens to sink the whole ship. The crew fear
for their lives and begin to throw things overboard, yet all this time,
Jonah sleeps, until the captain comes to him to say: "What meanest
thou, O sleeper? Arise, call upon thy God, if so be that God will think
upon us, that we perish not." (Jonah 1:6)

Jonah appears to ignore this request because the next thing that happens
is that they draw lots. The lot falls on Jonah and they ask who he is.
Jonah's reply seems to confirm that the Book of Jonah is something of
a satire for he says: "I am an Hebrew; and I fear the Lord, the God of
heaven, which hath made the sea and the dry land." (Jonah 1:9)

Even when they realise what is happening and even though Jonah asks
them to throw him overboard, at first the crew members still try to save
everyone by rowing hard for the shore, even praying to God not to let

---

[83]"It was not far from the town when the whale discovered he had no ticket" as Mark
Twain observed in 'The Innocents Abroad'.

them die for another's guilt. However, there is nothing they can do so they throw Jonah overboard at his insistence. The experience seems to make believers out of them, for they then make sacrifices and vows to the Lord.

Jonah is then swallowed by a fish (it is not a whale, in either the Bible or Qur'an, and only became one in the Middle Ages) and he stays there for three days and nights. With time to think and being so close to death, he remembers God and repents and prays, recognising God's power and his own puny nature. He recognises that God has "brought up (his) life from corruption" (Jonah 2:6) and promises he will sacrifice and give thanks. Thereupon the fish is commanded to "vomit" Jonah upon dry land.

On dry land Jonah is told again to go to Nineveh and is sped there in a third of the usual time. He announces that the city will be overthrown in forty days and the response is total repentance and total acceptance of God. By decree from the king of the city the population fasts, puts on sackcloth and ashes, and turns away from sin. When God sees this He "repented of the evil that he said he would do unto them; and he did it not." (Jonah 3:10)

However, Jonah is not pleased and prays to God, saying: "I pray thee, O Lord, was this not my saying when I was yet in my own country? Therefore I fled before unto Tarshish: for I knew that thou art a gracious God, and merciful, slow to anger, and of great kindness, and repentest thee of the evil." (Jonah 4:2)

I told you this would happen. That's why I did not want to take on the job then. I knew that whatever happened you would end up forgiving them, so I might just as well not have got involved.

God rebukes him for his anger so he leaves the city and sits in the shade of a booth to watch what becomes of the city. The booth does not give him enough protection so God sends a gourd to grow over him and protect him, a thing that pleases Jonah greatly. However, the next morning God sends a worm to destroy the gourd, and that day the heat is so great that Jonah faints in the heat and again wishes he were dead. This leads to the final dialogue between God and Jonah wherein the still unrepentant Jonah - he says: "I do well to be angry, even unto death" (Jonah 4:9) - is again rebuked for his anger. He is then made to face the comparison between the pity he, Jonah, had felt for a gourd that grew one night and perished the next, and the pity the Lord felt for Nineveh, a city of "more than six score thousand persons that cannot discern between their right hand and their left hand; and also much cattle?" (Jonah 4:11)

This last, apparently supreme, concern for cattle ends a story whose spirit is often at odds with what I could call the Sunday-school version. Closer in spirit to what might have been taught to children to establish a moral basis is the Islamic version.[84]

In the Qur'an, Jonah is also called Dhu'n Nun, which means "he of the fish" because he runs away and is swallowed by a fish. Jonah had been sent to call on his people in Nineveh to turn to God. They had ignored him so he had told them that they would be punished by God after forty days. Before forty days elapse, they do indeed turn to God and are not punished, but the people have by this time angered Jonah so much that he angrily (Lang calls it too much "personal involvement in his mission") leaves in a ship without waiting for any more instructions, "thinking that We would have no power over him" (21:87), that, having done as much as humanly possible, he will be permitted to leave.

The ship, however, is overloaded and is making too heavy weather of the voyage. The crew believe that it is because of someone on the ship and draw lots to discover whom. Jonah draws the short straw and is thrown overboard, whereupon a fish swallows him. If this situation might have led him to anticipate death, the miraculous salvation that follows must be a reminder of the timely repentance that the people he had preached to have just experienced. As he lays in the darkness of the belly of the fish he realises that he has deserted his role as Prophet and he repents, glorifying God with the words "there is no God except you – glory be to you – surely I have been a wrongdoer." (21:87)

---

[84] There is a significant mention in Christian tradition where the Gospel of Matthew says, "At the Judgement, when this generation is on trial, the men of Nineveh will appear against it and ensure its commendation, for they repented at the preaching of Jonah; and what is here (Jesus) is greater than Jonah." (Matthew 12:41)

Without this return of remembrance of God, Jonah would have stayed in the belly of the fish until the Day of Resurrection, but instead he is thrown out onto an empty shore and given the shelter of a tree while he recovers. When he has done so, he returns to the "hundred thousand" (37:148) of Nineveh and they repent. "When they believed, We removed from them the torment of disgrace in the life of the world and permitted them to enjoy life for a while." (10:98)

As can be seen, so many elements of the two stories are the same, yet they could hardly be more different in essence. In a Biblical cartoon version of the story children mock Jonah (literally *aggrieved* in Hebrew) with taunts of "Jonah the moaner" and James Crenshaw calls Jonah an antihero in his essay in the 'Oxford Companion to the Bible'. Mark Twain caps these with: "Jonah was disobedient, and of a fault-finding, complaining disposition and deserves to be highly spoken of, almost." To Muslims, though, this is once again rather shocking because this man is a Prophet.

There is some slightly unusual transposing of themes in the two versions in that, firstly, Jonah does actually prophesy warnings to a people about the iniquity of their ways, which is not as common among the Biblical Prophets as their Qur'anic counterparts. Secondly, Jonah does show disobedience to God (far more common in the Bible) in leaving his mission and he is punished for it – this being God's use of punishment as a corrective, to extend the point that was made in the chapter on Job.

Though similar in these ways and many other details, a key difference is that while Yunus is a Gentile (he was sent to "his" people of Nineveh), Jonah was an Israelite (who left from Joppa), making the story again unusual in the Bible in that God shows an interest in non-Israelites.

Another difference is what the structure of the Biblical story tells us about the character of Jonah. The first thing we see him doing is running away in the boat that he will lead into the eye of a storm. In the Qur'an, Jonah is in the city itself preaching. When the fish swallows them, Jonah has thus already obeyed God's will up to a point, while the Qur'anic Yunus has not. By the end of the story, Yunus will have

165

visited the city twice, Jonah just once. Possibly the writers of the Biblical story had to rearrange the structure of the story in order to give Jonah a connection to the Holy Land as a Jewish Prophet.

This structure seriously differentiates the moral scope of the two Prophets. Jonah being swallowed by the fish at the beginning uses up the most powerful symbol of the story without it having much affect on him. In his book on the Kabbalistic book, the Zohar, Gershom Scholem says that the story of Jonah "may be construed as an allegory of a man's life in this world." Jonah entering the ship is like a soul entering a human body where it becomes "aggrieved." The journey, and the attempted escape and the storm are like what happens to the body and soul in this life. However, "the story of Jonah" only refers to the incidents at sea and we are still left with a Jonah who is unreconstructed by the experience in the rest of the story.

It is thus only in the Qur'an, where Jonah repents when he looks death in the face like the people he has just angrily walked away from, and then experiences the mercy of God in being released alive from the fish, that we find something of the moral stature we hope to find in the Prophets.

Deedat, A. *What was the Sign of Jonah?* (1976) IPCI: Durban
Ibn Kathir, I. *Stories of the Prophets* (2003) Darrusalam: Riyadh
Lane Fox, R. *The Unauthorised Version* (1991) Penguin: London
Orwell, G. *Inside the Whale* (1940) Penguin: London
Scholem, G.S. *Zohar - The Book of Splendour: Basic Readings from the Kabbalah* (1971) Schocken Books: New York
Twain, M. *The Innocents Abroad* (2003) Penguin: London
Metzger, B.M. & Coogan, M.D. *Oxford Companion to the Bible* (1993) Oxford University Press: Oxford

10

JOSHUA

O Lord, we went forth like this thousands of years ago. We walked across arid deserts and the blood-red Red Sea in a flood of salt, bitter tears. We are very old. We are still walking. Oh, let us arrive finally.
  (Andre Schwarz-Bart)

The night before Yasser Arafat and Yitzhak Rabin signed the Oslo Accords on the White House lawn on 13 September 1993, US President Bill Clinton could not sleep and spent the night rereading all of the Book of Joshua and parts of the New Testament. The next day he gave a speech that talked about a shared future "shaped by the values of the Torah, the Qur'an and the Bible." The rest, as they say, is history. Though not a very happy one so far.

It would be interesting to know why he picked this book particularly; some have dubbed God "the Great ethnic cleanser" on the basis of it. Did it make Clinton more worried about what he might be unleashing? Did he feel he was working against fate, or what was written? Did it appear as a fulfilment? Did he feel better after reading it?

"The ... book of Joshua arouses strong passions: like its God's relation to his (sic) people, you either love it or you hate it. To my mind, it is the intersection of two great composers: J, who turned just-so stories into narrative, and D, the Jew in Exile, who worked from multiple sources and preached the book of the law. Its killings are beastly, and its speeches and stories are quite untrue, but it is an eloquent historian's masterpiece."[85] So says Robin Lane Fox, in his critical examination of the writing of the Bible.

Traditionalist archaeologist W.F. Albright loves it and refers to the "existing non-Jewish population" as being "a people of markedly inferior type," thus excusing anything. The book of Joshua has "a special position in the Israeli education system both as national history and as the cornerstone of Israel's national mythology" as Michael Prior

---

[85] Lane Fox (1991) p.186

167

says. The Israeli army strongly recommends the text for new recruits. Then on the other side, G.E.M. de Ste Croix writes that there is "little in pagan literature as morally revolting," and a lecturer at Tel Aviv University, Georges Tamarin, lost his professorship for publishing a paper on the negative effects of the uncritical teaching of the book on the nation's youth.[86]

"The book of Joshua provides the context for the subsequent story of Israel in the land..." as Adrian Curtis says in his study of the eponymous book about Joshua, and people go to the Book of Joshua, and his story as it appears elsewhere, because it is the crux of the whole story of the Children of Israel. Essentially, it justifies the taking of the land, and it does so in a very straightforward way. It is an apparent fulfilment of Yahweh's promises based on a covenant between two parties: the Children of Israel will obliterate polytheistic worship and take the land, and God will help them in doing so, beginning with the destruction of several cities. One People, One God, One Land, or "Land, leadership, law, Lord" as T.C. Butler, a modern commentator, nicely, and alliteratively, puts it.

There is also the direct continuity from Moses, Joshua having been nominated by him, and being, but for one other, the only survivor of the original fleeing Israelites. Such a tale is likely to toughen the sinews of anyone, then or now, required to perform acts of violence, and seems to have been designed for precisely that purpose.

However, Curtis continues that sentence above: "...against which the story of the people's unfaithfulness and disobedience is told." It is quite important, and the fact that the book of Joshua was written at a time of unfaithfulness and disobedience some hundreds of years after the purported invasion suggests it might reveal at least as much about its authors as it does about its subject.

The Biblical, and traditionally accepted, story is that Joshua entered the Promised Land and took it in a series of actions. The conquest of the

---

[86] Tamarin (1973)

central area - Jericho, Gibeon, Ai, Lachish and Hazor - is described in a way that implies the conquest of the whole land, the unity of the whole land reflecting the divine unity. No tribes come to terms with the people of Israel except the Gibeonites, and so ruthless wars of annihilation are permitted as "vengeance." Jericho, the first city encountered, has all its population massacred except the family of Rahab, a prostitute who helps Joshua's army take the city. As Garstang and Garstang state, ironically, considering this was just at the start of the Second World War:

"The destruction of Jericho was indeed an act unsurpassed in history, not so much for its frightfulness, as for the deliberation with which it was accomplished... there is no record of a determination comparable with this... in one awful holocaust." [87]

Though the Qur'an says very little explicitly about Joshua, two *Hadith* concur strongly with a Biblical story, making for an implicit vindication: "The sun has never been held back for setting except for Joshua," is found in a *Hadith* narrated by Imam Ahmad from Abu Hurairah, and this chimes with the battle in which "the Lord delivered the Amorites into the hands of Israel..." and Joshua said: "Stand still, O sun, in Gibeon..." (Joshua 10:12) Another from the same source will be mentioned later.

The slender number of Islamic references that seem to be consistent with the Biblical narrative are not really enough, though, to prevent us from accepting the current consensus among archaeologists and historians, that the evidence for any of this actually being so ain't necessarily there,[88] and that what most likely happened was far less epic, "a sequence of periods marked by a peaceful and gradual coalescence of disparate peoples into a group of highland dwellers

---

[87] Garstang & Garstang (1940) p.172
[88] David Rohl, mentioned in the chapter on Moses, moves the timeline back by 350 years to around 1500 BCE, making the invasion an event that occurred in the Middle Bronze Age. Though persuasive in many ways in terms of material evidence, the time shift makes David a figure of the Late Bronze Age. As the Qur'an mentions that David could make iron mail with his hands, this small detail would seem to make this thesis unsustainable from a Muslim perspective.

whose achievement of a sense of national unity culminated only with the entrance of the Assyrian administration," as Curtis expresses it.

He sums up this consensus, saying that Jericho was "probably no more than a hill fort"; Ai "a heap of ruins"; Gibeon "may not have been occupied"; and Hazor may have been "destroyed but it is not possible to be sure by whom."

In this process, the Hebrews may have been a catalytic small group, according to G.E. Mendenhall,[89] or it may have been that agricultural difficulties made cooperation between the tribes a necessity, according to D.C. Hopkins.[90] Either way, later chroniclers would be keen to paint this in as favourable light as possible; Prior actually calls the divine promises "retrojections into the past." As Muslims, we can accept the promises to some extent, as we have seen in the story of Moses, but much else can be seen in the light of these retrojections, from the ascendancy of nomadic Cain over pastoral Abel onwards. The question remains as to where we draw the line.

What has always been hardest for scholars and other sensitive souls is the scale of the slaughter the Bible seems to sanction. If we see it rather as a retrojection that is aimed to justify and strengthen the position of the Children of Israel at the time the book of Joshua is written, rather than the manifestation of the ethnic bias of the Lord of Creation, it becomes more understandable. We could consider the forming of the story in the light of a different cultural "myth."

The Grail Legend includes the story of Parsifal, the innocent, poor, fatherless boy who is chosen to be the knight who enters the magical castle to discover who the Grail serves. In the castle he is given a tremendous banquet. Finally, a woman comes in bearing the Holy Grail. He has been warned by his mother not to ask questions so he obeys her and asks nothing. The following morning when he awakes, the castle is empty. As soon as he crosses the drawbridge the castle disappears. After this people are furious with him for having come so

---

[89] Mendenhall (1962) pp. 66-87
[90] Hopkins (1985) p.222

close to discovering the meaning of the nation's sickness, yet ultimately failing.

The legend of Parsifal never really finishes in the original telling of the tale. The implication is that Parsifal enters the castle again when he is older and that he asks the right question. However, that part of the tale is not always recorded. It is as if there is a recognition that the western mind is not at the stage yet, in its evolution of consciousness, where it is ready for such truths. The implication is that the Grail, from which Jesus drank, serves him, but that Christians, among whom the legend grew, were not ready to accept that it served God.

Since the loss of Paradise the most compelling myths of the monotheistic religions have concerned the arrival at, or the creation of, a just world, a promised land, a kingdom of God. Crucial to this has been the question of timing, of readiness, of worthiness.

In 'Songlines' Bruce Chatwin argues that we are at our best, at our most human, when we are on the move. When we travel we are, in some profound way, more aware of who we are within ourselves, less defined or influenced by those around us who are like us when we are in one place, more open to the challenging awareness of others who are different or experiencing the same migration of the spirit. We are less inclined to be seduced by the notion that we have arrived.

The Children of Israel were closest to God when they spent forty years in the wilderness of the Sinai; it is a journey that seems unnecessary but for this crucial identity-forming experience. Christians make pilgrimages to atone for their sins. One of the five pillars of Islam is that Muslims are required to make a pilgrimage, the Hajj, to Mecca once in their lifetime. If we die on the Hajj we go straight to heaven, as martyrs.

It seems that this is an essential part of our nature, to move, to migrate. Arrival, home and roots are also important and they manifest themselves in different ways in different philosophies. They can be seen as a search for certainty in a universe that is paradoxical and ever changing. When the universe is at its most incomprehensible, its most dangerous, this haven is regarded as an absolute necessity and more important than any notional benefit to be derived from wandering in a hostile universe. Those who expressed their anger at Parsifal were less concerned with what his failure meant about the human condition than with the fact that he could have ended their suffering but did not. If not now, when?

This journeying, and the journey's end, is the crucial point of the story of Joshua. As we have stated, the faiths of Jews, Christians and Muslims all involve journeys of some type that break the cycle of life. In some profound way these three faiths, beginning with a small tribe, the Hebrews, broke the circle of cyclical faith. Life in other cultures and other belief systems was generally perceived to be cyclical, rather than historical. Things changed, but essentially remained the same. Something like harmony, balance, was their hallmark, a balance, of some sort, between masculine and feminine energies, yin and yang, or male and female gods. Perhaps in their deeper histories it was the earth, the yin energy and the goddess that were often central.

The monotheistic religions, with their perception of a masculine divinity, are more dominated by 'masculine', yang values: dynamism, energy, progress, movement, conquest. Home and stability remain important, but almost seem contradictory to the spirit of their faiths, which are seen as a progress towards a new "home" in the future. Hence the ritual importance of journeys.

These are often of a physical kind, but they are also symbolic. A journey implies a movement from one state to another. A journey can expose truths that it is possible for us to ignore when we are in the same place, involved with the habits of a sedentary life. A journey begs the question, Is it better to travel than to arrive? The answer, insofar as it is possible to answer such a question, depends on the time.

Throughout the history of Jews, Christians and Muslims there have been events of transformation, a grasping of destiny that has led to revolutions in consciousness and power: the massive expansion of the Islamic empire in the years following the death of the Prophet and the conquest of the "New World" are notable. All of these have had a geographical component. In the stories of the earlier Prophets we have a similar pattern. The first, mythically or historically depending on interpretation, was the eating of the forbidden fruit and the leaving of the Garden of Eden. Abraham had the land promised to his descendants and he lived in various parts of it, according to the Bible, owning none of it except the land where he and his wife were buried in Hebron, Il-Khalil. His descendants moved to Egypt where they lived for 400 years during which time they became enslaved. The flight from Egypt, commemorated every year at Passover, marks the end of this time of spiritual and physical slavery. The forty years of transformation in isolation in the pure spiritual space of the desert ends with the entering into, and conquest of, Canaan.

However, the dilemma the writers of the Bible faced in doing justice to this was that the Children of Israel did not seem to be much improved by their forty-year sojourn and had not done much better inside the Promised Land either. They thus resorted to a traditional mode of thinking and projected negative qualities on to the Canaanites, and they did it in spades. The Godly Children of Israel and the wicked Canaanites in Jewish eyes conformed to something like the spiritual human/unspiritual beast archetype, and this legacy has recurred in Jewish, and often Christian, reactions to the question of Israel ever since. If God, the writers could write, called on the Children of Israel to take Canaan by force, then it had to be done. In a way, they covered themselves with the reminder:

"It is not because of your righteousness or your integrity that you are going in to take possession of their land, but on account of the wickedness of these nations." (Deuteronomy 9:4-6)

The Children of Israel were not so holy, rather they were fulfilling God's plan, and if their quality could not be improved, then at least the worth of the opposition could be downgraded. Nonetheless, if they failed to live up to this task they could expect no special favour:

"If you defile the land, it will vomit you out as it vomited out the nations before you." (Leviticus 18:28)

According to the book of Joshua and beyond, the land now came to stand as the physical representation of God, of consciousness. (One God, One People, One Land). The Children of Israel's special task was

173

to hold to that consciousness at the same time as being dominant, in a position where it would be easy to be seduced by one's own ego and power. The struggle, in other words, did not end with the taking of the land. The struggle was not yet over. The beast, as represented by the "other nations", was vanquished, but it was not then to be supposed that the Children of Israel were in a state of grace. The shadow was still within them, as well as the light. They still had the potential to lapse back into unconsciousness. To prevent this, to remind them of whose is the ultimate power, the writers had God require that some visible, tangible yet symbolic act be performed to affirm the connection, the remembrance. The implication that they perhaps wished to communicate was that God and the land had not been taken to heart, and that a story that involved the sacrifice of all the inhabitants of the cities and their animals would be an appropriate way to remember, replicating as it did the sacrifice of a "lesser thing" when Abraham was about to sacrifice his son. Robert Johnson discusses this idea in a different context in 'The Psychology of Romantic Love', saying:

"When we refuse to integrate a powerful new potentiality from the unconscious, the unconscious will exact a tribute one way or another."

The powerful new potentiality, presence in the land, at the time of Joshua and at the time his book was written, required some action of equal impact in order for it to be accepted by the people who were still struggling to behave as a Chosen People.

As has been mentioned before, there is little in Islamic literature that seems to relate to this time, but there is one other relevant story that is mentioned in the *Hadith* about the stopping sun quoted above that occurred after the men of this Prophet (Joshua) had conquered the town:

"Then they all gathered what they found of the spoils of war. The fire then came to eat the spoils of war, but did not eat it. The Prophet then said: 'There is someone who has cheated from the spoils.' So he asked one man from every tribe to come forward and pledge to him. They all came to pledge to him, but the hand of one man stuck to the hand of the Prophet. He said: 'The cheat is from among you, so now let every one of your tribe come forward and pledge to me.' They came and offered their pledge to him, and the hands of two or three people got stuck to his hand and he said: 'You are a cheat. You took the spoils of war.' So they took out gold equivalent to the head of a cow. They put the gold together with the other spoils of war and the fire came and ate them."[91]

The implication is that the Children of Israel were required to restrain themselves and keep the intention of their actions pure. They were not supposed to be motivated by the love of plunder, and the Bible says much the same, but at the same time there is no mention of any kind of mass slaughter. In another mention of the twelve tribes, this time in the Qur'an, it says in a way that is reminiscent of the conditional promises of Leviticus and Deuteronomy quoted above:

"And God had taken the Covenant from the Children of Israel, and We appointed from among them twelve chieftains. And God said: 'I am with you, only if you establish prayer, pay the alms, believe in My Messengers and stand with them, and lend to God a good loan. So I will acquit you of your sins, and I will admit you to gardens beneath which rivers flow, so whoever of you disbelieve after that, surely he has gone astray from the Right Way." (5:12)

The message of the afterlife is barely mentioned in the Bible, so it is striking that it is mentioned in this *aya* of the Qur'an, at what must have been the time of Moses and Joshua, because, just at the time when the Children of Israel are contemplating "arrival" in a paradise on earth, they are suddenly reminded that there is a better place, and it is not the one they are about to enter. Arrival was as much about time as place, and in that sense, they had not "arrived finally." They were only half way there.

Albright, W.F. *The Archaeology of Palestine* (1956) Pelican: London
Chatwin, B. *Songlines* (1987) Picador: London
Curtis, A.H.W. *Joshua* (1998) Sheffield Academic Press: Sheffield
Garstang, J. & Garstang, J.B.E. *The Story of Jericho* (1940) Marshall, Morgan & Scott: London

---

[91] The *Hadeeth* concludes: "The spoils of war were not allowed for anyone before us. But when God saw our weakness and incapacity, he purified it for us."

Hopkins, D.C. *The Highlands of Canaan: Agricultural Life in the Early Iron Age, Social World of Biblical Antiquity 3* (1985) Sheffield: JSOT Press

Johnson, R. *The Psychology of Romantic Love* (1983) Harper Collins: New York

Mendenhall, G.E. *The Hebrew Conquest of Palestine* (1962) Biblical Archaeologist 25, pp. 66-87

Prior, M. *Ethnic Cleansing and the Bible: A Moral Critique* (2002) Holy Land Studies: Baltimore

Prior, M. *The Moral Problem of the Land Traditions of the Bible*, in *Western Scholarship and the History of Palestine*, Ed. Prior (1998) Melisende: London:

Rohl, D. *A Test of Time* (1995) Random House: London

Tamarin, G.R. *Essays on a Warfare State* (1973) Rotterdam University Press: Rotterdam

11

<u>DAVID</u>

Now I've heard there was a secret chord
That David played, and it pleased the Lord
But you don't really care for music, do you?
It goes like this
The fourth, the fifth
The minor fall, the major lift
The battle king composing Hallelujah
...
And even though
It all went wrong
I'll stand before the Lord of Song
With nothing on my tongue but Hallelujah
        (Leonard Cohen – 'Hallelujah')

The lyrics of the Leonard Cohen song capture the pathos that many find in the Biblical story of David: the beauty of the psalms; the disasters that in many ways David was responsible for, and still the yearning. A man, a king, a Prophet, who carries within him the potential for great sin and great goodness. The Islamic position finds the details of much of that story difficult to countenance (and may not care much for music, for that matter), yet, as we shall see, we can find much in these broad themes of beauty, guilt and yearning in our own tradition's understanding of David, Da'ud.

Because of his association with Jerusalem and his combined role of Prophet and king, David is one of the most important Prophets. Like Joshua, David is also something of a touchstone for the identity of modern Israel. There were great celebrations for the 3000 year anniversary of his takeover of Jerusalem in 1996, though this may have been partly an attempt to combat an opposite trend. As Professor Gavriel Moked of the University of the Negev said in an interview in *Haaretz* in 1999: "The worst thing that could happen to us is that we become cosmopolitans and end up knowing more about the Beatles and Kennedy's assassination than we know about King David."

There is, though, a serious question as to how much we know of him. Archaeology is not very helpful on this point, there being perhaps only the "House of David" inscriptions steles found in Tel Dan and Dhiban (the Mesha stele). Kathleen Kenyon, one of the foremost archaeologists of the Holy Land said:

"The united kingdom of Israel has a life span of only three-quarters of a century. It was the only time in which the Jews were an important political power in western Asia. Its glories are triumphantly recorded in the bible (sic), and the recollection of this profoundly affected Jewish thought and aspirations. Yet the archaeological evidence for the period is meagre in the extreme."[92]

In a book unambiguously titled 'The Invention of Ancient Israel', David Whitelam attempts to redress the historic weighting of interpretation towards Israel, believing this has much to do with the current imbalance in our perceptions of modern Israel. He aims to move towards the time when we can see "many diverse Palestines that go to make up the singular entity Palestine."[93] David particularly bothers him:

"The existence of the Davidic state as portrayed in the Biblical traditions is vital to this enterprise (modern Israel), hence the virulence with which any questioning of this master narrative is attacked."[94]

Worthy though this championing is, it is hard to see it becoming the dominant narrative approach, though it may well produce some interesting critical balance within the discourse. The main reason why archaeologists have ever gone a-digging in Palestine is precisely because they are interested in the cultural reference point they share with the history of the Holy Land, namely the fate of the Jews there. This is as much true for Christians as for Jews. Moreover, it is also, at the end of the day, the stronger cultural reference point for Muslims. Though Palestinian Muslims and Christians may superficially have more in common with the Canaanites who lost their land, on a deeper level, the Prophets who came to this Chosen People are our Prophets

---

[92] Kenyon (1979) p.233
[93] Whitelam (1995) p.169
[94] Whitelam (1995) p.167

too. (Suspicions even sometimes arise that the Jewish inhabitants of Palestine in the 7th century converted in large numbers to Islam.) Their monotheism is closer to our beliefs than the Canaanites' pagan idolatry, and to identify with or champion them too much is neither likely to prove popular nor, in the end, helpful. David and the rest are powerful figures and ours almost as much as anyone else's, so we might better engage with each other regarding how we understand what they mean in our search for meaning and peace than defend the historical role and rights of the Canaanites.

David may be the most famous king of Israel, but he was not the first. Both Islamic and Biblical traditions attribute that honour to Saul, or Talut as he is known in Islamic sources. I used to understand the closing words of Judges in a positive light ("In those days there was no king in Israel: every man did what was right in his own eyes. (Judges 21:25) thinking that this meant that everyone had such an individually developed sense of right and wrong that kings were not necessary. Happy days indeed. Rather, it means that everyone did what they felt like, usually a recipe for disaster. However, there is an implication in the Bible that they should have known better and should have been able to do without a king, but could not cope with the responsibility. This is the message that is communicated in the Bible by Samuel.

In the Bible, Samuel was one of the last of the judges and the last to be respected. His sons, whom he appointed, took bribes and perverted justice. This, and Israel's overall decline, caused a crisis for the people of Israel who demanded a king to govern them "like all other nations." In the Qur'an, the reason for the demand is phrased slightly differently for it says: "Have you not seen the chiefs of the Children of Israel, after Moses, when they said to a Prophet of theirs: 'Appoint for us a king that we may fight in the cause of God.'"(2:246)

In the Bible, Samuel sees this as an abdication of personal responsibility and a rejection of God. He warns the people that a king will mean a great loss of independence and wealth, and that if the people choose such a course and then complain of it God will not listen. In the Qur'an, the Prophet, who we assume to be Samuel, warns that if they are ordered to fight in the cause of God they may refuse. In both stories, the people insist and God says to Samuel that he should obey them. Thus, Saul, or Talut, is appointed.

In the Bible especially, this is a change of importance in the perception of the relationship between God and the Children of Israel. One person would now be responsible for carrying the hopes and dreams of the nation, and bearing the responsibility for their successes and failures. Responsibility is transferred from the heart of the individual, from the dwelling place of consciousness, onto the representative individual, the individual who now represents the nation. This idea contrasts with the Islamic understanding of the Prophetic role, which is essentially to guide people on the path to right worship of the One God.

According to the Bible, Saul, the first king of Israel, attempts to unite the tribes and to drive back the Philistines. He falls from favour when he disobeys the divine order to kill all the inhabitants and animals of a city he has captured. Instead, he and his men kill some of the animals and feast on them. The harsh punishment seems to be because this is a time when Saul has just taken on a new role among his people. It serves as a reminder that the Children of Israel only have power and success when God is acting through them, and that their power is nothing in its own right or when they forget God.

Saul then seems to go mad and David actually fights against him alongside the Philistines before finally succeeding him in around 1011, according to the generally accepted chronology. David's subsequent conquest of Jerusalem marks a change in the Children of Israel's approach to the land[95], and hence to belief. In terms of Jewish belief, as Hyam Maccoby explains:

"The land is the female element in Judaism. The land is not the mother – that would be a nomadic, dependant attitude – so much as the lover or bride, who expects not adoration or helpless dependency, but proper cultivation and husbandry."

---

[95] There is, however, a major discrepancy in the Biblical narrative in Judges 1:8 which records that after the death of Joshua "the men of Judah made an assault on Jerusalem and captured it, put its people to the sword and set fire to the city." Thirteen verses later it is recorded that "the Benjamites did not drive out the Jebusites of Jerusalem."

The symbolism of this interpretation corresponds to that which has been identified earlier, namely, the evolution of the story of the Children of Israel from a nomadic-oriented perspective to one that is settled in its perspective. However, because the central characters in the story so often fail to live up to expectations, there is also a built-in antithesis running through the narrative. If the correct relationship with the land, as symbol for God, is "husbandry", then the failure of that relationship is portrayed as infidelity and wantonly going after prostitutes. Thus, prostitutes are repeatedly found in the Biblical narrative, whether as symbolic, reminding presences, from the taking of Jericho; as characters in their own right; or as metaphors or similes. They serve to remind us of both the "bride" Israel's infidelity to God and of the cultic fertility practices that were such a common feature of the local religions.

This "Israel as bride" reaches its most potent representation in the city of Jerusalem. Here David spares the inhabitants, and is permitted to do so; Jewish survival is no longer threatened by this time and minds can turn to other things. One of these is the bringing of the Ark of the Covenant, which was believed to contain the Shekinah, sometimes understood as the presence and sometimes the feminine aspect of God, into the city, making Jerusalem the centre of Judaism from this time onwards. This can all be seen as the fruition of a process of change from a pure, unattached faith to one that is more related to a place.

The difficulties of "arriving" can be found in David's story but first we shall consider the overall context in which we hear the story. We are told in a *Hadith* that there have been 124,000 Prophets, that they have been sent to all nations, and that they have all brought the same message, of the unity of God and of our requirement to worship Him. The Children of Israel, though, are unique in receiving so many Prophets and in having so many identified by name in the Qur'an. The message may have been the same – submit – but in each case, the situation was different. They were told to submit to God in slavery and flight by Moses, as well as on the point of conquest. They were required to submit while under the leadership of Joshua when he invaded Canaan and to do the same when they had no king. They did not, but demanded a king, a controversial request. Neither under Saul in a position of defeat, nor David in victory, nor Solomon in peace did they submit. The pattern continued under, and was the reason for, the Great Prophets Isaiah, Ezekiel and Jeremiah, as we shall see, and by the time of Jesus, a fairly comprehensive patterned response to any situation had been established – no submission.

This begs the question, why so many sent to God's Chosen people? And what, dare we ask, is the meaning within this pattern? We assume that it is enough to know that other nations, all in fact, have had Prophets sent as guidance, and presumably not so many each, as is the case of the peoples of A'ad and Thumud. These were the nations that Hud and Salih, the only non-Biblical Prophets mentioned in the Qur'an, were sent to. We assume that these 124,000 Prophets were rejected, because no nations apart from the Children of Israel were monotheistic prior to the coming of Jesus, and none of these civilisations have survived.

Yet with the Children of Israel, we have detailed knowledge of their story, albeit sometimes dubious, and they have survived as carriers of their cultural legacy, their historical burden, their religious vocation. And all this, it seems, is precisely *because* they were stubborn: they had so many Prophets because they were stubborn and would not submit to God, and they survived because they were stubborn and would not submit to, call it what you will, fate, history. God. See how precious those "stiff necks" are? And how much trouble?

If this is a mixed picture, much the same can be said of the stories of the heroes of the Golden Era in the Bible. When their stories are first heard, often by young, audiences, the Biblical David and Solomon seem to be glorious figures. On closer inspection, though, we find that the shading, the details and the colours are not so bright. In fact, the Biblical David comes to be seen as a rather dark figure in the Judeo-Christian heritage. We will find a similar situation later with Solomon.

If we compare the pictures of the Biblical and Islamic Davids, they have much in common, in outline at least. However, the Islamic stories have little of the Bible's darkness. What is interesting is that the portrayal reflects the name of the faith, inasmuch as Judaism's focus is on a people chosen by God and Islam's is the relationship we have with God. The David of the Bible reflects the *people* he ruled, unflatteringly it should be said, while the David of the Qur'an reflects the *message* - submission - that he brought. In Islamic belief, the Prophets who came to the Children of Israel came to enjoin this same message from God - the message of Adam, Abraham and all - that it is our duty, and God is most pleased, when we submit to Him. Thus, pleasing God, a spiritual goal, should be our aim, rather than seeking political power or material gain, which are worldly aims. If either of these should come our way, they are to be considered as side effects. Of all the Prophets of Israel none were more blessed in this way than Da'ud and his son Suleyman, David and Solomon.

Though there are many similarities between the Biblical and Qur'anic stories, the balance of these two, the worldly and the spiritual, the cause and effect of God-consciousness or *Taqwa*, is completely opposite. While the Qur'an and *Hadith* glorify father and son's humility, the Bible stresses their power and glory. Ultimately, it depicts them as individuals who are unable to sacrifice their egos to "the dagger of self-discipline" and who succumb to the temptation of their worldly power to follow their *nafs*, their egotistical desires.

Despite the flaws in the Biblical David and Solomon, their reigns (a total of 73 years) are regarded by Jews as the highest point in their history. According to the Bible, David expanded Israelite territory enormously through his generalship, to include territory from what is now Egypt to Lebanon and Syria, and most significantly he took the city of Jerusalem and made it his capital. Solomon, who succeeded him, inherited this by-then peaceful kingdom and built the first temple on what, tradition says, is today the Haram Al-Sharif of Al-Aqsa.

When Israelis today speak of the eternal united capital of Israel or the Temple it is to this era they hark back to. Nonetheless even in the Bible there are implicit limits to seeing this as a *carte blanche* to Judaise Jerusalem. During the Jewish celebrations of 3000 years of Jerusalem as the capital of Israel, Israeli Daniel Gavron wrote that "Jewish pre-eminence (over Jerusalem under David) is an over-simplification"[96] and he highlighted four Davidic principles regarding the city. The first was that though Jerusalem was the capital it was shared with others. David neither massacred nor expelled the inhabitants (1 Judges 1:21).

---

[96] Gavron (1995)

Secondly, he expanded the city for newcomers (II Samuel 5:9) rather than displacing the existing residents. Thirdly, he respected their property rights, insisting on buying the threshing floor on which the Ark of the Covenant was to be housed (II Samuel 24:22-24). Fourthly, he co-operated with and integrated the inhabitants. His wife Bathsheba and, possibly, Zadok the High Priest were Jebusites.

Positive though this may be when applied to current realities, a more significant aspect of the Biblical David, and the biggest problem for Jewish and Christian interpretations of his life, is the theme of the paradoxical nature of his character. David possesses the twin streams of obedience and sin, "the tensions between (his) opposites", the David who is "just like everyone else only more so" and the hero. In 'The Oxford Companion to the Bible', David M. Gunn concludes his sketch of the king, one that mercilessly highlights these faults, by saying that it is these very unresolved tensions that "give him life."

The worst of these "tensions" is the "integrating" of Bathsheba, wife of Uriah, one of his generals. According to the Bible (2 Samuel 11:2-5), David spies her, takes her, and she becomes pregnant, all in the course of one evening and four verses. (She is not even ritually purified from her period). To cover his guilt, David summons Uriah from the campaign he is fighting in the south, so that he will sleep with her. However, conscious that his men are fighting, Uriah refuses to go to his wife, even when David gets him drunk, so David sends him on a particularly dangerous mission in which he is, as hoped, killed. Jung, strongly influenced by Christian belief as we have seen with Job, recorded a dream in which Uriah was in a tower that placed him higher than David. He saw in this the "guiltless victim" Uriah as a "pre-figuration of Christ, the god-man who was abandoned by God"[97] as Uriah was by David. The resonance both of Jesus being "born of David's line" and the parable of the lamb might have been at work here too.

After this, David marries Bathsheba but the first son dies as divine retribution for the sin. The second son is Solomon. Henceforward, the apparently unconditional promise of Yahweh given in Samuel 7 is revealed to have limits. David's third son Absalom kills his own half-

[97] Jung (1962) p.246

184

brother, David's oldest son, Amnon, for raping his sister Tamar. He then raises an army to fight David, thus beginning the demise of Israel at the moment of its creation.

With some understatement, Rupert Lane Fox calls all this "not unduly flattering", but he is inclined to accept that its detail is so meticulous that its source was someone writing at the time or soon after who had at least access to court sources and is thus closer to the truth than the later idealised versions of David's life. These later writers found the story so bothersome that they wrote the two Books of Chronicles which list the whole Davidic line from Adam onwards and tell the story of David as if all he did was achieve military victories and lay the groundwork for the founding of the Temple. As we have noted before, the Bible often stresses that the only important consideration in Chosenness is blood but in Chronicles even this is protected from too much scrutiny because the Children of Israel are sent plagues as punishment for the sin of trying to number the people in a census.[98]

Though some interpreters of the Bible have seen this as a change in worldview where now "all the threads are in God's hands", others, such as Edward Meyer, see it as "a purely secular work." For Muslims, the simplest way of approaching such profane and contradictory material could be to agree with the latter point of view and to see it as proof of God's words in the Qur'an which say that much of what is contained in the Bible we have has been concealed or changed (2:140; 2:146; 2:211). We have already seen discrepancies in many of the Biblical stories and with this, the Biblical David could be seen, not as a historical story, but as a projection by the writers of the Bible of the soul of Israel that at once condemns and justifies its continued sinning by attributing sin to its finest. Superficially the story says that sin brings divine retribution. However, the implicit, but overriding, message is that if David can be like this, how can his people be any better?

Such a rhetorical question seems legitimate in the context of the Bible, but if we compare the Biblical David's character and story with the equivalent in the Islamic tradition, we can learn something deeper.

---

[98] In the New Testament, it would be a census that linked Jesus with David's city.

In the Bible, after the required period of mourning for Uriah, Bathsheba marries David. Shortly after, God sends Nathan to David and tells him what seems to be a tale of unfairness in his kingdom: A rich man had a large flock of sheep and a poor man from the same city had just one little ewe lamb that was like a daughter to him. One day a traveller arrived and, rather than use one of his own flock, the rich man took the poor man's sheep to feed the traveller with. David is furious when he hears this and declares, "As the Lord liveth, the man that hath done this thing shall surely die, and he shall restore the lamb fourfold, because he did this thing and because he had no pity." (2 Samuel 12:5-6) Nathan lets him finish, and then replies: "Thou art the man." Despite all the things he has been given, and that yet might be given him, he has done evil in the sight of the Lord and "Now therefore the sword shall never depart from thine house." (2 Samuel 12:10)

David confesses that he has indeed sinned and is told that, though the Lord had put away his sin, the child that will be born to Bathsheba will die which, after seven days, it does. While the child is alive, David fasts and prays, but once it is dead died, he eats again. The second child that he has by Bathsheba is Solomon, whom the Lord loves. (Again, the second child is preferred). However, it is from this point that disasters assail the kingdom, as mentioned above.

In the Qur'an and *Hadith*, as king, David is blessed and is one of the Prophets particularly favoured by God. He defeats Goliath and is a success politically and militarily; he unites the twelve tribes of Israel and is given the knowledge of how to make chain mail: "And We made iron supple for him so as to make long coats of mail and to measure the links well." (34:11).[99] His political success is balanced by, rather than in opposition to, his spiritual gifts. God commands the mountains and the birds to sing their praises with him, those praises being the *Zabur*, the Psalms. (17:55).

When the information contained in various *Hadith* is added we are given a strong sense of a man of humility. According to Abu Hurayra in Al-Bukhari, the Prophet Muhammad said that recitation of the *Zabur*

---

[99] As we have seen in considering Joshua, this fact is given incidentally by the Qur'an, but it seems to rule out the possibility of Da'ud being a king during the Late Bronze Age, an argument David Rohl puts forward persuasively in 'A Test of Time'.

was easy for Da'ud, and also that he would only eat of what he had himself produced. In another *Hadith*, Ibn Umar reported that the Prophet Muhammad said:

"The prayer which God loves the most is the prayer of Da'ud. The fast which God loves the most is that of Da'ud. He used to sleep half the night, stand in prayer for a third and sleep for a sixth. He would fast every other day. He wore wool and slept on hair. He ate barley bread with salt and ashes. He mixed his drink with tears. He was never seen to laugh after his error (see below) nor to look directly at the sky because of his shyness before his Lord and he continued to weep for the rest of his life. It is said that he wept until plants sprang up from his tears and until tears formed ridges in his cheeks. It is said that he went out in disguise to learn what people thought of him, and hearing himself be praised only made him more humble."[100]

The error, and the reason why Da'ud should be such a man of grief, is not specified, but it is not unreasonable to suggest, based on context, hints and parallels, that it refers to some form of temptation (though this is by no means certain). The Qur'an tells how one day two men climbed into Da'ud's private chamber, frightening him greatly. They put him at his ease by telling him that they were brothers in dispute and wished to have his judgement on the matter. The one who did the speaking told Da'ud that his brother had ninety-nine ewes, while he had but one, yet his brother wished to look after it and had beaten him in argument on the matter.

Da'ud said: "He has undoubtedly wronged thee in demanding thy ewe to be added to his flock. Truly many are the (business) partners who wrong each other. Not so do those who believe and work deeds of righteousness, and how few are they?" (38:24)

As he said this some say that he must have asked himself whether he had the right to presume that he himself was one of the righteous, for he immediately realised that this was a trial from God. Had not the men disappeared as suddenly as they had arrived? Had not their case been strange to risk such an adventure, particularly for the brother with the

---

[100] *Ash-Shifa* of *Qadi Iyad: 1:2.24*

flocks? Had not he even been silent the whole time? So Da'ud fell down and asked for forgiveness and was forgiven. The Qur'an says: "O Da'ud! We did indeed make thee a vicegerent on earth. So judge thou between men in truth, nor follow thou the lust (of thy heart), for it will mislead thee from the Path of God." (38:26)

So, what is the meaning of the story of David, of Da'ud? And how does the parable of the sheep fit in to this?

To those raised on the Bible, David has been seen as an archetype, a man of both spirit and action, and the frequency with which he appears in literature and modern culture in the West, not to mention the thousand plus mentions in the Bible, shows how important a figure he is. Most people know the story of the triumph of faith over strength in David and Goliath, and many know the hymn 'The Lord's My Shepherd', which is an adaptation of Psalm 23, attributed to him, and that Jesus was born of David's line. Psalms attributed to him, such as the yearning of "Out of the depths I have called unto Thee, O Lord" (Ps. 130:1,2) and the beauty of "With my whole heart I have sought Thee" (119:10), are consistent with the *Hadith* concerning Da'ud's grief and faith. Yet the Bible's depiction (or depictions) of David makes him seem to be schizophrenic and at times even mad. He dances in a most exhibitionistic manner when the Ark is brought to the citadel (2 Samuel 6) and feigns madness during his time as an outlaw enemy of Saul. Mostly, to read David's story in the Books of Samuel and Kings is to be rather depressed because it is so dark, hence the corrective need of the Book of Chronicles. Nonetheless, Christians and Jews have been rather forced to accept this David, making a virtue of necessity at times. One commentator, Gordon Robinson, says:

"The plain fact which is so apparent in the Bible and in particular the Old Testament, is that such men, with all their strength and their weakness, 'their highest and their lowest, (their) pulses of nobleness and aches of shame' are the men whom God empowers, forgives, trusts and uses to achieve His great designs."

From the Muslim point of view, the plain fact is that these are the men that *the Bible* says God empowers. These portraits have been painted in dark colours by human hands and it is not possible to accept the story *in totum* because it differs not only in detail but also in spirit. The Qur'anic picture is similar but lighter. In the case of Da'ud, on the positive side he has the slaying of Jalut (Goliath), the *Zabur* (though these are not the same as the Biblical Psalms), the wisdom, the territorial expansion (implied) and a very God-fearing nature, fasting and praying, all of which can be found in the Biblical David. On the darker side, though some Islamic scholars would dispute this, there is a hint of shadow in the story of Da'ud's temptation concerning the matter that, in the corresponding story in the Bible, engulfs David and his whole family.

The central disaster of David's reign according to the Bible is the taking of another man's wife. This event does not appear in the Qur'an or any reliable *Hadith*, which may mean that it did not happen. However, the Divine command not to "follow thou the lust (of thy heart)", the "error" referred to in the above *Hadith* and the grief that followed it, and the parallel tales of the unjust men and their greed for sheep cannot, to my mind, be dismissed out of hand. With just a small, sardonic hint, a Christian writer, Jacques Jomier, summarises what another Muslim response could be:

"However much these incidents (38:21-26 concerning Da'ud and 20:92-94 concerning Moses) may remind the reader of the episode of David and Bathsheba... the Muslim relies on the terseness and silences of the Qur'an and rejects any exegesis that would impute grave offences to the sinless, infallible prophets. When David asks for and receives divine forgiveness in the Qur'an, it is to pause very briefly, without dismissing it immediately, over the mere idea of such a sin."[101]

If we pause slightly longer we notice subtle differences in the stories that may suggest significant differences in their interpretations. In the Bible it is clearly stated that David sinned in deed, and in the sheep story, the rich man had actually taken and slaughtered the poor man's ewe. In the Qur'an and *Hadith*, we are told that Da'ud committed an error and grieved and repented of it, and in the story, that the one brother had won the argument about the sheep. Whether he also received the sheep we are not told, though it is implied that he did not, because they were seeking judgement on the argument.

---

[101] Jomier (1997) p.82

In the same way, we do not know at what point in the process of the error Da'ud repented, and in the same way we can assume that *that*, one of Jomier's silences, is what the message is. Perhaps we do not need to know and are not *meant* to know; ambiguity is often surprisingly present in the Qur'anic text. In this context, just before telling the story of the owners of the sheep, the Qur'an says: "Be steadfast in the face of what they say and remember Our slave, Da'ud, possessor of strength. He truly turned towards his Lord." (38:17) As various *Hadith* say, we should neither gossip nor speculate about someone's inner life, nor bear false witness; God alone knows what is in our hearts. Such an answerless question should make us reflect on the answer within ourselves, as Da'ud did finally, rather than project sin onto others, as he did when first told the story of the sheep.

The question that remains at the end of a comparison of the lives of David and Da'ud is, What purpose does it serve to hold on to versions of a life of a king, albeit one of the greatest, when they were written some four hundred years after his death and when they are so detailed in describing the sins of their subject? To believe them requires a leap of faith into believing that this hero was driven solely by base desires and the confidence of perpetual forgiveness, a credo that can hardly ennoble. Accepting the Qur'anic Da'ud means losing nothing of the essential glory of this first great king of Israel, and neither does it mean dismissing what may have been the weakest moment of his life. It merely means relegating it from its central position in the Biblical story. In the terms of a current secular credo, that what you focus on expands, it allows the shadow to take on a manageable size, and to be seen as, ultimately, liveable with. The alternative, of celebrating, as Israel did in the 1990s, 3000 years of Jerusalem as the capital of Israel through the Biblical story of David, is to enshrine this internal chaos as a source of national pride and identity, and to renounce both the wish and the possibility of moving on.

Blenkinsop, J.A. *Gibeon and Israel* (1972) Cambridge University Press: London
Gavron, D. *Would David have approved?* (1995) Palestine-Israel Journal of Politics, Economics & Culture, Vol. II, No. II
Ibn Kathir, I. *Stories of the Prophets* (2003) Darrusalam: Riyadh

Jomier, J. *The Great Themes of the Qur'an* (1997) SCM Press Ltd: London

Jung, C.G. *Memories, Dreams, Reflections* (1972) Fontana: London

Kenyon, K. *Archaeology in the Holy Land* (1960) Praeger: New York

Lane Fox, R. *The Unauthorised Version* (1991) Penguin: London

Maccoby, H. *The Day God Laughed* (1978) Robson Books Ltd: London

Moked, Prof. G. (15 Oct 1999) Haaretz: Tel Aviv

Robinson, G. *Historians of Israel* (1962) Lutterworth: London

Whitelam, D. *The Invention of Ancient Israel: The Silencing of Palestinian History* (1996) Routledge: London

12

SOLOMON

Solomon was a secular person: a man of his world and age to the bottom of his heart, if he had a heart.
        (Paul Johnson – A History of the Jews)

These are tough, perhaps surprising, words from a man who is something of a champion of the Jews. Solomon was their big moment. He and his father were the Golden Era. So how is it that the crown is so tarnished? How has the Great Solomon's legacy so developed that it is associated with satanic circles and world-controlling freemasonry? What is going on?

A place to start is the striking difference between the stories of the rulers of the Golden Era in the Bible and Qur'an. If the most striking difference between David in the Bible and Da'ud in the Qur'an is the intensity of the shadow of the former, the most striking difference between Solomon and Suleyman is the intensity of the light of the latter. This is so much so that the Golden Era of the Biblical Solomon becomes an untenable notion, though this is not the case with the Golden Era of Suleyman, and for this there may even be some archaeological evidence. The implications of this are profound.

Most of the components of the stories of Solomon and Suleyman are shared, such as the wives, the wisdom, the Temple, the visit of the Queen of Sheba (of Saba in Islamic tradition). However, what we find when we read the Bible story of Solomon is that it seems to miss the magic and majesty of Suleyman in the Qur'an, a splendour befitting a man who combined both prophecy and political power. To take just one example, in the almost universally known story of the two women and the baby, the Biblical version names them as prostitutes.

In Jewish and Christian tradition these magical qualities only seem to exist in the Talmud and in Jewish legends of Solomon and to have survived in an underground form in Masonic ritual. One Jewish legend of the Shamir[102] interestingly seems to contain expanded details of the Qur'anic story's building of the Temple.

In fact, by the end of the Bible version, the Solomon we read about is seen as vain, greedy and foolish, and it is he who is seen as the chief reason why the united kingdom of Judea and Samaria splits apart. This is one of the problems Jews, and particularly Jewish Israelis, face in the rancorous "Is the Bible true?" debate - "Damned if it is, damned if it ain't." Perhaps it is this feeling of being let down that fuels the negative light in which Solomon is often shown.

Nonetheless, there are moments of majesty. Early on, the Biblical Solomon has a dream in the course of which we realise that he is still a child. In the dream God asks what He shall give Solomon. Solomon replies:

"I am but a little child... And thy servant is in the midst of thy people whom thou hast chosen... Give thy servant therefore an understanding mind to govern thy people, that I may discern between good and evil, for who is able to govern this thy great people?" (1 Kings 3:7-10)

God is pleased that Solomon has asked for wisdom rather than riches or the lives of his enemies and says:

"Behold, I give you a wise and discerning mind, so that none like you has been before you and none like you shall arise after you. I also give what you have not asked, both riches and honour." (1 Kings 3: 12-13)
[103]

Though in the Biblical story Solomon emerges very much without the latter, the spirit of the promise compares with Suleyman's prayer in the Qur'an when he prays that God "give me a kingdom the like of which no one else after me will ever have." (38:35)

---

[102] King Solomon and Ashmedai, from the Mayse Book, Book of Jewish Legends (Picador)
[103] Though Midrash Mishlei 1:1 says that Solomon, as king, fasted 40 days in order to be granted wisdom

This is the same spirit we see in the two stories that show Suleyman's wisdom. Though Da'ud is a glorious figure, his son, Suleyman is more so. Da'ud is surely wise, but there are two recorded instances, in the Qur'an and *Hadith*, of Da'ud giving a judgement that is improved upon by his young son. In one, a man comes to Da'ud complaining that the sheep of a neighbour have strayed in the night and grazed in his field. Da'ud initially decides that the sheep should be given to the wronged owner as compensation. However, eleven year old Suleyman says that the owner should only keep the sheep until he has received full compensation in the form of lambs, milk and wool, whereupon the sheep should be returned to their original owner. (21:78)

On another occasion, according to the Prophet Muhammad in a tradition transmitted by Abu Hurayra, there are two women who each have a child. However, one of the children is stolen by a wolf. They present their case to Da'ud who finds in favour of the older woman. When they go to Suleyman for his judgement he asks to be brought a knife that he can cut the child in half so that they might share it. The younger woman immediately says: "Don't do it! May God have mercy on you. It is her child!" Her instinctive selflessness shows her to be the real mother, so Suleyman finds in her favour.

The former story does not appear in the Bible but the latter does in almost exactly the same form except that the child is killed by one of the mothers rolling on to it and, as mentioned above, there is the detail of the women being prostitutes (1 Kings 3:16). In a holy book it is surprising to find such an appearance but this is by no means the only appearance of prostitutes in the Bible, as has been noted before. They appear, as here, as an incidental detail and elsewhere as figures whose licentiousness is central to the story. It is as a metaphor, though, that harlotry most tellingly appears, a metaphor that is used to describe the relationship of the Children of Israel and God, particularly in their worship of other gods. (See Hosea 1:2: Leviticus 20.5; Judges 2:17; Jeremiah 3:1) Because of this, each narrative appearance serves as a reminder of this metaphor, and here is one at the heart of the most famous story of the most famous king who was most famous for both his wisdom and his relationships with women.

In his relationships with women, both Bible and Islamic sources, the Qur'an and *Hadith*, credit Suleyman with a large number of wives. Both traditions point to the wrongs that occur as a result of this, but the wrongs are of a totally different order. In the Bible, the distinctive Israelite quality of Solomon's society is weakened by the number of non-Israelite wives Solomon has, including the Pharaoh's daughter and princesses of Moab, Ammon and Edom. According to the Bible, this brings about Solomon's fall from grace because, in his old age, he is affected by these wives and begins to worship other gods and does "evil in the sight of the Lord" (1 Kings 11:6), building temples for many of them. Despite divine warning, Solomon persists so God tells him that, after his death, the kingdom will be rent in two, although Jerusalem will be saved.

In the Islamic sources, it seems that Suleyman, like perhaps all the Prophets, is tested at his weakest point. How is he, perhaps the most blessed of all kings, to avoid imagining that all this power and splendour is a reward for his own merit? One night he proudly declares that he will sleep with seventy of his wives and that each of them will bear a son who will fight for God. A companion says to him, "Insha'Allah" ("God willing") but Suleyman does not say it - according to a *Hadith*, he forgets. No wife becomes pregnant that night except one who delivers "half a child" (perhaps one that is stillborn), one that has been associated by some with an *aya* in the Qur'an – "And We placed on his throne a body." (38:34) Another interpretation of this body on the throne is that Suleyman becomes very ill while at the height of his power and then realises how weak he is and how dependant he is on the power of God. Whichever is true, and God knows best, he is at his lowest and it is when Suleyman realises his fault that he prays: "My Lord, forgive me and give me a kingdom the like of which no one else after me will ever have. Verily art Thou the one who giveth." (38:35) Thus, at the heart of the Islamic Suleyman's power is a humility that the Biblical Solomon only shows in childhood.

Through his repentance, Suleyman finds favour with God and his wish is granted. If indeed some of these gifts do manifest only after this incident, we can imagine that Suleyman has indeed passed the test. A further sign of this humility is to be found in the story of the ant. All

Suleyman's forces are on the march, men, *jinn*, birds, "all kept in order and ranks" (27:17) and they arrive at a valley where there are many ants. One of the ants tells the rest to make haste to their habitations in case Solomon and his forces crush them by mistake. Suleyman smiles when he hears this speech. Suleyman, the greatest of kings, smiles at the speech and the respect of the ants, not because it is ridiculous or amusing, but because the greatest king on earth can also understand, and therefore see himself from the point of view of one of the smallest creatures on earth. To the ants, he is a king who may heedlessly crush them, so his response is to pray for guidance, as he sees his importance compared to God's on a similar scale, and to pray that "I may work the righteousness that will please Thee" (27:19) rather than do what might merely please (great) men.

It is through his relationship with animals, namely the hoopoe or *hoodhood* bird, that Suleyman hears of the land of Saba, or Sheba, and that country's queen, Balqis. The bird tells him of the country's riches and the queen's glorious throne, but also of the queen and her people's worship of the sun. "The Devil had made their works seem fair to them" (27:24) as it is explained in the Qur'an. Therefore, Suleyman sends the bird back to the queen with a letter calling her to God. One Muslim storytelling tradition has it that the hoopoe causes the sun-worshipping queen to miss the sunrise by covering her window with his wings (there are shades of the death of Da'ud here). When the queen wakes in dismay, the hoopoe throws the letter in her face.

The queen has, in many ways, an enlightened kingdom and she responds by asking her council for guidance, as she usually does, and they in turn defer to her judgement after saying that their country's usual response is to wage "vehement war." (27:33). She decides to send gifts to see what Suleyman sends in return, and thus determine whether he is a king or Prophet. What he sends is the gifts back, with a message:

"Will ye give me abundance in wealth? That which God has given me is better than He has given you! It is only you who rejoice in this gift. Go back to them, and be sure we shall come to them with such hosts as they shall never be able to meet." (27:36-37)

Because of this, the queen decides to accept Suleyman at his word and she comes to him in peace. To test her using a symbol of her monarchical dignity and power, Suleyman decides to have the queen's throne brought to his court. He will then disguise it to see if she recognises it. He asks his court who can bring the throne and is given two affirmatives, one from Ifreet, a large and powerful *jinn*, and one from one who has knowledge of the Book. Both of them say that they can bring the throne almost instantaneously. Even in this small detail, faced with the choice of the physical magic of the *jinn* and the spiritual "magic" of the holy man, Suleyman chooses the latter, thus confirming his intention to glorify God rather than himself.

When the Queen of Saba arrives, she does indeed recognise the similarity of the throne, but she does so because many things have happened - she has been given knowledge in advance and has recognised that Suleyman is a Prophet and that *his* gifts are God-given. She has consequently submitted to God, and now sees differently, with inner sight. It is suggested that the throne looks better.

Suleyman also tests the quality of her sight by commanding his builders to build a lofty palace with water flowing under a glass floor. When Balqis sees this, she instinctively raises the hem of her dress to avoid getting wet, an Islamic storytelling addition at this point has this action revealing her hairy legs. When Suleyman tells her that the floor is paved with crystal, rather than feeling angry, she thanks him. Her words show that she is thinking beyond merely the outer appearance of the thing:

"O my Lord! I have indeed wronged my soul. I do submit, with Suleyman, to the Lord of the Worlds." (27:44) [104]

The sincerity of her previous submission is tested and she passes the test. As is the case with her erroneous worship of the sun, there is often more to things than meets the eye. Most traditions suggest that they then married, though this is not specified.

---

[104] In one elaborated telling of the story, Suleyman sees that the queen has shapely, though rather hairy, legs when she raises her dress. The *jinn* advise him about the benefits of depilatories to amend this.

This story in the Bible is superficially very similar, though the main point seems to be to show recognition of Solomon's glory. Unusually, it has fewer details than the Qur'anic version, to the point where the queen is virtually ignored, a fact that later storytellers in the Judaic tradition would rectify, as we shall see. The Queen of Sheba has heard of Solomon's wisdom and of his name "concerning the Lord" (1 Kings 10:1) so she comes with a huge retinue, and gifts of gold, stones and spices. The Hebrew word *bo*, meaning 'come', we met in the Moses' story. What was not mentioned there is that it can also be used to mean 'to enter', and is thus often used to mean sexual intercourse, and this is just one example where the Biblical text has given a sexual ambiguity to the story. We shall see more soon.

Sheba also comes to test Solomon with "hard questions," an ambiguity that has given enormous scope for advancing various interpretations. One version of one of the questions in the *Targum Shemi* sees it as a riddle where a woman says to her son, Your father is my father, your grandfather is my grandfather, you are my son and I am your sister. Solomon correctly guesses that the mother is one of Lot's daughters. Though not spiritually uplifting it is at least Biblical; the *Zohar*, the medieval book of the Kabbalah, identifies the Queen as a filthy witch questioning him to discover the use of serpents.

Solomon answers all her questions and when she has seen all the glory of his court and his worship of the Lord there is "no more spirit in her." (1 Kings 10:5) She has lost the battle of wills. The phrase "He gave her all her desire" in verse 13 regarding her questions makes another reference that could easily be interpreted sexually. One way or another, everything surpasses her expectations and she says: "Blessed be the Lord your God, who has delighted in you and set you on the throne of Israel! ("On His throne as His king" in 2 Chronicles 9:8) Because the Lord loved Israel for ever, he has made you king, that you may execute justice and righteousness." (1 Kings 10:9) In return, she is given many gifts and returns home with them. Significantly, gifts play a significant part – hers to him are not returned according to the story in Kings, as they are in the Qur'an. However, in 2 Chronicles 9:12 "King Solomon gave the queen of Sheba all she desired, whatever she asked, besides her gifts in return for what she brought him" sounds like a slightly clumsy way of saying that he *did* return the gifts. After all this, the story ultimately merely confirms the ethnic specificity of "Solomon's God" and does not lead to conversion or marriage (she was a non-Israelite), though there is an understanding that they slept together.

Christian tradition sees much of the Hebrew Bible, or Old Testament, as allegory that relates to Jesus. Thus, the Venerable Bede, writing in the 8th Century and reworking the marriage symbolism we have seen in Jewish tradition, sees Sheba's questions as being like the Church eager to know Christ. "To know in the Biblical sense" is used to this day as a euphemism for sexual intercourse, a dominant theme in the story of Solomon in all traditions. The other significant mention in Christian tradition gives "the Queen of the South" an important appearance at the time of the Final Judgement "when this generation is on trial … (when she will) ensure its commendation, for she came from the ends of the earth to hear the wisdom of Solomon; and what is here (Jesus) is greater than Solomon." (Matthew 12:42)

Though she does not have a strong presence in the Biblical telling, the elaborations in various stories cast the queen in a very negative light and she is portrayed as anything from a riddler to a demon. In the latter case the hairy legs that we find in the Islamic version are goat's feet, or Sheba's whole body is covered with hair. Some commentaries say that she is descended from one of the concubines of Abraham (an implicit slur on Hagar), and others that the night spent together either produces Nebuchadnezzar, later scourge of the Jews and destroyer of the Temple, or it leads to his birth, thus making one of the greatest of the Jews the father of one of the Jews' greatest enemies. By the middle ages, in the Kabbalah, and later in 17th and 18th Century Germany, the Queen of Sheba has assumed diabolical significance as Lilith, the queen of the demons or, as mentioned above, a filthy witch.

This raises interesting questions as to why, and what the truth, or at least meaning, is. One of the appeals of the story of Solomon and Sheba is the meeting of two very different rulers. They are crucially Jewish and non-Jewish in the Bible, and "muslim" (in the deepest sense) and non-muslim in the Qur'an. However, they are also very different in other ways. They are male and female; north and south; black and white, at least when viewed through a eurocentric prism; and

199

even, in some tellings, purveyors of different kinds of magic. This is a classic set-up for, or result of, all kinds of psychological projection, including the sexual.

In the Jewish tellings particularly, these become more extreme over time, as we have seen, while in the Ethiopic Christian tradition, interestingly, the "shadow" projections are reversed. In the Ethiopic telling, Sheba is impressed by Solomon, and vice versa, to the extent that he wants a son by her. He organises a banquet of heavily flavoured food that will leave her thirsty after and then invites her to stay in his tent. She agrees on the condition that he does not touch her, and he agrees to that on the condition that she take nothing of his. She wakes up thirsty, drinks his water and thus has to pay the penalty, resulting in the birth of a son Menelik. He later comes to Jerusalem to study, and takes the Ark of the Covenant with him when he leaves. The story explains the uniqueness of Ethiopian Christian culture and how, Ethiopians believe, Ethiopia became the home for the Ark.

If wisdom was his intellectual hallmark, in some traditions at least, Solomon's greatest physical achievement was the building of the Temple for this Ark of the Covenant. This was most symbolic of, and in some ways the reason for, his glory. In the Bible, the Ark is sometimes described as containing the Ten Commandments (1 Kings 8:5), sometimes as containing the Commandments and other relics from Exodus (Hebrews 9:4), and sometimes as containing the presence of God Himself (Numbers 10:35-36). Colin Thubron, drawing on the first tradition, describes the first Temple: "No god stood in its night, only the tablets of the Law: morality, for the first time, overawing the fetish for an idol."

1 Kings 6 and 7 describe the building in great detail: its size and style; how the stone was prepared at the quarry so that no sound of metal should be heard (1 Kings 6:7); its golden opulence; the two cherubim made of olive wood, ten cubits high, in the inner sanctuary and the carvings of cherubim that covered the woodwork; where and how the bronze basins and pots were made, and by whom (King Hiram of Tyre); and a sea that was supported on a dozen bronze oxen.

In the Qur'an there are echoes of these details as well as something of the supernatural nature of the construction:

"And to Solomon (We subjected) the wind, its morning was a month's journey and its afternoon was a month's (journey) and We caused a fount of copper to gush forth for him by permission of his Lord, and (We gave him) certain of the *jinn* who worked before him by permission of his Lord. And such of them as deviated from Our command, them We caused to taste the punishment of the flaming fire. They made for him what he willed: temples and statues, basins like wells and cauldrons built into the ground." (34:12-13)

Such vivid, concrete descriptions in both Bible and Qur'an beg the questions that hover behind all these stories: How true is this? Is it true at all? What is the evidence?

Unfortunately perhaps, the 'Golden Age' of David and Solomon is also what most archaeologists and historians call a 'Dark Age' in terms of archaeology. Commenting on this and the age from David to late in the Biblical narrative, Robin Lane Fox confirms that there is some correspondence between archaeological evidence and the Bible, citing the overlapping pottery of the sites at Tirzah and Samaria and how they relate to the movement of the palace of King Omri; the match of the Siloam tunnel and the one described in 2 Kings 20 that King Hezekiah had made to bring water to Jerusalem; and the siege ramp at Lachish built by Sennacherib in 701 BCE and evidence of the Babylonian siege of Jerusalem in 587 BCE (see chapter on Isaiah). However, that's about it and as he says: "One change of palace, a tunnel and two sieges are not exactly the living heart of Biblical truth."

To abbreviate what consensus there may be in an emotive argument that has even had Israeli archaeologists attacking each other (Professor Ze'ev Herzog, teacher of Archaeology at Tel Aviv University calls the Golden Age "an imaginary historiosophic creation"), it could be said that the Bible perhaps overstates the opulence and power of Jerusalem and that the cities mentioned in association with Solomon – Hazor, Gezer and Megiddo – were "like villages" (Fox), with a "civilisation… not of a very high order" (Kenyon) and "meagre in scope and power" (Herzog). Many places and books have been associated with Solomon,

Solomon's Stables at both Megiddo and Jerusalem, his pools at Bethlehem, and various ivory carvings, as well as the Book of Wisdom and the Song of Songs in the Bible, implying plenty of wealth and wisdom. However, connections between these and Solomon have mostly been disproved, leaving the question of how wealthy and powerful Solomon was, and also how he gained this wealth. Most answers suggested have involved looking south.

One possibility is that the economic basis of Solomon's wealth, however great it was, was a trade deal with Hiram, King of Tyre, mentioned above as the Phoenician king who did the metalwork for the Temple and also supplied timber (1 Kings 9:11). However, the same chapter also mentions that Hiram built Solomon a navy and he provided Solomon with men and ships in return for use of the harbour near Eloth (after which present-day Eilat is named) at Ezion Geber. (1 Kings 9:26-28) This would have given the Phoenicians access to the east and Solomon the revenue for the toll charges and it has also been used to validate the visit of the Queen of Sheba. Professor Abraham Malamat believes that the visit was a result of the danger the deal posed to her Sheban economy, particularly its camel trade. The "hard questions" he believes were economic and that it was a case of "political affairs, not romantic *affaires*." These are interesting and possible and do not necessarily contradict a surprising possibility suggested in the Qur'an that also involves the south.

Both Tel al-Khalifa to the north west of Aqaba in present-day Jordan, and Timna, north of Eilat in present-day Israel, have been identified as sources of copper or smelting sites and the possible bases of Solomon's wealth[105] and both are located near Ezion Geber (possibly located on the Coral Island in the Gulf of Aqaba, also known as Pharaoh's Island, *Jezirat Firaoun*),[106] from where the copper was traded with the Ophir of the Bible for gold. Kathleen Kenyon makes the point that Tel al-Khalifa is very badly situated as a place to smelt copper except that it is near Timna, which *did* produce copper, and is in the path of the wind

---

[105] Fox discounts this as a possibility, saying the only copper Solomon had came from the north. He suggests raiding or chariot trading as potential sources of wealth.

[106] 1 Kings 22:48 mentions Jehosophat as building merchantmen to sail for Ophir for gold but that they were wrecked at Ezion-Geber. This would suggest that the place of building was near the place of production but not the same place, which would fit geographically with the Coral Island.

that blows up the Araba Valley, wind that was used in the smelting process.[107] The copper and the wind relate interestingly to what is said of Suleyman in the Qur'an as quoted above: "And to Solomon (We subjected) the wind, its morning was a month's journey and its afternoon was a month's (journey) and We caused a fount of copper to gush forth for him by permission of his Lord" may seem, in that verse, to be referring specifically to the Temple but its frame of reference may be much wider.

The following part of that *aya* may also relate to a part of the Bible version: "And (We gave him) certain of the *jinn* who worked before him by permission of his Lord. And such of them as deviated from Our command, them We caused to taste the punishment of the flaming fire. They made for him what he willed: temples and statues, basins like wells and cauldrons built into the ground." (34:12-13) This and the "despised toil" in the *aya* that follows perhaps suggest a different meaning of the forced labour that the Bible says was one of the causes of Solomon's unpopularity.

There may be no archaeological evidence for the Temple, ("yet" as Herschel Shanks wrote, responding to Herzog the following week) but its semi-magical creation by the *jinn* is something Muslims take as a given because it says so in the Qur'an, a fact that is commemorated in the current architecture. Near the Dome of the Rock in the Haram al-Sharif is a building, an unprepossessing building to the north of the mosque, named Suleyman's Throne. It commemorates the verse following the one quoted above, for it is said that it was here that Suleyman was sitting, leaning on his staff and watching the work of the Temple nearing its completion, when he died:

"And when We decreed death for him, nothing showed his death to them save a creeping creature of the earth which gnawed away his staff. And when he fell, the *jinn* saw clearly how, if they had known the unseen, they would not have continued in despised toil." (34:14)

Had they known, they would not have completed the Temple.

---

[107] The display boards for tourists at Timna, however, do depict the draft being produced by foot bellows.

In the Bible, it says: "Concerning this house which you are building, if you will walk in my statutes and obey my ordinances and keep all my commandments and walk in them, then I will establish my word with you, which I spoke to David your father. And I will dwell among the Children of Israel, and will not forsake my people Israel." (1 Kings 6:12-13)

According to the Bible, when the Temple is finally completed, the Ark of the Covenant is carried up to the place and placed beneath the wings of the cherubim with great ceremony, with Solomon and the priests "sacrificing (so many) sheep and oxen that they could not be counted or numbered." (1 Kings 8:5) When it is in place, Solomon stands before the altar and, spreading forth his hands to heaven, says: "O Lord, God of Israel, there is no God like thee, in heaven above or earth beneath… keep with thy servant David what thou has promised him."

Then, quoting David's last words to him, he says: "There shall never fail you a man before me to sit upon the throne of Israel, if only your sons take heed to their way, to walk before me as you have walked before me." (1 Kings 8:23 & 25)

The Temple, he prays, will be a special place for oath taking and prayers in general and will even have a universal mission. Solomon prays: "When a foreigner, who is not of thy people Israel, comes from a far country for thy name's sake (for they shall hear of thy great name, and thy mighty hand, and thy outstretched arm), when he comes and prays toward this house, hear thou in heaven thy dwelling place, and do according to all for which the foreigner calls to thee, as do thy people Israel, and that they may know that this house which I have built is called by thy name." (1 Kings 8:41-43) So powerful is the wish concerning this person – "do according to all for which the foreigner calls to thee" – that this single "foreigner" could be seen to refer to none other than the Prophet Muhammad who, as we shall see, "comes and prays toward this house" in the Night Journey, (though it could be any one of us).

It is not, however, the spiritual aspect of the Temple that the Bible stresses as much as the physical and political. It describes how, as well

204

as the building of the House of the Lord, which took seven years, Solomon took thirteen years building five other buildings as part of the complex: the House of the Forest of Lebanon, the Hall of Pillars, the Throne Room or Judgement Hall, his own palace, and a palace for his Egyptian wife. As Graeme Auld, another jaundiced Biblical scholar, says, the Temple in the context of these is "more of a royal chapel, an adjunct to the palace, simply one of the buildings of state. The architectural symbolism which our text appears to allude to almost presents Solomon as Yahweh's landlord than his tenant."

Sometimes the religious and the political are reflections of the other. According to the Bible, the Ark of the Covenant is removed from the (lower) city of David to this higher place, which marks the change of status of Jerusalem from local to central religious centre. The building of the Temple leads to a centralisation of worship that is paralleled by a centralisation of political power. The army is expanded enormously, with huge chariot and cavalry regiments being stationed in the chariot cities of the kingdom, as well as in Jerusalem (1 Kings 10:26). Local tribal ties are weakened as people look towards, and pay increased taxes to, the centre, a phenomenon that affects both Israelites and the old Canaanite population. As the latter assimilate themselves into Israelite society so too does Israelite society absorb some of their ways. Foreign trade also brings foreign ways. All this, and the foreign wives and their foreign gods mentioned above, the increase in taxes, the involvement of Israelites in forced labour, the creation of a new rich Jerusalem elite at the expense of the old local upper class and a growing gap between rich and poor are the reasons the Bible gives for the kingdom's decline after Solomon's death.

With all this, by the end of the Biblical account it really becomes necessary to remind ourselves that this is a golden era, because the glory of Solomon has been irredeemably tarnished by his chroniclers in the Bible. His image is one of overweening power and uncheckable lust, weaknesses that create a kingdom whose structure simply collapses when he dies, and whose spirit is prostituted to idols. However, it is on these foundations, literally and metaphorically, that many would have the third Temple built. They await the finding of a pure red heifer whose sacrifice will restore the ritual purity of the site where the Dome of the Rock and Al-Aqsa now stand.

Like his father David, the Biblical Solomon contains both shadow and light. He is a meeting of saint and sinner, monotheist and pagan, servant and overblown triumphalist. He is all too human. His magical qualities, missing in the Bible, appear in the Talmud, in Jewish legend and have a symbolic role in freemasonry. In the latter, mentioned in a study of the symbolism of freemasonry, there is an insight we could use to understand the Biblical Solomon and the development of his "mythology" since: "Whenever anything is perceived in such a way that it appears to exist separate from its divine source, its complement also appears to exist to provide a balance for it." In the Bible, Solomon is portrayed as significantly untouched by divine grace, so a superficial Solomon has been left, a by-word for wisdom. Also, though, a kind of "shadow" Solomon, or "shadow" partner such as the Queen of Sheba, has developed to balance this should-be golden image of Solomon. Though some commentators point to the bad deeds of Biblical figures as proof that they existed (something like, If these chroniclers were trying to write the Bible only to advance the Israelite cause, they would not include all this libel), this is not necessarily proof enough.

A kind of contrariness has actually been a feature of the Biblical narrative, as we have seen from Adam onwards. It is not new to Solomon, nor David, but seems to come from a frame of mind that is trying to reconcile the impossibilities of being Chosen and especially beloved of God, and that God being the universal One God.

For whatever reason, this "shadow Solomon" with all his contradictions, has been enshrined within the Judeo-Christian canon. Jews have spent thousands of years trying to come to terms with that, while Christians have partly done so by casting that shadow onto the Jews as a kind of scapegoat. It is not surprising that this projection is so strong in the case of Solomon, the highest point in Jewish history. Thus, even black magic draws on Solomonic images and rituals – and at its heart lies this debased Solomonic Jerusalem. Was it coincidence that the identifying number on Israeli Jerusalem car number plates used to be 666? Someone chose the number. If the finest can breed such a legacy, what hope is there for the rest?

Ironically, the logic is that Jews and Christians can only glorify Solomon by letting go of Solomon and embracing Suleyman. Both the Bible and the Qur'an agree that Solomon's reign was the highest point in Jewish history -"none like you shall arise after you" (1 Kings 3: 13) as God told him, and "give me a kingdom the like of which no one else after me will ever have" (38:35) as Suleyman asked. It was an unrepeatable time. What Jews have been Chosen for, what they have been brought back to Palestine for, cannot be to repeat it.

Rather, it is Solomon's prayer concerning "a foreigner, who is not of thy people Israel (who) comes from a far country for thy name's sake... and prays toward this house," (1 Kings 8:41) that we should heed. There were to be no more like Solomon, not from the House of Israel anyway. By the time "a foreigner" came, may peace and blessings be on him, the House of Israel would have run its course in establishing the worship of the One God in the Holy Land, for the time being perhaps. That legacy would now be carried by one from the House of Ishmael. The Prophet Muhammad's successor, 'Umar, would actually take Jerusalem and it was under him that a simple wooden mosque was built on the place of the termination of the Prophet's Night Journey and his ascension to the heavens. (The Dome of the Rock was built sixty years later). Coincidentally perhaps, this is the third holiest place of worship in Islam so there are, in fact, two reasons that we, as Muslims, believe that the third Temple has already been built.

In the end, (and that could be taken quite literally), there is a paradox confronting those who would rebuild the Temple and reinstate the glory of Solomon through the blood of animal sacrifice. It seems profoundly undignified to countenance the destruction of the Al-Aqsa mosque, which is at once "Israel's" most unmistakable landmark and a building which is unique in being a monument to transcendent monotheism (Israel's Millennium Dome in deed!), to erect a glorified slaughterhouse.

This is not to say that the role of the Jews as Chosen People has ended. What it does mean is that the term "Chosen" needs a different spin. Their role is exemplary, their covenant conditional. The rest of us can see what happens when we do not submit, in any situation, when we give too much to our egos. The Jews may yet bring blessings to humanity in this, God willing, but just because it does not happen in the way that has been traditionally expected, there is no reason why the new way should not be right. Or good. And a new Golden Age may yet grow from the darkness that currently rests over Jerusalem.

Auld, A.G. *Kings - The Daily Study Bible* (1946) St. Andrew Press: Edinburgh
Clarke, E.G. *The Wisdom of Solomon* (1973) Cambridge University Press: London
Herzog, Z. *Deconstructing the Walls of Jericho* (29 Oct 1999) Haaretz: Tel Aviv
Kenyon, K. *Archaeology in the Holy Land* (1960) Praeger: New York
Kirk MacNulty, W. *Freemasonry – A Journey Through Ritual and Symbol* ()
Lane Fox, R. *The Unauthorised Version* (1991) Penguin: London
Magnusson, M. *Archaeology & the Bible* (1972) Bodley Head Ltd/BBC London
Pritchard, J.B. *Solomon & Sheba* (1974) Phaidon: New York, inc.
Silberman, L.H. *The Queen of Sheba in Judaic Tradition*
Montgomery Watt, W. *The Queen of Sheba in Islamic Tradition*
Ullendorff, E. *The Queen of Sheba in Ethiopian Tradition*
Watson, P. *The Queen of Sheba in Christian Tradition*
Shanks, H. *Nor is it necessarily not so* (5 Nov 1999) Haaretz: Tel Aviv
Thubron, C. *Jerusalem* (1969) Heinemann: London
<u>Williamson, H.G.M. *Israel in the Book of Chronicles* (1977) Cambridge University Press: London</u>

13

ELIJAH

*(He) gravelled the Prophets of Baal every way he could think of. Says
he, You don't speak up loud enough; your god's asleep, like enough, or
maybe he's taking a walk; you want to holler you know – or words to
that effect; I don't recollect the exact language.*
(Mark Twain – 'The Stolen White Elephant')

Twain's Elijah is necessarily, typically comic, though in spirit not a
world away from the Elijah who Magnus Magnusson describes as "a
weird and alarming... declaratory sage" who erupted out of the desert,
hairy and dressed in a leather loin cloth.[108] Robin Lane Fox concedes
that he must have been "hard to live with." Recovering his equanimity,
Magnusson's psychological diagnosis is that Elijah "represented the
primitive desert conscience of the Children of Israel." The last Prophets
we saw were dressed in royal finery, and here we see the other end of
the spectrum in terms of social position. The Biblical Elijah is very
much the outsider and is critical of all, rulers and courtiers.

In the Qur'an there is little detail concerning Ilyas, as Elijah is known,
except for a mention of his personality and the specific mention of his
preaching against Baal worship. This could suggest that the essence of
the story is sound (we find a similar quantity of detail concerning Job/
Ayyub) and there is, in fact, not much in the Biblical version that is
inconsistent with this brief Qur'anic sketch. We find the call to *taqwa*,
the fear of God; the reproval of the most despised sin in Islam, *shirq*,
the worshipping of partners beside God, in this case, Baal; and the
reminder of the Abrahamic roots of the people's faith. We could
therefore look at the story and for the most part, let it stand, though
there are some inconsistencies.

Elijah, whose name means "Yahweh is my God", was, like many of the
Prophets in the Bible, a Prophet in the Northern Kingdom of the
divided monarchy (Israel, or Samaria) between around 873 and 843
BCE and the stories concerning him in the Bible show him trying to

---

[108] Magnusson (1977)

209

keep the belief and practice of monotheism alive during the reigns of Ahab and Ahaziah. They both prayed to Baal and his consort Asherah for the winter rains and summer dew according to 1 Kings 17and18, and Ahaziah also sought healing from them (2 Kings 1). Often solitary and, to some, austere and even mad, Elijah brought the message that people should worship God alone, and that kings were accountable to God through the word they received through Prophets like himself. He prophesied that there would be no rain until he gave the word.

The first of these kings, Ahab, seems to have been a brave and successful military leader according to Chronicles (where his portrayal is rather positive), but he became Elijah's first foe because, according to 1 Kings 16:33 he "did more to provoke the Lord God of Israel to anger than all the kings that were before him." His sin was much to do with his Phoenician wife Jezebel and his prostrating himself to her god Baal and building a Temple to the same in Samaria. (1 Kings 16:31-32) After admonishing Ahab, Elijah is told by God to go and dwell by a brook where he drinks and is fed by ravens. (This is the usual translation but the word, *crybym*, can also mean Arabs if pronounced in another way). The first sign that the drought that will be central to Elijah's message has come to the land is when the brook dries up, though God continues to sustain Elijah and the family he stays with, and heeds Elijah's prayer for the life of his host's son. While this continues, the drought and famine take hold elsewhere until God commands Elijah to show himself to Ahab.

Elijah's reputation has also spread in this time. Ahab has heard of him through his servant Obadiah's meeting with Elijah, and he greets him with the words: "Art thou he that troubleth Israel?" Elijah replies: "I have not troubled Israel, but thou, and thy father's house, in that ye have forsaken the commandments of the Lord, and thou hast followed Baalim." (1 Kings 18:17-18) This is the closest point to the second mention of Ilyas in the Qur'an where his explicit mission to turn his people away from Baal is mentioned: "Will you not have *taqwa*? Why do you pray to Baal and turn away from the Best of Creators, God, your Lord and the Lord of your forefathers?" (37:125-6) In much the same way as the Bible, though in a considerably "terser" way, the Qur'an then says that they denied him and would be punished.

In the Bible, Elijah challenges Ahab to prove that the king's purported gods are greater than God and tells him to bring four hundred and fifty priests to Mount Carmel. The place that is particularly associated with this is a cave below the mount's summit, near modern Haifa, where Elijah is believed to have spent the night in prayer before the rainmaking confrontation the following day. On that day the confrontation takes place in which the deity who can end the drought is revealed, and where the idea that both God and gods can be worshipped simultaneously is ended once and for all.

Elijah commands the four hundred and fifty to dress a bullock and lay it on wood and call down the fire of their gods onto the wood. This they do but nothing happens. So Elijah dresses a bullock and lays it on wood and builds an altar of twelve stones, one for each tribe, and has a trench dug around the pile and commands water be poured over it all, not once, not twice, but three times, and he then calls on the God of Abraham to let it be known that He is "God in Israel." (1 Kings 18:36) At this point, the fire falls and burns everything. The people fall on their faces, declaring that God is the Lord, Baal's false prophets are slain and it rains.

The battle is not yet over, though, for Ahab flees and tells Jezebel what has happened. She dares God to do the same or worse to her if she does not do the same to Elijah within a day so Elijah flees back to the roots of his forefathers' faith, first to Beer Sheba and then to Mount Horeb, as Mount Sinai is sometimes known. There he asks God to take his life "for I am no better than my fathers." (1 Kings 19:4) God sustains him thereafter and then in an encounter where God speaks to him in a "still, small voice" he is told to go to Syria to anoint Hazael to be king over that place. After this he is then to anoint Jehu son of Nimshi to be king of Israel and Elisha son of Shaphat to be Prophet after his, Elijah's, time. The significance of these three is explained: "It shall come to pass that him that escapeth the sword of Hazael shall Jehu slay: and him that escapeth from the sword of Jehu shall Elisha slay." (1 Kings 19:17) He is also told that he is not alone, but there are still seven thousand men who have not bowed down to Baal. Thus, as well as being Lord of the elements, God is seen as having the authority to choose earthly rulers, both of Israel and beyond.

Elijah next confronts Ahab after Jezebel has a landowner, Naboth, put to death in the name of Ahab for refusing to sell or exchange his vineyard next to Ahab's palace in Samaria. In the vineyard Elijah curses Ahab and his wife and descendants: "In the place where dogs licked the blood of Naboth shall dogs lick thy blood, even thine." (1 Kings 21:19) On hearing this Ahab repents and is himself forgiven by God, though he is told the curse will still fall on his son's house. There seems to be an editorial attempt to ignore this because the original prophecy is later fulfilled. After Ahab is killed by chance in battle his bloodstained "chariot was swilled out at the pool of Samaria, and the dogs licked up the blood, and the prostitutes washed themselves in it, in fulfilment of the word the Lord had spoken." (1 Kings 22:38) As Robin Lane Fox points out, this event is described in 2 Chronicles 18:33-4 as happening to an unnamed king. He suspects that there has been some splicing here, particularly as the Kings version also describes Ahab as dying and "sleeping with his fathers," in other words, peacefully. He suspects that the author, the Deuteronomist, uses this authentic, though unspecific, story to blacken the image of Ahab.

After Ahab's death, the curse on the descendants manifests first when Ahab's son Ahaziah is sick and sends messengers to enquire of Baalzebub the god of Ekron whether he will recover. Elijah intercepts the messengers and asks them why they are going to enquire of Baal when there is God. He says that Ahaziah will not rise from his bed, a message that he repeats when he meets the king in person in Samaria, and the prophecy duly comes to pass.

Finally, Elijah is taken up to the heavens in a whirlwind on a chariot of fire after he has crossed the Jordan with Elisha. As a Prophet who thus did not die Elijah comes to have future significance. In the final words of the Jewish Bible it says he will return: "Behold, I will send you Elijah the Prophet before the coming of the great and dreadful day of the Lord: And he will reconcile fathers to their children, and children to their fathers, lest I come and smite the earth with a curse." (Malachi 4:5-6)

The New Testament also connects his return with the Day of Judgement, though at one point says that this has already happened: "And they asked him, saying, Why say the scribes that Elias must first come? And he answered and told them, Elias verily cometh first, and restoreth all things; and how it is written of the Son of man, that he must suffer many things, and be set at nought. But I say unto you, That Elias is indeed come, and they have done to him whatsoever they listed, as it is written of him." (Mark 9:11-13)

As well as the brief description of his mission mentioned above, Ilyas is also mentioned in the Qur'an in Surat al-An'am, where he is named alongside Zakariyya, Yahya and 'Isa as being "from among the righteous" (6:85) whom God chose and guided to the straight path. In Islamic tradition, he is sometimes associated with Al-Khidr, the Green Prophet, whom Moses met in the Sinai. According to a *Hadith* recorded by Bukhari he was so named because after sitting on barren land, green plants would grow there. This figure is often found in Islamic writings, a Prophet who is always with us but may take different guises and who appears at different times through the ages – here the dirtiest beggar, there a holy man. The implication is that whoever we meet and deal with, we should always treat them with respect and courtesy, for there may be more to them than is apparent. The connection between the two may be because in bringing the rains, Elijah brought the return of greenery to barren land, symbolically re-establishing the roots of faith in the spiritual desert, and also because Elijah did not die but ascended into the heavens. The idea of a Prophet of this sort is not confined to Islam; in the Gospels the crowds wonder if Elijah has returned when they see John the Baptist.

Ibn Kathir, I. *Stories of the Prophets* (2003) Darrusalam: Riyadh
Lane Fox, R. *The Unauthorised Version* (1991) Penguin: London
Magnusson, M. *Archaeology & the Bible* (1972) Bodley Head Ltd/BBC London

14

ELISHA

*The poetic genius of my country found me, as the Prophetic bard Elijah
did Elisha – at the plow, and threw her inspiring mantle over me.
  (Robert Burns)*

Elisha was Elijah's successor, receiver of the Prophetic mantle, as
described by Burns, and he prophesied in the Northern kingdom.
Unlike the solitary Elijah, he is a man associated closely with people,
with companies of prophets and with kings. He is first mentioned in the
Bible when Elijah returns from the Sinai, as we have seen in the
previous chapter, after having been instructed to anoint Elisha "as
prophet in your place... and whoever escapes from the sword of Jehu,
Elisha shall kill." (1 Kings 19:17) He finds Elisha ploughing his fields
with twelve oxen and covers him with his mantle, symbolising the
succession of prophethood that will eventually come to pass. Elisha
immediately offers to say farewell to his parents and follow Elijah,
though Elijah says that he has made no claim on him to do so: "Go
back again; for what have I done to you?" (1 Kings 19:20) Elisha
follows, nonetheless, slaying, cooking and distributing the meat from
his oxen before he does so.

The next time the Bible talks of Elisha, he is still with Elijah, and
travelling with him. Elijah, sensing that he is about to be taken to
heaven by a whirlwind, asks Elisha to stay behind at both Bethel and
Jericho but Elisha insists on staying with him, aware of what is about to
happen to his master. When they reach the Jordan, Elijah rolls up his
cloak and strikes the river, which parts in front of them. After they have
crossed, Elijah asks Elisha what he wishes for before Elijah departs.
Elisha replies: "I pray you, let me inherit a double share of your spirit."
(2 Kings 2:9) Elijah acknowledges that this is a difficult thing but says
that if Elisha witnesses his departure it will be so. The chariot and
horses of fire then come down and take Elijah away. Elisha tears his
clothes and, picking up Elijah's fallen mantle, returns to the Jordan. He
strikes it with the cloak again and says: "Where is the Lord, the God of
Elijah?" (2 Kings 2:14) The waters part, and he recrosses.

214

When he returns to Jericho the "sons of the Prophets" first of all declare that "the spirit of Elijah rests on Elisha" (2 Kings 2:15) and then persuade the reluctant Elisha to send out a search party, which searches for Elijah for three days. While in Jericho, Elisha performs a miracle, purifying the town's water, and after leaving, curses some boys on the way to Bethel who call him "baldhead." Two she-bears proceed to tear forty-two of them apart.

Elisha's powers are shown again when kings Jehoram of Israel and Jehoshaphat of Judah go to fight against the rebellious King Mesha of Moab and the army runs out of water. Elisha makes the streams run and the water slakes the thirst of the Israelites but appears to the Moabites as blood, making them think that the Israelites have fought among themselves. They rush in in search of spoil and are defeated. They flee but, although Elisha had promised that they would be given into the hands of the kings, Moab saves himself by offering his son as a burnt offering. At this point the forces of Israel withdraw.

Elisha performs further miracles, such as creating a fount of oil for a woman who is poor. He transforms a pot of poisoned gourds into an edible meal. He gives a son to a rich woman who had treated him well and brings him back to life when he dies prematurely, a story that is similar to the raising of the dead by both Elijah and Jesus. It is so similar to the Elijah story that some narrative confusion could be suspected. In a story that prefigures Jesus' feeding of the five thousand, he feeds a hundred men with twenty barley loaves.

While these miracles could be described as populist, others, such as those performed against the people of Moab, were done in the service of the kingdom. Elisha also orders Naaman, the leper king of Syria to bathe seven times in the Jordan, curing the king's leprosy and precipitating something of a recognition that "there is no God in all the earth but in Israel" (2 Kings 5:15). This story is mentioned in the New Testament as showing that God cares for non-Israelites, sometimes in preference to Israelites. "And many lepers were in Israel in the time of Eliseus (Elisha) the Prophet; and none of them was cleansed, saving Naaman the Syrian." (Luke 4:27) Elisha also plays a role in ending Syrian raids on Israel. (2 Kings 5:23)

Such is the respect that the Syrians hold for Elisha that when their king Ben-Hadad falls sick he sends for Elisha to heal him. The Syrian king sends to him Hazael, whom Elijah was commanded to anoint but never did, with gifts to ask whether Ben-Hadad would recover. Elisha tells Hazael: "Go, say to him, 'You shall certainly recover,' but the Lord has shown me that he shall certainly die." (2 Kings 8:10) He then weeps because he sees, explicitly, what this man will do to the people of Israel. Hazael cannot understand why Elisha should imagine a servant, a "dog", such as himself should precipitate such fears. Elisha tells him: "The Lord has shown me you are to be king over Syria." (2 Kings 8:13) Accordingly, Hazael returns to his king, tells him he will recover, and then smothers him to death. Hazael then becomes the one who carries out the Lord's work in fighting the corrupt descendants of Ahab and Omri.

The third part of Elijah's Sinai instruction is then put into operation by Elijah's successor: "It shall come to pass that him that escapeth the sword of Hazael shall Jehu slay: and him that escapeth from the sword of Jehu shall Elisha slay." (1 Kings 19:17) After saying there can be no peace while "the harlotries and sorceries of your mother are so many" (2 Kings 9:22), Jehu kills Joram, son of Ahab and king of Israel, King Ahaziah of Judah, and finally Jezebel, who he orders to be thrown from a window. She is trampled on by horses and eaten by dogs, as Elijah had prophesied. Jehu proceeds to rid Israel of Baal worship and is told by God: "Because you have done well in carrying out what is right in my eyes, and done to the house of Ahab all that was in my heart, your sons of the fourth generation shall sit on the throne of Israel." (2 Kings 10:30)

As is often the case, though the words suggest an unconditional offer, the next sentence tells us that Jehu continues the sins of Jeroboam, and the next paragraph tells us that the Lord begins to "cut off parts of Israel" through the enemies of Israel such as Hazael. Jehu has the dubious distinction of being the only Israelite king to be depicted by a contemporary artist, prostrating himself before the Assyrian king Shalmaneser, a sculpted relief that is in the British Museum, an event that took place in 841 BCE, the same year as Jehu's coup, according to Biblical archaeologist Michael Astour. He explains Jehu's assassination of Joram as an attempt to appease Shalman and prevent further

216

reprisals. The Bible does not mention this surrender but Lane Fox suggests that it marked the point at which the Judah-Israel alliance's ability to hold back the Assyrians ended. Placing it at this date also refutes the dates the Bible gives for Ahab and his sons.

Misbehaviour continues through the reign of Jehu's son, Jehoahaz, and Jehoahaz' son, Jehoash or Joash (2 Kings 13 contradicts itself as to whether this is one or two people). Israel continues to disobey the law of God and "did not depart from the sins of Jeroboam" and Syria continues to attack her. It is during the reign of Joash that we witness the death of Elisha and one more chance for Israel to behave faithfully. Joash comes to the sick Elisha, greets him with the same words that Elisha said to the about-to-depart Elijah, and is told to take a bow and arrows and shoot an arrow eastwards through the window. He then pronounces: "The Lord's arrow of victory, the victory over Syria! For you shall fight the Syrians in Aphek until you have made an end of them." (2 Kings 13:16) He then tells him to strike the ground with all the arrows. The king only strikes the ground three times and Elisha's last words are: "You should have struck five or six times; then you would have struck down Syria until you had made an end of it, but now you will strike down Syria only three times." (2 Kings 13:19)

There is one more miracle left in Elisha. A dead man thrown into the grave of the Prophet comes back to life. In a similar way Israel seems to come back to life after the death of one who is anointed. Following the death of Hazael the Syrian, his son Ben-Hadad begins to suffer defeat at the hands of Joash.

Much of the Biblical story of Elisha is consistent with the Islamic understanding of Prophethood, though Elisha's refusal to allow his servant, Gehazi, to his master's religion is not. This means that there is not a great necessity for a major retelling in the Qur'an. Of Al-Yasa, as he is known, there are two references in the Qur'an, both of which attribute qualities to him rather than tell his story. He is named as belonging to the "chosen" or "the company of the good" (38:48), along with Isma'il and Dhul Kifl, in Surat Sad, while in Surat al-An'am we read: "And Zakariyya and Yahya and 'Isa and Ilyas – each of them was from among the righteous; and Isma'il and Al-Yasa and Jonah and Lot

– and we favoured each one of them in all the worlds, as well as some of their forefathers and their descendants and their brothers; and We chose them and guided them to a straight path... These are the ones to whom We gave the Book and the wisdom and the Prophethood; so if they disbelieve in it, then We will certainly entrust it to a people who do not disbelieve in it." (6:85-89)

Here the Qur'an states what the Bible does not. The Bible contains blessings and promises that seem eternal but, as we saw with both David and Solomon, a Biblical eternal promise is dependent on righteousness. The Qur'an states that the promise and the blessing will go to another people if the initially chosen people continue to disbelieve. Al-Yasa, prophesying in a kingdom that is now divided, is near the end of the chain of Prophets.

Though Al-Yasa's story is not told in the Qur'an, parts of it are found in Islamic tradition. According to Ibn Kathir: "Ibn Is'haq said that Qatadah narrated from Hasan Basri, saying: Al-Yasa came after Ilyas, peace be upon them. He called his people to the way of God, and followed the laws and *Shari'ah* revealed to Ilyas, till he passed away." Also, Abdur Rehman Shad tells the story of the meeting of Ilyas and Al-Yasa:

"One day Ilyas (peace be upon him) passed through the fields while the owner, Al-Yasa, was busy in ploughing. No sooner had the owner seen the Prophet than he abdicated his own work and approached Ilyas (peace be upon him) in hot haste. Al-Yasa began to follow him. The Prophet was much surprised and remarked: Why do you accompany me after leaving your work? Al-Yasa retraced his steps and fetched his ox. He slaughtered it, lit the fire and cooked the beef. He fed Ilyas, his companions and many other guests to seek the pleasure of God. The Prophet was much pleased with his host for his sincerity, hospitality and righteousness. When Ilyas (peace be upon him) was about to depart, Al-Yasa expressed his keen desire to live in the company of his honourable guest for the rest of his life and serve him wholeheartedly as his humble servant. As the noble attitude of Al-Yasa had enamoured Ilyas (peace be upon him), the latter afforded him permission without hesitation."

The same chapter also contains the story of the end of Ilyas' life: "When the Prophet Ilyas (peace be upon him) was on his death-bed, he wished to bid him farewell. Al-Yasa was not prepared to leave him. Then Ilyas asked him to express any of his desires to be fulfilled. Al-Yasa said: I wish that God may bestow blessings upon me in the same way He has blessed you. The Prophet Ilyas (peace be upon him) supplicated and invoked the blessings of God on his successor. His prayer was granted. God chose Al-Yasa as His Prophet after the death of Ilyas (peace be upon him). He derived spiritual magnificence from the company of his guide and became the favourite of God."

The personal sacrifices that are required to follow Elijah are great at this time but as the Children of Israel grew further away from God, from Allah, following the way of the Lord became demanding. Jesus, for example, refers to Elisha's summons specifically when a would-be follower says that he will follow him: "I will follow thee; but let me first go and bid them farewell, which are at home at my house. And Jesus said unto him, No man, having put his hand to the plough, and looking back, is fit for the kingdom of God." (Luke 9:61-62)

Abdur Rehman Shad, *From Adam to Muhammad (Peace be upon them)* (1978) Kazi Publications: Lahore
Astour, M. *841 B.C.: The First Assyrian Invasion of Israel (*Jul.-Sep. 1971) Journal of the American Oriental Society, Vol. 91, No.3
Ibn Kathir, I. *Stories of the Prophets* (2003) Darrusalam: Riyadh
Lane Fox, R. *The Unauthorised Version (*1991) Penguin: London

15

<u>ISAIAH</u>

How beautiful are the feet of them that preach the gospel of peace.
(Handel – 'The Messiah')

Taken from Isaiah, this line is from the famous Oratorio by Handel, and he means it to refer to Jesus, the Messiah. In the course of this chapter we shall consider that it may not have done originally, and we shall consider some of the message that the Book of Isaiah contains, some of the most moving and uplifting of the whole Bible in its vision of peace, as is witnessed in the timeless appeal of Handel's work.

The supposed author, Isaiah, was not a king like David or Solomon, nor a complete outsider, like Elijah, but a courtier in the southern kingdom of Judah whose career spanned over fifty years in the second half of the eighth century BCE. The book of Isaiah is consequently one of the longest in the Hebrew Bible, with only Genesis and Psalms being longer. Its authorship has been disputed and it is often seen as containing a First Isaiah, who prophesied in the time Hezekiah, a Second Isaiah, who prophesied in the reign of Cyrus in the 6th Century, and sometimes even a Third Isaiah. It is also believed to have been written at least a hundred years after the death of Isaiah himself, with parts perhaps being as recent as the 4th Century BCE. Thus, the "prophecies" of what would happen, especially in terms of the Assyrians and Babylonians, were written after the events had happened. For all these reasons, it is often a contradictory book and, as a result, it often means very different things to different people.

For Jews, Isaiah is the first of the Great Prophets, for he is considered to be the Prophet who announces a different relationship between God and Israel, one that changes from formalism and Temple worship towards something of the heart, a change from fear to love. There are two aspects though, to the "Jewish Isaiah". He is both a stern warner who rages at his people, and a bringer of good news who confirms Israel's blessing.

The "Christian Isaiah" takes this one step further and, of all the books in the Jewish Bible, it is to Isaiah that Christians turn to most for prophecies of the coming of Jesus as Messiah. It is sometimes even called the Fifth Gospel. Some of these are the same predictions that are used by Jewish interpreters but they are seen from a different viewpoint.

There is, though, another Isaiah, one who is perhaps the most surprising, to non-Muslims at least, and he is the "Muslim Isaiah". Muslims look at many of Isaiah's prophecies, some of which are the same prophecies as those singled out by those who hold the above views and some of which are not, and see these, not as predictions of the coming of a Messiah in the future, nor of Jesus as the bringer of a universal faith two thousand years ago, but as predictions of the coming of the Prophet Muhammad, "the burden of Arabia" as it says in Isaiah 21:13.

The book is 66 chapters long and can be seen to fall into five sections of approximately equal length. Four of the five are addressed to the people of Jerusalem under threat from the Assyrians, chapters 40-55 being addressed to the exiled Babylonian community in the 6th Century BCE by "the Second Isaiah", who hails King Cyrus as the Lord's anointed. The common themes are an attack on arrogance and what Robin Lane Fox identifies as sins arising from human self-assertion "exercised against the natural order of God and His creation." There are also appeals to justice and to righteousness and the importance and holiness of Zion and Jerusalem.

Such is the power and the resonance of the words of Isaiah that they have inspired victims of injustice through the ages. However, the Isaiah of the Bible is not a rebel; he was in fact against the near-rebellion caused by the reforms that he had inspired and Hezekiah had carried out. Though the times were fraught with danger, Isaiah advocated that Judea spurn alliances and rely on God alone, though he was no pacifist. In the beginning he saw the Assyrians' success as punishment for Israelite sins, but when he felt the latter had exceeded their divine task he urged King Hezekiah to resist. Essentially, he demanded a risk of faith, one that required a miracle, and one did happen, according to the Bible (2 Kings 18 and 19), in the siege of Jerusalem (mentioned in passing above in 'Solomon'). According to the Biblical account, following the siege of Lachish, (where there are remains of the siege ramp that is shown on the Lachish relief in the British Museum), Sennacherib sent three generals and a great army against Jerusalem. Buying him off had availed him none, so King Hezekiah, urged on by Isaiah, refused to surrender. Then one night "the angel of the Lord struck down 5180 of the Assyrian army. When they woke in the morning, all around were dead bodies. So Sennacherib, king of Assyria, departed and returned to Nineveh." Oblique confirmation that Sennacherib was less successful at Jerusalem than Lachish is found in the blustery tone of the Sennacherib cylinder, a six-sided cuneiform tablet:

"As for Hezekiah, him I shut up like a caged bird in his royal city of Jerusalem. I built earthworks against the city walls and whoever came out of the city was made to pay for his crimes. Those of his cities which I had captured, I took away from his kingdom. I increased the tribute which he paid me and a yearly tax. As for Hezekiah, he was frightened by the splendour of my power and his best troops deserted him."

Between the two documents, both a successful bribe by the Jerusalemites and a reverse in the fortunes of the Assyrian war machine are possible, given that both sides have an interest in "spinning" the story their way.

Whatever did happen, however, there was no spiritual renewal. If anything, Isaiah felt that perhaps he had hardened hearts, though perhaps this was the divine plan. Thus, what also comes through increasingly, and often, it seems, reluctantly, are quite specific hints and predictions concerning an altogether different destiny and, specifically, an Arabian Prophet.

The first section, to the end of Chapter 12, attacks the arrogance and hypocrisy of "the rulers of Sodom" (1:10), Jerusalem's leaders, and calls for a new form of faith, one centred in the heart, rather than the practices of the Temple:

"Bring no more vain oblations; incense is an abomination unto me; the new moons and Sabbaths, the calling of assemblies, I cannot away with; it is iniquity, even the solemn meeting. Your new moons and your appointed feasts my soul hateth: they are a trouble unto me; I am weary to bear them. And ye spread forth your hands, I will hide mine eyes from you: yea, when ye make many prayers, I will not hear: your hands are full of blood. Wash you, make you clean; put away the evil doings from before mine eyes; cease to do evil; learn to do good; seek judgement, relieve the oppressed, judge the fatherless, plead for the widow." (Isaiah 1:13-17)

With repentance and willingness and obedience, though, "ye shall eat of the good of the land." (Isaiah 1:19) However, as we will find with Ezekiel, Isaiah does not expect that this will happen, though he stresses again and again that obedience is an option. When he experiences a vision of heaven, God tells him: "Go, and tell this people, Hear ye indeed, but understand not; and see ye indeed, but perceive not. Make the heart of this people fat, and make their ears heavy, and shut their eyes; lest they see with their eyes, and hear with their ears, and understand with their hearts, and convert, and be healed." (Isaiah 6:9-10)

Isaiah does, though, promise a better time when, famously, swords shall be beaten into ploughshares (Isaiah 2:4) and "the wolf shall dwell with the lamb" (Isaiah 11:6). This will be in the last days when the "the Lord's house shall be established in the top of the mountains, and shall be exalted above the hills; and all nations shall flow into it." (Isaiah 2:2) Great victories will be achieved against the enemies of Israel (Isaiah 11) and a saviour will come, a prophecy that has been interpreted as affirming the coming of a Jewish Messiah, or Jesus as Messiah, or the Prophet Muhammad:

"For unto us a child is born, unto us a son is given: and the government shall be upon his shoulder: and his name shall be called Wonderful, Counsellor, the mighty God (translated as "hero" in one version, "Godlike in battle" in another), the everlasting Father, the Prince of Peace. Of the increase of his government and his peace there shall be no end, upon the throne of David, and upon his kingdom, to order it, and to establish it with judgement and with justice from henceforth even for ever." (Isaiah 9:6-7)

This, and: "Therefore the Lord himself shall give you a sign; Behold, a virgin shall conceive, and bear a son, and shall call his name Emmanuel" (Isaiah 7:14) have been seen by Christians particularly as predictions of Jesus' birth.

However, if the house of Jesse (Isai in Hebrew) is an abbreviation of the house of Ishmael as one commentator, Dr Jamal Badawi, suggests, quoting Cheyene in the Encyclopaedia Biblica, then the tenor of the prophecies points beyond Jesus:[109]

"And there shall come forth a rod out of the stem of Jesse, and a branch shall grow out of its roots: And the spirit of the Lord shall rest upon him, the spirit of wisdom and understanding, the spirit of counsel and might, the spirit of knowledge and of the fear of the Lord; And shall make him of understanding in the fear of the Lord: and he shall not judge after the sight of his eyes, neither reprove after the hearing of his ears: But with righteousness shall he judge the poor, and reprove with equity for the meek of the earth: and he shall smite the earth with the rod of his mouth, and with the breath of his lips shall he slay the wicked. And righteousness shall be the girdle of his loins, and faithfulness the girdle of his reins." (Isaiah 11:1-5)

The following four verses, initiated by the word "then", describe an end-time scenario, of lions and calves walking together, and this is followed by: "And in that day there shall be a root of Jesse, which shall stand for an ensign of the people; to it shall the Gentiles seek: and his rest shall be glorious." (Isaiah 11:10) Though this verse is quoted by Paul in reference to Jesus in Romans 15:12, it does not mean that the reference *is* to him, perhaps any more than it could be a reference to the Prophet Muhammad. As we shall see when we consider Chapter 21 of Isaiah, the language is so open to interpretation that it is tempting to subscribe to the old adage that even the Devil could quote scripture for his own purposes. That, though, would be too easy. The difficulty we face is that maybe at least some of the truth of all religious texts is dependent on how they inspire us to live them out; that truth is in application, not just interpretation.

---

[109] Badawi (1997)

224

In the case of Isaiah, on the whole it is hard to see a distinctive point of view within the prophecies the book contains, in the first section at least. They are favourable one moment, but not the next, and seem to be about Isaiah's times at one point, and some indefinite time at another, at one moment historical time, the next – to Muslim ears – the Day of Judgement.

In the second section, until the end of Chapter 27, the pattern continues as Isaiah prophesies concerning the nations. Again it is suggested that great good will come to Israel but also great calamity. In the vision of "the desert of the sea" Isaiah recounts how a watchman sees "a chariot with a couple of horsemen, a chariot of asses, and a chariot of camels" (Isaiah 21:7), where the chariot has been seen as symbolic of David's entry into Jerusalem, the ass as Jesus' entry, and the camels as those of the Prophet Muhammad's successor, Omar, on his entry to the city. Though Jewish commentator Saadya translates this as an event that was fulfilled by the Babylonians ("he saw…"), ibn Ezra makes it a conditional prophecy ("when he sees…"). It is worth noting that there is considerable debate, according to Mackintosh[110], about what the watchman actually saw (or will see).

The later part of this chapter elaborates on what Isaiah calls this "grievous vision." It gives what some Muslims have seen as a description of the Prophet Muhammad's flight from Mecca to Medina. There he was taken in and protected until the tables turned and he was in a strong enough position to defeat the inhabitants of Mecca within a year at the Battle of Badr and then to return to Mecca in triumph. If we compare the King James and New English version, we can both see glimpses of this, as well as some of the ambiguity of these prophecies:

"The burden upon Arabia. In the Forest in Arabia shall ye lodge, o ye travelling companies of Dedanim. The inhabitants of Tema brought water to him that was thirsty, they prevented with their bread him that fled. For they fled from the swords, from the drawn sword and from the bent bow, and from the grievousness of war. For thus saith the Lord unto me, Within a year, according to the years of an hireling, and all the

---

[110] Macintosh (1980)

glory of Kedar shall fail... the mighty men of the children of Kedar, shall be diminished: for the Lord God of Israel hath spoken it." (Isaiah 21:13-17, King James Version)

In this passage, as elsewhere, Kedar can be seen as referring to the Arabs. Kedar is named by the Bible as the second son of Ishmael (Gen. 25: 13) and in Ezekiel 27:21 Kedar is synonymous with Arabs in general. However, to see some of the difficulties of interpretation, we can compare this with a modern translation of the same passage where we find:

"With the Arabs:[111] an oracle. You caravans of Dedan that camp in the scrubs with the Arabs, bring water to meet the thirsty. You dwellers in Tema, meet the fugitives with food, for they flee from the sword, from the sharp edge of the sword, from the bent bow, and from the press of battle. For these are the words of the Lord to me: Within a year, as a hired labourer counts off the years, all the glory of Kedar shall come to an end; few shall be the bows left to the warriors of Kedar. The Lord God of Israel has spoken." (Isaiah 21:13-17, New English Version)

After his tour of the region, in the third section to the end of Chapter 39, Isaiah returns to denouncing his own people. He does this with a vengeance. He rails against the drunkenness of the priests, the Temple's "tables... full of vomit and filthiness" (Isaiah 28:7-8) and then asks who the one shall be who can receive knowledge. "Them that are weaned from the milk, and drawn from the breasts" (Isaiah 28:9) is his answer to himself.

This is the first of several parts of this section that could be seen to refer to the Prophet Muhammad. In the Night Journey (Al-'Isra) the Prophet is offered two cups, one of wine, the other of milk, when he arrives at the site of the Temple in Jerusalem. His choice of milk at the place where wine had caused desecration changed the drinking of wine

---

[111] Some believe *b'arab* means "in the evening," while others think that it can mean both. The Hebrew letters *ain*, *rah* and *bet* can mean 'Arab', 'evening' or 'to be sweet or pleasing'. Incidentally, *ma'ariv* is the evening prayer for Jews in Hebrew; it is *maghrib* for Muslims in Arabic, meaning "the place of the west" (i.e. where the sun sets).

in Islam from something discouraged to something forbidden outright.

Another part can be seen as referring to the Revelation of God's message to the Prophet. The Qur'an was revealed to the Prophet Muhammad over a period of twenty-three years and the word of God, transmitted to him in Arabic by Jibreel, the Angel Gabriel, was often a shattering experience that initially left the Prophet speechless and fearful of his sanity. All this is echoed in the same chapter:

"For precept must be upon precept, precept on precept; line upon line, line upon line; here a little and there a little: For with stammering lips and another tongue will he speak to his people." (Isaiah 28:10-11)

When Jibreel first came to the Prophet, he commanded him: "Iqra!" which can mean both to recite and to read. "I am not a recite," the Prophet replied; he was unable to read. In a *Hadith* he continued that this happened three times, each time the angel crushing him to his limit and then releasing him, the same dialogue each time, until Jibreel said:

"Read! In the Name of your Lord Who has created (all that exists). He has created man from a clot of blood. Read! And your Lord is the Most Generous Who has taught (writing) by the pen. He has taught man that which he knew not." (Qur'an 96:1-5)

This is prefigured exactly in Isaiah's prophecy in the following chapter:

"And the book is delivered to him that is not learned, saying, Read this, I pray thee, and he saith, I am not learned." (Isaiah 29:12)

The fourth section of the book, from Chapter 40 until the end of Chapter 55, is addressed to the Babylonian community and again calls the people back to the worship of One God and to the rejection of idolatry. At the opening of Chapter 40, we find another reference to a destiny that is possibly beyond Israel, saying that Jerusalem should take comfort for her wars have (or possibly will have) ceased:

"The voice of him that crieth in the wilderness, Prepare ye the way of the Lord, make straight in the desert a highway for our God." (Isaiah

40:3)

In Arabic, the word *Shari'ah*, usually the term given to the system of Islamic law, originally meant simply a straight track that led to an oasis.

As the section progresses, the prophecies become more specific and in Chapter 42 we find more references to a Prophet who comes: (a) with a law (b) for the Gentiles and (c) is not discouraged until (d) he achieves this aim, criteria that Jesus does not fulfil. It begins:

"Behold my servant, (*mustifa*[112] in Hebrew) whom I uphold; mine elect, in whom my soul delighteth; I have put my spirit upon him; he shall bring forth judgement unto the Gentiles. He shall not cry, nor lift up, nor cause his voice to be heard in the street.... He shall bring forth judgement unto truth. He shall not fail nor be discouraged, till he have set judgement in the earth: and the isles shall wait for his law." (Isaiah 42:1-4)

The same chapter then talks of the former things coming to pass and the singing of a new song, but in the villages of Kedar. Though this passage does not say specifically that God's servant is from Kedar, which are the villages of Arabia and home of the forefathers of the Quraysh, (it only says that the people of Kedar, along with the many other peoples, should rejoice) it is the only place specifically named and it mentions things that relate to the Prophet Muhammad, such as that this Prophet "shall prevail" and that he would arouse jealousy.

"I the Lord have called thee in righteousness, and will hold thine hand, and will keep thee, and give thee for a covenant of the people, for a light of the Gentiles; to open the blind eyes, to bring out the prisoners from prison, and them that sit in darkness out of the prison house. I am the Lord: that is my name: and my glory I will not give to another, neither my praise to graven images. Behold, the former things are come to pass, and new things do I declare: before they spring forth I tell of them. Sing unto the Lord a new song, and his praise from the end of the earth, ye that go down to the sea and all that is therein; the isles and the

---

[112] *Al-Mustafa* is one of the names by which the Prophet Muhammad is known.

inhabitants thereof. Let the villages lift up their voice, the villages that Kedar doth inhabit: let the inhabitants of the rock sing, let them shout from the top of the mountains. Let them give glory unto the Lord, and declare his praise in the islands. The lord shall go forth as a mighty man, he shall stir up jealousy like a man of war: I shall cry, yea, roar: he shall prevail against his enemies." (Isaiah 42:6-13)

This end part is translated in the New English Bible as: "The Lord will go forth as a warrior, he will rouse the frenzy of battle like a hero, he will shout, he will raise the battle cry, he will triumph over his foes." Again, this is a closer description of the Prophet Muhammad than Jesus, a point strengthened by the person being called "messenger" (*rasool*) in verse 19.

The fifth section, from Chapter 56 until the end, begins with the announcement that the Lord's "salvation is near to come, and (his) righteousness to be revealed," (Isaiah 56:1) and carries forward this developing vision of the Arabian destiny by recalling the Ishmaelite line of Abraham's family and their restoration:

"Neither let the son of the stranger, that hath joined himself to the Lord, speak, saying, The Lord hath utterly separated me from his people... (Let) also the sons of the stranger, that join themselves to the Lord, to serve him, and to love the name of the Lord, to be his servants, every one that keepeth the Sabbath from polluting it, and taketh hold of my covenant; Even them will I bring to my holy mountain and make them joyful in my house of prayer." (Isaiah 56:3 & 6-7)

After this universal vision, there is an astonishing, though typical, change of tone to, "All ye beasts of the field, come to devour." (Isaiah 56:9) It is as if the writer is horrified that destiny is passing from the hands of Israel, and he is also dictating, for the chapter finishes with the Biblical equivalent of, I've had enough, let's drown our sorrows: "Come ye, say they, I will fetch wine, and we will fill ourselves with strong drink; and tomorrow shall be as this day, and much more abundant." (56:12)

The next day, though, brings more of the same: prophecies that arguably enlarge the compass of divine blessing and guidance beyond the people of Israel. It is usually assumed that the city referred to is Jerusalem. However, there are hints that it is not:

"Arise, shine; for thy light is come, and the glory of the Lord is risen upon thee. For behold, the darkness shall cover the earth, and gross darkness the people: but the Lord shall arise upon thee. And the Gentiles shall come to thy light, and kings to the brightness of thy rising. Lift up thine eyes round about, and see: all they gather themselves together, and thine heart shall fear, and be enlarged; because the abundance of the sea shall be converted unto thee, the forces of the Gentiles shall come unto thee." (Isaiah 60:1-5)

To this point, Christians would be happy with this quotation, but then we are told who these Gentiles are; they are the descendants of the children of Abraham who were born of Keturah, Abraham's wife after Hagar and Sarah. Genesis 25 names all of these peoples as the children of Keturah, except Kedar who was a son of Ishmael but who was, like the others, Arab:

"The multitude of camels shall cover thee, the dromedaries of Midian and Ephah; all they from Sheba shall come: they shall bring gold and incense; and they shall shew forth the praises of the Lord. All the flocks of Kedar shall be gathered together unto thee: they come up with acceptance on mine altar, and I will glorify the house of my glory." (Isaiah 60: 5-7)

Some believe that the "flocks of Kedar (that are)...gathered together" refer to all Arabia uniting under the Prophet Muhammad's leadership to adorn "the house of my glory" (the Ka'bah in Mecca). Though the chapter continues with: "Foreigners will rebuild your walls..." (60:10) and "Your gates will always stand open..." (60:11) in a way that strongly suggests Jerusalem (as does "...and will call you the city of the Lord, Zion of the Holy One of Israel." (60:14) this could be a point where the editors edited different prophecies together on the assumption that all references were to the Messiah, Jerusalem and Israel, where in fact some of them were not.[113]

---

[113] This understanding could be applied to Isaiah 61:1 where it says: "The Spirit of the Sovereign LORD is on me, because the LORD has anointed me..." which is quoted in

The final chapter (66) sees the dominant themes of the book coming together. The blessings, the need for a new way of praising God, the warnings, and the one to come. A rhetorical question is asked: "Where is the house that ye build unto me? And where is my place of rest?" (Isaiah 66:1) And then: "All those things have been, saith the Lord: but to this man will I look, even to him that is poor and of a contrite spirit, and trembleth at my word." (Isaiah 66:2) This cannot be Isaiah, who is not poor. Nor did Jesus tremble. But this is what God wants now in place of sacrifice.

We are then told that they did not hear. The Lord called but received no answer. And *they did not hear.* We can ask ourselves, Who did hear? Whose name means that God heard him? Who was the survivor of an earlier sacrifice and who was made to leave by his brother's mother? The answer is Ishmael, and here also things get turned around:

"Hear the word of the Lord, ye that tremble at his word; Your brethren that hated you, that cast you out for my name's sake, said, Let the Lord be glorified: but he shall appear to your joy, and they shall be ashamed." (Isaiah 66:5)

The remainder of this section alternates between trial and triumph, chariots like a whirlwind and the comfort of Jerusalem, whereto shall go all the nations. This culminates with the closing two verses that contain one of the few visions of the fire in the Hebrew Bible, immediately after what appears to be an optimistic end:

"For as the new heavens and the new earth, which I shall make, shall remain before me, saith the Lord, so shall your seed and your name remain. And it shall come to pass that from one new moon to another, and from one Sabbath to another, shall all flesh come to worship before me, saith the Lord. And they shall go forth, and look upon the carcasses of the men that have transgressed against me: for their worm shall not

---

the New Testament in Luke 4:18 by Jesus when he says that he is the "Messiah" (Anointed One).

die, neither shall their fire be quenched; and they shall be an abhorring unto all flesh." (Isaiah 66:22-24)

So disturbing have Jews found this end to one of the most important books of the Hebrew Bible that when it is read in Synagogue, the section beginning "the new heavens and the new earth" is often repeated at the end.

As such an important figure, it is necessary to consider Isaiah's place in Islamic tradition. Isaiah is not mentioned in the Qur'an and maybe in Islamic terms he should not be considered as a Prophet because, according to a *Hadith*, all of the Prophets were shepherds; Isaiah, a lifelong courtier, does not seem to have had any such opportunity, though he mentions them frequently. It is perhaps worth considering what it was, or is, that makes shepherds such appropriate mouthpieces for God. A shepherd is usually solitary, but not entirely alone, because he (he is usually a he) is surrounded by, and responsible for, many other living creatures. It is a job that does not require 100% concentration, but it does require a high level of awareness, while allowing time to reflect, to listen to an inner voice, or, as in the case of Da'ud, to sing praises. If it is not a sole, or first, occupation, it allows space for this reflection on other things. Most important of all, and hardly separate from the above, shepherdhood is a rural occupation, where one is intimately in touch with the elements. This is very much the realm of God, of Allah.

As a courtier, Isaiah's position would have been very different. A courtier's worldview might be compared to that of a political journalist, who is at the centre of power, but sees only the centre of power. Isaiah lived during the second half of the eighth century BCE during the reigns of four kings of Judah - Uzziah, Jotham, Ahaz and Hezekiah - and saw Judah's fortunes deteriorate sharply during that time. There is also the sense that, no matter how critical one is of that environment, it is still one's environment and the sense of supra-personal separation that, say, a shepherd would have would be lacking. Thus, there is a tension between Isaiah's wish to offer hope to the Children of Israel and the overwhelming necessity to warn. Through all this there breaks through, reluctantly it seems, prophecies of a different kind, such as the ones quoted above that point to an Arabian destiny for monotheism. Though he may not understand all that he says, or wish it, he cannot avoid saying it.

Though Isaiah is not mentioned by name, passages of the Qur'an contain a similar message to that of Isaiah, particularly in the last chapter:

"Hast thou not seen those unto whom a portion of the Scripture hath been given, how they believe in magic (*jibt*) and the evil one (*taghut*), and how they say of those who disbelieve: 'These are more rightly guided than those who believe.' They are those whom God hath cursed, and he whom God hath cursed will find none to help him." (4:51-52)

Finally, the Qur'an does say that the Children of Israel sometimes killed their Prophets. A strong Talmudic tradition asserts that this was the fate that met Isaiah in the reign of the idol-worshipping King Manasseh. Islamic tradition has it that he was fleeing his enemies when a tree opened to conceal him. Unfortunately, a portion of his cloak was left outside, identifying his place of concealment, and his pursuers cut the tree in half, killing him.

It is not likely that he was mourned greatly by some of the powerful of the day, including some of the priests of the Temple and in his description of the Suffering Servant, often seen as a prophecy concerning Jesus, we can see Isaiah himself:

"He was wounded for our transgressions, he was bruised for our iniquities: the chastisement of our peace was upon him; and with his stripes we are healed. All we like sheep have gone astray; we have turned every one to his own way; and the Lord hath laid on him the iniquity of us all." (Isaiah 53:5-6)

When the question of authorship is considered, with most authorities believing that the books were written so far after Isaiah's time, it is hard to trust the book(s) entirely. It seems to be a very human thing in which the soul of Israel seems to be struggling with itself through the author(s). It is at one moment reassuring, the next, sensing where this perilous state of affairs is leading. Where it is leading - to the coming of a servant of the Lord, or perhaps two - seems to break through this timeless struggle of Israel with God almost against the will of the writer, or writers, confronting them again and again with predictions of all nations worshipping God and it being the Children of Ishmael who leads them.

If it is accepted that the words of Isaiah were not entirely as they have been recorded in the Book of Isaiah, then we need to consider the motivations of those who recorded them. Certainly Jewish writers would wish to keep their own destiny as a central feature. Isaiah is critical of his people, but he describes God's judgement taking place, not in post-historical time, but towards the end of historical time, which allows for a period of peace, and again not having to face a final judgement.

What is most interesting though, and more important, is not what was distorted or added, but rather, what was not left out. The Islamic thesis seems so credible in Isaiah (and elsewhere) because, until the coming of the Prophet Muhammad, the verses that have been highlighted here would have appeared to Jews and Christians as simply more obscure Biblical byways. In the light of the events of the life of the Prophet Muhammad, they begin to look more like highways, a straight path, albeit heading in an unexpected direction. The extreme reluctance of the telling of the vision of Arabia at the start of Chapter 21 suggests perhaps that the direction was not so much unexpected as unwished for.

This is an unashamedly partisan position, because it selects what is useful to its argument and counts it as more than the rest. I would argue, in view of the above, that it is the only way of reconciling the paradoxes of the text. Yes, the blessings on the tribe of Israel are confirmed, though not in quite the way they have been traditionally seen. Yes, the Children of Israel are warned, and called on to worship and love God, though others will also be called. Yes, there will be a Judgement, but after the end of historical time, not before. Yes, Isaiah tells of the coming of the anointed one, the Messiah, though perhaps more than one, and not only Jesus. And yes, there is only One God, and the Prophet Muhammad is His Prophet.

Isaiah is credited by many with beginning Judaism, a religion that is almost distinct from the religion of the House of Israel. It could be argued that his message implicitly recognised that the kingdoms of David and Solomon, Da'ud and Suleyman, were the highest points that Israel would ever attain and that a different way of relating to God needed to be found. This needed to be one that could cope with the inevitable earthly punishments that were to follow, until such a time as a spiritual reformer would come to reform the House of Israel in the form of Jesus, 'Isa, and a spiritual and political reformer come to all the nations, in the form of the Prophet Muhammad. His coming seems to have been recorded elsewhere, as we have mentioned before and shall see in more detail later when we consider the Prophet himself, but it is surely the book of Isaiah, more than any other, that accounts for what the Qur'an says about the Arabian Jews at the time of the Prophet:

"And lo, it (the message of the Prophet Muhammad) is in the Scriptures of the men of old. Is it not sufficient evidence for them that the learned of the Children of Israel recognise it?" (26:196-7)

Badawi, Dr. J. *Muhammad in the Bible* (1997) International Islamic Publishing House: Riyadh
Ibn Kathir, I. *Stories of the Prophets* (2003) Darrusalam: Riyadh
Lane Fox, R. *The Unauthorised Version (*1991) Penguin: London
Macintosh, A.A. *Isaiah XXI – A Palimpsest* (1980) Cambridge University Press: London
Roberts, M. *The Ancient World* (1979) Nelson: Oxford

16

JEREMIAH

...And I was rummaging around in the attic and I found the original copy of the Bible. Which was nice.
  (The actor Patrick Nice – The Fast Show)

Around 623 BCE, laws that were claimed to have been written by Moses were found, possibly by the later Prophet Jeremiah's father. They were found during the Temple renovation programme of King Josiah by the High Priest and had survived the purges of Josiah's father and grandfather. The discovery came at an opportune time, something that could be interpreted both cynically or as a sign of God's omnipotence, because the Kingdom of Judah was in danger from both without and within. The laws were embraced by the king, who "tore his robes" and then went on to enforce them as the literal rule of God. However, Josiah was a rare thing, a good king, and the kings who followed were less enthusiastic. Nonetheless, there was always a significant group of champions of the new/old law, one of whom was Jeremiah.

From what we learn in the Bible, and this is an area of some doubt, because the Greek version of the book is over 10% shorter than the (probably later) Hebrew version, Jeremiah did not bring a palatable message, nor one that seemed very relevant at first with the waning of Assyrian power. People were following the form of what they believed was the right religion, and the Assyrians were not a threat, so there seemed to be no need to change. In fact, people seemed to treat religion as a form of divinely-sanctioned nationalism, despite the warnings of Isaiah one hundred years previously and the example of the destruction of Israel by the Assyrians. They were doubtless encouraged by the perceived holiness of Jerusalem itself and played the game of power politics to counter the power of Babylon, the new imperial threat, allying themselves with other small states in the region as well as with Egypt.

Jeremiah spoke out against this, prophesying that Jerusalem would wear the yoke of Babylon, which he illustrated by wearing one himself, and that the city faced a terrible doom, with only one way to avoid this fate. In Chapter 24 he compares the people to two baskets of figs – the "good figs" being exclusively those who submit to the Babylonians and the "evil figs" being those who do not. It was a message that was rejected by both rulers and people; when King Jehoiakim heard these prophecies, he cut them up and burned them, forcing Jeremiah to flee in fear of his life. When, in 597 BCE, Jerusalem was surrendered to the Babylonians and the last King of Judah, Zedekiah, was appointed by the Babylonians themselves, still the nationalists plotted. Jeremiah warned that the Babylonians would come again, and take the city, and burn it with fire (37:7, 8) at which the princes put him in prison (37:15-38:13) where he was when the city was taken in 586 BCE. Finally, the Babylonians could stand no more and destroyed the Temple, an event that is mentioned in the Qur'an in the Chapter named *Bani Isra'il – The Children of Israel*:

"Then We clearly declared to the Children of Israel in the Book: 'Twice you will work corruption in the earth and will act with great arrogance.' So, when the time for the fulfilment of the first prophecy drew near, We raised against you some of Our servants who were full of might, and they ran over the whole of your land. This was a prophecy (verily) fulfilled." (17:4-5,)

For his stance against his people's nationalism, his endless prophecies of doom and his counsel of submission both before the city's capture and after, Jeremiah was regarded as a traitor and a heretic; the Babylonians actually wanted to reward him, which probably did not help. As Robert Davidson says in 'The Oxford Companion to the Bible':

"If the fall of Jerusalem had not vindicated his stance, we might be reading now, not the book of Jeremiah but the book of Hananiah or of some of the other prophets with whom Jeremiah clashed."

Jeremiah is similar to Isaiah in many of his criticisms. Throughout his time as prophet he rails against the Jews' cry of "I will not serve" (Jeremiah 2). He also attacks the religious practice of cultic devotion to the high places and compares it to harlotry (that motif again). He cites the fate of Israel as being a result of doing the same (3:6-9), calling Israel and Judah "treacherous sisters". Furthermore he attacks the lewdness of the people ("neighing after his neighbour's wife"), prefiguring Ezekiel, and he talks of harlots again, but this time not as a metaphor but as a literal description of the people's behaviour. Before the destruction he announces that "a nation from afar" will come to destroy and desolate but he always warns that it is not too late; God's favour could still be retained through returning to following His laws. Then, in desperation, he announces that God has abandoned His "beloved", regarding them as strange to Him, like animals that have become as unconscious of their relationship to God, and hence their humanity, as the pagans around:

"I have forsaken mine house, I have left mine heritage; I have given the dearly beloved of my soul into the hand of her enemies. Mine heritage is unto me as the lion in the forest; it crieth out against me: therefore have I hated it. Mine heritage is unto me as a speckled bird, the birds round about are against her; come ye, assemble all ye beasts of the field and devour." (Jeremiah 12:7-9)

However, like both Isaiah before and Ezekiel after, he knows that the ears will not hear: "Therefore thou shalt speak all these words unto them; but they will not hearken to thee: thou shalt also call unto them; but they will not answer thee." (7:27)

Yet he continues, because it is God's will and God's message. What is offered, particularly after the destruction of Jerusalem, is a hope, not of a national Israel, but of something beyond, specifically with the Babylonian exiles. Jeremiah also speaks of a new heart (31:31-34) that will replace the old (3:17), a prophecy that the New Testament will refer back to as justification for Jesus in 1 Corinthians 11:25 and Hebrews 8:6-13. These glad tidings come after the fall of Jerusalem, after the lesson might be assumed to have been learned, at a time when Jeremiah has been allowed by the Babylonians to remain and preach. There will be a new covenant and the Jews will change: "Deep within them I will plant my Law, writing it in their hearts…" (31:33), but not in Jeremiah's lifetime. Christians see this being fulfilled in the life of Jesus, though the time reference could be more modern:

"In his days Judah shall be saved, and Israel shall dwell safely: and this is his name whereby he shall be called the Lord Our Righteousness. Therefore, behold, the days come, saith the Lord, that they shall no more say, The Lord liveth, that brought up the Children of Israel out of Egypt; but, The Lord liveth, which brought up and led the seed of the House of Israel out of the north country, and from all countries whither I had driven them; and they shall dwell in their own land." (23:6-8)

This, possibly, aside, the books of Jeremiah do not appear to be full of allusions to anything specifically post-Jewish, unlike Isaiah. However, there is one telling reference to the area of Arabia:

"For pass over the isles of Chittim, and see; and send unto Kedar, and consider diligently, and see if there be such a thing. Hath a nation changed their gods, which are yet no gods? But my people hath changed their glory for that which doth not profit." (2:10-11)

As we have seen previously, Kedar, as a son of Ishmael, is Arab and the flocks of Kedar would indeed be gathered. They had not changed their gods "which are yet no gods" at this stage, but under the Prophet Muhammad they would do so, offering instead their allegiance to the One God. In the time of Jeremiah, the Children of Israel seemed, spiritually speaking and literally, to be heading in an entirely contrary direction.

Also, in Jeremiah 28: 9, it is written that if a prophet prophesies peace, he will be recognised as the one truly sent by the Lord when those prophecies come true. As we will see, Jesus said he did not come to bring peace on earth but division (Luke 12: 51-53). Islam, which means "peace", is closer to the message of the Prophet Muhammad, who both prophesied and brought peace.

Davidson, R. in Metzger, B.M. & Coogan, M.D. *Oxford Companion to the Bible* (1993) Oxford University Press: Oxford
Ibn Kathir, I. *Stories of the Prophets* (2003) Darrusalam: Riyadh
Kenyon, K. *Archaeology in the Holy Land* (1960) Praeger: New York
Lane Fox, R. *The Unauthorised Version (*1991) Penguin: London
Wikipedia, *Jeremiah*

17

EZEKIEL

Ezekiel cry 'Dem dry bones'
Ezekiel cry 'Dem dry bones'
Ezekiel cry 'Dem dry bones'
Now hear the word of the Lord.

Ezekiel connected dem dry bones
Ezekiel connected dem dry bones
Ezekiel connected dem dry bones
Now hear the word of the Lord.

Dem bones, dem bones gonna walk around
Dem bones, dem bones gonna walk around
Dem bones, dem bones gonna walk around
Now hear the word of the Lord.
          (Popular song)

Though Ezekiel was a contemporary of Jeremiah, his place of prophecy was in exile while Jeremiah's was in Jerusalem. He thus offers another geographical perspective on the business of righteous guidance. He was deported to Babylon in 598 BCE just before the Babylonians captured Jerusalem for the first time and, according to the opening verses of the Book of Ezekiel, he received his calling as a Prophet four years later. Many of the verses thereafter talk of the destruction of Israel and Judah that had already taken place. They aim to shake the Jews out of their complacency by causing Jerusalem "to know her abominations" (Ezekiel 16:2) before she went the same way and to reject her false prophets who were prophesying peace and visions of peace when "there is no peace." (Ezekiel 13:16)

Like Jeremiah, whose close identification with his message is expressed through such means as the "Yoke of Babylon", Ezekiel also graphically illustrates his message through his life and actions. When he starts prophesying, he begins by knocking a hole in the wall of his house and leaving through it with his worldly goods, thus enacting the violence and suddenness of the leaving of Jerusalem that he would prophesy. Robin Lane Fox quotes G. Josipovici who says:

"We are here dealing with something more than symbols or emblems: there is a drive towards total identification of the individual, even to the point of taking a whole group's into one's own body."

This identification even extends to Ezekiel's response to the death of his wife. The Lord tells Ezekiel: "Son of man, behold I shall take away from thee the desire of thine eyes with a stroke," and commands that he not grieve. Just as God had taken his wife, so too would He take by the sword the desire of the eyes of the people: the Temple and the sons and daughters in Jerusalem. "Thus Ezekiel is unto you a sign... and when this cometh, ye shall know that I am the Lord."

The message as expressed through Ezekiel is a sign that appeals to all the senses. In a vision in which Ezekiel sees God and His heavenly chariot, God shows His Prophet a written scroll, which Ezekiel eats (and therefore digests), describing it as being "as honey for sweetness" in his mouth.

In his words, he speaks of other tastes to highlight his message. One of the themes of his prophecies is what some commentators have called the contradiction between Ezekiel the champion of personal responsibility and Ezekiel the Prophet of divine intervention. At one point he dismisses the proverb that says that the fathers have eaten sour grapes and the children's teeth are set on edge, saying that we are all responsible for our own salvation:

"The soul that sinneth, it shall die. The son shall not bear the iniquity of the father." (Ezekiel 18:20)

Yet paradoxically, in a later verse he prophesies a change in heart that will mark a sea change for the people of Israel, although it will be a change that is carried out by God:

"A new heart will I give you, and a new spirit will I put within you: and I will take away the stony heart out of your flesh, and I will give you an heart of flesh. And I will put my spirit within you, and cause you to walk in my statutes, and ye shall keep my judgements, and do them." (Ezekiel 36:26-27)

In one of his most well known visions, which 'Dem Bones' sings of, Ezekiel sees a vision of something like this happening in the desolation of exile. He is carried in the spirit of the Lord to a valley, which is full of dry bones. God speaks to him and says of the bones:

"Behold, I will cause breath to enter into you, and ye shall live: And I will lay sinews upon you, and will bring up flesh upon you, and cover you with skin, and put breath in you, and ye shall live, and ye shall know that I am the Lord." (Ezekiel 37:5-6)

Afterwards, God tells him that the bones are the House of Israel and that God will restore them to the land with his spirit in them.

Though Ezekiel is not named in the following, the description in the Qur'an of the vision of the destroyed town (Jerusalem) and of God's powers of restoration are witnessed in the following verse and are believed by many commentators to refer to him:

"Or consider the one who, when passing by a town which had fallen into ruins, said, 'How can God bring this town back to life after its death?' So God made him die for a hundred years, and then brought him back to life, and asked, 'How long have you been here?' He replied, 'I have been here for a day, or for some of the day.' He said, 'No, but you have been here for a hundred years. Look at your food and drink which have not rotted, and look at your donkey. And, that We may make thee a token unto mankind, look at the bones, how We arrange them and cover them with flesh!' And when this was shown to him, he said: 'I know now that God is able to do all things.'" (2:259)

Though he is sometimes known as Hizqil in Arabic, Ezekiel has also been linked to Dhul Kifl in the Qur'an, where he is described as being a man of steadfastness, of patience and constancy, like Isma'il and Idris, and has been admitted to God's mercy as one of the "righteous" (21:85-86). Elsewhere he is named with Isma'il and Al-

Yasa (Elisha) as one of the chosen (38:48).

If Ezekiel and Dhul Kifl are one and the same, we see that one of his hallmarks is his patience. Christopher T. Begg, in 'The Oxford Companion to the Bible', describes him as "an outwardly stoical, highly self-controlled and somewhat passive personality," citing as an example God's command that he not grieve for his beloved wife when she died. This implies that he might well have been due a long wait before he saw the change of heart that he had prophesied. If we consider what happened after the return from Babylon in 546 BCE, it does not seem to have wrought profound changes, and certainly not enough to justify itself as the fulfilment of the vision of the dry bones. If we interpret the Qur'an's "one hundred years" as a very, very long time, rather than as a literal hundred, we could infer the same and that it has not happened even until now.

What did happen, though, was the physical restoration of Jerusalem and, to some extent, of Jewish power, after the return from exile in 539 BCE under Cyrus, king of Persia. God, though, was not "sanctified in them in the sight of many nations" (39:27). Over the next 500 years or so, having run it in exile, as a nation the Children of Israel ran the gamut of politico-religious experience in the Promised Land. After the revolt of Judas Macabeus, they achieved a brief period of independence from 142 to 104 BCE, which was followed by 40 years of civil war until the semi-welcomed occupation by the Romans in 63 BCE. By this time a belief that this was "the End of Days" was growing, and with it the anticipation of the coming of the Messiah who would deliver them; they seemed unable or un-destined to deliver themselves.

During all this time, the extensive prohibitions that had been listed by Ezekiel in 18:5-9 were not honoured: keeping justice; obeying the law; not eating in the mountains nor worshipping idols; being sexually faithful and clean; being charitable; honouring debts and not taking interest on loans. The Great Hebrew Prophets were solace and direction to some at least of the Children of Israel at, during and after their worst time – the time of destruction and exile. The Children of Israel were offered, or perhaps promised, a new heart – offered if we regard these matters on the human plane, promised if we see it on the level of the Divine. On the human (and collective) plane, they failed, and would be expelled a second time. On the Divine (and microcosmic) plane, though, the promise was fulfilled – a Jew came who did have a new heart. And that was Jesus.

Ibn Kathir, I. *Stories of the Prophets* (2003) Darrusalam: Riyadh
Lane Fox, R. *The Unauthorised Version* (1991) Penguin: London

18

JOHN the BAPTIST

What does it matter? If He is to wax, I must wane.
(Gustave Flaubert, in 'Herodias')

In 'Apocalypse', Neil Faulkner says that John the Baptist's arrest "cleared the field" for Jesus' ministry and, as Flaubert puts it above, there is something tragically essential in the rise and demise of John the Baptist in the Bible. Implicitly, this is so for the Islamic understanding of this Prophet. However, as Christian commentator M.S. Seale says, the Qur'an has very little to say about Yahya,[114] as John the Baptist is known, particularly his later life. Though Seale acknowledges the respectful references, as a Christian he wishes for a clear mission statement and some linkage to Jesus. Indeed, the only connections are indirect. Peace is invoked on the birth, death and resurrection of both; accounts of the births of the two are found next to each other in the Suras entitled 'The House of Imran' and 'Maryam', (their family connection to each other is given) and John's father Zakariyya is "curiously", according to Seale, credited with sheltering Mary during her pregnancy. (3:32)

Regarding family, there is a family connection in both the Biblical and Qur'anic narratives. According to Luke, (1.5) John was the son of the priest Zechariah, just as the Qur'an says that he was the son of Zakariyya, though a *Hadith* says that Zakariyya was a carpenter as well as a Prophet. In both narratives, the father is married to a woman (Elizabeth in the New Testament) who is Mary's "kinswoman", though presumably much older. This is not stated directly in the Qur'an, though if she were family, it is therefore less "curious" that Zakariyya's home is where Maryam is assigned for care before the annunciation of Jesus.

---

[114] Seale also expresses puzzlement at this use of name, claiming that Yohanna is a more accurate equivalent.

The annunciation to Zakariyya of his coming son while he is worshipping is similar in both narratives: he is told he and his wife will have a blessed son as an answer to their prayers, despite their age. Ibn Kathir says that he had prayed for a son because he understood the miraculous supply of fruits that were out of season to Mary (3:37) as being analogous to him and his wife producing a child "out of season." In Luke "he will be great in the eyes of the Lord. He shall never touch wine or strong drink. From his birth he will be filled with the Holy Spirit; and he will bring back many Israelites to the Lord their God." (1:25-27) The Qur'an says he is "noble, chaste and righteous" and of Zakariyya's wife, "We healed his wife for him." This is followed by a period when the father cannot speak, until the time when "these things happen to you" in Luke 1:20, and for three nights in the Qur'an. (19:10) In the Qur'an, it is specified that the name is a first, while in the Bible the name is mentioned in Luke 1:61 as being a name that *nobody in the family* has. It is when the people question Zechariah about the name and he writes down that the child's name shall be John that he speaks again. At some point after this he prophesies:

"And thou, child, shalt be called the prophet of the Highest: for thou shall go before the face of the Lord to prepare his ways; to give knowledge of salvation unto his people by the remission of their sins, through the tender mercy of our God; whereby the day-spring from on high hath visited us, to give light to them that sit in darkness and in the shadow of death, to guide our feet into the way of peace." (Luke 1:76-79)

The Qur'an says: "O Yahya, hold fast to the Book." This message was probably given to him in his childhood because this immediately precedes the *aya* where the Qur'an says: "And We gave him wisdom when he was a boy, and compassion from Our presence, and purity – and he had *taqwa*, and he was kind to his parents, and he was never tyrannical or rebellious." (19:12-14) In *Ash-Shifa*, Qadi Iyad says that the children used to ask why Yahya did not play with them and were met with the reply of someone who knew from a young age why he was here: "Was I created for playing games?"[115]

---

[115] Qadi 'Iyad: 1.2.10

A little later the same book says: "Mujahid said, 'Yahya's food was herbs. He used to weep out of fear of God until the tears made ridges in his cheeks. He used to eat with the wild animals to avoid mixing with people.'" (Ash-Shifa' of Qadi 'Iyad: 1.2.24)

This is a tradition similar to that found in Luke who says that John grew up strong and was in the wilderness for most of his life, at least until he began prophesying in his own right to the people of Israel. He is first seen elsewhere in the New Testament in this light as an ascetic, living on locusts and wild honey, and dressed in the simplest traditional prophet's clothing of camelhair covering with a leather girdle.

When John begins his mission, Matthew says that he fulfils Isaiah's prophecy of "the voice of one crying in the wilderness, Prepare ye the way of the Lord, make his paths straight." (Matthew 3:3 referring to Isaiah 40:3) Mark 1:3, Luke 3:4 and John 1:23 say the same.

At the beginning of the Book of John we read: "He was not that Light, but was sent to bear witness to that light." (John 1:8) He was to (re)open the way for all those who had been excluded from the authentic worship of God, to receive the repentance of the people of Judea and to wash them clean of their sins to prepare them for the one who was to come. As he says:

"I have baptised you with water; he will baptise you with the Holy Spirit." (Mark 1:8)

Baptism, unlike circumcision, did not exclude women and, as Walter Wink writes in the Oxford Companion to the Bible, both John's dress and use of metaphor identified him with "the lowly". His message was that being a descendant of Abraham was not enough to guarantee salvation, and that this lineage was, if anything, being abused by those of that line who imagined that nothing else was required of them except their genes. One day, when many Pharisees and Sadducees came for baptism, he said:

"O generation of vipers, who hath warned you to flee from the wrath to come? Bring forth therefore fruits meet for repentance: And think not to say within yourselves, We have Abraham to our father: for I say unto

247

you, that God is able of these stones to raise up children unto Abraham." (Matthew 3:7-9)

He elaborated that any tree that did not bring forth good fruit would be cut down and thrown into the fire. Very similar words are used in Luke 3:7-9 but are addressed to "the multitude" rather than just the Pharisees and Sadducees and when the multitude asks what to do he says that anyone who has two coats should give to those who have none and similarly with food.

Such was the power of his oration and the manner of his birth that all the Jewish people, according to the contemporary historian Josephus, regarded him highly. (Josephus speaks more and better of him than he does of Jesus). He was "a good man (who) commanded the Jews to exercise virtue, both as to righteousness to one another and piety towards God, and so to come to baptism."[116]

Some did, in fact, actually think that John the Baptist was the Messiah himself. "When the Jews sent priests and Levites from Jerusalem to ask him, Who art thou? And he confessed and denied not; but confessed, I am not the Christ. And they asked him, What then? Art thou Elias? (Elijah) And he saith, I am not." (John 1:19-21) In Matthew, in contradiction to this, however, Jesus *does* refer to John as being Elias: "Elias truly shall first come, and restore all things, but I say unto you, that Elias is come already, and they knew him not... then the disciples understood that he spake unto them of John the Baptist." (Matthew 17:11-13)

The new rite that celebrated this was baptism in the Jordan. As Joshua had led the people through the river to take possession of the land before, so now baptism by immersion in the same river would be the sign of the new Israel. The twelve stones referred to in Matthew 3:9, the ones that had been raised at the time of Joshua at the parting of the river, would become twelve new tribes if repentance was not forthcoming. Jesus, the one who will come after, "shall baptise you with the Holy Spirit, and with fire." (Matthew 3:11 & Luke 3:16)

---

[116] Josephus *Ant.* 18.5.2

Though similar in form to cleansing before Temple worship, this baptism was closer to the purification that preceded conversion, though spiritual rebirth through immersion in (running) water was quite new. John has been linked to the Essenes at Qumran, to the point where the promotional film at the site now says that he left in controversial fashion, and one of the Dead Sea Scrolls[117] refers to the purificatory rite of bathing in "seas and rivers" before entering the Covenant. This "peculiar and solemn act" according to Geza Vermes, is a symbolic purification by the "spirit of holiness":

"For it is through the spirit of true counsel concerning the ways of man that all his sins shall be expiated that he may contemplate the light of life. He shall be cleansed from all his sins by the spirit of holiness... and when his flesh is sprinkled with purifying water and sanctified by cleansing water, it shall be made clean by the humble submission of his soul to all the precepts of God."

Josephus explains in a similar way that the baptism that John carried out was not for the remission of sins committed before but for the purification of the body after the purification of the soul had been carried out.

The baptism of Jesus marks the beginning of his ministry because when Jesus has been baptised by John, Matthew says: "Lo, the heavens were opened unto him, and he saw the Spirit of God descending like a dove, and lighting upon him: And lo a voice from heaven saying, This is my beloved Son, in whom I am well pleased." (Matthew 3:16-17) The same incident is described in Mark 1:10-11 in exactly the same words.

With Jesus confirmed in his mission, John now "wanes." Because of his teachings, and particularly because he reproves Herod for his adultery with Herodias,[118] his brother Philip's wife, John is imprisoned in Mechareus (Miqawer in present-day Jordan), one of Herod's palaces.

---

[117] *Community Rule III, V*
[118] In Flaubert's novella *Herodias*, Herod, complains: "People are most unfair to me, for when all is said and done, Absalom slept with his father's wives, Judah with his daughter-in-law, Ammon with his sister and Lot with his daughters."

According to the New Testament, he would have been put to death immediately but for fears of popular insurrection, though Josephus says the opposite, that he is executed to *stop* him doing this, so incendiary is his eloquence – "it would be much better to strike first." There is ambiguity in the Bible too, where Herod "liked to listen to him, although the listening left him greatly perplexed." (Mark 6:20)

While he is in prison, John sends a message asking: "Are you the one who is to come or are we to expect some other?" Jesus' reply talks of his own miracles and good news, implying, though not saying, that he *is* the one. Then, as the one who has prepared the way, Jesus calls John the greatest of the Israelite prophets: "Verily I say unto you, among them that are born of women there has not risen a greater than John the Baptist: notwithstanding he that is least in the kingdom of heaven is greater than he." (Matthew 11:11)

This section is one that Muslim scholars have pointed to as describing a Prophet after Jesus. According to Ahmed Deedat, "the least" referred to here can only be a prophet who is still in the kingdom of heaven, and who is "the least", the last, in other words, the Prophet Muhammad. Personally, I do find it a little difficult to be completely persuaded by this interpretation of this particular phrase. However, the question John has just asked about "some other" suggests that even *he* thought there might be another, even though he had seen Jesus and baptised him. It seems that it is a bit late in the day to be asking this question now if there is some contradiction between Jesus being the Messiah *and* the one, though none if he were asking if Jesus were the Messiah *or* the one.

On the same line of argument is an earlier occasion, when John the Baptist is asked a final question by the priests and Levites as to who he is: "He confessed, and denied not; but confessed, I am not the Christ. And they (the priests) asked him, What then? Art thou Elias? And he saith, I am not. Art thou that prophet? And he answered, No." (John 1:20-21) "That prophet," argues Deedat, can only be the one who has been spoken of since Deuteronomy 18:18, namely the Prophet Muhammad.

Whatever the exact nature of his message, John's imprisonment was to end with his death. At a great feast, Herod, by now infatuated with Herodias' daughter Salome, promises the girl anything after she has danced for him.[119] On her mother's request she asks for John's head on a platter. Herod is reluctant, but he has given an oath in front of the people he is eating with and is thus forced to give the order. On being given the head, Salome presents it to her mother. Matthew records that the followers of John bury him (14:12) and that, on hearing the news, Jesus goes by ship to "a desert place apart." (Matthew 14:13)[120] For his part, Herod's army is destroyed in battle with Aretas, the father of Phasaelis, who had been divorced to allow Herod to marry Herodias, a battle that was fought over the divorce issue. This event, Josephus says, the Jews attributed to God's punishment.

The earlier quoted Qur'anic *ayat* concludes: "Peace be on him the day he was born, and the day he died, and the day he will be brought back to life." (19:15) His grave is believed to be in at least two places – the Umayyah Mosque in Syria and in the ancient town of Samaria (now Sebastya) near Nablus.

Deedat, A. *Muhammad (Peace be upon him) – The Greatest* (1990) IPCI: Durban
Deedat, A. *Muhammad (Peace be upon him) – The natural Successor to Christ* (1990) IPCI: Durban
Deedat, A. *What the Bible says about Muhammad (Peace be upon him)* (1995) IPCI: Durban
Faulkner, N. *Apocalypse – The Great Jewish Revolt Against Rome AD 66-73* (2002) Tempus: Stroud
Flaubert, G. *Herodias* from *Three Tales* (1961) Penguin: London
Ibn Kathir, I. *Stories of the Prophets* (2003) Darrusalam: Riyadh
Josephus, *Antiquities of the Jews* (2006) Cosimo Inc.: New York
Lane Fox, R. *The Unauthorised Version* (1991) Penguin: London

---

[119] In Mark 6:24-5, Salome goes out to ask her mother what to ask for. In excavating Miqawer, archaeologists found two adjoining rooms at the site and identified them as adjoining dining rooms, concluding that the guests had been separated by gender at the meal.

[120] It is at this point that the crowds follow him and he performs the miracle of the loaves and the fishes.

Qadi 'Iyad *Ash-Shifa (Muhammad: Messenger of Allah,* Translated by
'Aisha Abdur-Rahman Bewley (2004) Medina Books: Riyadh
Seale, M.S. *Qur'an and Bible (*1978) Croon Helm: London
Vermes, G. *The Dead Sea Scrolls in English* (1962) Penguin: London

19

JESUS

Why can't everybody wait and see? If the Messiah comes saying, 'Hello, it's nice to see you again,' then the Jews will have to concede. If, on the other hand, he comes saying, 'How do you do?' then the entire Christian world will have to apologise to the Jews. Until that time, why don't we just live and let live?
(Amos Oz's Grandmother)

The most obvious disagreement regarding Jesus is between Jews and Christians; he was a Jew, but he is the central figure in Christianity, the religion that takes its name from what Christians believe was the reason for his coming, namely to be the Christ, Greek for Messiah. Amos Oz' grandmother, understandably, omits a third interested party – the Muslim one – which has much to say about him too, as we shall see. However, the principle of her comment seems to be sound; though all faiths feel endorsed by their Books, there is an ambiguity within and between them that requires faith, patience, understanding and openness in dealing with the Other. Though this has been true with all the Prophets so far, it becomes especially important with Jesus because each faith, in one way or another, defines itself in relation to him.

Somewhat over two thousand years ago, the Children of Israel did expect something momentous. The brief period of Jewish independence and expansion under the Hasmoneans (the Maccabis) between 142 and 102 BCE seems to be the time that is mentioned in the Qur'an in the Chapter entitle 'Bani Isra'il', also sometimes called 'The Night Journey':

"Then we granted you an upper hand against them, and strengthened you with wealth and children, and multiplied your numbers. Whenever you did good, it was to your own advantage; and whenever you committed evil, it was to your own disadvantage." (17:6)

The former part of the verse could encompass these times of independence, the fact that as much as a tenth of the population of the Roman Empire was Jewish, and that, as Neil Faulkner says, Herod was "the greatest king since Solomon". It would be hard to argue that he did great service to his faith but, like Solomon, he did build the Temple and, in terms of other buildings, no ruler has left a greater number of palaces around the Holy Land. If this is so, then the latter part of the verse seems to refer to the breakdown into civil war after the brief period of independence and the partly wished-for Roman takeover, all of which caused great soul-searching among the Children of Israel. Death, immortality and divine judgement became matters of debate and the subject of writing, and the feeling grew that this anguish was leading to the "End of Days". The key event in this time would be the coming of the Messiah, but what this Messiah was expected to do was to challenge the Romans. Jews did not anticipate that he would, first and foremost, challenge *them*, which is essentially what Christians and Muslims believe. As Jesus in many ways did not match Jewish expectations, the question as to how Jesus was and is seen by Jews, as Clive Lawton says, "doesn't come into our frame of reference." He is as relevant to them as, he compares, Muhammad is to Christians. (So, more than you think, we say.)

Jesus, miraculously born of a virgin mother, who ascended to heaven at the end of his life to await his return to earth for a final confrontation at the end of days, is a figure common to both Muslims and Christians. It is the arguments as to the nature of Jesus that divide - the God-in-person, the Trinity - beliefs that seem to be essential to the Christian belief that theirs is the final revelation. From a Muslim point of view, though, they are arguments that, in trying to elevate Jesus, obscure part of his universal significance, not as the Prince of Peace, but as his forerunner.

From the Muslim point of view, but not only, Jesus was a Jew and the Messiah. He did not come to bring a new religion but to re-form Judaism, to put within it a heart of flesh rather than a heart of stone - where the Word of God as given to Moses had been written in stone, the Word that Jesus brought was in his heart, "the Word made flesh." Muslims see the Jewish response as part of a familiar pattern; as they had done before, the majority of Jews rejected both Prophet and message. However, this time there would be no more messengers, not sent to the Jews alone anyway. As "a mercy to the worlds", Muslims can see how his time on earth could lead to a spreading of the worship of One God in the years after his life and view this as a mercy from God. At the same time though, a religion founded in his name does not neatly fit the struggle/submission paradigm that this book at least has tried to describe, a fact that may suggest that we are all missing something.

In the Church of the Holy Sepulchre in Jerusalem, beneath the site of the place Christians believe the crucifixion took place, is a place that is known as the Chapel of Adam. The place was identified, legend has it, following a dream by Saint Helena, the mother of Roman Emperor Constantine, and the skull of Adam was found there. Its position for early Christians gained its significance from the symbolism of the blood of Jesus flowing down and washing away the sins of the first man.

We have no way of knowing the geographical truth of this but what it highlights is the position of Jesus in Christian belief and the necessity of his coming to vanquish humanity's 'Original Sin'. Christians believe humanity was innately flawed by the sin of Adam's disobedience in the Garden until Jesus died to cleanse humanity of that flaw. Thence, people had only to believe in him, or Him, to be saved and to receive eternal life. In contrast, Muslims believe that our Adamic nature means that we are clay animated by the breath of God and so contain reflections of all the supreme attributes of God (who, among many attributes, is the Compassionate, *Al-Rahman*, the Merciful, *Al-Raheem*). Our flaw is that we have the susceptibility to be tempted by Shaytan because, according to the *Hadith* mentioned before, except for Jesus and his mother Mary, our hearts have all been touched at birth by Shaytan. He tempts us through our earthly natures, our appetites, (as we saw when we considered Adam), and he can assume many guises to do so. Thus, what we need is knowledge of a way to live with this nature, which we believe we have in Islam. We see Jesus, among others, as being an example of how to live with this nature, rather than as performing its cosmic reparation.

In comparing Jesus as he appears in the Bible, or at least in traditional Christian belief, with Jesus ('Isa) in the Qur'an there appear to be four further differences. The first of these is that the life and meaning of the Qur'anic Jesus is described relatively briefly and simply, while the life and meaning of the Jesus of the Bible are depicted in both an extensive and often contradictory way. This difference amplifies the other three main differences, these being: who Jesus came for; his nature - whether Prophet and Messiah, or Son of God, or God Himself (from which comes the uniqueness of God or the existence of the Holy Trinity); and finally, the appearance or fact of the Crucifixion. We can say that 'Isa, the Jewish Messiah, a human Prophet of supernatural birth, serving God, and not being crucified despite appearances, essentially characterises the Islamic viewpoint, (though we will return to this last point later), while Jesus as the supernatural Son of God, one of the Holy Trinity, crucified for humanity's sins, broadly (though not entirely) characterises the Christian.

The question of whom Jesus came to helps us to focus on where the sense lies in these points of view. Even if we consider Jesus as he is depicted in the Synoptic Gospels (those of Matthew, Mark and Luke) he seems to have come for the Jews alone. In Matthew we read:

"These twelve (disciples) sent forth, and commanded them, saying 'Go not into the way of the Gentiles, and into any city of the Samaritans enter ye not. But go rather to the lost sheep of the house of Israel.'" (Matthew 10:5-6)

He preached the coming of the kingdom of God (though he also described the kingdom of God as here already, but existing as a seed that was beginning to grow) and called the people of Israel into it, using parables of weddings and feasts (Luke 14:15-24 & Matthew). These parables were used because they were things that most would recognise, though Jesus also refers back to Isaiah (6:9-10) who said that the people would hear but not understand, and see but not perceive.

Similarly, in the Qur'an, Jesus, 'Isa, the son who was born to Maryam, the Angel Gabriel (Jibreel) said would be "a Messenger to the Tribe of Israel" (3:48), and "a pattern for the Tribe of Israel" (43:59). He would be the last of a succession of Jewish Prophets, "confirming what was revealed before him in the Torah and a guide to those who have *Taqwa* (fear of God)" (5:46); he would be taught by God in wisdom, in the

Book, the Torah and the *Injeel* (the Gospel). However, he would also be of universal significance - "a sign for mankind, a mercy from Us" (19:21), a "sign to all the worlds" (21:91) and "illustrious in the world" (3:45). Significantly though, he did not intend to found a new faith. That would come later, chiefly through Paul, as we will see. Inasmuch as this brought belief in God to many people, Muslims have no problem seeing in this a "mercy" and "sign to the worlds." However, this is not the same as recognising the establishment of a new religion, particularly one that has a different conception of God to the one that existed in Judaism. Having said that, the Qur'an also says that Christians are closer to Muslims than Jews, in a way that suggests that here spiritual differences are greater, and more important:

"You will find the most vehement of mankind in hostility to be the Jews and idolaters. And you will find the nearest of them in affection to be those who say: Look! We are Christians. That is because there are among them priests and monks, and because they are not proud." (5:82)

Some people also relate the last two verses of the opening chapter of the Qur'an to these three Peoples of the Book, respectively, Muslims, Jews and Christians:

"Guide us to the Straight way. The way of those on whom You have bestowed Your Grace, not (the way) of those who have earned your anger, nor of those who have gone astray." (1:6-7)

There are doctrinal differences, though, and the biggest difference between Christianity and Islam concerns the very nature of Jesus, and hence of God. Surat Al-Ikhlas ('The Chapter of Purity') in the Qur'an is said in a *Hadith*, a saying of the Prophet Muhammad, to be equivalent to half the Qur'an. It says:

"God is One, the Eternal God. He begetteth none, nor was He begotten. None is equal to Him." (112:1-4)

It asserts unambiguously the uniqueness of God and, in "He begetteth none", specifically states that a Son of God, in the literal sense, is anathema; God was not his father.[121] Another verse says: "Those who say: 'Verily God is the Messiah, son of Maryam,' have indeed disbelieved." (5:17)

It seems fair to say that, as the central plank in Christianity's whole foundation, neither Jesus the Son of God nor Jesus as God in human form finds anything like unambiguous expression in the New Testament either. When, addressing Jesus as "Good Master", a rich man asks what he should do to inherit eternal life. Before he gives his reply, Jesus says: "Why callest thou me good? None is good, save one, that is, God." (Luke 18:19) These are not the words of one who thinks HE is God. Mostly the 'Son of God' claim rests on how you read the Gospel of John and that, as we shall see, is debatable, too.

Though Muslims do not see Jesus as God, he is nonetheless different. Like Adam, he was born without a father. Also, unlike the Prophets of the Jewish Bible, he does not seem to speak words given to him by God. As Christian commentators Cupitt and Armstrong put it: "On the contrary, he speaks with great immediacy and freedom on his own authority, often without appealing to the authority of either God, scripture or tradition."[122] Though the Qur'an says that his words were from God – "I spoke to them only what you commanded me"[123] - this does not contradict Muslim belief that the essence of the message was the same as all the Prophets before. As we have mentioned, Muslims often understand the Book he brought, the *Injeel,* to be his heart, and this book was, by definition, written by God.

The Qur'an also says that he was even more blessed than some of the Prophets - "And of these messengers We have made some to excel others... and We gave 'Isa son of Maryam clear signs and strengthened him with the pure spirit." (2:253) What was different about him was an essential purity of spirit. Expressed in the above-mentioned *Hadith* transmitted by Abu Hurayra, the Prophet Muhammad said, "There is

---

[121] South African Ahmad Deedat, in 'Christ in Islam' makes the point that the effect of using the word 'begotten' makes us think that the father will look the same. Thus, the "begotten Son" who we see depicted invariably as a white man in churches will, the mind is bound to think, have a father, God, who is also white.
[122] Cupitt & Armstrong (1977) p.64
[123] 5:117

no-one born among the Tribe of Adam who is not touched by Shaytan at the time of birth - and it is the touch of Shaytan which makes a child cry when it is born - except for Maryam and her son." (Al-Bukhari)

Though Jesus is, according to Professor Tarif Khalidi, "more than any equivalent Prophetic figure... placed inside a theological argument rather than inside a narrative," some of these arguments are clarified by the telling of the story, first considering "Maryam and her son."

In both tellings of the story, there is something like the Annunciation. In the Qur'an, Mary is identified as "preferred above (all) the women of creation" (3:42), who has withdrawn to a secluded "chamber looking East" when the angel Gabriel comes to tell her that she will bear the Messiah Jesus. When she asks how this can be "when no mortal has touched me", the angel says that God only has to say, "Be!" and it is, a word that has been linked with the very creation of the universe, and the saying: "In the beginning was the Word, and the Word was with God." In contrast, the New Testament specifies the Holy Spirit as the agent of the conception. Matthew says that she "found she was with child by the Holy Spirit" (Matthew 1:19), while in Luke the exchange when the angel visits her in Nazareth is more developed. It begins as in the Qur'an with Mary asking how she could bear a child when she is a virgin, to which the angel says: "The Holy Spirit will come upon you, and the power of the Most High will overshadow you; and for that reason the holy child to be born will be called 'Son of God.'" (Luke 1:35-6) In both cases, Mary is betrothed to Joseph who is, we are told, of David's line, an important point because the Messiah was to be of that lineage, but irrelevant because Joseph is not supposed to be the biological father. The effect of this, though, is to encourage the mind to think the unthinkable: that he is.

The events before the birth of Jesus are thus very similar in form but profoundly different in implication, to the point where some Christians could say, "God became a baby." This is not to say that the child was not remarkable. An event not found in the Bible is described in the Qur'an, when Maryam takes the child back to her people. On seeing the child, they immediately conclude the worst and say: "O Maryam, you have indeed come with something deceitful! O sister of Haroun, your father was not a wicked man and your mother was never

259

immoral!" (19:28) Obeying the command to keep her silence, her reply is simply to point at the child, who begins speaking: "Verily I am the slave of God. He has given me the Book, and He has made me a Prophet, and He has made me blessed wherever I may be, and He has made the prayer and the *zakat* (almsgiving) obligatory for me as long as I live, and He has made me obedient towards the one who bore me, and He has not made me tyrannical or ungrateful - and peace be on me the day I was born, and the day I die, and the day I shall be brought back to life!" (19:33)

That the people around knew they were in the presence of someone special is highlighted by a commentary made by Sayyid Mawdudi on this incident. He makes the point that Mary was not an unknown woman, but a God-fearing and devout one of the house of Aaron whose guardian was the highly respected Jerusalem patriarch, Zechariah. She had lived a life of devotion, secluded for much of the time in the Temple. Thus, pregnancy and birth would hardly be unnoticed, and the refutation from the mouth of the infant would be an event that many would know about and remember, should this child grow up to claim himself to be a Prophet, as of course he did. Mawdudi says:

"Now, if those people still refused to recognise him as a Prophet, and instead of dutifully following him, charged him with being a criminal and sought to crucify him, they should be dealt a punishment more severe than that meted out to all other peoples."

The narrative version of the life of Jesus is perhaps less important than any other Prophet because it is what his life (and particularly his end) meant that is crucial. Very little is recorded of the time from his birth to the time of his ministry. Then, when 'Isa began teaching, his message was to bring the Children of Israel back to the teachings of Moses in accordance with the Torah, "to make plain some of that about which you differ" (43:63) and "to make some of what used to be forbidden for you lawful for you." (3:50) He brought the *Injeel*, the Gospel, though this was not a written book. Rather, he was "the word made flesh." The wisdom he had he carried in his heart and it showed in his actions and words. He healed the blind and the lepers, he raised the dead with the permission of God, he breathed life into a clay bird he had made and it became a live bird, (actions that could easily be connected with

Divinity if you so chose), and he could tell people what they had eaten and what they had stored away at home, all in the name of God, of Allah.

Of his life, even Jewish writers can find little that is fundamentally disconcerting. Much, in fact, is very familiar; he is Jewish after all. Clive Lawton plays down some of the more radical changes he announced, claiming that they are merely rhetorical points that are typical of Jewish discourse and are not to be taken literally. Jewish scholars such as Joseph Klausner and Jacob Neusner have criticised him, respectively, for focusing on the ethical over the national and for focusing on heaven over earth, though these charges are relative and could be argued or compared to many Biblical Prophets from before, particularly the Great Prophets, Isaiah, Jeremiah and Ezekiel. Geza Vermes calls him a great man and says that he had "genius… (and)…laid bare the inner core of spiritual truth and exposed the essence of religion as an existential relationship between man and man, and man and God." He, and all of them, can say these things without their sense of themselves as believing Jews being threatened. Essentially, Jews believe that there was nothing fundamental about their faith that needed reforming, so a Messiah who only brought such a message was unnecessary.

Christians and Muslims, on the other hand, believe that, in the end, his message proclaimed something different to the religion that was being practised by the Children of Israel at that time, most particularly by the Jewish priesthood, the Sadducees and Pharisees, and something different to the political struggle the revolutionaries wanted, and it is because of this that he was rejected by the majority of the Jewish people.

Most of the gospels agree that after the death of John the Baptist, Jesus went up to Jerusalem to take his message to the people there and this is when he "cleansed" the Temple of its moneylenders. This, according to Professor John Dominic Crossan of De Paul University, symbolically destroyed the Temple, but in the short-term at least, it brought him into conflict with the religious authorities. According to the Qur'an as well as the New Testament, they plotted to have him killed, fearing that as well as threatening their authority, Jesus was likely to provoke a violent

Roman reaction. If there is truth in the story of the robber or insurrectionist Barabbas, whose crucifixion Pontius Pilate unsuccessfully offered to the crowd as an alternative to that of Jesus, both sides of the Jewish community, rebels and reactionaries, tried to have Jesus killed. However, according to the Qur'an, they did not succeed: "And they planned, and God planned - and God is the best of planners." (3:54)

It is this, the end of Jesus' time on earth, which provides the final departure point for Muslims and Christians, but also for Christians and Jews. In the New Testament, at the farewell meal on the eve of Passover, *Pesach,* Jesus speaks of his coming death as the climax of his life. He associates the bread that he breaks with his person, and the wine with his blood, his death, and he tells the disciples that the kingdom of God lies beyond his death. In many ways the origins of Christianity lie in a transformation of imagery that begins here. For Jews, the passage from slavery to freedom is commemorated at this same Passover meal, the *Seder.* For Christians, the New Covenant is commemorated at communion, which recalls this Last Supper at the feast of Passover. In Christian symbolism this meal not only represents the transformation of the bread and the wine into body and spirit, but it also transforms Judaism into a universal faith. For Christians, the People are now the Gentiles *and* the Jews, rather than just the Jews, and the whole world becomes Israel, God's kingdom, rather than just the Promised Land of Israel.

On the level of story there is a change here, and on the level of symbolism there is a requirement that something like a sacrifice is required to mark this birth of a new consciousness. Drawing on a belief related to sacrifice, there is the need for something undeserving of full human sympathy to carry the sin. This is the origin of the term scapegoat, where that thing was literally a goat, recalling Abraham's sacrifice. However, in common usage, a scapegoat refers to a person, and that is what happens here.

The traditional Christian depiction of the disciples at the meal and after is that they are a group, with the exception of Judas who is the one who is different, the one who is the outsider. In some Medieval Passion plays, and in Christian mythology since, Judas often appears as if he is

262

the only Jew. There is some doubt as to whether he really existed and whether he was the Betrayer. However, there is little doubt that he was a mythical, psychological and theological necessity. Howard Jacobson, in the television programme 'Sorry, Judas!' calls him a "shadow Jesus", a point Hyam Maccoby elaborates on:

"The reason is that the violent death of the divine sacrifice, while it brings salvation to the community, cannot be thought of to have been wished by the community. There has to be, therefore, an evil figure, or group of figures, on whom the death can be blamed. This is the Black Christ, who sacrifices his soul for the community of believers, while the White Christ sacrifices only his body. Judas brings salvation no less than Jesus, but this can never be acknowledged, for the company of the saved must preserve their attitude of mourning for the death of the necessary sacrifice."

The personal tragedy of Judas within the myth is that he loved Jesus but felt unloved by him, and that he was merely doing what he had felt inwardly compelled to do. What may not have been wished by the community was desired by God, that: "One of you shall betray me." According to all four gospels, a rare piece of unanimity, this is Judas' role.

In the Garden of Gethsemane after the Last Supper, Judas leads the Temple police (and Roman soldiers according to the Gospel of John) to arrest Jesus, and shows them the one they are to arrest with a kiss. In this kiss of betrayal Judas thus becomes the representative Jew parting company with Christians. For a brief moment there is a union of "good" and "evil" before Jesus departs into sanctity, and Judas into Hell, a Hell that Christians would often feel free to try and replicate on earth for Jews in the coming centuries.

For this, Hyam Maccoby calls him "the archetype of the Betrayer, without whom the drama of redemption would have been incomplete." Howard Jacobson puts it more angrily, saying: "Load all the obloquy on the one apostle whose name means Jew, and the Church can wash its hands of its Hebrew origins."

Jacobson, as mentioned, calls him a "shadow Jesus," and in him we can see merging the individual and collective personae. As an individual, he is the weak link in the group that surrounds Jesus who helps those hostile to him to capture him. Due to the "unfortunate coincidence" of his name, he is naturally identified with the Jewish people, which Hyam Maccoby believes to be a logical inference from the Gospel story. Both were possessed by Satan, both rejected Jesus and both paid through suffering a pitiable death. "Judas plays out on an individual level the role of treachery assigned to the Jewish people." In light of how convenient all this is, Howard Jacobson's reasonable request is that Christians not only apologise to Judas, but that they actually thank him. He thought along the lines of having him canonised by the Catholic Church. (There is a Saint Judas in some Orthodox Churches). He received an honest, though discouraging, answer from Kevin Thomas of the Catholic Media Office:

"Judas is a figure for we Christians of what we are like when we are not good Christians."

This is the same pattern as that which traditionally characterises the relationship of Christians and Jews (and later, Muslims, and other Others), the external "darkness" delineating the boundaries of the Christian "enlightened" self-image. "The Jews are what we good Christians are not." Perhaps the main trouble with the accepted Christian story is the inappropriately pure self-image the 'divine Jesus' loans them, and what this has done to the Christian perception of the Other. The first group to suffer from this was the Jews.

Much of the diabolisation of the Jews is attributed to the Gospel of John, usually regarded as the most historically unreliable of the Gospels. It includes the supremely damning phrase: "Your father is the devil and you choose to carry out your father's desires." (John 8:44) Much of the anti-Jewish invective concerns the Jews' collective refusal to heed Jesus' message and one such exchange carries particular significance in setting the pattern of Judeo-Christian relations over the next two thousand years.

The confrontation takes place when Jesus is walking alone through the Temple and is confronted by angry Jews; he has, after all, recently thrown out the moneylenders. The argument culminates in Jesus saying "I and my father are one," (John 10:30) which is seen as a defining point where Christians see Jesus as saying straightforwardly who he is and the Jews are seen as saying that Jesus is committing blasphemy and twisting everything to reject the truth that he brings.

How accurate this confrontation is we do not know, but even based on what it actually contains, it is not possible to strongly sustain the argument that this is about the Divinity of Jesus. As Ahmed Deedat points out in 'Christ in Islam', the context of this one line in the confrontation means that Jesus is saying that "I and my father are one" in *purpose*, not power, nor knowledge, nor nature. This would mean that it is not only the Jews twisting words, if indeed they did, but Christians too.

"One in purpose" is consistent with the Muslim point of view, which sees Jesus as Prophet and Messiah. Jews may have rejected him and they may have accused him of blasphemy, but these are two separate issues that may have been conflated by Christian writers after. What is certain for us is that Jesus would not have made a blasphemous claim of this sort. Thus, from the Muslim point of view, both parties were wrong in different ways and at different times. Jews were wrong at the time to reject him as Messiah and Prophet, and Christians have been wrong since in seeing that rejection as being on the basis of a rejection of Christ's divinity.

This should considerably lessen the vehemence of Christian vilification of Jews for this supposed reason, because something like two wrongs do not make a right. It is a classic case of psychological projection, in fact, where the (Christian) self cannot recognise the flaw in itself but can see a flaw in the Other, its shadow self, "the Jew," which it proceeds to hate, in magnified form. Tragically for both parties, no amount of persecution of that Other will satisfy the self, because the self will always feel the nagging sense of its own wrongness within.

This is not to say that at least some Jews, for whatever reason, did not wish to silence Jesus. According to the Gospels, he has a hearing in front of the Jewish authorities and they conclude that there are enough grounds for him to be tried by the Romans for high treason. The

265

Gospels then say that he is condemned to death by them and crucified with two criminals. He dies on the same day and is buried by sympathisers. To Christians, what happened next, after Jesus' death, is more important than anything he achieved in his life for, according to Christian interpretation of the New Testament, he rose bodily from the grave, thus triumphing over death and cleansing humanity of Adam's primordial sin, before ascending to heaven to sit at God's right hand.

The Muslim understanding is different. According to most understandings of the Qur'an, though there was the Jewish wish for the death of Jesus, and his ascension into heaven took place (a mosque in Jerusalem commemorates it), there was no crucifixion, at least, not of Jesus. As Seyyed Hossein Nasr says: "This is one irreducible 'fact' separating Christianity and Islam, a fact that is placed there providentially to prevent a mingling of the two religions." The relevant words from the Qur'an begin with:

"And they (the Jews) did not kill him and they did not crucify him, but it appeared so to them." (4:157)

If we read this common translation, there is immediately some apparent ambiguity in these words, because they could mean that someone else did the crucifying, such as the Romans, (which was the case), rather than that he was not crucified. In other words, it is a question of whether 'they' or 'kill' or 'him' or 'crucify' are stressed. Because of this, some translations are more explicit, though only through implication. Thus, one says that: "…only a likeness of that was shown to them", rather than "…but so it appeared to them." This is a far more active sense that suggests that there was a substitution of the crucified person.

This is probably more of a disputed area in Islam than we are generally aware of. Writing in 1929, Rev. James Robson says:

"The learned have differed concerning his death before his being raised up. Some say, 'He was raised up and did not die.' Others say, 'No, God made him die for three hours.' Others say, 'For seven hours, then He brought him back to life.' And those who say this are expounding His

266

saying (Exalted is He!), 'Verily I will cause you to die and will raise you to myself.' (3:55)"

This final quoted line can also be translated as "I will take thee and raise thee..."[124], though the word *mutawafeeka* generally carries the meaning of taking in death.

In a less globalised world, it is possible that debate on such issues as this[125], would have been of little direct interest to the majority within the faith nor to those with little awareness outside it. In modern times, where we are more aware of our Others, such internal debates could be perceived as showing weakness to "our enemies," which could discourage debate for different reasons. A mirror silence around the non-divinity of Jesus within Christianity may be for a similar reason. After all, if Muslims start believing in the crucifixion and Christians start believing that Jesus was not the son of God, where will we be?[126]

As if in answer to this question, the specific chapter continues:

"And verily those who disagree with this cannot be sure - they have no knowledge about it except their speculation. They did not kill him for certain. God took him up to Himself. And there is not one of the People of the Book who will not believe in him before his death - and on the Day of Standing he will be a witness against them." (4:157-159)

It has to be said here, by a Muslim who accepts the Qur'an as the literal word of God, that He, in His Infinite Wisdom, has done it again and left a thread of ambiguity running through a defining incident. As we have seen, there is no cast-iron certainty around that other major would-be sacrifice, Abraham's son. We cannot exactly, any of us, say for certain whether it was Isaac or Isma'il, and we cannot definitively say whether it was Mecca or Jerusalem (or Nablus for that matter).

So too here. This section and its translations are half bracketed-inference within bracketed-inference (see footnote for three more

---

[124] Yusuf Ali translation
[125] And the identity of the would-be sacrificed son of Abraham, among others.
[126] Um, believing the same thing?! And if Jews can no longer reject Jesus for claims that he is the son of God...?

versions)[127] that almost ask as many questions as they answer. The Hilali/Khan version infers the common Muslim belief that a likeness was substituted for Jesus, but we do not find such an explicit understanding in the other two versions. All that is stated for certain is that the Jews did not kill him, thus releasing Jews from the centuries-old anti-Semitic blood libel. There is then the ambiguity in 4:159 as to whether "his death" refers to the death of each one of the People of the Scriptures (therefore in chronological time), or whether it refers to the death of Jesus (presumably at the time of the Last Judgement, though possibly if he died on the cross). At this point, whichever it is, the People of the Scripture will understand. Asad says that it is the former and that they will believe *at the moment* of their deaths, while Pickthall understands that they will believe in him some time *before* their deaths, while Hilali/Khan say that they "must" do this, implying "or else..."

---

[127] And because of their saying (in boast): "We killed Messiah Jesus, son of Maryam, the Messenger of Allah," - but they killed him not nor crucified him, but it appeared so to them [the resemblance of Jesus was put over another man (and they killed that man)], and those who differ therein are full of doubts. They have no (certain) knowledge, they follow nothing but conjecture. For, surely, they killed him not. But Allah raised him up (with his body and soul) unto Himself (and he is in the heavens). And Allah is Ever All-Powerful, All-Wise. And there is none of the People of the Scripture (Jews and Christians) but must believe in him (Jesus, as only a messenger of Allah and a human being) before his [Jesus', or a Jew's or a Christian's] death, (at the time of the appearance of the angel of death). And on the Day of Resurrection he (Jesus) will be a witness against them." (Hilali & Khan)
"And because of their saying: We slew the Messiah, Jesus son of Mary, Allah's messenger - they slew him not nor crucified him, but it appeared so unto them; and lo! Those who disagree concerning it are in doubt thereof; they have no knowledge thereof save pursuit of a conjecture; they slew him not for certain. But Allah took him up unto Himself. Allah was ever Mighty, Wise. There is not one of the People of the Scripture but will believe in him before his death, and on the Day of Resurrection he will be a witness against them." (Pickthall)
"And their boast, "Behold, we have slain the Christ Jesus, son of Mary, [who claimed to be] an apostle of God!" However, they did not slay him, and neither did they crucify him, but it only seemed to them [as if it had been] so; and, verily, those who hold conflicting views thereon are indeed confused, having no [real] knowledge thereof, and following mere conjecture. For, of a certainty, they did not slay him: nay, God exalted him unto Himself – and God is indeed almighty, wise. Yet there is not one of the followers of earlier revelation who does not, at the moment of his death, grasp the truth about Jesus; and on the Day of Resurrection he [himself] shall bear witness to the truth against them." (Asad)

but also the possibility that they will not, if they are really wicked. They also allow that the death referred to could be that of Jesus.

It is interesting, and surely intentional, that we are left with these mysteries within the greater mystery of faith. As with the sacrifice of Abraham, these are defining events, and yet we are not sure. No Jew has satisfactorily explained why the Jews' very disobedience made God choose them as His People; no Christian has properly explained the contradictions around who, or what, Jesus was; and no Muslim has fully explained why Jesus seems to be more important in all of our futures than the Prophet Muhammad (peace be upon them both), nor, for that matter, why the Chosen People are now back in the Holy Land, nor why the Islamic world is languishing so badly in its worldly performance. What the Qur'an seems to suggest, through the words of Jesus, is that some error is understandable, and even forgivable:

"And when God will say (on the Day of Resurrection): O Jesus, son of Mary! Did you say to mankind: Take me and my mother as two gods beside God? He says: Be glorified! It was not mine to utter that to which I had no right. Had I said such a thing, You would surely have known it. You know what is in my mind, and I know not what is in your mind. You, only You, are the knower of Things Hidden. I spoke to them only what you commanded me, (saying): Worship God, my Lord and your Lord. I was a witness of them while I lived among them, and when You took me You were the Watcher over them, and You are Witness over all things. If You punish them, they are Your slaves, and if You forgive them (they are Your slaves). You, only You, are the Mighty, the Wise." (5:116-118)

What is perhaps a little shocking here for some Muslims who are prone to call even Christians *mushriq*, people who attach partners to God, the most detested of all sins in God's eyes, is that Jesus is asking for forgiveness for those (some, at least) who commit *shirq*! Which is nice. In fact, to reverse an oft-quoted trism, it sometimes seems that human beings are extremists by nature and that religion is a moderating influence. (Or could or should be).

At least part of the reason why Muslims have not said much about the Crucifixion is that it is not theologically important. As has been mentioned, for Christians the crucifixion of Jesus and his resurrection represents the cosmic reparation of the universe, while for Muslims, Jesus' death is not necessary. However, Muslims do believe that Jesus was taken to heaven, where he will wait until the Final Days, at which point he will return to vanquish the anti-Christ, the *Dajjal*, and as the world is getting smaller and this day is, by definition, getting nearer, it seems necessary to try and answer the question, What did happen to Jesus?

One interpretation is the substitute crucifixion, as suggested by Halili/Khan. Personally, I do not feel (not very intellectual this) that could have been the case. Some people point to the Gospel of Barnabas as a text that explains this, but as a text it is too perfect in its fit into the Muslim position, in a way that cannot even be said of the Qur'an (or any religious text I know of). Paradoxically, this undermines its credibility because it does not seem to be the way God works. (Mysterious ways).

Slightly more convincing is something outlined by Deedat in three booklets[128], that Jesus was taken down on Good Friday and that he was still alive at that point, though barely, perhaps. Deedat points out that in the New Testament, when asked for a sign by the Pharisees, Jesus himself implies that he will not die:

"An evil and adulterous generation seeketh after a sign; and there shall no sign be given to it, but the sign of the Prophet Jonas: For as Jonas was three days and three nights in the whale's belly; so shall the Son of man be three days and three nights in the heart of the earth." (Matthew 12:39-40)

The words are strongly put, and include the words "there shall be *no* sign…but the sign of the Prophet Jonas," this despite all the other miracles that he had performed and would yet do. "He is putting all his 'eggs' in one basket," as Deedat says. The important point about Jonas,

---

[128] See bibliography

Jonah, is that he was *alive* for three days and three nights in the whale.[129]

This then leads onto his explanation of Jesus' encounter with Mary Magdalene outside the tomb. She has come bearing oil to anoint him (or, possibly, massage), not a Jewish practice for the dead, according to Deedat, despite the fact that Jesus is supposed to be covered by "half a hundred weight" of aloes and myrrh. He deduces that she was not expecting to see a corpse, but a still-live Jesus. Among other things, she came to take him away, not something she would likely have been able to do alone had he been dead.

When she arrives she is shocked to find the tomb open and Jesus gone, so she cries, which would be because this was not what had been planned if the story is as told in John and we are trying to fit it to Deedat's thesis. However, a man she assumes is a gardener addresses her, and then reveals himself to be Jesus. He asks her not to touch him, which Deedat takes as a sign that his wounds are still painful.

Ahmed Deedat makes much of the distinction between a resurrected body, a spiritual event and the term that is used in Christianity for Jesus' rising from the tomb, and a resuscitated body, a physical recovery, which is what he believes happened. The resuscitated Jesus feels pain on the Sunday, but allows disciples to touch him after at least a week has past (according to both Luke and John); he is disguised out of fear of capture by the Jews and is unrecognisable, at first, which would not be the case if he had been resurrected in the way he himself describes resurrection in Luke 27-38. In this incident, he is answering the Sadducees who do not, as an article of faith, believe in resurrection (which in itself may explain why it became such a polarising issue between the Jews and the new Christians). It is clear that what Jesus describes in Luke is what takes place *after* the Final Judgement at the End of Time, and it is also clear that it is a spiritual resurrection. In other words, he is talking about a different kind of resurrection to that which Christians believe happened to Jesus himself after the crucifixion, when he is still very much bodily present. If this is the case, then we have a confusing use of a key word that is used to mean

---

[129] Deedat also points out that the Christian tradition of three days and three nights between Good Friday and Easter Sunday is mathematically flawed.

two different things, rather than, as Deedat seems to argue, a misrepresentation by Christians in saying that Jesus experienced spiritual resurrection when it was actually physical resuscitation. In fact, Christians seem to say something between the two, (confusing because both physical and spiritual). Norman Anderson puts it as follows:

"His deathless Spirit returned to His mutilated human body; His body was instantly and miraculously changed into a new, spiritual body – different from His mortal flesh and blood, but recognisable nonetheless."[130]

Norman Anderson also gives two other strong arguments in favour of the resurrection having taken place in the form he describes it here. The accounts in the New Testament are rather too lifelike to have been made up to suit a particular position, and also the subsequent behaviour of the disciples, going from dejection to zealous proselytising, often ending in martyrdom, could not be based on something these disciples knew to be fraudulent. He points out that Mary Magdalene, a former prostitute (interesting, in the optimistic sense, given that this has been the recurrent metaphor for the Jewish people[131]), is the first to see him, and others too have commented on how the crucifixion devastated the disciples. As Clive Lawton says: "After the crucifixion, the Disciples did not sit around calmly and reassure each other that everything was going according to plan."

Looking at this short period of time, one realises that it is central to the perceived identity of all peoples of the book, either by defining or defining by exclusion. Yet it seems that all "those who disagree concerning it are in doubt thereof; they have no knowledge thereof save pursuit of a conjecture," or in some doubt at least, and yet all have built formidable fortresses around these positions. Muslims categorically say that there was no crucifixion; Christians categorically

---

[130] Anderson's use of the upper case in, for example, "His body…" has been retained, though this is not a notation used by Muslims when discussing Prophets (though they do get an upper case 'P'). Capitals are only be used by Muslims when referring to God, which may be why Anderson uses it, though he never explicitly identifies Jesus with God.

[131] …and slanderously wrong according to a tradition that has culminated in Dan Brown's *Da Vinci Code*.

say that Jesus was God in human form; and Jews believe this to be absolute heresy and Jesus unnecessary, so the resurrection is irrelevant.

Perhaps it is understandable that this is so; we all wish for clear identity markers to delineate core beliefs. Yet if this study has shown anything, I hope it is that, just as we are all sons and daughters of Adam and Abraham, we share many core beliefs, most central of which is the belief in One God. This ultimately implies one truth, and I believe that the paradox of the 'Holy Trinity' of Judaism, Christianity and Islam is resolvable. Each people experiences the truth of its faith through a different aspect of its self: the Jews through themselves as a people, with a genetically encoded propensity to struggle; Christians through the person of Jesus, and his sacrifice, and Muslims through our relationship of submission, Islam, with God, which, being the right way of course, makes us prone to a certain dismissal of the others. Because of this, each is looking at God in a subtly different way and cannot quite "get" the position of the others, so the other becomes Other, not part of us, not like us. Yet this certainty is based on illusion.

So, Jesus came to the Children of Israel. They rejected him, as God knew they would because they were stiff-necked and blocked-eared, mostly, and that is why He had Chosen them, because they *did* struggle with Him. The Jews were so disconcerted by Jesus that they did plan to have him killed "but God is the best of planners" and the Romans did it. He was crucified, he appeared to die, and perhaps really, or nearly, did, and was taken to a tomb where God said, "Be alive again!" and he was, just as Bible and Qur'an say he brought people back to life. In surviving in this way, he did convince his followers that he was both what and who he said he was, which was not God nor literal Son of God, but the kind of Messiah the Jews were not expecting, and then he ascended to heaven. Though challenging to the accepted wisdom of all three, it retains something essential of each, and none of this outright contradicts their respective scripture. For example, Muslims may find some support in the words of Jesus quoted earlier, just after his birth when he defends his mother:

"And peace be on me the day I was born, and the day I die, and the day I shall be brought back to life!" (19:33)

If this, and God alone knows, is what happened, it was certainly not the narrative that informed the stances that different groups took after Jesus ascended. After they had recovered from the shock of seeing Jesus again, the disciples and Jesus' other followers spread the teachings of their master to other Jews. Soon, though, the message became more universal, rather than Jewish, through the teachings of Paul.

Paul was initially both a practising Jew and, unusually, a Roman citizen. He had never actually met Jesus but had experienced conversion from persecution of, to belief in, Christianity whilst on the road to Damascus. After this, he believed that Jesus had been revealed in him (Galatians 1.16) and was the literal Son of God and that it was his mission to take this message to the gentiles. Thus, his influence on Christianity reflects his own path, moving from the particular (the Jewish) to the universal (Roman).

This led to a doctrinal struggle with the original disciples and the subsequent loss of the two most distinctive features of Jewish life among Jesus' followers, circumcision and a kosher diet. As the religion became less Jewish in practice, the Jewish language of the Messiah, possibly increasingly with divine qualities, gave way to the more culturally familiar notion (to the non-Jewish pagans and non-Palestinian Jews to whom Paul preached) of a divine redeemer visiting the earth. In initiating this, it is *Paul* who appears to be the founder of a new religion, at whose centre was the resurrection. Carl Jung actually says that Paul was the earliest source for this, an event Jung sees as purely psychological. The religion that Paul founded was one that was in some ways monotheistic, but that was ambiguous (or wrong) about the nature of Jesus in a way that would later allow the concept of the Holy Trinity to become the cornerstone of the Christian Church. In this, as in other ways, Pauline Christianity does not accord with what Jesus taught or intended, though this is not the usual Christian position, a fact that must be partly because Christians without a Jewish background (i.e. most of them) are likely to feel more comfortable with a Christianity being a religion for non-Jews.

One significant effect of this shift in Christian [132] doctrine was that it moved the goalposts, so to speak, in what Jews were supposed to believe in. Had Jesus' followers remained a recognisably Jewish Messianic sect, events may have vindicated them, especially the destruction of the Temple that Jesus himself had predicted, and other Jews may have followed them. However, by the time of the rebellion of 66 CE, Christianity had more or less set off on a new path, appealing to different people.

Jung has an interesting explanation as to how this leap of faith happened, from Jews to a wider gentile public. As he puts it: "The story of the Resurrection represents the projection of an indirect realisation of the self that had appeared in the figure of a certain man."[133] In explanation, he goes on to say that the old (usually localised) gods had become insignificant and that "their power had been replaced by the concrete one of the visible god, the Caesar." This was a form of 1st century globalisation where the Roman Empire finds parallel representation in the modern "American Empire" and it seems to require some internal searching of the self for something to help rise above the loss of identity this can create. Thus, Jesus defeating death at the hands of the Romans provided an "indirect realisation of the self" to anyone who was experiencing loss of identity or power to the Romans. It was ultimately attractive to the Romans too, particularly as the New Testament both shifted the blame for Jesus' death away from them and offered a form of belief that echoed their paganism. This more universal idea of God and the moral character of the faith ultimately seemed more in tune with their position.[134] Jesus, and Paul's interpretation of his life and death, thus met an internal, collective need among the people of the Mediterranean, that was partly shaped by political realities, but which was also spiritual. As Sam Keen, a philosopher who has been contributing editor of a psychology journal, writes:

---

[132] The term was first used in Acts 11:26

[133] Jung (1999) p.249

[134] Jung is derisive of this, saying: "But this substitution was as unsatisfactory as that of God by the communistic state. It was a frantic and desperate attempt to create – out of no matter how doubtful material – a spiritual monarch, a *pantokrator*, in opposition to the concretized divinity in Rome. (What a joke of the *esprit d'escalier* of history – the substitution for the Caesar of the pontifical office of St. Peter!)." *ibid.*

"Man is spirit incarnate, at once a citizen of two kingdoms... As an archetype of man, Jesus exemplifies the notion that virtue and divine inspiration can never be separated because man is created in the image and substance of God."

The two kingdoms are the kingdom of the body and the kingdom of the spirit, an echo of which we find in the words of Jesus, when he says: "Render unto Caesar what is Caesar's, and to God what is God's." (Mark 12:17) Both kingdoms have paradoxical demands, and it often seems that if we are fulfilling ourselves within one world, the other world will be in a state of chaos, uncertainty or neglect, and that it will thence demand attention, as a friend put it, to stop you getting cocky. Our life stories, and those of peoples of the world, are firstly about survival, but ultimately about how we integrate these two sides of our lives.

Another writer elaborates on this duality being reflected in Jesus with these words:

"The incarnation tells us of the paradox of two natures: of divine love and human love mixed in one vessel, contained in one human being.... In this image is reflected the dual nature of every human, the two loves that legitimately claim our loyalty, and the synthesis we should make between the two. The Incarnation shows us that the divine world and the personal world coexist within each human being. It is when the two natures live together in a conscious synthesis that a person becomes a conscious self."

This idea of "God within us" can sound blasphemous if treated as an absolute, but Jews are quite comfortable with the notion of the Divine spark within all of us and both Bible and Qur'an describe our creation as being from clay, animated by the breath of God. This message, this idea, is in fact very close to that which the Jews understood in their vision of the Land, where the Chosen People live in the Promised Land, and for Muslims, Islam is nothing more and nothing less than the Divine system for living this duality of the earthly, animal self (the clay) and the spiritual (the breath of God).

Thus, if Jews did not see him as the Messiah, they did not need to be told again by 'Jesus as metaphor' that life was at once physical and spiritual. To re-quote Clive Lawton: "He doesn't come into our frame of reference." However, for the "new Christians", as a suddenly dawning birth of self-awareness it could be rather unbalancing to the collective self. In fact, they would spend much of the next millennium identifying with the spiritual, submissive aspect of Jesus before embracing a more physical archetype in the form of the crusader that would dominate Christian consciousness for at least the second millennium.

This can all be seen, and disputed, with hindsight but at the time, this would not have been the obvious outcome of those few days following the crucifixion. There was another, more immediate struggle, more within the Jewish frame of reference. According to the New Testament, Jesus had foretold the destruction of Jerusalem: "Do you see these great buildings? There will not be left here one stone upon another, that will not be thrown down" (Matthew 24:2:). Though many did not believe *in* him, they nonetheless believed *like* him that this was the end of days and that the confrontation between the Romans and the Jews was its greatest sign.

There had been revolts among the Jews since the time of Jesus' birth, with regular massacres in response. To mention but two events, there were two thousand crucified by the Romans in 4 BCE and three thousand Passover pilgrims slaughtered in the Temple court, not by the Romans but by Archelaus, one of the sons of Herod, demonstrating the depths of the class split within Jewish society. As today, this level of suffering among people defined by faith produced a murderous anger that seemed to be its antithesis, and also perhaps made the anger of the minority more powerful than the majority's natural preference for avoiding conflict.

Jews, though, apart from class, were further divided among themselves. There were several groupings: the Temple-based, ritualistic Sadducees, disbelievers in the after-life, pro-status quo, representative of the ruling class and sometimes despised for their collaboration with the Romans. Then there were the middle class Pharisees, the most important group

277

(and Jesus' main competitors according to Fox), the "proletarian democratisers of tradition", as Clive Lawton describes them, who were concerned with teaching how to live the best life in this world, though also believers in the after-life. There were also the unworldly Essenes, who awaited the Messiah in their remote Dead Sea community in Qumran and believed only in the authority of God. Also outsiders were the Zealots, or *Sicari*, freedom fighters or terrorists, depending on your point of view, who believed it was a cardinal sin to obey earthly rulers and that rebellion was a religious duty, and, of course, there were the Jewish followers of Jesus themselves. Finally there were the majority of the population who were poor and lived in villages and mostly wanted peace but who may well have felt that, in the end, "not too fight was worse," as Faulkner says.

There was also a large non-Roman gentile population, only a few of whom were by belief Christian. According to Karen Armstrong, the relationship of Jews and Romans was not purely antagonistic. With a population of one tenth of the Empire, Jews were a sizeable minority whose moral character and "more encompassing divinity" were attractive to an entity that was trying to outgrow its total reliance on force and pantheon of gods. She cites good relations between the two in Palestine, though this apparent contradiction perhaps suggests rather how deep the internal Jewish splits were.

The irony, the not particularly helpful might-have-been, is that rather than there having been the founding of Roman Catholicism in the 4th century, there could have been a reformed Roman Judaism in the 1st under Jesus instead. If only... But though Jesus had what could be called something for everyone[135] – he was as well-versed as the Sadducees, debating Mosaic law in the Temple at the age of twelve; as innovative as the Pharisees, preaching of a compassionate God; as holy as the Essenes, and as revolutionary as the Zealots – none could identify fully with him. For the Sadducees, his teachings seemed to make their role as guardians of a Temple-centred religion redundant; he was too critical of the worldliness of the Pharisees ("Ye shut up heaven against men!" Matthew 23); to the Essenes' elite position he was

---

[135] The four Gospels are said by some to represent four of his different aspects: Matthew, his humanity; Mark, his prophetic nature; Luke, his priestly character, and John, his heavenly origin.

threatening; and he was not political enough for the Zealots. Each group was more guided by its own self-importance, where what was needed was a novel, epoch-marking submission to this man of God. For His own reasons, God had Chosen a people who would not do this, who were stiff-necked. Thus, the Children of Israel lived up to their name as those who struggled with God, but this time they did not prevail.

Tension and incidents continued until 66 CE when Roman procurator Gessius Florus seized a large amount of money from the Temple and massacred a number of furious Jewish complainants. This led to the Temple priests refusing to carry out the established sacrifice to Caesar, thus breaking all ties with Rome. This in turn led to dispute between the Zealots and those Jews who wished to reconcile with Rome, a dispute that the Roman garrison at Jerusalem first tried to suppress but that, in so doing, led to them being surrounded. Though Herod Agrippa II, the Jewish king of the Galilee, mediated and the soldiers surrendered under terms, they were attacked and slaughtered by the Zealots as they marched out unarmed. Thus, should the Syrians of, say, Caesarea choose to massacre almost the entire Jewish community of that city, some 20,000 people, as they did, Gessius Florus could only feel vindicated, and maybe pleased.

With such enormous loss of life, revolt became unstoppable and spread throughout the country. The near-successful Roman capture of Jerusalem by Cestius Gallus turned to defeat as the retreating army was attacked at Beth-Horon, but by now the Romans were determined to end the troubles once and for all. Vespasian, credited for this and later deeds as the man who saved the Roman Empire, ruthlessly led his army through the Galilee, crushing all resistance, and finally laid siege to Jerusalem. Civil war in Rome saved Jerusalem temporarily, with Vespasian returning there to become emperor, but his son Titus resumed the campaign.

The siege, which began in spring 70CE, was bloody and desperate and lasted some five months, the Jews inside starving and fighting desperately with the Romans, but also so badly among themselves that, according to Josephus, a Jewish former governor of the Galilee who had gone over to the Roman side, many Jerusalemites wished for

Roman victory. Finally, though Titus may have wished to spare the Temple, when the Romans broke through they showed no mercy to the inhabitants, and slaughtered them as the Temple area burnt out of control. As Josephus wrote:

"The Temple Hill, enveloped in flames from top to bottom, appeared to be boiling up from its very roots; yet the sea of flame was nothing to the ocean of blood, or the companies of killers to the armies of killed: nowhere could the ground be seen between the corpses, and the soldiers climbed over the heaps of bodies as they chased the fugitives."

The destruction, with a reference back to the earlier Assyrian destruction, is mentioned in the Qur'an in the following verse:

"So, when the time of the second prophecy drew near (We raised other enemies that would) disfigure your faces and enter the Temple as they had done the first time, and destroy whatever they could lay their hands on." (17:7)[136]

Thousands had died in battle or from hunger. Of the survivors, some were executed, others were cast into slavery, or amphitheatres or sent to Rome. Significantly, legend has it that one, Rabbi Yohannan Ben Zakkai, was smuggled out of the city in a coffin during the siege; the zealots would not let him out "alive". He had opposed the confrontation with the Romans and advised submission to Caesar, believing, unlike the Zealots, that the ultimate fate of the Jews was dependant on obedience to God, not on military strength. He believed

---

[136] Some commentators, most recently Shaikh Bassam Jarrar in '2022 –The Decline of Israel', discount this as being a reference to the Roman destruction on the basis that the preceding verse 6 doesn't match the situation of the Jews in Palestine at this time. (I would disagree. See comment on 17:6 at the beginning of chapter). Instead, they place the second destruction in the future, it being possible for a past tense to refer to a future prophecy. I still think that the general context, and especially verse 4 of the same chapter – "And We decreed for the Children of Israel in the Scripture: indeed you would do mischief in the land twice and you will become tyrants and extremely arrogant," – suggests a reference to the Roman period, though God knows best. Also, for the second destruction to be an event in the future, Israel would have to destroy Al-Aqsa mosque and rebuild the Temple. It seems unwise to invest in such a vision if a more positive interpretation is available.

Jews would be better stateless, and was thus an ideal leader of post-destruction Jewry. All he required from the Romans was religious freedom and he foreswore the use of power in dealing with them. With Roman permission he set up a Pharisaic community near Jerusalem at Yavne and this became the foundation of a new conception of Judaism, one that was not land-dependant, and which would be the doctrine of most Jews until after the Second World War. It is ironic that again, from the apparent death of a Jewish religious leader in Jerusalem, a faith should not so much survive as be reborn. As Yanai Ofran says:

"Christianity also began as a decentralistic Jewish movement that offered a pocket-sized religion that could follow the believer wherever he went. But Christianity, a universal religion whose latter-day versions reduced the practical obligations of its adherents to nearly none, adjusted to the new reality with greater ease than did the religion established by Ben Zakai and his pupils. As opposed to Christianity, they preserved Jewish nationalism and, of course, the practical obligations as well."

Whether Temple-based Judaism as it had been at the time of Jesus' preaching needed renewing or not was now beside the point. In making this choice, inasmuch as it was a choice, the only means of survival open to Jews was to suppress any martial instincts they had, the martial instincts they had drawn on to take Canaan centuries before, because they were no longer appropriate.

Linda Grant identifies this, the *shtarker*, the strong fighter for Israel, as being one of the triangle of archetypes of the Jews. She highlights Samson (and Ariel Sharon in modern times), but almost any of the major figures of the Jewish Bible from Joshua onwards qualify. The other aspects are the *mensch*, which means literally a human being but implies one who is honoured and righteous, and the *nebbish* (think Woody Allen), who is "someone you feel sorry for," as defined by Leo Rothstein, author of 'The Joys of Yiddish'. Moses was the finest balance of these qualities and, as we have noted, he was not allowed to enter the Promised Land. Instead that task had fallen to the warrior Joshua, and it was this *shtarker* spirit that the Children of Israel had relied on to deliver them from adversity, though the whole tenor of the Jewish Bible suggests that the Jewish people were supposed to move on from this to find the balance that existed within Moses, but to live it in the Promised Land. The Prophetic warnings of the Great Prophets and, ultimately, Jesus, were to this end, where Jesus coming as Messiah represents the fulfilment of Isaiah's warnings. This is clearly not how he is seen by the Jews. Geza Vermes, for example, believes that the fact that no attacks were made on Jesus' followers after his death proves that Jesus was not a political Messiah. This is true up to the point where we say he was not a political Messiah in the way that had been expected; in other words, he was no *shtarker*. However, Muslims at least, believe that he was a *mensch*.

The fighting qualities of the *shtarker* now stood redundant after the Fall of Jerusalem. They were, if anything, shameful. Jews, in effect, were forced to suppress a part of themselves, and culturally they became somewhat disembodied. From preferred position, the Children of Israel suddenly became homeless, recalling the development of their namesake Jacob's relationship with his twin Esau. The two are often seen as representatives of the Jews and the Gentiles or Christians, where Esau is like the physical, political Other to the Jews, with whom they will implicitly be reconciled. He is, and they are, the Jews' shadow, and it is no accident that Esau is related to the Arabic version of Jesus' name, 'Isa.

The destruction of the Temple and the dispersal of the Jews with this new understanding of their religion marked a major step in their history, as great as the initial conquest of Canaan. Yohanan and the rabbis, and Jewish thinking until the 20th century, saw it as divine retribution for failing to live according to God's law in the land and failing, also, in loving God.

The Christians also saw the destruction as God's punishment, though their interpretation was necessarily different. They saw it as punishment for rejecting Jesus as the Messiah, and later as the Son of God, and also, they believed, for murdering him. Norman Perrin, one-time Associate Professor of New Testament at the Divinity School of the University of Chicago says:

"The destruction of Jerusalem and the Temple by the Gentiles sent a shock wave through the Jewish Christian world whose importance it is impossible to exaggerate. Indeed, much of the subsequent literature, both of Judaism and Christianity, took the form it did precisely in an attempt to come to terms with the catastrophe of 70 AD."

If the Jews had been in competition with the Christians before this time for the souls of the idolaters, the destruction of Jerusalem effectively ended their role as a proselytising faith.[137] The trauma of its loss now became an essential feature of belief and ritual - the glass crushed underfoot at weddings is accompanied by the words "No joy is complete without remembrance of the destruction of Jerusalem" - and an acceptance of guilt for failure to live in the land became a characteristic trait. Stateless, most Jews became passive as far as national history was concerned.

This emasculation left Jews vulnerable. Previously Jewish belief and those of their neighbours had been different, but based on an entirely different world-view. The Jews, being monotheistic, were if anything, more intolerant than their polytheistic neighbours. Anti-Jewish feeling had existed before Jesus in Egypt, for example, where there had been strong anti-Jewish feeling under the Greeks, but generally Jews were not seen as a threat. This climate of distrust now changed to something more virulent. Now Jewish and Christian beliefs were in direct contradiction in their interpretation of the life of Jesus and the fall of Jerusalem. As the balance of power swung towards the Christians, the Jewish position became more and more tenuous.

This marginalisation of the role of the Jews, something that Christianity has never been entirely comfortable with, has been at least part cause of Christian anti-Jewish feelings ever since as it has allowed Christians to project their own insecurity about their faith onto a weaker Other. Fear of this disconfirming Other actually increased after

---

[137] There were, though, the Khazars. They were a warlike tribe from the Black Sea, bounded by Christians and Muslims. To maintain their independence while upgrading their status in the eyes of God, they converted top-down to Judaism in the 9th Century. Many eventually emigrated to eastern Europe where they intermarried with the existing Ashkenazim Jews there, thus injecting a bit of aggression into the Jewish gene pool. One argument that is sometimes made by Palestinian Muslims is that this means that many Israeli Jews are not the real Bani Isra'il who were God's Chosen, and therefore have no rights as Jews. For obvious personal reasons, among others, I am less sympathetic to the idea that one's faith is something given by birth or blood.

Christians ceased to see their own truths as self-evident in the 19th Century, and particularly in the 20th Century in the Holocaust. However, this fear can also be seen at the inception, where something that was pure and literally heaven-sent was adapted to suit this world which was, at that time, effectively Roman and polytheistic. Some idea of how far this adaptation went becomes apparent when we know something of the beliefs of Paul's hometown, Tarsus. The town, in what is now Turkey, was then the centre for the Romanised Babylonian mystery cult of Mithraism in which a god known as *sol invictus*, the sun god (which even allows a pun on "son of God" in English), was born on 25th December. This god died by self-sacrifice for the sins of human beings, dying in the form of a bull. His flesh and blood were then eaten as a way of redemption. So familiar was all this that St Augustine called this the devil's ploy, a shadow Christianity designed to make Christians into unbelievers. Rather, it was perhaps this familiarity that made unbelievers into Christians, with Christianity finally becoming the dominant religion of the Western world after Constantine's conversion in 325 CE. The polytheistic strain of the religion and its essential hybridisation became enshrined thereafter in the doctrine of the Trinity.

From this we can see that, though in Islam Jesus has significance for Jews, Christians and Muslims, in the Final Judgement it is said that only the Islamic understanding of Jesus that will be accepted. In this understanding, Jesus is the Prophet through whom the worship of One God began its transition from the particular (from the Children of Israel) to the universal, the fruition of which would come with the Prophet Muhammad, as the Qur'an says Jesus himself prophesied:

"And (remember) when 'Isa son of Maryam said, 'O Tribe of Israel, verily I am the Messenger of God to you, confirming what was (revealed) before me in the Torah, and bringing news of a Messenger who will come after me, whose name is the Praised One (Ahmed).'" (61.6)

A similar message is to be found in the New Testament, as we shall see in the following chapter. Even from Paul, often deemed responsible for the loss of the purity of Jesus' teachings, we find that in one letter that he seems to recognise the destiny that was coming and the necessary limitations of his work:

"But when that which is perfect is come, then that which is in part shall be done away." (1 Corinthians 13:9)

As a result of Jesus' life and his passing, humanity's relationship with its Creator stood in a different form. In a sense, the role the Children of Israel had been chosen for, receiving the Messiah, had been rejected. Instead of a faith for all mankind coming through them, something of the spirit of universalism and divine unity had passed into Christianity, albeit in adapted form. As a Jewish writer, Alfred Lilienthal, put it:

"Jesus was in the line of the great Hebrew prophets. Jesus' reiterations of Jeremiah, Isaiah and Ezekiel went unheard among nationalists preoccupied with the struggle for national freedom and racial solidarity. The Judean rabble, in rejecting the offer of Pontius Pilate to release Jesus and in choosing Barabbas, the insurrectionist and murderer, did more than turn their back on the preacher from Nazareth. They pushed Judaism off the road of universalism and thus encouraged the building of a new faith around Jesus' preachments. Christianity, as a denationalisation of the Hebrew ideal, was promulgated as a universal religion for gentiles."

Without the people who had been living with the belief in one God to lead them, the new Christians found it easiest to build their new religion's foundations, both literally and metaphorically, on those of the old, and in doing so, to obscure them. Thus, in a religion increasingly shorn of, and antagonistic to, its Jewish identity, a god-man whose death promised everlasting life was a more meaningful and familiar figure than a Jewish Messiah or a Prophet, even though these ideas remained in theory, and apparent contradiction. Also, without the structure of the Jewish faith, Christianity had an amorphous quality. At its best, the heart was its guide - an echo of the idea that "The Book" that Jesus brought was his heart. However, aside from some rituals concerning the Last Supper, the founding fathers had to define a whole system of beliefs around that heart, resulting in Christianity taking diverse forms the world over, absorbing beliefs and rituals wherever it is practised, and often seeming to merely cover polytheistic paganism with a monotheistic veneer. Yet this was the new Chosen People.

For the Jews, according to Lilienthal again, 'Chosen' changed: "Their relationship to God was subordinated to their relationship to one another."

A struggle over symbols and definitions would be one of the hallmarks of the relationships between the two faiths. For Christians, Jesus was "God with a face", an intermediary between God and man, which contrasts with the direct relationship of Judaism (and Islam for that matter). However, as Christianity has lapsed and the life and message of Jesus have become less meaningful, for Christians (whether ex-, nominal or practising), his co-religionists, the Jews themselves, have often come to be seen as the intermediaries. This is true for the perception of the Christian world of the massive 'recrucifixion' of the Jews in the Holocaust and also of the Jewish reincarnation as secular Israelis – like the Westerner, but nearer God, theologically and/or geographically. There are many cultural, social, psychological reasons why it is so but it does seem that, as an American journalist, Walter Kerr, says:

"What has happened since World War II is that the American (and hence, my addition, Western) sensibility itself has become part Jewish, perhaps nearly as much Jewish as anything else. (And) it goes right to the bone, all the way in."

In Islam, Jesus is special. Unlike all the other Prophets except Adam, his birth was miraculous. Unlike all the other Prophets, his heart at birth was pure and untouched by Shaytan. (The Prophet Muhammad's was purified when he was six). Unlike the other Prophets before him, he is a supra-historical figure. He came at a particular time, but left it to await his return at the End of Days. In these ways, he is uniquely blessed to be a sign. He is a sign who has been seen, but whose message, the destination, has been misread or rejected.

In Matthew, Jesus says: "Think not that I am come to send peace on earth: I came not to send peace but a sword." (Matthew 10:34) It seems that he did. Much is made, by both Jews and Christians, of the role of the Jews in the development of human consciousness, our perception of right and wrong, and our sense of the oneness of God. In the light of the Holocaust there are understandable attempts to see Jews in as positive a light as possible. Essential though this is, it seems that this analysis does not go deep enough. It could be argued - and I intend to - that the Jews, "just like everyone else, only more so", were indeed "the Chosen People" precisely because of the stiff necks that even Moses chided them for. The refusal to submit was given dramatic life in the story of Jacob who wrestled with the man/angel/god/God at the river and was renamed Israel, in Hebrew, "He who struggles with God." And that was to be the role of the Children of Israel. To live through the logical consequences of this struggle. To be reminded and warned by their Prophets. (Though, as the Qur'an says, all nations have been sent Prophets, none have had as many as the Children of Israel). To reject those Prophets. And to be expelled, not once, but twice, for doing so. But to survive. And bear witness. And yet still believe that they were, are, right.

Yet before the second expulsion, they were given one last chance, which they rejected. The change that was needed was in their hearts and they could not make it. As it was written that they would not make it.

Thus, the path of *most* resistance, to the will of the Almighty, was shown to be futile, even illusory, a message that was there for all humanity to read, if they chose to. So what was the alternative? At the time there was no explicit universal one, though Christianity seemed, in some ways, to fit. The path of *least* resistance was instead to come from a descendant of Abraham's first son, Ishmael, rather than his second one, Isaac - the Qur'an says that this religion is the primordial one, the original religion of Adam, who had also had one occasion of disobedience. It is called Islam, submission to God, and it is also related to the word *Salaam*, which means peace. Jesus was not the Prince of Peace, but he highlighted the choice.

287

The choice is between continuing to struggle with God and with submitting to Him, and here the sword that Jesus brought could remind us of the sword that Solomon brought to the child, implying that ultimately there is only one way to serve God, or even to believe in God. Accepting that in many cases we have been travelling down the wrong path, or have even rejected the notion that there is a path, requires repentance and a return to the primordial path. The repentance that is required to make the heart ready recalls a story whose image is familiar to Jews and Christians.

In the Jewish story, a king's son goes astray and sends word to his father that he has done too much and has gone too far to ever come back. But the father sends a reply saying: "Come to me as far as you can, and I will come to meet you the rest of the way."

The Christian story is the story that the New Testament records of the prodigal son, who takes his inheritance and squanders it. In choosing to take the riches of this world rather than to be patient and to serve he reminds us of the choice that Jesus did not take when Satan offered him dominion over all he surveyed when he withdrew to the Jericho wilderness after his baptism. (Perhaps the choice of dominion represents the majority Jewish expectation of the Messiah as temporal leader, so Jesus was in a sense tempted with the role that would belong to the one who came after him). The riches of the world are their own reward and ultimately transient and, as the son sits in a foreign land, so hungry that he is tempted to eat the food that he is feeding to pigs, he thinks that his father's servants eat better than he, and he decides to return and beg forgiveness. As he approaches, his father sees him and runs to embrace him. The son tells him: "Father, I have sinned against heaven, and in thy sight, and am no more worthy to be called thy son." (Luke 15:21) The father, though, tells a servant to kill a fatted calf, and a celebration begins.

During the celebration, the older brother returns and he is angry that he has never had anything like such treatment. (And I sometimes think that we Muslims are like that older brother). The father says to him: "Son, thou art ever with me, and all that I have is thine. It was meet that we should make merry, and be glad: for this thy brother was dead, and is alive again; and was lost, and is found." (Luke 15:31-2)

As we read in the story of Ezekiel, God, Allah, can restore a city, or the life of a living creature. Or even a nation. The son is restored by the forgiveness of his father. But as Primo Levi, a survivor of the Shoah, the Holocaust, would say many centuries later, for there to be forgiveness there first has to be repentance. Jews, Christians and Muslims would do well to reflect whether we as believers have sinned before we begin to cast stones.

Anderson, J.N.D. *The Evidence for the Resurrection* (1966) Inter-Varsity Press: Downers Grove

Cupitt, D. & Armstrong, P. *Who Was Jesus?* (1977) BBC: London

Deedat, A. *Christ in Islam,* (1986) IPCI: Durban

Deedat, A. *Resurrection or resuscitation?* (1978) IPCI: Durban

Deedat, A. *What was the Sign of Jonah?* (1976) IPCI: Durban

Deedat, A. *Who Moved the Stone?* (1975) IPCI: Durban

Faulkner, N. *Apocalypse – The Great Jewish Revolt against AD 66-73* (2002) Tempus: Stroud

Johnson, R. *We: Understanding the Psychology of Romantic Love* (1983) Harper Collins: New York

Josephus, *Antiquities of the Jews* (2006) Cosimo Inc.: New York

Jung, C.G. *On Resurrection* from *Jung on Death and Immortality* - Selected and Introduced by Jenny Yates (1999) Princeton University Press: Princeton

Keen, S. *Fire In The Belly: On Being a Man* (1991) Bantam: New York

Kerr. W. (14 Apr 1968) New York Times, quoted in Ernest Van Den Haag *The Jewish Mystique*

Khalidi, Prof. T. *Jesus through Muslim eyes* (18 March 2002) BBC Lent Talks

Lawton, C.A. *Jesus through Jewish eyes* (18 March 2002) BBC Lent Talks

Lilienthal, A.M. *The Other Side of the Coin,* (1965) Devin-Adair: New York

Maccoby, H. *Judas Iscariot and the myth of Jewish Evil* (1992) Free Press: New York

Maccoby, H. *Was there a traitor at the Last Supper?* (1992) The Independent: London

Merr, B. *Jesus, a faithful Jew* (11 Feb 2000) Haaretz: Tel Aviv (reviewing Joseph Klausner's *Jesus of Nazareth* in Hebrew)

Nasr, S.H. *Jesus Through the Eyes of Islam* (28 July 1973) The Times: London

Neusner, J. A *Rabbi argues With Jesus* (27 March 2000) Newsweek: Amsterdam

Ofran, Y. *Inventor of a Portable Judaism* (9 May 2000) Haaretz: Tel Aviv

Oz, A. *Rabbi Jesus* (21 March 2000) Guardian: London

Robson, Rev. J. *Christ in Islam* (1929) John Murray: London

Sanders, E.P. *In Quest of the Historical Jesus* (15 November 2001) New York Review

Sayyid Abu A'la Mawdudi *Towards Understanding the Qur'an, Vol. V.* (1995) The Islamic Foundation: Leicester

Seale, M.S. *Qur'an & Bible – Studies in Interpretation & Dialogue* (1978) Croon Helm: London

Vermes, G. *The Dead Sea Scrolls in English* (1979) Pelican: London

Vermes, G. *Whatever historians say, Jesus was a great man* (8 April 2001) Independent on Sunday: London

20

MUHAMMAD

Maybe that camel, not a donkey, will bring the Messiah. After all, that camel has been here forever.
(Policeman on duty in Jerusalem before 'Y2K')[138]

Unsurprisingly, there was a funny atmosphere in Jerusalem in 1999. Unsure quite how to pitch Israel as a religious destination, the Government Tourist Authority ran advertisements in Britain that showed the Dome of the Rock and said:

"In the land where the Millennium began, the Dome has already been built."

And:

"We've already got our Millennium Dome."[139]

I like to think of this as an admission, though I accept that it may have been unconscious and unintentional, but an admission nonetheless, of two omissions in Jewish theology and belief. These are: that Jesus was indeed the Messiah, and that the Dome of the Rock is the third Temple, built as it is on the spot of the Prophet Muhammad's ascension to the heavens from Jerusalem. I believe that this realisation is what the whole saga of the repeated expulsions and returns has been about, the final act in the (till now) apparently endless struggle with God. This, this rendezvous with destiny, this squaring of the circle of the paradox of free will and predestination, struggle and submission, this alone can explain the suffering that preceded and followed 1948, whether Jewish or Arab, Israeli or Palestinian, both Muslims and Christians. Explain and thence, God willing, heal. It has happened, it is out there. All we need to do now is catch up.

---

[138] *Jerusalem Post, 31 December 1999*
[139] Around this time I visited a display in the Jewish Quarter of the Old City in Jerusalem that showed plans and other paraphernalia that were being prepared for the rebuilding of the new temple, the third, as other Jews wish. As I left I heard a young boy ask his mother: "When will there be a fourth temple?"

If this has not been, till now, an idea whose time has come, it is because we have not been able to see it right. We have already seen in the previous chapter how Jesus has been seen by Jews, Christians and Muslims, in terms of his role (Messiah or otherwise), his nature (son of God or otherwise) and his end (crucifixion or otherwise, and resurrected or otherwise). The same can also be said of the recognition of how the Prophet Muhammad, peace and blessings be upon him, is referred to and described in the Bible.[140]

The idea is at first surprising, but some considerations should be borne in mind. Firstly, in the course of translation from the Semitic languages of Hebrew and Aramaic (both of the same root as Arabic), obvious resonances and references are sometimes lost, either accidentally (because translators were not expecting to find the Prophet Muhammad) or deliberately (they had found him and wanted to hide him). Secondly, most readers of the Bible are not Muslims, and so they are not looking for the Prophet Muhammad there. If they are Jewish, they are looking for a Messiah at the end of time. If they are Christian, they are looking to make prophecies point to Jesus, either his First or Second Coming.

If we consider these two factors together we can see that one reason for changing the Bible would be to project and protect a particular point of view. However, because of this focus, it seems that scribes have ignored parts of the Bible which they saw as obscure or unimportant (because they were not looking for anyone beyond their own group) but which actually open up a whole new story if studied on their merits. We have seen this earlier, particularly in the text of the books of Isaiah.

Thus, if we see that the whole vast pageant of monotheism is actually leading to the coming of a universal religion both after Jesus and beyond the land promised to the Children of Israel, then these obscure prophecies or prophecies attached to others can be seen in a very different light. Again and again it seems that, although plans have been made to conceal the message that the Truth lies beyond the pages, and the central people, of the Bible, the evidence of that message, and

---

[140] According to Husayn Jisri, in *Risalat Al-Hamidiya*, there are 114 such references.

sometimes its concealment, is found in the Bible itself. And then the work of a greater planner can be seen.

The first such prophecy comes as early as the Torah itself. At the end of the life of Jacob, the dying patriarch gathers his sons and blesses them and tells them what will "befall you in the last days" (Genesis 49:1). To Judah he says: "The Sceptre shall not pass from Judah, and the Lawgiver from between his feet, until Shiloh come and to him belongeth the obedience of peoples." (Genesis 49:10) In an analysis of the language and content of this verse Professor Abdul-Ahad Dawud disagrees with the Christian assertion that Shiloh refers to Jesus. Jesus, he says, reasserts the Law of Moses rather than bringing any new laws himself and he does not try to accept the 'Sceptre' of temporal power. He is also of the line of Judah, so, even if the sceptre is seen as his, it has not passed from Judah's line. Professor Dawud looks at possible meanings of 'Shiloh' and finds that the word itself could signify either 'he to whom it belongs' or 'tranquil, peaceful, trustworthy, quiet', either of which would be appropriate in describing the Prophet of Islam.

The next such passage is the one we considered earlier in which Moses tells the people that the Lord had told him:

"I will raise them up a Prophet from among their brethren, like unto thee (Moses), and will put my words in his mouth; and he shall speak unto them all that I shall command him. And it shall come to pass, that whosoever will not hearken unto my words which he shall speak in my name, I will require it of him." (Deuteronomy 18:18)

There is also the passage when, before his death, Moses blesses the Children of Israel:

"The Lord came from Sinai, and rose up from Seir unto them; he shined forth from mount Par'an, and he came with ten thousands of saints; from his right hand went a fiery law for them." (Deuteronomy 33:2)

The gentile, non-Israel, import of this message is emphasised by the words that follow: "Yea, he loved the people; all his saints are in thy hand: and they sat down at thy feet; *every one* shall receive of thy words. Moses commanded of us a law, *even* the inheritance of the congregation of Jacob." (Deuteronomy 33:4-5)

Without understanding these words as referring to the Prophet Muhammad, they make very little sense.

A further example of this is to be found in the Song of Songs, sometimes attributed to Solomon, which reads: "His speech (or mouth) is most sweet, and he is altogether lovely (or desirable). This is my beloved, and this is my friend, O daughters of Jerusalem." (Song of Songs 5:16)

What is surprising is that the word in Hebrew for 'lovely' (or 'desirable') is *Muhammadeem* and that, furthermore, a *Hadith* states that God said to the Prophet: "O Prophet Muhammad, I take you as a friend just as I took Abraham as a friend."

Later still, in a study of the seventh chapter of the Book of Daniel, Professor Abdul-Ahad Dawud describes Daniel's vision of the four beasts as being symbols of empires to come, the Chaldean, the Persian, the Greek and the Roman. The first three are bad but not described in detail because, Professor Dawud says, they are pagan. The most powerful and dangerous of these is the fourth, which has iron teeth and brass nails and grows horns. In the vision, one of these horns – which he says corresponds to the Christian Constantine - grew and "made war on the saints and prevailed against them; Until the Ancient of Days came, and judgement was given to the saints of the most high; and the time came when the saints possessed the kingdom." (Daniel 7:21-22) Professor Dawud sees "the saints" as being those who believe in one God, unlike the Trinitarian Constantine. He believes that the "Ancient of Days" is the Prophet Muhammad. In fact, this does not correspond to the general usage of that term nor to the verses that come before, though it referring to God is not incompatible with the reference still being to Muhammad.

294

In these preceding verses, though, there is further support for this inference because a connection could be made between the prophecy and the Prophet Muhammad where there is a description of something that sounds like the *Isra'* and the *Mi'raj*, the Night Journey to Jerusalem and the ascent into the heavens:

"I saw in the night visions, and behold, one like the Son of Man came with the clouds of heaven, and came to the Ancient of Days, and they brought him near before him. And there was given him dominion, and glory, and a kingdom, that all people, nations, and languages, should serve him: his dominion is an everlasting dominion, which shall not pass away, and his kingdom that which shall not be destroyed." (Daniel 7:13-14)

Furthermore, immediately prior to this we read that "the judgement was set, and the books were opened," (Daniel 7:10) where the Hebrew word used for 'judgement' is *dina*, a word that has the same root as the Arabic word *deen*.

The books of two later prophets of the Jewish Bible also contain prophecies that could be understood to confirm the reversion of this *deen*, the burden upon Arabia, to the line of the elder of Abraham's sons: "God came from Teman and the Holy one from Mount Par'an. Selah. His glory covered the heavens, and the earth was full of his praise." (Habakkuk 3:3)

"The Holy one" could refer to the Prophet Muhammad, coming from Mount Par'an, which, as we have seen, is associated with Mecca. Then, in the Book of Haggai we read of the glory of two houses of God, the second of which is the greater:

"And I will shake all nations, and the desire of all nations shall come: and I will fill this house with glory, saith the Lord of Hosts. The silver is mine, and the gold is mine, saith the Lord of Hosts. The glory of this latter house shall be greater than that of the former, saith the Lord of Hosts: and in this place will I give peace, saith the Lord of Hosts." (Haggai 2: 7-9)

Finally, in the last book of the Jewish Bible, Malachi, which literally means 'My angel', who would be the angel Gabriel, Jibreel in Arabic, we find a prophecy that seems to be another reference to the *Isra'* of the Last Prophet, the journey that would take place between the two houses some centuries later, and which we noted a hint of through Solomon before.[141]

"Behold, I will send my messenger, and he shall prepare the way before me: and the lord, whom ye seek, shall come suddenly to his Temple, even the messenger of the covenant, whom ye delight in: behold, he shall come, saith the Lord of Hosts." (Malachi 3:1)

As we shall see later, this journey would be the seminal point in the history of the worship of one God, Allah, a point that asserted both continuity and transformation. On a practical level, one important achievement was the formalisation of the numbers of prayers to be prayed daily, a number that was arrived at with the help of Moses, as we shall see. This itself is appropriate, because in the Bible Moses' practices in preparation for speaking with God are described more than any others, though they were practices that had always been performed by the Prophets. They included many practices that are part of daily prayer in Islam, such as bowing to the ground:

"They (Moses and Aaron) fell upon their faces: and the glory of the Lord appeared unto them." (Numbers 20:6)[142]

The removal of shoes and washing before prayer are also described for Moses: "And He (God Almighty) said, Draw not nigh hither: put off thy shoes from thy feet, for the place whereon thou standest is holy ground." (Exodus 3:5) There is also: "Moses and Aaron and his sons washed their hands and their feet thereat: When they went into the tent of the congregation, and when they came unto the altar, they washed as the Lord commanded Moses." (Exodus 40:31-32)

---

[141] (1 Kings 8:41-43)
[142] This had also been mentioned for Abraham in Genesis 17:3.

As we have seen, following the destruction of Jerusalem in 70 CE relations between the followers of Jesus and the Jews who had rejected him deteriorated as Jews ceased to be a political power. Moreover, to Christians, the destruction seemed to be a decisive punishment for ignoring prophecies out of pride. However, Jesus himself brought tidings of the coming of another Prophet who had roots in the Jewish Bible and disqualified trinitarian Christians from declaring that they, once and for all, were the new Chosen People.

One place this has been mentioned is in the story of John the Baptist, as we saw above:

"Verily I say unto you, Among them that are born of women there hath not risen a greater than John the Baptist: notwithstanding he that is least in the kingdom of heaven is greater than he." (Matthew 11:11)

As we have seen, Ahmed Deedat sees "the least" as the last. Also, when John the Baptist was asked who he was "he confessed, and denied not; but confessed, I am not the Christ. And they (the priests) asked him, What then? Art thou Elias? And he saith, I am not. Art thou that prophet? And he answered, No." (John 1:20-21) "That prophet," as we saw, seems to be the one who has been spoken of since Deuteronomy 18:18.

However, the most striking example of looking forward is to be found in the Gospel of John where Jesus consoles his disciples about his imminent departure:

"Let not your heart be troubled, ye believe in God, believe also in me... And I will pray the Father, and he shall give you another Comforter, that he may abide with you for ever; Even the Spirit of truth." (John 14:1, 14:16-17)

The Comforter, in other words, will be a man, like Jesus, and there will be no more after him, and he will be a trustworthy man, the Spirit of truth.

"But the Comforter, which is the Holy Spirit, whom the Father will send in my name, he shall teach you all things, and bring all things to your remembrance." (John 14:26)

The writer seems to wrongly equate the Spirit of truth with the Holy Spirit, that which had been with David and Jesus. That being so, it seems illogical that Jesus would need to ask God to send him. And it has already been said that the Comforter will be human.

"Hereafter I will not talk much with you: for the prince of this world cometh, and hath nothing in me." (John 14:30)

Here the Comforter is equated with the Spirit of truth, a distinct entity from Jesus, and in the following this is further emphasised by the prophecy that the Comforter will speak well of Jesus, again as of a distinct entity. The numerous references to Jesus in the Qur'an and *Hadith* support this.

"But when the Comforter is come, whom I will send unto you from the Father, even the Spirit of truth, which preceedeth from the Father, he shall testify of me." (John 15:26)

In Chapter 16, Jesus speaks of the nature of the mission of the Comforter, as well as the conditions of his coming:

"Nevertheless I tell you the truth; It is expedient for you that I go away: for if I go not away, the Comforter will not come unto you; but if I depart, I will send him unto you. And when he is come, he will reprove the world of sin, and of righteousness, and of judgement."(John 16:7-8)

To reprove could carry a notion of "testing again", or restating, the moral limits of man – defining sin, defining righteousness, and judging between the two. He would be able to do this because he would be a pure instrument of divine transmission, and an example in his conduct:

"But when he, the spirit of truth, is come, he will guide you in all truth: for he shall not speak of himself but whatsoever he shall hear (from God) that shall he speak: and he will show you things to come. He shall

glorify me: for he shall receive of mine and shall show unto you."
(John 16:13-14)

The words in English seem strongly to signify the coming of the
Prophet Muhammad, but if we look at the translation of the word
'Comforter' from its original Greek, *Paraclete*, this sense becomes
stronger still. *Paraclete* means, more than a comforter, an advocate, a
word with a legal sense to it.[143] The Prophet was both the bringer of a
"fiery law" and has the role of being our advocate on the Day of
Judgement when, insha'Allah, he will save people from the fire. A
Hadith states that on that day he will say: "Go and take out of Hell (the
fire) all those who have faith in their hearts equal to the weight of... a
mustard seed."[144] When we consider that the Greek word *Periclyte*
means "the Praised One" we are as close as we can be to the Qur'anic
verse that states that 'Isa brought "news of a Messenger who will come
after me, whose name is the Praised One." (61.6) "The Praised One" in
Aramaic, Jesus' language, means 'Hamad', and in Arabic 'Ahmad'. As
Sulayman Shahid Mufassir says, it is possible that they were *both*
written, but in the process of copying, one was omitted, something that
has happened with other words and sentences. As he says:

"There is no one else in all history that John 14:16 *et seq.* could refer to
but the Prophet Muhammad bin Abdullah, peace be upon him... Only
one man stands as Counsellor and Advocate (*Paraclete*) for mankind
for all the ages to come, Praised (*Periclyte*) by God and some 800
millions of the human family."[145]

It is for all of these reasons that, as the Qur'an says, the Jews were
expecting a Prophet from Arabia and it is because of this that many
fled there after the destruction of Jerusalem in 70 CE. In Arabia, they

---

[143] The American Bible Society translates the word as 'Counsellor' and in the Gideon's
Bible as 'Helper'.
[144] *Bukhari Summarised* - 9:601-O.B.
[145] Misunderstanding of the Muslim position on this is recorded in a book written in
1688 (*The Present State of the Ottoman Empire*, book 2, Chapter 12, p.131) written by
a Paul Rycaut. He records that he had met a group of extremely orthodox Muslims in
Bosnia called the Poturs, or Kadizadelers, who "nonetheless mixed in some
Christianity." Among other things, he says, "They believe yet that Mahomet was the
Holy Ghost promised by Christ."

established large communities in the area of Medina where they eventually came to occupy a position of power, though by the time of the Prophet they were more like a balance of power between the tribes of the Aws and the Khazraj. There were no Jews living in Mecca but Jews venerated the Ka'bah as an outlying Temple that had been raised by Abraham. One notable Jew, Al-Hayyaban, migrated from the relative luxury of Syria to Medina precisely because of what had been foretold but died at the time of the Prophet's first revelation. He said, "His hour is close upon you. Be ye the first to reach him, O Jews; for he will be sent to shed blood and to take captive the women and the children of those who oppose him. Let that not hold you back from him."

However, if the Children of Israel thought Jesus had had the right faith but the wrong message, their attitude to the Prophet Muhammad could be seen as something opposite – the right message (Prophet for all humanity) but the wrong faith (Gentile). Once again, their willingness to submit was to be tested, but in a different context. The result, except in a few cases, was to be the same. Bahira, a learned Christian who recognised Muhammad's Prophethood before it had been revealed, warned him specifically that the Jews would be envious and a danger to him.

Once the Prophet began his call to Islam, the attitude of the Jews can be described as "in favour of the message but against the messenger", as Martin Lings puts it in his *Seera* of the Prophet. When the Quraysh asked the Jews of Yathrib (Medina) what they, having knowledge of Scripture and Prophets, thought of the veracity of the Prophet's message, the rabbis told them to ask three questions. "If he tell you of them, then he is a Prophet sent by God." The questions concerned the young men who left their lands in days of old and what happened to them; the traveller who went east and west to the ends of the earth; and the Spirit, and its nature. The story runs that, when asked, the Prophet Muhammad was unable to answer the questions through revelation at first because he did not say, "Insh'Allah" (God willing). As Martin Lings points out, this impressed people by its authenticity; had he been an extemporising poet, he would not have risked "losing the audience" through such a shoddy performance. Nonetheless, many still did not believe him. Or rather, they *would* not.

300

This became increasingly clear as time passed. During the Prophet's life it has been calculated that only 39 Jews actually embraced Islam. One of these was Safiyya, the wife of Kinanah. She was a pious woman who was offered freedom or marriage to the Prophet after her husband had been killed at the siege of Khaybar. She chose the latter. One of the reasons for this was that she had overheard her husband and another of the Jews of Khaybar, Huyay, talking about the Prophet before meeting him, saying that he could not be what he said he was. On their return they had been deeply troubled, because they had realised that he *was* a Prophet, though their opposition did not cease.

Another significant Jewish convert to Islam was Abdullah Ibn Salaam. He described his first meeting with the Prophet Muhammad:

"When God's Messenger emigrated to Medina, I went to see him, as did everyone else. He was sitting amidst a group of people when I went in, and saying: 'Give food to others and greet them." His speech was so sweet and his face so charming that I said to myself: 'I swear by God that one with such a face cannot lie.' Without delay I declared my belief in him."[146]

The Qur'an states that the People of the Scripture recognise Muhammad as a Prophet as they recognise their sons (2:146) and after his conversion, Omar asked Abdullah if he had recognised God's Messenger. He replied: "I recognised him. I may doubt my children, my wife might have deceived me, but I have no doubt about God's Messenger being the Last Prophet."[147]

In a *Hadith*, Abdullah questions the Prophet as to the meaning of a dream he had had:

"(In a dream) I saw myself in a garden and there was a pillar in the middle of the garden, and there was a handhold at the top of the pillar. I was asked to climb it. I said, 'I cannot.' Then a servant came and lifted me and I climbed, and then got hold of the handhold, and I woke up

---

[146]Ibn Hanbal, 5:451
[147]Mukhtasar Tafsir Ibn Al-Kathir, 1:140

still holding it. I narrated that to the Prophet who said, 'The garden symbolises the garden of Islam, and the handhold is the Islamic handhold which indicates that you will adhere firmly until you die.'"[148]

His conversion was especially problematic for the Jews because they held him in such high esteem that they called him "the lord, son of a lord." After his conversion, he asked the Prophet to hide him in a room and summon the Jewish scholars of Medina to ask about him and his father. When they were gathered, Muhammad asked them what they thought of Abdullah and his father. They said, "They are among our noblest and most learned people."

"How would you react if he affirms me?" the Prophet asked.

They said this was impossible, at which point Abdullah appeared and told them that he had converted. They immediately changed their tune, saying:

"He is the most wicked among us, and the son of the most wicked."

Another Jewish outward denial of this truth was when Abu Sufyan of the Quraysh met with Jewish leaders actually within the *Ka'bah* and asked them which group they believed had the better *deen*. The Jews said: "You Quraysh have the better *deen*."

It was not that the Prophet did not know all this. Nonetheless, in Medina he established a covenant with the Jews of mutual loyalty and protection. The two faiths had equal status, Jews would only be required to follow their own laws and there was no requirement of them to recognise the Prophethood of Muhammad. They were taken at their word. "If they incline to peace, then make peace with them and put your trust in God," (8:61) the Qur'an says, an injunction that still stands. It was only if they acted against the Muslims that they would face the consequences.

---

[148]Bukhari 9, no. 142

One Jewish group, the Qaynuqa, chose to do this. In 624 after the Muslims' victory at Badr, this tribe remained haughty and relations were strained. In an argument between a Muslim and a Jew in the market over an indecent practical joke played by the Jews, blood was spilled on both sides. Muhammad reminded them of their treaty obligations and asked them to become Muslims:

"By doing so you will be making a loan to God that will bring you marvellous interest," to which they replied that God must be very poor to need to borrow from them who were not.

Angered by this blasphemy, the Prophet demanded that they convert, to which they responded: "Thou art proud indeed by reason of thy victory over soldiers of no account. Try now to attack us and thou wilt see that we are no way like thy fellow-countrymen of Mecca. If we fight you, you will know we are men of war." The Prophet walked out and the Jews chose to make a fight of it, withdrawing to fortified positions, sure that their skills and the promised reinforcements would be more than adequate to dispose of the Muslims. However, no reinforcements came and after two weeks they surrendered unconditionally. The Prophet favoured cutting their throats, according to Gulen, but the intercession of Abdullah Ibn Ubbayy, "the hypocrite," saved them. It is important to note that despite the Qur'anic injunction: "If thou overcomest them in war, then make of them an example, to strike fear into those that are behind them, that they may take heed," (8:57) the Jews were only banished without their belongings[149] rather than killed.

The Prophet's approach to the Jews can be seen as one of patience in the face of hostile thought, and action in the face of hostile acts. Typifying this was the killing he ordered of Ka'b ibn al-Ashraf in 625. He was the chief of the Bani Nazir and a poet who had satirised the Prophet and called on the Quraysh to take revenge for Badr the year before, as well as trying to cause a renewal in the hostility of the Aws and the Khazraj tribes in order to win back the Jewish position as holders of the balance of power. When the Jews of the Bani Nazir tribe complained to Muhammad, he said:

---

[149] Ibn Hisham, 3:58

303

"If he had remained as others of like opinion remain, he would not have been killed by guile."

After this, he went among them, possibly to negotiate compensation, and invited the Jews to make a special treaty in addition to the covenant, which they did. Dinet and Ibrahim suggest that they were also financially compensated. After the agreement had been made, however, while seated in the shade of a house, the son of Jahsh ibn Ka'b climbed onto the roof with the intention of dropping great rocks that had been stored there onto the Prophet. He became aware of this at the decisive moment, moved out of harm's way and returned to Medina. The attempted murder led to an order to leave, refusal because of the declared support of "Abdullah the Hypocrite", declaration of war, siege, surrender and the banishment of the Bani Nazir. Under the terms of the treaty, the Jews were only allowed to keep a limited number of camels per person and whatever it could carry, but with the camels in single file, their curtains thrown open to reveal the enormity of their owners' wealth, the Jews marched out to the tune of fife and drum. Such arrogance was noted, as was the potential booty should defeat catch up with the Jews again.

Following the victory at Badr the Muslim position strengthened in Medina. The treaty between Jews and Muslims was enough to restrain the Jews from waging outright war, and perhaps the hope that the Quraysh would do the job for them, but following the much closer Battle of Uhud in 625, relations broke down completely.

A further campaign was launched by the Jews and Quraysh in 627, which was stopped at the Battle of the Trench. Leading up to this, a deputation of Jews from the Bani Nazir, including Sallam Ibn Abi al-Huqayq, Huyyay Ibn Akhtab, who had been expelled from Medina, and some of the Bani Wa'il, had visited Mecca to offer an alliance that increased the ranks of the Confederates (the Quraysh and their supporters) that would also come to include the Ghatafans. Huyyay Ibn Akhtab then encouraged Ka'b ibn Asad, the Prince of the Jewish tribe of the Bani Qarayzah, to join them. Despite the Covenant that existed between the Muslims and the Medinan Jews, he said: "Who is this Prophet of Allah of whom ye speak? There exists no treaty between him and us." This denial was an act of great treachery because Ka'b knew the weak points of the Muslim's defences.

Though this was an apparently formidable alliance, a mixture of innovation, some clever sowing of distrust and divine intervention undid it. Firstly, the trench, which gave the battle its name, was a Persian tactic, brought by Salman Al-Farisi. The Prophet chose defensive tactics because of the hypocrites and Jews and had the inhabitants dig a trench around the unprotected parts of city. The rightness of such tactics was borne out by events; despite their treaty, the Jews did not to support the defenders but rather contacted the enemy and stopped selling to Medinans. The appalling weather then aided the defenders, making life harder for the attackers and also allowed Naim Ibn Mas'ud, a prince of the Ghatafans who had become a Muslim during the siege, to move around the Confederates' camp without being seriously challenged and to sow the distrust that unstuck the glue of their forces. The Prophet Muhammad declared that war is achieved by guile ("war is treachery") and Naim's guile was to tell the Jews that they should take hostages from the Ghatafans and Quraysh as security because they were not fighting on their own area and would abandon them. He then told the Quraysh that the Jews would not fulfil their promise and had promised hostages to the Muslims in return for their pardon, telling the same to the Ghatafans. Thus primed, the alliance immediately fell apart when the Jews requested the hostages. The weather then became too much. After 27 days, a harsh east wind destroyed the Confederates' tents, their fires were extinguished, and rain and sand were blown at them. These signs led to the abandonment of the siege.

For their treachery, the Bani Qurayzah were immediately besieged by the Muslims and finally surrendered after 25 days. They were offered Islam and five accepted, three having known Al-Hayyaban in their childhoods. The Prophet was sent a deputation by the clan of Aws asking for mercy for these Jews who were former allies, but he was less enthusiastic about pardoning them because of the greatness of their treachery. He asked the deputation: "Will it satisfy you, men of Aws, if one of yourselves pronounce judgement on them?" and they agreed. Muhammad appointed Sa'd ibn Mu'adh, one of their chieftains, and he decreed that the men should be slain for breaking the treaty, to which the Prophet said: "Thou hast judged with the judgement of God from above the seven heavens." Huyay, one of the seven hundred to die, said to the Prophet before his death: "I blame not myself for having opposed thee, but whoso forsaketh God, the same shall be forsaken." This is the man who had spoken with Safiyya's husband about the Prophet, as we have mentioned.

It is important to notice that, though stern retribution is permitted, it was rarely the choice of the Messenger and that in this instance there was a clear opportunity for mercy to be claimed. Similarly, in another instance of action taken against the life of the Prophet when magic was used by Labid, a Jewish resident of Medina (undone, literally, by the recitation of the last two chapters of the Qur'an) no action was taken. Nor was any taken against the Jewish woman who poisoned the Prophet after the Muslim victory at Khaybar, which was the last confrontation between the Muslims and Jews in Arabia.

The Treaty of Hudaybiyah in 628 suspended hostilities against the Quraysh and meant that Muhammad was free to act against his other enemies, who were now most notably the remaining Jews. The final conflict took place at Khaybar in 628 in the sixth year of the *Hijra* and it contains many of the features of other Muslim-Jewish confrontations: the Jews were numerically superior and confident of winning because their fortifications at Khaybar were proverbially impregnable, but they were disunited and were let down by promised reinforcements; the Ghatafans were cut off from reaching them and, fearing an attack from their rear, headed home. As the Qur'an says: "Ill feeling is rife amongst them. Thou countest them as one whole, but their hearts are divided." (59:14) The Muslims fought "in ranks as if they were a close-built block" (61:4) and took one fortress after another. In defeat it was agreed that the Jews would go into exile – again there was no slaughter – but this time they would leave without possessions (remembering the over-proud display of before). The Prophet added the further clause that anyone found trying to do so would be put to death. Kinanah, the Jewish leader agreed.

It seems that the prevailing attitude among the Jews was that they were beaten and that the Prophet really was who he said he was. However, they insisted on only following Moses and the Torah, and the Prophet permitted them to do so. Nonetheless, this leader of the Jews, Kinanah insisted on trying to conceal his riches, angrily dismissing counsel not to from his own people. Given that he had established those seven years before that he was not dealing with a normal adversary, this seems to be a suicidal form of pride and indeed he was discovered and executed.

Following Khaybar, the Prophet allowed some of the Jewish date farmers to stay, as well as two further Jewish settlements of Fadak and Wadi l-Qura, which had been in league with Khaybar. They claimed that only they knew how to cultivate the dates and were allowed to stay in return for half their crop on the understanding that if the Prophet later ordered them to leave, they would do so (which, in fact, he did). However, following Tabuk, the Prophet made a treaty with Jewish and Christian settlements to the north of Arabia in the Aqaba region that gave them protection.

This final act shows that there was no policy of hostility, nor any implacable malice, in the Prophet's treatment of the Jews. As far as events of that time went, the Jews were enemies as long as they behaved as such. The enmity was towards their crimes or actions, not towards their religion

That the Prophet was not troubled by the Jews was because he was able to rise above their hatred of him. After all, he had literally risen above their holy city. The Prophet Muhammad and Jerusalem are connected for two reasons. Firstly, Jerusalem was the direction of prayer, the *qibla*, for all Muslims until the first year of the *Hijra*, 622, twelve years after the Prophet Muhammad's Prophethood began, when he received a revelation that changed it to Mecca. This did not take place, though, until one year after the second most significant night in the history of Islam, the night of the *Isra'*, the Night Journey to Jerusalem. Jerusalem was, thus, central, then superseded, but it remained, and remains, a place of profound importance for Muslims, for whom it is the third holiest place, precisely because it is so important for Jews and Christians, the People of the Book.

"Glory to God who did take His Servant for a Journey by night from the Sacred Mosque to the Furthest Mosque whose precincts We did bless, in order to show him some of Our Signs: for He is the One Who heareth and seeth all things." (17:1)

One night, before the *Hijra* to Medina, the Prophet went to visit the Ka'bah as he often did. While there he felt tired and fell asleep. In a *Hadith* (I I 264), he tells how Gabriel shook him awake and led him to a winged white beast named Buraq that was part ass and part mule. With Gabriel's guidance they flew to Jerusalem where he was met by a company of Prophets, including Abraham, Moses and Jesus. When he prayed on the site of the Temple they formed a congregation behind him and followed him in prayer. After the prayer he was offered two vessels to drink from, one containing wine, the other containing milk. He was faced with the choice of corruption (wine is a fruit juice in degenerated form) or purity (milk is described as pure, *khalisan,* in the Qur'an). He took the milk and left the wine, after which Gabriel said: "Thou hast been guided unto the path primordial, and hast guided thereunto thy people, O Prophet Muhammad, and wine is forbidden you."

The Prophet Muhammad was then taken from the rock in the centre of the site of the Temple up to the heavens in the same way as Elijah and Jesus before him. As he passed through each of the seven heavens he saw again the same Prophets he had prayed with in Jerusalem. He had prayed with them before in their earthly forms but he saw them now in their "celestial reality" as Martin Lings describes them in his biography of the Prophet. Joseph had the splendour of the moon at its full and had been given more than half of the existing beauty of the world, and he particularly praised the beauty of Aaron too. The beauty of the smallest piece of Paradise was better than the whole world, he said, and a woman from Paradise "would fill the space between Heaven and here below with light and fragrance."

Above the seven heavens he reached the Divine sphere about which nothing is said except that he reached the Lote Tree of the Uttermost End. According to a commentary based upon the sayings of the Prophet, the Lote Tree marks the end of knowledge, whether human or angelic. Beyond is the hidden mystery, the unknown and the unknowable, known to God alone:

"When there enshroudeth the Lote Tree that which enshroudeth, the eye wavered not nor did it transgress. Verily he beheld there the greatest of all the signs of his Lord." (53:16-18)

The Divine Light descended upon the Lote Tree and covered it, and everything else, and the Prophet beheld it without looking away. It was here too that the Prophet Muhammad received the command of fifty prayers a day, and also the creed of Islam, which contains the essence of the nature of Prophethood:

"The messenger believeth, and the faithful believe, in what hath been revealed unto him from his Lord. Each one believeth in God and His angels and His books and His messengers: We made no distinction between any one of His messengers. And they say: we hear and we obey; grant us, Thou our Lord, Thy forgiveness; unto Thee is the ultimate becoming." (2:285)

On their descent, the Prophet and Gabriel passed the same Prophets. As the Prophet Muhammad said:

"On my return, when I passed Moses, and what a good friend he was unto you, he asked me: 'How many prayers have been laid upon thee?' I told him fifty prayers every day and he said: 'The congregational prayer is a weighty thing, and thy people are weak. Return unto thy Lord, and ask him to lighten the load for thee and thy people.' So I returned and asked my Lord to make it lighter, and He took away ten. Then I passed Moses again and he repeated what he had said before, so I returned again, and ten more prayers were taken from me. But every time I returned unto Moses he sent me back until finally all the prayers had been taken from me except five for each day and night. Then I returned unto Moses, but still he said the same as before, and I said: 'I have returned unto my Lord and asked him till I am ashamed. I will not go again.' And so it is that he who performeth the five in good faith and in trust of God's bounty, unto him shall be given the meed of fifty prayers." (I.I. 271)

When they had made their return to the Rock - tradition has it that there is a footprint there still - they returned to Mecca by the same route, arriving back in the *Ka'bah* the same night. The Prophet returned to the house of his cousin where he had been staying and, after leading them in the dawn prayer, told the household where he had been. At this stage, the Prophet had many enemies among the leaders of Meccan society, the family of the Quraysh, so his cousin implored him to tell no one of what had happened because it would lead to even more insults being heaped upon him. Perhaps there was a hint here that she disbelieved him in some way but the Prophet's response was to say: "By God, I will tell them."

As his cousin had feared, many of the Quraysh were delighted with the news, because it seemed to prove finally that the Prophet Muhammad was indeed mad. They all knew full well that it took a month at least to get to Jerusalem. With mischievous intent, some men went to see Abu Bakr, one of the first, and certainly one of the most respected, converts to Islam, and they asked him what he thought. Suspecting a trick he accused them of lying, but they assured him that he was in the Mosque at that very moment speaking about the journey. In an instant Abu Bakr showed the trust that he felt for the Prophet by retorting: "If he so saith, then it is true. And what is so surprising about it anyway? He telleth me that Tidings come to him from Heaven to earth in one hour of the day or night, and I know him to be speaking the truth. And that is beyond what you joke at." (I.I.265)

God knows how important this public expression of belief at this time was, and Abu Bakr sensed that it was, for he went to the Mosque to repeat his words: "If so he saith, it is true." Because of this the Prophet gave Abu Bakr the name *as-Siddiq,* which means "the great confirmer, or witness, of the truth."

The obvious mocking response to the story began to look shakier still over the coming days because, in the course of its telling, the Prophet would describe the camel caravans he had overtaken on the way, predicting when they would arrive in Mecca. When they duly started to arrive as predicted and as described, any disbelief or lack of faith looked unfounded. At first the Prophet only told Abu Bakr and his close companions of the ascent into heaven, confining his public telling

310

to the actual journey itself but over the coming years people learned more of the details. This was often in response to questions, questions that would indicate a readiness to hear answers that, if they had been told initially in the story, would have been too hard to take in all at once.

This event gave a transcendent dimension to the Prophet's message, a connection with the chain of Prophets and the importance of this other Holy City and this other Holy Land. But the return to Mecca emphasised that our closest earthly proximity to God was beyond Jerusalem. The return metaphorically put Jerusalem behind the Prophet Muhammad, who now had to focus on his increasingly insecure position in Mecca and on protecting what, with God's grace, he had created. And it was because of this that the Prophet Muhammad and his followers made the *Hijra*, the migration, to al-Medina Yathrib, the city of Yathrib, most commonly known simply as Medina.

It was here that the Prophet Muhammad was to put Jerusalem behind him literally as well as metaphorically. It was still revered, but it was part of a revered past where the message of One God, Allah, had been the responsibility of one people. Muslims would now look to the future and to Mecca, the centre of the universal faith, whilst acknowledging the sacredness of the past and Jerusalem, the centre of the particularist Judaic faiths. Since the time of Jacob, the worship of One God had been carried by the Children of Israel, Isaac's line, and their self-proclaimed successors, the new Children of Israel, the Christians. Through God's will they had, respectively, been expelled twice from the Holy Land for failing to live according to the Laws of God; and created a religion that, for all its goodness and love for the heart of Jesus, was, with its Trinity and its veneration of pictorial representations of Jesus and Mary, not exactly God-centred. With patience, the line of Ishmail would now step forward and take its place.

Until this time, the Prophet had always taken great care to face in the correct direction when praying. When he had been in the Mosque in Mecca he had faced in the direction of the *Mihrab*, the prayer niche, in the Jerusalem wall, and had set his direction by sun or stars when outside. Now, after the *Hijra*, living in Medina and on the eve of war with Mecca, the centrality of that place, rebuilt centuries ago by Ishmail and his father Abraham, was confirmed by a Revelation:

"We have seen the turning of thy face unto the sky; and now We shall turn thee a way that shall well please thee. So turn thou thy face towards the Inviolable Mosque; and wheresoever ye may be, turn ye your faces towards it." (2:144)

Jerusalem was now literally, as well as metaphorically, behind him.

Badawi, J. *The Prophet Muhammad in the Bible*
Bukhari, *Sahih Al-Bukhari 9*, Darrusalam: Riyadh
Dinet, E. & Beb Ibrahim, S. *The Life of Muhammad; The Prophet of Allah*, (1973) Taj: Karachi
Gulen, M.F. *The Prophet Muhammad – Aspects of His Life, Vols. 1 & 2* (2000) The Fountain: Fairfax Va.
Levy, G. *Sentimental Journey* (Sept 30 2005) Haaretz: Tel Aviv:
Lings, M. *Muhammad: His Life Based on the Earliest Sources* (1987) Inner Traditions: Vermont
Mufassir, S.S. *Jesus in the Qur'an*
Schimmel, A. *The Prophet's Night Journey and Ascension* (1998) Q-News: London

Conclusion

Islam's single most defining characteristic is unity - unity of belief, of origin, of people, of purpose, and, of course, of God. The meaning of the word Islam is submission, in the root of which we also get the word *salaam*, peace. The implication of this is that peace will come, and will only come, from submission to the power and wisdom in the universe that is far, far greater than our own, that of God, of Allah. If we look at the names of the other two monotheistic faiths, we find a contrast. Jews define their beliefs and identity around a tribal name, Judah, or Israel, which itself means "he who struggles with God", though Isaiah's straight path in the desert remains a possibility. Christians define themselves around the name of a man whose very nature is disputed, by them at least. The focus of these two faiths is not essentially upon God, as is shown clearly in these names and in much of what they say about their own faiths. It is, respectively, on the Jews as a people, and on Jesus.

The attitude of the two faiths to their Books reflects this concern and, if there has been another way to God, one that has been right under their noses, it has not been seen because of this. The very limitations of this world-view have probably saved some of the prophecies that have declared something other than this from being taken seriously enough to be destroyed. However, there remains the problem that the very Jewish-Christian belief system that has produced minds of intelligence and brilliance has also discouraged the development of spirits that are ready or willing to submit to the final revelation of God. This has been sent, not to God's Chosen People, not to a white European, not even to Jerusalem, but to an Arab in a city in the middle of a desert.

The two greatest limiting factors in the way Jews and Christians see the Prophet Muhammad are, respectively, the Jewish expectation that the Messiah will be a supernatural figure of the line of David who will vanquish Israel's foes, and be Jewish; and the Christian non-expectation of another messenger until the second coming of Jesus at the end of time. The Prophet Muhammad, of the line of Ishmael, proclaiming the perfected religion of Islam, a faith, a *deen*, that is both the faith of the mostly Jewish Prophets who preceded him *and* a

313

universal faith for all people, does not fit into this picture. However, that is, as I have argued, a responsibility to be laid at the doors of those who have kept those faiths alive rather than a fault of the God-centred essence of those faiths. Essentially, Islam rises above the debate as to who the only or new Children of Israel are, whether Jews or Christians, by embracing them both and proclaiming that we are all Children of Abraham, and ultimately, of Adam, and all, if doing it right, 'muslim', with a small 'm'. If we are open-minded enough about it, Islam even allows for the central pillars of Judaism and Christianity to stand, these being respectively, that the Jews are the Chosen People, and that Jesus is central to humanity's salvation. It's win-win-win theology.

In *this* picture, Jesus was the last *Jewish* Prophet, calling Jews back to God and heeding Isaiah's counsel to rely on Him alone. He was the Messiah who promised God's kingdom on earth. What he was not was the political leader who would found this kingdom, nor was he a religious leader come to found a new faith. Both of these tasks were to be carried out by the last of the Prophets, the Prophet Muhammad. The moment when his calling ceased to be a particularist, Arab one, and became a universal one was when he was awoken by the Angel Gabriel to be taken to Jerusalem, there to pray and to ascend into the heavens to meet the Lord of All. This did not happen in Mecca; it happened in Jerusalem, and could only have happened in Jerusalem. But the House of Peace, the House of God, was elsewhere, and it was to there that the Prophet Muhammad returned, and it is to there that we now, as Muslims, turn.

In the light of this, the Israeli Government Tourist Authority advertisement of 1999 that says "In the land where the Millennium began the Dome has already been built" could look like an implied acceptance of the Prophets Jesus and Muhammad, peace be upon them both, given a sense of humour and a bit of imagination. A glimmer of light in hard hearts? Though probably not planned that way it could be seen as something a little like the *Shahada*. As the Qur'an says:

"And they planned, and God planned, and God is the best of planners."

If there were grounds for optimism in the words of this advertisement, uttered as the Israel-Palestine peace process moved towards its denouement, they were given a serious reality check by the outbreak of the Al-Quds (Jerusalem) *Intifada* at the end of the following year, 2000. The Camp David talks earlier in the year, between Yasser Arafat and Ehud Barak, presided over by Bill Clinton, had seemed to come close to making a definitive, final settlement of the whole problem. Ultimately though, the breaking point was not the fate of the Palestinian refugees, nor settlements, nor final borders, but the fate of Jerusalem and particularly its central point, the Al-Aqsa/Temple Mount complex. Though neither of the protagonists (nor, for that matter, their peoples) are particularly religious in an overt, practising way, they were unable, for political, psychological and ultimately religious reasons to accept anything less than sovereignty over the area.

It seems that it had to be so, that there is no political, "worldly" solution to this crisis, that there is no half-and-half compromise in "owning the access point to God." The baby cannot be cut in half. There is but one way to God, and until that is taken to heart, the dominant relationship between those who currently claim it will be struggle and not peace. God, through the Prophet Muhammad, has put before us, essentially, a very simple choice in how we relate to Him, a choice of struggle with God, or submission. Ultimately, the answer can only be sincerely found through patience rather than violence but nonetheless that question is, and will remain, Do we choose Israel or Islam?

Shalom

Salaam

Printed in the United Kingdom by
Lightning Source UK Ltd., Milton Keynes
139081UK00001B/96/P